Children's Literature and Capitalism

Critical Approaches to Children's Literature

Series Editors: **Kerry Mallan** and **Clare Bradford**

Critical Approaches to Children's Literature is an innovative series concerned with the best contemporary scholarship and criticism on children's and young adult literature, film and media texts. It addresses new and developing areas of children's literature research as well as bringing contemporary perspectives to historical texts. The series has a distinctive take on scholarship, delivering quality works of criticism written in an accessible style for a range of readers, both academic and professional. It is invaluable for undergraduate students in children's literature as well as advanced students and established scholars.

Published titles include:

Clare Bradford, Kerry Mallan, John Stephens & Robyn McCallum
NEW WORLD ORDERS IN CONTEMPORARY CHILDREN'S LITERATURE
Utopian Transformations

Margaret Mackey
NARRATIVE PLEASURES IN YOUNG ADULT NOVELS, FILMS AND VIDEO GAMES
Critical Approaches to Children's Literature

Andrew O'Malley
CHILDREN'S LITERATURE, POPULAR CULTURE AND ROBINSON CRUSOE

Christopher Parkes
CHILDREN'S LITERATURE AND CAPITALISM
Fictions of Social Mobility in Britain, 1850–1914

Michelle Smith
EMPIRE IN BRITISH GIRLS' LITERATURE AND CULTURE
Imperial Girls, 1880–1915

Forthcoming titles:

Elizabeth Bullen
CLASS IN CONTEMPORARY CHILDREN'S LITERATURE

Pamela Knights
READING BALLET AND PERFORMANCE NARRATIVES FOR CHILDREN

Kate McInally
DESIRING GIRLS IN YOUNG ADULT FICTION

Susan Napier
MIYAZAKI HAYO AND THE USES OF ENCHANTMENT

Critical Approaches to Children's Literature
Series Standing Order ISBN 978–0–230–22786–6 (hardback)
978–0–230–22787–3 (paperback)
(*outside North America only*)

You can receive future titles in this series as they are published by placing a standing order. Please contact your bookseller or, in case of difficulty, write to us at the address below with your name and address, the title of the series and the ISBN quoted above.

Customer Services Department, Macmillan Distribution Ltd, Houndmills, Basingstoke, Hampshire RG21 6XS, England

Children's Literature and Capitalism

Fictions of Social Mobility in Britain, 1850–1914

Christopher Parkes

First published 2012 by
PALGRAVE MACMILLAN

Palgrave Macmillan in the UK is an imprint of Macmillan Publishers Limited, registered in England, company number 785998, of Houndmills, Basingstoke, Hampshire RG21 6XS.

Palgrave Macmillan in the US is a division of St Martin's Press LLC, 175 Fifth Avenue, New York, NY 10010.

Palgrave Macmillan is the global academic imprint of the above companies and has companies and representatives throughout the world.

Palgrave® and Macmillan® are registered trademarks in the United States, the United Kingdom, Europe and other countries.

ISBN 978–0–230–36412–7

This book is printed on paper suitable for recycling and made from fully managed and sustained forest sources. Logging, pulping and manufacturing processes are expected to conform to the environmental regulations of the country of origin.

A catalogue record for this book is available from the British Library.

A catalog record for this book is available from the Library of Congress.

10   9   8   7   6   5   4   3   2   1
21   20   19   18   17   16   15   14   13   12

Printed and bound in Great Britain by
CPI Antony Rowe, Chippenham and Eastbourne

This book is dedicated to Judith and to my parents, Katherine and David

Contents

Series Preface

The *Critical Approaches to Children's Literature* series was initiated in 2008 by Kerry Mallan and Clare Bradford. Its aim is to identify and publish the best contemporary scholarship and criticism on children's and young adult literature, film and media texts. The series is open to theoretically informed scholarship covering a range of critical perspectives on historical and contemporary texts from diverse national and cultural settings. It aims to make a significant contribution to the expanding field of children's literature research by publishing quality books that promote informed discussion and debate about the production and reception of children's literature and its criticism.

Kerry Mallan and Clare Bradford

Acknowledgements

I should like to thank the Lakehead University Senate Research Committee for providing research funds. I should also like to thank the librarians in the Osborne Collection at the Toronto Public Library, where some of the early research for this book was conducted.

My colleagues in the Department of English at Lakehead University deserve thanks for their encouragement and support.

Some of the discussion contained in Chapter 3 was previously published in my article "Treasure Island and the Romance of the British Civil Service", *Children's Literature Association Quarterly*, 31.4 (2006): 332–45. Copyright © 2007 Children's Literature Association. Adapted with permission by the Johns Hopkins University Press.

Introduction

At the end of Britain's first industrial revolution, the child emerged as both a victim of and a threat to capitalist society. The sight of the suffering child, exploited as cheap labour in the nation's factories, appeared to prove that capitalist society could not properly accommodate its most vulnerable members, that it could only use them up and destroy them. Consequently, the image of the innocent child, damaged and destroyed by its participation in the commercial world, came to represent a distinct challenge to the future of capitalist society as it rendered all too obvious the lack of sentiment contained within the market economy. The purpose of this book is to examine the ways in which Victorian and Edwardian authors developed narratives that were fundamentally concerned with redefining the relationship of the child to the marketplace in order to accommodate the child within capitalist society. The solution to the problem of the child as a victim of commercialism and industrialization came, as I shall argue, in the form of a rhetorical strategy that equated the spirit of capitalism with the spirit of childhood. By locating capitalist ingenuity at the level of the child, the authors with whom I am concerned are responsible in part for transforming the child from the victim of capitalism into its ideal participant. During the nineteenth century, the spirit of childhood and the spirit of capitalism became virtually synonymous as authors argued that children are defined by an innate curiosity and invention, the kind that leads to capitalist innovation. Ultimately, once children were rendered the living embodiments of the capitalist spirit, they could no longer be seen to be victimized by that which was fundamentally a part of them.

British romanticism had argued at the end of the eighteenth century that children should be sheltered and protected from industrial and commercial activity. Following the lead of Rousseau, it essentialized the child as an innocent child of nature, a kind of noble savage whose purist form is found not in human society but in the natural world. According to Penny Brown, the romantic view of childhood was born out of an adult "sense of uncertainty and vulnerability, and of simplicity, innocence and feeling in the face of the increasingly dehumanising industrial age" (6).[1] In the 1780s, artists and authors began to depict children as inhabiting an ideal state beyond the bounds of commercial society. Thomas Gainsborough's painting *Cottage Girl with Dog and Pitcher* (1785), for example, depicts a barefoot peasant girl holding a puppy that seems to share her wistful expression.[2] There are no adults or physical structures present in the scene to indicate that she is anything other than a child of nature. She is clearly very poor, but the sentimentalism of the picture renders her such an object of aesthetic pleasure that we would no more put shoes on her than we would the little dog. With his *Ode: Intimations of Immortality* (1804), William Wordsworth presents what is perhaps the period's most idealized version of the child as the poem argues, in effect, that the child is far superior to the adult, having been born into the world possessing within him or her all the knowledge of the universe. Growing up and becoming socialized represents for Wordsworth the unlearning and forgetting of this knowledge.

As scholars of child labour and child protection have demonstrated, the romantic view of childhood was responsible in part for initiating the gradual removal of the child from the workplace that took place in nineteenth-century Britain.[3] The many Factory Acts of the period, beginning with that of 1802, set limits on the age of child labourers and the number of hours they could work until, by the time of the 1901 act, the minimum age for child labour was 12.[4] The acts were motivated by the larger belief that a child should remain separate from the marketplace in order to be granted a proper childhood. According to Hugh Cunningham, the ideal childhood was to be spent "in a home divorced from economically productive activity" (*Children of the Poor*, 230). Similarly, Monica Flegel writes in her study of the National Society for the Prevention of Cruelty to Children (NSPCC) that childhood was to be "a protected, carefree time and space that should be enjoyed by all children, regardless of class" (13). The ideal family home was to be a space in which the child was neither produced by, nor implicated in, the production of the family income. Flegel notes how the period witnessed "the transformation of the child from an economically useful member of a household to an 'economically worthless but emotionally priceless' figure in society" (13).[5] As children were increasingly removed from the economy, their value as labour decreased while their sentimental value increased dramatically. As they were made non-participants in the marketplace, their economic agency was deferred to the future where it could not corrupt their innocence.

In many ways, British romanticism represented a break from the evangelical tradition of early eighteenth-century Britain, which had argued that children should not be sheltered from commercial society but raised as active participants. Brown notes how this tradition of child-rearing "stressed the need for strict discipline, constant watchfulness for sin, the early breaking of the child's will and absolute obedience to parents" (6–7).[6] The child is a site of disorder that requires constant monitoring for signs of even the slightest deviation from correct behaviour. In texts such as Isaac Watts's poem, *Against Idleness and Mischief* from his *Divine Songs for Children* (1715), for example, children are to perform useful labour throughout the course of a day, just like the "busy bees" that "improve each shining hour", so that they never experience an idle moment.[7] If romanticism insulated the child from labour, the evangelical tradition immersed the child within it but, in both cases, the child remained a passive subject lacking agency and autonomy in the labour market.

As Marah Gubar argues in her study of nineteenth-century children's literature, *Artful Dodgers*, the child in the nineteenth century became a contested site where the romantic and evangelical views competed for control. The fascination with the child as an innocent and the fascination with the child as a prodigy came together to produce the Victorian "cult of the child", which, she notes, is "a cultural phenomenon that reflected *competing* conceptions of childhood. More specifically, it was the site where the idea of the child as an innocent Other clashed most dramatically with an older vision of the child as a competent collaborator, capable of working and playing alongside adults" (9). She adds, "members of the self-proclaimed cult of the child expressed their allegiance to the ideal of unconscious innocence even as they demonstrated a profound fascination with knowledgeable, experienced, and remarkably competent children" (15). Capitalist society, as I have indicated, required the child to be a figure that could participate in commercial activity and yet remain innocent and uncorrupted. During the course of the nineteenth century, a particular kind of child evolved in children's literature, one characterized by a charming curiosity that is displayed only when the child participates in commercial society. This child of Victorian and Edwardian fiction possesses a well-developed imagination and an enormous capacity for imaginative play, which usually takes the form of acting out scenes taken from favourite books or from adult activities witnessed in everyday life. Rather than corrupting the child's imagination, participation in commercial activity allows for the release of a natural capacity for ingenuity that is just as innocent as it is precocious. This charmingly innocent prodigy turned the "cult of the child" into what might be better described as the "cult of the imaginative child"[8] as the child's curiosity became conflated with capitalist invention.

The emergence of the imaginative child can be traced back to Maria Edgeworth's many advice handbooks for parents, including *Essays on Practical Education* (1801), which discusses the importance of educational toys in a child's development. While children in the Edgeworthian home are not directly implicated in the production of the family income, they are in training for their future careers as the child's playroom is meant to dissolve the line between work and play. Whereas children were once encouraged to covet fashionable toys, such as finely painted coaches, Edgeworth argues that the imaginative child will naturally despise useless toys that exist only to display the family's wealth. Practical children will soon discover, she argues, that all they can do with fashionable toys is break them:

> as long as a child has sense and courage to destroy his toys, there is no great harm done; but, in general, he is taught to set a value upon them totally independent of all ideas of utility, or of any regard to his own feelings. Either he is conjured to take particular care of them, because they cost a great deal of money; or else he is taught to admire them as miniatures of some of the fine things on which fine people pride themselves. Instead of attending to his own sensations, and learning from his own experience, he acquires the habit of estimating his pleasures by the taste and judgment of those who happen to be near him. (3)

In order to provide a proper childhood, Edgeworth's audience of parents is to construct the playroom as a classroom or a workshop that will allow their offspring to develop a kind of practical curiosity. In her model of parenting, toys are no longer bound up in the material circumstances of the home but are instead reconfigured as a means of stimulating innovation and ingenuity. Her manuals articulate a radical shift in thinking about the space of the home as they construct the child as a subject that is profoundly un-embedded in the material conditions of the home, as a subject that is granted an economic future that is not pre-determined by the family's socio-economic position.

The "self-help" movement, which came to prominence in Britain largely through the work of Samuel Smiles, whose writing career began with *Self-Help* (1858), a volume devoted to the habits of industry of successful businessmen, grew out of Edgeworth's notion that the child's playroom should be a training ground for participation in capitalist society. Smiles's main contribution as a writer is to locate the spirit of capitalism in childhood rather than adulthood and to argue that it is only the child who is truly in possession of ingenuity and invention. In *Life and Labour* (1887), for example, he writes that the Victorian age of invention is the result of the talent and genius of young people rather than the studied wisdom of adults:

> Most great men, even though they live to advanced years, have merely carried into execution the conceptions of their youth. The discovery of Columbus originated in the thoughts and studies of his early life. Newton's discovery of the law of gravitation was made at twenty-five, and he carried out no new work after forty-four. Watt made his invention of the condensing steam-engine at thirty-two, and his maturer years were devoted to its perfection. Youth is really the springtime of inspiration, of invention, of discovery, of work, and of energy; and age brings all into order and harmony. All new ideas are young, and originate for the most part in youth-hood, when the mind is thoroughly alert and alive, ready to recognize new truths; and though great things may be done after forty—new inventions made, new books written, new thoughts elaborated—it is doubtful whether the mind really widens and enlarges with age. (145)

According to Smiles, because innovation and invention are child-like qualities, child development must by definition involve the awakening and emergence of a capitalist spirit. In *Men of Invention and Industry* (1884), he writes of James Watt the inventor of the steam engine:

> Even when a child Watt found science in his toys. The quadrants lying about his father's carpenter's shop led him to the study of optics and astronomy; his ill health induced him to pry into the secrets of physiology; and his solitary walks through the country attracted him to the study of botany and history. (18)

Similarly, he tells the story of John Harrison, who won the famous contest in the eighteenth century to measure longitude at sea with his invention of a very accurate clock to be mounted on board ships.

Harrison's solution, we are told, was inspired by a moment in his childhood when, as he was lying in his sick bed, "a going watch was placed upon his pillow" (77). In the self-help movement, it is only the simplest objects—those that are available to any child regardless of the family's wealth—that are likely to stimulate the child's imagination. Every child, therefore, has the capacity to transform his or her material circumstances into a brighter future if he or she refuses to become embedded in the family home. The tools of social mobility, in other words, are everywhere available if only the child is child-like enough to recognize them.

The version of childhood constructed by the self-help movement was very much based upon the values of the nineteenth-century middle class, which not only believed in the virtues of hard work and industry but became obsessed with the ability of its children to compete in the labour market. Just as capitalist society needed to promote the concept of social mobility so that it could no longer be seen to victimize children, so it required that competing working-class and upper-class versions of childhood be over-written by a middle-class version of childhood. Working-class and upper-class views of childhood needed to be displaced by a middle-class view of childhood, one in which the child is defined by a potential for innovation and ingenuity in order to construct the child as that which cannot be victimized by capitalist society. Just as it was argued that working-class children born into poverty had the same potential for performing ingenuity and invention as middle-class children, so it was argued that upper-class children born into a life of privilege had been denied the circumstances that would demand that they perform ingenuity and invention. In Henry Mayhew's account of the working lives of the poor in the mid-Victorian period, *London Labour and the London Poor* (1851), a poor boy selling food in the street is asked what he wants to be when he grows up, a question that seems to hold very little meaning for him. He replies, "No I wouldn't like to go to school, nor to be in a shop, nor be anybody's servant but my own. O, I don't know what I shall be when I'm grown up. I shall take my chance like others" (123). Even as the boy is overwhelmed by his poverty he refuses to become part of a middle-class narrative of social mobility. Instead, he pledges allegiance to his fellow street vendors by refusing to imagine a future in which he is a shop clerk making his way up the social ladder. According to the self-help movement, however, it cannot be capitalism or the British class system that robs him of his childhood when it is childhood itself that will allow him to develop the tools necessary to escape poverty. Typically, children like the street vendor were depicted as old before their time, as grotesque figures who had allowed the circumstances of their birth to define their economic destinies too early in life, rendering them little adults. Likewise, upper-class children were often constructed as inferior children because of their over-reliance on the family's fortune. For example, prior to reforms in the 1850s that required its candidates to pass an examination, the British civil service was often derided as the place where an aristocratic family could be rid of its untalented offspring. Upper-class children were not very good at being children because, it was argued, they did not have to develop their capacity for ingenuity given that the family could always use its aristocratic connections to arrange suitable employment. Relying on the family's money and connections suddenly meant that the individual had not fully grown up and had not properly left home. The popularity of self-help meant that even the wealthiest and most comfortable members of society could be made to feel guilty about relying on inherited wealth. Both working-class and upper-class children were inferior children because they were not seen as using their natural capacity for ingenuity to reconstruct or re-imagine the material conditions of the family home.

It is the purpose of this study to examine the role played by nineteenth- and early twentieth-century children's literature in re-configuring the child as a subject that cannot by definition be victimized by capitalist society. While the majority of the texts covered here are typically considered children's literature, I also include texts that are not necessarily for children but that are very much concerned with the representation of the child and childhood. This study focuses in particular on some of the most well-known authors of the period—Charles Dickens, Robert Louis Stevenson, E. Nesbit, Frances Hodgson Burnett, and L.M. Montgomery (a Canadian author often studied as part of the British tradition)—and argues that they were instrumental in transforming the child from a victim of capitalism into its ideal participant as they equate capitalist ingenuity and invention with childhood development. It is my goal to re-contextualize their work so that we may better appreciate the contributions they have made to the larger argument about the position of the child within the British labour market of the nineteenth and early twentieth century.[9] It is my intent to remain within the British tradition in order to explore how British romanticism's conceptualization of childhood as separate and apart from capitalist society has been far too dominant in discussions of children's literature. It has caused us to focus almost exclusively on what capitalist society has done to the child rather than on what the child has done to capitalist society. The stability of capitalist society, I argue, was entirely contingent upon its ability to accommodate what was, at the end of the eighteenth century, its greatest threat.

Chapter 1 provides an overview of the problem of exploitation faced by nineteenth-century youths in the labour market and the ways in which Victorian authors of religious tracts, serial publications, biographies, and novels began to address the fears of a young readership that was increasingly anxious about its ability to compete. British youths were worried about being victimized by dead-end jobs like clerk and apprentice which, at the start of the century, were firmly rooted in the evangelical tradition's construction of youth employment as punishment. The tradition argued that as part of a national youth problem, young workers needed hard work and discipline to keep them on the right path and to keep them in their proper place in the social hierarchy. More sympathetic authors, however, began to focus on the career ambitions of British youths such that they re-imagined dead-end employment as a material context out of which young people could create better job opportunities.

Chapter 2 explores the ways in which Dickens's novels articulate the role of the child within nineteenth-century family capitalism. At the same time that both *David Copperfield* (1850) and *Great Expectations* (1861) represent the Victorian family firm as the ideal business, they criticize the exploitation and lack of innovation contained within it. The strategy of Dickens's narrative is to dis-embed the child in the family home such that he or she, while remaining imaginatively attached to the family business, is not victimized by it by being forced from birth to act as a source of cheap labour. The child is the site of Dickens's transformation of the family firm into an innovative business as he or she draws inspiration from its sights, sounds, and objects in order to reconfigure it as a new and improved commercial enterprise.

Chapter 3 demonstrates that Stevenson's adventure novels are fundamentally about the making of the modern professional. Within the romantic landscapes of *Treasure Island* (1883) and *Kidnapped* (1886), Stevenson's boy heroes Jim Hawkins and David Balfour are in training to become a civil servant and a lawyer, respectively, even as they inhabit romantic landscapes populated by pirates and rebel highlanders. As they work to impose the bureaucratic machinery of state on lawless regions, they absorb the spirit of romance and adventure possessed by figures like Long John Silver and Alan Breck into their professional identities. Whereas the private, libidinal self was once suppressed or victimized by the Calvinist merchant class in order to present its business practice as devoid of any duplicity, it is incorporated into the professional identity in Stevenson's adventure narratives such that it allows him or her to become a powerful social actor.

Chapter 4 argues that in Nesbit's novels *The Story of the Treasure Seekers* (1899) and *The Railway Children* (1906), the Edwardian version of the imaginative child comes into focus as children are depicted as able to circulate in the commercial world of adults while remaining entirely innocent. Her children are involved in some rather questionable business practices as they try to rescue the family from poverty but, because they are playing, they are never embedded in and corrupted by crass commercialism. In *The Story of the Treasure Seekers*, the Bastable children manage, because they are such delightful children, to make both industrial capitalism and colonial domination appear as so much innocent child's play. Likewise in *The Railway Children*, the child's playroom is connected to the industrial landscape of Britain such that the two resemble each other. The railway industry is no longer a blight on the rural landscape but an imaginative project born out of the child's playroom.

Chapter 5 examines the ways in which Burnett's novels *A Little Princess* (1905) and *The Secret Garden* (1911) are concerned with a kinder, gentler form of education, one that eliminates the tracking or streaming involved in the Victorian school system by granting a common curriculum to children from various social classes. In *A Little Princess*, the princess figure is presented to girls as a means of resisting the education system's tracking of children according to their class positions. Her storytelling, which allows her to play at being a princess, enables girls from every class and social position to resist being embedded in material contexts; it is that which allows even the most pitiable domestic servant to resist poverty. In *The Secret Garden*, the boy who is placed in the female space of the garden classroom interprets the natural world from the perspective of a scientific discoverer. The female power of the garden heals the sickly aristocrat so that he can become a powerful member of capitalist society. Colin articulates the position of the modern boy within the kinder, gentler education system as he becomes a model for the scientific discoverer inside a feminized classroom. His lack of "embeddedness" in the natural world allows him to discover and exploit the technology lying dormant within the female space of the garden.

Chapter 6 examines two novels from L.M. Montgomery's series of Anne novels, *Anne of Green Gables* (1908) and *Anne's House of Dreams* (1917), and the ways in which they allow the female subject as a victim of economic marginalization into the labour market by elevating the female life history to the level of a job qualification. Before

Montgomery's novels, women were certainly not encouraged to tell their own life stories of pain and suffering. Indeed, a woman who drew attention to her pain and suffering or complained about her lot in life violated traditional feminine codes of conduct. But as women were forced to suppress their life histories, they became victims of a capitalist society, which, in upholding traditional womanhood, denied them full participation in the marketplace. Montgomery's novels, however, construct female histories of pain and suffering as a qualification for professional employment and, in doing so, transform victimization itself into a valuable commodity.

In the light of British romanticism, it is tempting to argue that the participation of children in capitalist society represents a corruption of their essential innocence. Children and children's authors, we may feel, are not to concern themselves with such a crass and mercenary subject. But as children's authors moved beyond the romantic view of childhood to focus on the career aspirations of young people, they helped transform youth employment from a site of discipline and punishment into a site where ambitions are fulfilled. No child could be trapped and exploited when his or her natural curiosity and capacity for invention could turn dead-end employment into an opportunity for innovation. Once this argument gained traction, it became virtually impossible for any child to be seen as exploited by the marketplace. At the same time, however, the argument absolved capitalist society of any responsibility for the individual's lack of success, placing the blame instead on the shoulders of children who had failed to discover their innate talent for innovation; who had failed, in other words, to perform childhood properly. As I shall demonstrate in the next chapter, a lot of what made nineteenth-century Britain an exciting and dynamic period for children and adolescents was the fact that at the same time the labour market was difficult to navigate, the age itself became known as the age of invention, a time when every day seemed to bring another incredible scientific or technological innovation. The child was no longer a delinquent who had to be forced to perform labour to keep from committing the sin of idleness, and the child was no longer an innocent who had to be kept apart from the corruption of commercial society. Childhood became, for better or for worse, the site of a dynamic and enterprising form of capitalism.

1
Avoiding Dead Ends and Blind Alleys: Re-imagining Youth Employment in Nineteenth-Century Britain

In Dickens's *Our Mutual Friend* (1865), a poor law clerk is asked about his chances of one day advancing to the bench. He expresses a strongly held belief in social mobility even as he concedes that he will probably not benefit from it, that he will not rise up to become a judge: "The boy virtually replied that as he had the honour to be a Briton [...] there was nothing to prevent his going in for it. Yet he seemed inclined to suspect that there might be something to prevent his coming out with it" (85). Social mobility is precisely about making sure that a young lad like Dickens's law clerk "goes in for" becoming a judge even as he knows the odds are against it. One of the questions that continues to be debated by historians is the extent to which improved education and literacy levels translated for the working classes into social mobility and the movement into professional employment. While there were many individual cases in which an increase in education translated into an increase in social position, in general, social mobility was, for the nineteenth-century poor and working classes in Britain, statistically non-existent. According to David Vincent, "In the early years of the twentieth century, with the industrial economy firmly established, over 90 per cent of the sons of labouring men were themselves working with their hands at the time of their marriage" (130). Based on the actual statistics, therefore, Dickens's young clerk is right to doubt that he will ever become a judge.

The purpose of this chapter is to examine the ways in which youth employment was constructed in the first half of the nineteenth century as a solution to the threat posed to the social order by the nation's young people. Writers and commentators on the so-called "youth problem"

11

championed employment as a means of keeping youths warehoused within rigidly hierarchical workspaces so that the danger posed by their desire for social mobility could be contained. The framing of youth employment in terms of rigid discipline, however, threatened to extend exploitation and victimization well into adolescence. In order to release the nation's youth from victimization, the space of youth employment needed to be reframed as one that could not only discipline and control the nation's youth but allow those with talent to pursue their ambitions and to aspire to a higher socio-economic position. Writers began to focus in the second half of the century on the idea that despite the often severe forms of discipline built into so-called "dead-end" or "blind-alley jobs", they still afforded young workers with a material context out of which more ingenious and inventive youths could fashion much better careers. As I proceed with my overview of the position of British youths within the nineteenth-century labour market, I want to examine how authors who were aware of the frustrations of young workers began to re-imagine youth employment as a kind of necessary trap for ambitious youths. Writers of many different kinds of texts argued that it was only out of the material conditions of a seemingly dead-end job, such as clerk or apprentice, that true ingenuity and innovation could emerge. Such a representational strategy reconfigured youth employment as a disciplinary space without victims as it effectively reconciled the competing claims of social control and social mobility.

The clerk and the evangelical tradition

Sally Mitchell notes in *The New Girl* that early in the nineteenth century the job of clerk offered one of the better chances for social mobility for working-class girls, providing them as it did with something more exciting and lucrative than domestic service. By the end of the century, however, clerking had been reduced to a low-paying job offering no opportunity for promotion:

> The number of female clerks exploded from 6,000 in 1881 to 125,000 in 1911. Early in the Victorian period boys who began as clerks might expect to rise into management, but as businesses and civil service expanded, clerical work was subdivided and made routine; upward mobility became rare; and the pay eroded to working-class levels. (43)

In her analysis of the nineteenth-century banking industry, Ellen Jordan describes how, by the 1890s, the job of bank clerk was specifically set aside for women. Due to rapid expansion, banks were forced to hire male clerks from the working classes. Because they had a system of merit-based promotion, it was feared that talented working-class individuals would have to be promoted to management positions. Banks decided to hire women as clerks instead because women were resigned to the fact there was no possibility of their being promoted. The job of office clerk, which at the beginning of the century had been an avenue for upward mobility, had become by the end of the century a dead-end.[1]

Apprentices were just as likely to find their hopes of social mobility dashed as the apprenticeship system broke down in the nineteenth century. Young workers were lucky to finish their apprenticeships as employers tended to fire them just as they were about to complete their training and become skilled tradesmen. Hugh Cunningham notes how the use of machinery and an increase in the division of labour "made it possible to employ boys on routine jobs which had no element of training in them, and from which they would be dismissed when they became too expensive" (*Children of the Poor*, 183). Employers were not compelled and could not be trusted to give apprentices proper training or to allow them to complete their apprenticeships.

At the same time that Britain's industrialized economy witnessed a large number of young workers moving into urban areas to take up jobs as clerks and apprentices, the idea that the nation had a youth problem on its hands emerged. As Jenny Holt notes, the idea of a youth problem gained currency in the eighteenth century as a result of the "socio-economic 'crisis' in youth identity [that] occurred when artisans and farmers stopped using long indenture between 1750 and 1844" (25). The depopulation of the countryside caused "masterless, unanswerable, working-class adolescents" (25) to flood into urban areas. In addition to an increasing rootlessness on the part of young workers, there was a sharp rise in competition in the labour market due to both an increase in life expectancy and the frequency of sudden economic downturns. According to Holt, the new youth culture was bound together by a shared postponement of adulthood. Adolescence came into view as a distinct time of life as large numbers of youths became "alienated by lack of professional employment and the subsequent delay of marriage prospects and proper citizenship" (25).[2] Crime became re-imagined as a youth problem rather than an adult problem and, consequently, youth employment was framed as a social good, a type of charity that could keep young people off the streets and out of prisons. Despite differences in class and economic status, young people were increasingly lumped together as a problem that could only be solved by employment. Consequently, in industrialized Britain, clerking and apprenticing became not just a particular kind of employment but a particular kind of disciplinary space able to incorporate young people from all backgrounds and economic statuses into one labour pool. Clerical jobs and trade apprenticeships came to be imagined as occupations that could not only exploit the labour of young people but keep them warehoused.[3] From the young worker's point of view, however, they were positions to be left behind for more exciting prospects.

The idea that the clerk's position is designed to restrain both ambition and sexuality is found in George Lillo's eighteenth-century sentimental tragedy, *The London Merchant* (1731), which tells of the downfall of George Barnwell, a young office clerk who is seduced by Sarah Millwood, a prostitute who convinces him to steal from his employer and murder his wealthy uncle. The play is an early example of a text that lumps British youth together as a sociological problem. It came to the stage at a time when, as I have indicated, the industrial revolution was just beginning to create great numbers of anonymous office workers toiling away in obscurity in the big city. It went on to have a long run in the nineteenth century as employers paid to have it produced so that they could force their clerks to attend performances as part of their training.[4] Barnwell's story is designed to create the clerk as single-mindedly devoted to his work so that he has no other interests that might lead him astray. Barnwell's dilemma as an adolescent is that he must restrain his sexuality and ambition in order to make himself an obedient employee but, at the same time, he must be able to deploy his ambition and sexuality in order to become a mature adult. In the end, the young clerk is hanged for his crime so that he may stand as a warning to all adolescents who might attempt to challenge their employer's authority. Once Barnwell is ritually expelled from the community and the text, the good businessman, Mr Thorowgood, emerges as a figure whose private life is as pure and innocent as his business affairs. As Max Weber argues, the Calvinism of the merchant class completely erased any boundary between public and private life.[5] Because of his involvement in the world of money, the merchant had to perform innocence in the form of self-restraint at all times. While the aristocrat could attend masquerades, the merchant had to eliminate any hint of duplicity from his life in order to prove himself a scrupulous trader.

The pressure on the apprentice to remain entirely enclosed within his job and to repress his sexual desire is evident in many of the evangelical publications of the period. In the anonymous tract entitled *The Apprentice* (c.1845), for example, the author warns the apprentice that he is to spend his leisure hours learning only about his trade. He must not read adventure novels while on the job for they will only overexcite him. Anything other than a trade manual is equated with a kind of pornography that must be kept hidden. The author advises:

> above all things, do not fall into the exceedingly reprehensible prac-
> tice of taking books with you into the shop—secreting them behind
> the shelves, or in some snug drawer—and stealing away from them
> from time to time when you think you can do so unobserved, or at
> every unoccupied moment. (70)

The trade manual is satisfaction enough for the apprentice, according to the author: "it will distinguish you from the mere pounds, shillings, and pence automaton, which illiberal writers and speakers describe a shopkeeper to be" (70). As it is in Lillo's play, career frustration is made to resemble sexual frustration while the only relief offered to the young apprentice is to sublimate his desire by becoming an even better employee.

Edwin Hodder's didactic novel *The Junior Clerk* (1864) brings together clerks from different classes and social positions to create a portrait of urban youth culture. The main character, George, is from a poor family but soon falls in with a group of more sophisticated clerks described as a "fast set" (42). He is corrupted by the evil Harry Ashton, a dissipated aristocrat who favours billiards, gambling, and anti-religious lectures at the university. Eventually, George forges a cheque to cover his gam-bling debts and dies of a brain-fever alone in his shabby lodgings. Like the heroine of a popular romance novel, he is seduced by a reckless nobleman who uses him and throws him away. The story requires the poor clerk to avoid getting mixed up with gentlemen like Ashton and to suppress any desire for social mobility. Such narratives are designed to convince young workers that it is possible to achieve wealth and sta-tus using fair means, that they should remain patient and obedient and wait for a kindly employer to promote them.

Children from middle-class homes, as I have indicated, tended to pin their hopes of escaping unskilled jobs on finding professional employ-ment. In the last half of the nineteenth century, many professions underwent a process of reform in which their standards of practice and entrance qualifications were modernized. The middle classes under-stood that the acquisition of qualifications and credentials would be its primary means of distinguishing itself in the labour market. In young-adult literature, a type of adventure narrative emerged combining an account of the protagonist's struggle to become part of the nation's management class with the kind of rollicking action found in the penny dreadful.[6] This narrative synthesizes the work performed by the modern professional with a landscape of pure romance in order to make the professional career better able to capture the young reader's imagination. Meanwhile, for youths born into what might be described as practical homes, ones in which the parents were middle-class industrialists or working-class tradespeople, becoming a scientific discoverer or inventor came to represent an ideal path to achieving mobility in the marketplace. Great discoveries and inventions were so widely reported that a kind of patent fever took hold of the nation's youth. Biographies of inventors, which became an enormously popular genre, made children believe that in one eureka moment they could make a patentable discovery or invention that would make them rich and famous. For young people destined to face a competitive job market where the value of their labour was low, inventing a patented product looked like a very effective means of bypassing the labour market entirely. Readers of such biographies were taught that creating an exciting new product like the steam engine or the wireless telegraph was a much easier way of achieving success than selling one's labour. Inventing came to represent the quickest way of using practical knowledge to ascend to the top of the industrial class. These two forms of literature—the adventure story and the inventor's biography—came to represent, in many ways, an important form of career counselling. For some, it was the only real advice they were given on how to realize their career goals. In both cases, children were encouraged not only to strive for social mobility but to begin to acquire childhood experiences not just for their own sake but for the sake of their future employment. In an age when negotiating one's way in the job market was made very difficult by the lack of defined career paths, children were encouraged to take it upon themselves to find a way to stand out from the competition. As the jobs of clerk and apprentice threatened to victimize their ambitions, British youths required narratives that would allow them to turn dead-end employment into an opportunity for advancement.

The middle-class professional and fiction for the young

In the first half of the nineteenth century, James Mill announced that the middle-class had become Britain's management class: "The people of the class below are the instruments with which they work; and those of the class above, though they may be called their governors, and may really sometimes seem to rule them, are much more often, more truly and more completely under their control" (qtd in Simon, 78). Within this management class, there is an important distinction to be made between industrialists and professionals.[7] Throughout the nineteenth century, there remained in general a distrust of commercial and industrial men. Thomas Carlyle argues in *Past and Present* (1843), for example, that the British identity had become defined too much in terms of the nation's commodity markets and its bureaucratic machinery. Whereas other countries had produced great composers and great artists, England had produced only one Shakespeare because, as he argues, British artistry and invention had been "reduced to unfold itself in mere Cotton-mills, Constitutional Governments, and such like" (135). He writes, "The saddest news is, that we should find our National Existence, as I sometimes hear it said, depend on selling manufactured cotton at a farthing an ell cheaper than any other People" (157). Businessmen and industrialists were depicted as rather unimaginative figures that reduced human endeavour to nothing more than the pursuit of profit as they ignored more imaginative forms of production and innovation.

In *British Imperialism, 1688–2000*, P.J. Cain and A.G. Hopkins offer a useful description of the nineteenth-century professional, a figure who they argue falls somewhere between the landed aristocrat and the industrialist:

> This newly formed gentlemanly class, paternalist in its assumptions and held-together by a club-like spirit which resulted from a common educational and social background, was deeply suspicious both of landed indolence and of the world of trade and everyday work. But though they had to break free of aristocratic control in order to develop, both the ideology and the practice of these service-based professions were much closer to aristocratic ideals than they were to those of industry, especially as regards over their own time, their ability to charge fees rather than to depend upon salaries or wages, their contempt for mere money-making and the personal rather than mechanical nature of their work. (119–20)

The development of a professional class involved combining the gentleman's belief in aristocratic codes of conduct with the industrialist's belief in practical and technical training.[8] Monica F. Cohen in her study of professionalization, notes that the term "professional" as it indicates "a livelihood or calling socially superior to a trade or handicraft" (81) was not in usage until the latter part of the nineteenth century. By the end of the century, however, its meaning had crystallized around three criteria:

(1) expertise or specialization, often in an esoteric or abstract form of knowledge;
(2) associations and institutions that 'gate keep' by conferring and/or recognizing the training or education necessary and sufficient for such specialization;
(3) an ethic of social good attendant on the performance of that expertise (although not necessarily on an efficacious performance) by which society is persuaded of a professional's right to resources and rewards (Cohen, 39–40)

The hallmark of the professional, that which sets him or her apart from the upper-class statesman or the middle-class industrialist, is technical expertise put into practice for the greater good of society. While in practical and utilitarian circles, industrialists were often celebrated as figures who were working for the greater good as they built and improved the nation's economy, those who were running cotton mills employing children working for low wages were unlikely to garner as much sympathy as the medical doctor working to rid the nation's water supply of cholera.

Proprietary schools and utilitarian schools for the middle classes emerged at the beginning of the nineteenth century as a response to Britain's rapid industrial expansion. Practical subjects such as mathematics and drafting, as opposed to the classical subjects offered in public and grammar schools, were combined with a strict disciplinary regimen to produce young workers who would be able to drive economic development. By the end of the 1880s, however, proprietary schools were mostly bankrupt while almost no utilitarian schools, despite the plans drawn up by Jeremy Bentham and others, had actually been constructed. The failure of utilitarian education in Britain can be attributed, in part, to the privileging of professional labour over industrial labour. The middle classes were not keen on a practical form of education divorced from the public school and grammar school models because they wanted to be perceived as the right sort to run the nation. Despite the new interest in practical education, it was still an age in which the civil service exam, even after mid-century reforms, required knowledge of classical languages. In one of the few utilitarian schools built, Hazelwood, which was set up by the Hill brothers in Birmingham, the disciplinary mechanisms were designed to create a kind of robotic efficiency in its students. As Brian Simon describes it, "the bell was rung 250 times a week, on each occasion signalling a definite action" (82). The utilitarian school was to train children to be diligent in performing repetitive tasks such that they would form a class of British citizens constantly working to improve industry by making it more efficient. As Simon writes, it

> places and keeps boys in a condition in which there is little opportunity of doing wrong. Their time is completely occupied: their attention is constantly fixed; they are never idle; they never deviate from a steady and regular course: whence the habit is founded of doing everything in its proper hour and place. (84)

The problem with such schools, as Dickens's *Hard Times* (1854) so scathingly argues, is that they can only grind out graduates with imaginations more suited to regular work habits than creativity and innovation. The schools gained little traction with the middle classes because they were not too dissimilar to charity schools for the poor, which constantly treated their pupils as convicts in need of punishment.

From 1800 to 1914, the number of professional associations grew from seven to over sixty and to this number can be added the various non-qualifying associations aspiring to professional status.[9] Because it is beyond the scope of this chapter to provide an overview of so many different types of professions, I shall briefly focus on five: doctor, lawyer, civil servant, nurse, and schoolteacher. These, I would argue, were some of the most well known to children and adolescents of the period and some of the most well represented in literature. All five of these professions underwent a process of modernization, which standardized their knowledge, practice, and entrance qualifications. Three of these were also responsible for the opening of the professional ranks to women as medical schools unlocked their doors to female candidates, nursing became a legitimate occupation for middle-class women, and the female schoolteacher replaced the old-fashioned governess. The drive to professionalize occupations, to standardize their practices and accumulate bodies of technical knowledge around them, emerged at a time when the middle classes feared that the professions were already overcrowded. By the early twentieth century, these five professions were no longer constructed around apprenticeships but required study at a college or university followed by a standard entrance examination. In this way, entry into overcrowded professions was limited to those who could obtain recognized credentials.

Medical doctor became a modern profession in England with the passing of the Medical Act of 1858, which established the medical register. While there were still a number of different ways to become qualified to be on the register, the Medical Act required licensing through the three branches of medicine: the physicians, surgeons, and apothecaries.[10] Certainly, there remained a large difference between the experience of the London surgeon who often made enormous sums of money and the country physician who often struggled to establish a reliable network of paying customers, but being listed on the register meant that both figures were certified as the pre-eminent authority within their spheres of practice. The local healer practising ancient folk medicine and the travelling quack peddling fake cures were excluded from practising in any official capacity and, in this way, the Medical Act solidified the position of the doctor as part of a professional class with power over the class below. As Mary Poovey has shown in *Making a Social Body*, sanitary legislation and improved standards of hygiene meant that the homes of Britain became subject to rules set down by medical authorities.[11] The poor and working classes were colonized by the larger nation and, in the process, were consolidated as a market for professional services.

Women were allowed entry into the medical profession because of the conventional wisdom of the time that female patients should be treated by female practitioners. The majority of pioneering female doctors was drawn from middle-class families. Elizabeth Garrett Anderson was the first woman to appear on the medical register, having been licensed by the Apothecary Society in 1865. Another pioneering female doctor, Sophia Jex-Blake, was admitted to Edinburgh University in 1869 to study medicine but was ultimately refused a medical degree. She eventually gained her degree in 1877 after having founded the London School of Medicine for Women in 1874.[12] As Kristine Swenson notes, women became doctors in order to "treat their sex" (7). While domestic ideology dictated that women should not work outside the home, sexual propriety dictated that male doctors should not treat female patients. What the experience of women's entry into medicine highlights is the extent to which the female professional had to maintain a connection to domesticity even as she trained for and competed in the labour market. Female medical students and doctors constantly faced the charge that their work, particularly that involving surgery and dissection, would harden and de-feminize them. They were allowed into the profession not for their technical ability or expertise but as caregivers who would administer to female patients just as they would administer to family members.

In the legal profession, the split between the gentleman's breadth of knowledge and the industrialist's practical training played out as a split between barristers and solicitors on the one side, and attorneys on the other. While barristers and solicitors were drawn from the upper classes, attorneys were drawn from both the middle and working classes. The training of barristers and solicitors was far less practical because their value was very much class-based; their good breeding made them the right sort to be handling the affairs of other gentlemen and of the nation. An attorney, in contrast, often began as a copy clerk at the age of 10. If he impressed the attorney, he would then article. His training was on the job and completely immersed in the day-to-day operations of the firm. The attorney may have been drawn from the lower orders but his technical mastery of legal proceedings made him essential. According to W. Wesley Pue, attorneys developed their technical knowledge of the law by offering lectures to apprentices. He writes, "Symbolically such programs endorsed the value of precise training in matters of practice as a method of gaining admission to the profession" (251). The barrister, embarrassed by his own technical inadequacies, hit back at the attorney by claiming that he was, as Pue writes, merely "a mechanical agent for carrying out the practical processes of the profession" (255). The 1846 Report on Legal Education attempted to build a bridge between the two sides in order to standardize legal training. It sought to create a new "scientific jurist", by directing legal training towards the unification of a broader education with an education in legal procedures. According to Pue, "The proposals called for both branches of the legal profession to become both learned (in literature, languages, and abstract thought) *and* skilled in the peculiar subject matter or technical competence that was of relevance to their clients" (263). The attempt to synthesize aristocratic and utilitarian practices within the profession remained a tension throughout the second half of the nineteenth century. Because apprenticeships continued in the last half of the century, there was no motivation for attorneys to be trained as gentlemen before pursuing their practical studies and, because being called to the bar did not yet require that an examination be passed, barristers were not forced to prove their legal expertise as a qualification for entry.

The British civil service was modernized by the Northcote-Trevelyan Report of 1853, which sought to transform it from a dumping ground for the indolent aristocracy into an efficient bureaucracy managed by talented individuals.[13] The report divided the civil service into two tiers—managers and clerks. Managers were to be university educated individuals from the upper and middle classes who could pass the civil service exam. Trevelyan insisted that the exam should remain connected to a gentleman's education, that it should test knowledge of classical languages, literature, history, and geography. Such an exam was to favour a candidate possessing both an upper-class breadth of knowledge and a middle-class proficiency at writing exams. Harold Perkin notes that, as a result, the civil service slowly changed from "a predominantly upper-class, major public school educated elite, to a predominantly middle-class, minor public and grammar school-educated cadre recruited typically from the sons of small business men and the lesser professionals" (91). The qualified middle-class candidate replaced the well-bred gentleman as the civil service looked to identify talented rather than aristocratic candidates.

The story of nursing in the nineteenth century is the story of turning what was once a disreputable occupation on a level just above the prostitute into a heroic profession on a level just below the doctor. As Lee Holcombe writes in *Victorian Ladies at Work*, very few women in mid nineteenth-century Britain wanted to become nurses because of the deplorable conditions:

> The nurses of the day lived and worked in appalling surroundings; their work was considered a particularly repugnant form of domestic service for which little or no education and special training were necessary; their living was meagre indeed; and not surprisingly, their ranks were recruited from among the very lowest classes of society. (68)

According to Swenson, the "tenacious link between the nurse and the working-class prostitute" (5) continued until Florence Nightingale's experience in the Crimean War transformed the nurse into the "lady with the lamp", a figure of heroic self-sacrifice. Nightingale envisaged nursing as providing employment for both working- and middle-class women. Nursing colleges connected to hospitals were eventually set up so that young women could gain qualifications. As the nurse gained legitimacy, however, she continued to be looked upon with suspicion by doctors because she threatened to appropriate some of their professional responsibilities. Swenson writes, "Because she threatened the status of medical men and the traditional role of the Victorian woman, the nurse was professionally subjugated to her 'superior', the doctor, and culturally re-domesticated in the press and fiction" (6). The battle for nursing to become an acceptable career for middle-class women was won only when it was fashioned as an extension of work done in the home, not as an encroachment into the specialized expertise of the doctor. Nightingale herself, as Poovey argues, promoted nursing as a form of housekeeping.[14] Even as young women entered jobs that would eventually require expertise, such expertise had to be downplayed in order to emphasize the connection of women's labour to the home.

The new female schoolteacher, as opposed to the old governess, represents a profession in which academic performance became, not surprisingly, a necessary job qualification.[15] Under the pupil-teacher system, good students with good grades were already leading classrooms. According to Vincent, the transition from student to teacher represented one of the clearest paths from school to the workforce:

> For those who performed outstandingly well at their lessons, the introduction of the pupil teacher scheme in 1846 provided an immediate extension of the system of examination and advance. Through a combination of practice and further testing, bright children could move directly into the nascent teaching profession, with the most successful eligible for Queen's Scholarships and another two years at a training college. (127)

A gifted child could move from being the pupil to being the teacher based solely on her academic performance. According to Mitchell, teaching afforded the most opportunity for social mobility as female teachers were often drawn from the working classes:

> The elementary schoolteacher was likely to be the daughter of a tradesman or even a labourer. Usually herself from a state-supported school, she began at fourteen as a "pupil teacher"—but after passing an exam at eighteen, she went to a training college and, later in the period, sometimes to a university. (35)

While the female schoolteacher was certainly one of the lesser professionals in terms of social position, she was instrumental in extending the influence of women beyond the home.

The early feminist writer Emily Davies, as Jordan notes, argued for the same education for both girls and boys so that young women could obtain independent and lifelong professional careers. Jordan writes:

> if women were to be able to pursue the standard upper-middle-class careers of physician, barrister, upper-division civil servant, and (for those with independent incomes) politician, they must be admitted to university education; and to fit them for university education, they must pursue the same secondary curriculum as boys. ("Making Good Wives", 456)

She notes, however, that Davies was almost alone in promoting independent careers for women. Most feminist writers tended to promote the idea of the "accomplished married woman" ("Making Good Wives", 448). Time spent in the workforce was useful for a woman not in and of itself but because it gave her more value in the home. For a middle-class woman lacking property, a working life before marriage increased her value by sending the message to a prospective husband that she could stand on her own if necessary. The idea that a woman should be educated to become proficient in a particular area of expertise was not promoted either. A woman's education, it was argued, should not be about overloading the mind with facts but should instead be about sound moral reasoning. If a woman's role was to be a good wife and mother, then her good judgement was to make her the moral authority in the household.[16] Jordan argues, however, that many women working in factories chose to marry not simply to conform to domestic ideology but because housework offered better working conditions and, in some cases, increased the family's income by reducing the need to pay others for domestic services ("Exclusion of Women", 278). At the beginning of the twentieth century, domestic science classes were being offered for women at local technical colleges. Women who had technical knowledge of household management were left to take control of the home as male members deferred to their superior know-how.[17] Professionalization worked at the domestic level as domestic science training gave married women the technical authority to control the home.

While authors of the evangelical tradition tended to view the labour market in terms of its ability to impose self-restraint and self-denial on the nation's youth, authors who were more concerned with the ability of middle-class children to compete began to view the labour market in terms of its ability to fulfil childhood ambitions. Rather than confining young workers to the office, the tradesman's shop, or the warehouse, more child-friendly authors released youths into the wide world to make their mark and to come of age. The quest to find suitable employment became conflated with the release of youthful energy as protagonists were allowed to pursue fulfilling work. Juvenile delinquency, which the evangelical tradition had argued was lying within every child, came to be depicted as something that if controlled properly could be incorporated into the identity of the modern professional. Authors concerned with the obtainment of professional employment argued that the young middle-class hero, in order to be a leader in society, must not be entirely innocent. Whereas the danger lurking within the working classes was to be strictly controlled and punished, the middle-class individual was required to have some experience of vice and corruption in order to be able to recognize and control it in others. The middle-class professional became, in other words, a figure that could make vice and corruption work for the good of the nation. If the need for academic study and the obtainment of technical expertise threatened to keep the child confined within a disciplinary space, then the dangerous adventures to be had by the professional represented the reward for such perseverance. In young adult literature, the movement into professional employment came to be told through adventure narratives in which the spirit of adventure, when combined with technical expertise, turns into the spirit of entrepreneurship and nation-building. The studious youth, as opposed to the more physical youth, had to find an adventurous spirit lying within that would allow him or her to break out of dead-end employment and take his or her place in the nation's management ranks.

The school story is the genre in which we might expect to find young protagonists working to pass examinations in an effort to gain entry into the professional ranks. The public school story as it is epitomized by Thomas Hughes's *Tom Brown's Schooldays* (1857) is, however, usually about building character of the kind that will allow the pupil to take his rightful place at the top of the social hierarchy. Career training and résumé building are not as important in school stories as the social interaction of day-to-day school life and the physical exertion of participating in tough sports like rugby football. Academic performance is typically only one small part of the making of the successful public school boy. The jobs the students will undertake in later life are almost never referred to because of the understanding that well-bred children will inevitably rise to their rightful positions. As Holt notes in her study of public school stories, they "often neglect or denigrate science, technology, and modern languages, or anything else related to industry or the economy" (5) in favour of an Arnoldian "inculcation of skills necessary to citizenship and statesmanship" (5). While school stories, in general, tended to follow the model of Hughes's book in stressing character as important above all else, academic performance became more significant in stories set in provincial boarding schools for the middle classes. Protagonists still built their characters on the playing field but they were increasingly shown as training for a particular professional career.

In contrast to stories set in older, more established boarding schools, those set in newer, more regional schools tended to mix children of different classes together in a single classroom. In Talbot Baines Reed's *Adventures of a Three-Guineau Watch* (1883), for example, the fictional boarding school of Randlebury includes poor scholarship students, middle-class students from professional families, and entitled sons of country squires. In Reed's story, pupils from all three groups are depicted in the same academic setting in order to play out a competition to decide which class should have control of the nation. The narrator of the story, a pocket watch that makes its way from one character to another, witnesses the development of three middle-class boys, Charlie, Jim, and Tom, who grow up to become a military officer, a doctor, and a clergyman, respectively. Meanwhile, the son of the local squire, Gus, is depicted as "one of the smallest and most vicious boys at Randlebury" (53), a boy whose sense of privilege has ruined him:

> He was the son of a country squire, who had the unenviable reputation of being one of the hardest drinkers and fastest riders in his county; and the boy had already shown himself only too apt a pupil in the lessons in the midst of which his childhood had been passed. He had at his tongue's tip all the slang of the stables and all the blackguardisms of the betting-ring; and boy—almost child—as he was, he affected the swagger and habits of a "fast man," like a true son of his father. (53–4)

Gus falls into the aristocrat's dissolution far too early in life as he emulates his father's bad habits. In contrast, the school's working-class scholarship student, George, does not grow up at all. He confines himself to his room as a celibate as he studies to win a lucrative fellowship but, because he has neglected his health, he dies of a fever before he can reap the benefits of his hard work. The three middle-class boys, in contrast, play just enough sports and study just hard enough to become well-rounded professional men. Tom, however, eventually undergoes a period of dissolution, which culminates in him being thrown out of medical school. His first misstep occurs when he begins to frequent a burlesque theatre with his old classmate Gus. Later, he shows up on the ward intoxicated:

> At last, about six months ago, Tom was found tipsy in the dissecting-room at the hospital and cautioned by the Board. A fortnight later he was found in a similar state in one of the wards, and then he was summarily expelled from the place, and his name was struck off the roll of students. (132)

After being stripped of his professional status, he descends into criminality until he is saved by his friend Jim who bails him out of jail. Tom eventually finishes his medical degree and finds redemption on the battlefield as an army doctor. Unlike Gus and George, he is redeemable because he is able to combine his experience of vice and corruption with hard work and industry to forge a professional identity for himself. Despite being a clergyman, Jim must also have experience with corruption when he moves from the tranquil countryside to take up an urban curacy where vice and criminality are rampant:

> Instead of fresh country air he had now to breathe the vitiated air of close-courts and ill-kept streets; and instead of an atmosphere of repose and innocence, he had now to move in an atmosphere of vice and disorder, from which very often his soul turned with a deep disgust. (188–9)

In order to become a complete clergyman, he must leave the innocent world of the country and expose himself to vice. The professional who works for the greater good must have some familiarity with vice and corruption in order to deal with the poor in their own environment. Moral purity, in fact, disqualifies him from doing the dirty work of cleaning up the nation. In order to become a doctor on the battlefield or a clergyman in a poor parish, the professional must be as comfortable in dangerous areas as the military man.

Emigration to the much less competitive colonial labour market represents in many adventure stories an attractive alternative to languishing in dead-end employment. G.A. Henty's *In the Heart of the Rockies* (1895), for example, opens with what is perhaps the most forthright expression of the anxiety experienced by British youths as they faced a tough job search in a competitive labour market. The story of the adolescent hero, Tom Wade, begins when he is newly orphaned and must begin to earn his own living. Because his education has been cut short and his middle-class family lacks the connections that might help him find suitable employment, he decides to forsake Britain for the American west. He tells his sister,

> I can be of no use here, Cary. What am I good for? Why, I could not earn enough money to pay for my own food, even if we knew anyone who would help me to get a clerkship. I am too young for it yet. I would rather go before the mast than take a place in a shop. I am too young even to enlist. I know just about as much as other boys at school, and I certainly have no talent anyway, as far as I can see at present. I can sail a boat, and I won the swimming prize a month ago, and the sergeant who gives us lessons in single-stick and boxing says that he considers me his best pupil with the gloves, but all these things put together would not bring me in sixpence a week. (1)

Tom acknowledges that his qualifications are only good for a military post or a clerkship and that his future lies, therefore, in America where he does not need a specialized talent in order to compete. He recognizes that his lack of talent forces him to use his physical strength in the much less competitive colonial labour market.[18] Rather than go boldly into the colonies as a conquering hero, Henty's unqualified protagonist slinks off to America to take his chances in exile.

Many writers of adventure fiction began, however, to depict employment in the colonies as the severest form of dead-end employment, as a space that no amount of ingenuity could transform, in order to downplay the lure of the lack of competition to be found in distant locales. Charlotte Maria Tucker's *The Lake of the Woods* (1889),[19] for example, reverses the usual hero's journey as it is told from the perspective of the son of a military officer, Alfred Gaveston, who grows up in the colonies rather than in Britain. Alfred is the victim of his father's military career, which ensures that, despite his being a talented lad, he goes uneducated in the backwoods of Canada. As Captain Gaveston tells his daughter at the outset of the story, he himself had to emigrate to Canada because he could not compete back home: "I saw no other means of securing independence; I would not be a burden on my relations; better a life of honourable labour in a free country, than the vain struggle to make my way in some over-crowded profession at home" (6–7). He laments that while he joined the military because of his lack of ability, his son is much better able to compete back home:

> "Alfred was made for something better than felling trees," said the captain, sadly. "Amy, when I find how your brother's mind is developing, what a grasp of thought he possesses, how he masters every difficulty before him, I sometimes bitterly regret that I ever brought my family to settle in Rupert's Land, to bury talents such as his in a wild unsettled country like this! [...] Had he been at school he would have risen to be the head of it; were he to enter a profession, he would win his way to distinction." (6)

In Tucker's story, Canada requires only cheap physical labour and thus it provides Alfred with no opportunities to move into the management class. The colonial setting is suitable for a youth lacking intellectual abilities but, for the more academically gifted child, it is a wilderness where there is nothing but physical exertion. Poor Alfred is embedded in manual labour almost from birth as the wilderness setting cannot educate him properly or provide the means for proving himself worthy of better employment. He lacks the material context out of which he can begin to build a professional career for himself. Tucker's novel excises from the child's imagination the idea that escaping to the colonies can somehow offer a release from exploitation as it demonstrates that only back-breaking labour is required in the undeveloped world. The problem with the colonies is that they embed the youth in the kinds of manual labour that cannot properly be turned into a professional career.

As Kelly Boyd has shown in his study of Victorian periodicals for boys, adventure stories began to focus on careers in the domestic economy rather than careers in the colonial economy. In earlier stories, the young hero emigrates to the colonies because he possesses only the old-fashioned qualifications of physical strength and courage but, in later stories, he possesses a particular technical skill. Boyd notes how the periodicals began to portray white-collar employment as a heroic part of the larger imperial adventure: "Young readers needed to be moulded into proper men who could take their place in the imperial project, whether as overseas administrators and merchants, or as loyal acolytes back home" (49). He notes how at the end of the century periodicals shifted their focus to very precise careers such as pharmaceutical dispensing, which had very little to do with imperialism. Young lads leaving for the colonies could escape Britain's overcrowded job market but stories increasingly reminded them that if they were to become part of the nation's management class they would have to possess some kind of technical expertise.

What we find then is that the dead-end job became integrated into the making of the middle-class professional. Running away to the colonies in order to skip over a period of training provided by a job like clerk or apprentice does not give the youth the materials out of which he or she can achieve the technical skill and administrative experience necessary to become a professional. Harold Bindloss's novel *True Grit* (1904), which is greatly indebted to the Stevensonian adventure story (the subject of Chapter 3), demonstrates how the job of clerk allows the young professional to acquire technical expertise even as it exploits him. The middle-class youth requires such a disciplinary space, according to the narrative, because it forces him to unlock the potential lying within him. Without the frustration produced by the dead-end job, the boy hero cannot be forced to find his ingenuity and invention. The young hero, Benson, is able to combine the administrative skills he acquires as a shipping clerk with the military skills he acquires during his adventures in Africa to obtain a job as a high-ranking civil servant. As he toils away in a warehouse in Liverpool, where goods from all over the globe arrive, he imagines the adventure available to him in the world beyond his workplace. He tells a fellow clerk, "Those ships set one thinking. [...] Sometimes when I'm extracting from the warehouse books I dream about the men who grew the grain, and while I wonder how they live and whether they work as hard as we do, the office gets choky and small" (83). While he certainly dislikes being a clerk in a warehouse, it provides him with a material context out of which he can begin to fashion a better career. By studying his situation in the warehouse and the nature of the work being done, Benson comes to understand that he belongs in management: "He began to understand that if England was great and powerful, it was this strenuous labour her greatness was based upon, and that the men who could control and direct such tremendous energies did more to hold her foremost than general or admiral" (129–30). He then leaves Liverpool behind for Africa where he eventually becomes connected to the colonial office and, after displaying his bravery during a violent native uprising, he is finally given a prominent position in the civil service. The studious lad with accounting skills is granted control of the national phallus—the ability to control and direct the energy of the national body—after proving himself to be tough enough to do the tough work of imperialism.

If we turn to novels featuring the female professional, we find that she also requires a period of confinement in order to release the potential within her. While Charlotte Bronte's *Jane Eyre* (1847) is certainly not an adventure novel, it is about the female protagonist's desire to break out of dead-end employment to become part of the larger project of nation building. It is about the creation of the female schoolteacher out of the old-fashioned governess, a transformation that plays out in terms of sexual constraint. As a middle-class orphan without any family connections, Jane falls to the level of charity-school girl as she becomes an inmate of Lowood institution. Under the tutelage of her teacher Miss Temple, however, she is able to gain enough experience as a pupil-teacher to advertise her services in the newspaper. Unfortunately, she finds that her first job is a blind alley as it puts her to work in Thornfield Hall as a governess to only one student, an aristocratic French girl. Jane uses her confinement, however, as the catalyst for discovering her identity as a middle-class schoolteacher. As she struggles to escape the fate of the mad woman in the attic, a woman who is literally locked inside the home, she shines a light into the dark corners of the manor house to find that which must be exposed so that the home can be subjected to middle-class standards. While the colonial subject, Bertha, is restrained and controlled by the patriarch, Jane deploys her sexuality in the form of ambition.[20] She escapes from the job of governess, which shuts her up in the home, to become a modern schoolteacher connected to the bustling commercial world lying beyond the aristocrat's retreat. She constructs out of the material context in which the governess is exploited a more modern job that releases her from confinement. In the final scene, she cuts the hair of the badly burned and dishevelled Rochester in order to colonize him on behalf of the middle classes.[21] Rochester has returned back to a wild and natural state but when she picks up a pair of scissors to cut his hair she proceeds to re-civilize him. She wields the national phallus in a way that releases her sexual energy and that restrains his corrupt sexual energy.[22] Jane's story proves that a young schoolteacher cannot rely on an advertisement placed in a newspaper to find work in the management ranks. She must prove herself to be a reformer and an innovator within the dead-end space of youth employment before she is worthy of professional status.

By the end of the nineteenth century, the purpose of the female career novel was to reconcile the audience's desire to be both plunged into physical danger and rescued from economic marginalization. Novels about young women in the medical profession became popular as they depicted female nurses and doctors as occupying exciting and important positions in society. As Martha Vicinus argues, even though nursing came to be promoted as a safe and respectable profession, young women were able to recognize its potential for adventure: "Beneath the rhetoric lay a desire to see life that was ordinarily hidden from a middle-class girl. She found cases of venereal disease, delirium tremens, malnourished children, and tubercular mothers that more than met her expectations" (104). In Eva Jameson's novel *The Making of Teddy* (c. 1904), for example, a young unmarried nurse takes time out from her job on the ward changing linens and bed pans to go into the homes of the poor as an inspector figure and, in the process, ends up circulating among some very unsavoury characters. During her work in the slums of London, she rescues the boy of an alcoholic mother from a gang of thieves that tries to turn him into a house breaker. As the young nurse rescues the boy, she proves she is more than just a typical ward nurse, that she has the same heroic spirit as Florence Nightingale. Just like the male professional, she cannot be entirely innocent if she is to be able to patrol the mean streets of London. Despite the fact that Jameson's novel was published by the Religious Tract Society, it has coded into its dangerous action scenes the desire of the heroine to discover dark secrets, including her own ambition and sexuality, lying hidden beneath the veneer of respectable society. While women were initially allowed entry into professional occupations such as doctor, nurse, and teacher because of their connections to care-giving and domesticity, it became apparent that, if they were to become inspector figures whose job it was to reform the homes of the poor, they could not be represented as entirely pure and innocent.

Many female career novels of the period are constructed, however, by marriage-plots in which female ingenuity is closely controlled by a male suitor. Female doctors are often cast as adventurous figures who administer to poor patients in bad neighbourhoods but they usually remain under some kind of surveillance. In Margaret Todd's *Mona MacLean, Medical Student* (1894), for example, the protagonist becomes a doctor in a London slum, a setting that places her in danger but that also keeps her confined within domestic ideology as she operates as a care-giver who treats her own sex. While she must go into dangerous areas to extend health and hygiene standards to the poor, she eventually settles down to marry a paternalistic male doctor who has helped her to pass her examinations after she has spent years failing to pass them on her own.[23] After failing her exams, Mona retreats to a dead-end job in a woman's clothing shop only to be discovered by a sympathetic male doctor. She uses the frustration of unskilled employment to motivate her to make one final attempt to pass but, in the end, she requires the help of an older and wiser husband who rescues her from her Cinderella-like obscurity.

Mona's story demonstrates the extent to which female ingenuity and ambition continued to be equated with the threat of female sexuality.

In nineteenth-century narratives in which the protagonist is a young professional-in-training, the protagonist typically fights against his or her own exploitation in the labour market. Unlike the neutered clerk or apprentice, the professional is a figure who is allowed to embrace ambition as a kind of sexual energy that is required to break out of dead-end labour and to do the work of nation-building. Indeed, the more academically inclined, middle-class child has to find an adventurous spirit lying within in order to make technical expertise work for the good of the nation. Crucially, the dead-end job the young protagonist is trapped in is no longer a space that victimizes and exploits him or her. It is no longer a space to run away from as it is integrated into the narrative as the material context that will allow him or her to gain expertise. Without a job like clerk or apprentice, the young worker has no place to even begin to imagine becoming a professional. Even as the adventure story maintains the need to confine young workers as part of the youth problem, it constructs the dead-end job as the material context out of which a better career can be made and, in doing so, allows the ingenuous youth to leave his less talented co-workers behind.

Working-class youths and the self-help movement

Throughout the nineteenth century, various education commissions made the case that in order for Britain to stay ahead of other industrialized nations its workers would have to be better educated, better able to function in an increasingly complex work environment. The need for a better educated workforce in order to meet the demands of complex industrial production became conflated with the promotion of social mobility in the nineteenth century. The problem for working-class youths, however, was that the two had very little to do with each other. While the Forster Act of 1870, which made education compulsory until the age of 12, is often thought to have been an important step towards extending the possibility of social mobility to the masses, it was more about fitting young workers into the increasingly more abstract spaces of industrial production. Young industrial workers had to become more disciplined in their habits in order to become accustomed to modern workspaces. Consequently, inculcating them with middle-class standards of discipline became a means of replacing the mentality of the small workshop or guild where work was performed on a piecemeal basis with the mentality of the efficient, mechanized factory where work was performed according to a rigid schedule.[24] The promotion of social mobility became part of a strategy to adapt working-class children to abstract space rather than to ensure their ability to move into the middle classes. As Michael J. Childs notes in *Labour's Apprentices*,

> Late Victorian writers were proud that "there is being prepared, there now seems within measurable distance of completion, the ladder that will enable any English boy and many girls to accomplish the ascent from the gutter to the highest teaching of the University." This process, however, involved a formidable series of curricular, financial and cultural hurdles, including one whereby the boy "is to be separated from the class in which he was born and his brains recruited for the governing minority". (43)

The problem with compulsory education was that it was in no way tailored to the specific needs of working-class children. The middle-class codes of conduct, which were supposed to help working-class children become disciplined enough to climb the ladder, were designed to alienate them from their working-class homes and communities in which they were embedded and to recruit their brains for the new reality of the efficient factory floor. Before the Forster Act, the Revised Code of 1862 radically transformed state-funded elementary schools by tying their funding to mechanical measures of success, such as regular attendance and examination scores. It was designed, according to Vincent, to disconnect working-class children from their homes and to remake them as middle-class subjects:

> the Revised Code with its clearly defined standards were associated with the move towards an exam-based meritocracy in the middle class. In both cases the paper qualifications were designed to erode the pervasive influence of birth and family connections in the sphere of occupation. Just as the professional and Civil service exams were to replace nepotism and patronage, so the structured curriculum [...] was at the centre of the attack on the working-class family. The hierarchy of attainment in the schools would challenge the scale of values in the home, and the evidence of ability represented by a completed education would substitute for the recommendation of a parent or a relation to an employer. (120)

Working-class children would have to learn to attend school regularly and pass examinations like middle-class children if they were to start their climb.[25] At the same time, however, working-class children were subjected to a rigid code of discipline designed to teach them that they were essentially meant for manual labour.[26] They were sent, in other words, a mixed message that told them a) they were born for working-class labour and b) working-class labour is repugnant. Even as working-class children were told they should strive for something more, they were being trained for mechanized labour. Such a strategy was effective for adapting working-class subjects to the modern factory in which the worker is often not required to have a skilled trade. By identifying less with the skilled tradesman and more with the white-collar worker, the industrial labourer became less embedded in working-class traditions even as he or she was unlikely to move up in social status. The industrial labourer and the clerk began to resemble each other as both operated within an abstract workspace rather than within the materially dense space of the family workshop.[27]

Childs's analysis of working-class education, however, warns us not to overestimate the education system's ability to undermine working-class values. We should not, he argues, underestimate the ability of the child to maintain his or her working-class identity when faced with the coercion of the classroom:

> As a formative influence, the school could not compete with the omnipresent realities of working-class life in the home, the street and the workplace. Social control, or ideological indoctrination by the middle class, paradoxically had little overt success because of the pervasive economic control exercised by the same class and because of the responses to this environment created by the working-class family. (50)

As he notes, the school system entrenched class divisions by putting working-class children into separate elementary schools that were much different from public and grammar schools. While he is right to downplay the idea that education reform could somehow eliminate working-class culture, it did bring working-class culture within a new disciplinary vocabulary. Even as the gospel of social mobility was preached in ragged schools and elementary schools, the education system was not in any way reformed to meet the specific needs of poor and working-class children. Rather than setting up working-class children for success according to the standards of their own community, the Revised Code set them up to fail according to middle-class standards. Universal education, which many parents and children strongly resisted, subjected the working classes to statistical measures of aberrant behaviour. According to Cunningham, the "science of childhood" that emerged in the period subjected poor children to analysis that correlated, for example, "the height and weight of schoolchildren with their living conditions" (192).[28] While Childs argues that many youths left school as soon as they could, that "they voted with their feet as soon as possible and headed into the inevitable, yet seemingly free and exciting, world of work" (50), after 1870 they did so not as proud rebels but as delinquent school leavers. Working-class culture was not eradicated by education reforms, just as it was not eradicated by sanitary legislation and other forms of state intrusion, but it was increasingly constructed as an inferior version of middle-class culture. The working-class child was certainly not eradicated but he or she was increasingly constructed as an inferior version of the middle-class child.

Because the apprenticeship system of the nineteenth century was in a state of crisis, many working-class youths when they left school were denied entry into skilled trades. As Childs describes, young labourers were trained up to the point of becoming semi-skilled only to be let go by the firm at the age of 18 or 19 as younger, cheaper labour was hired. British youths moved from one unskilled job to the next as they found it difficult to stay with one firm and to move up into jobs requiring specialized skills.[29] As the apprenticeship system broke down, vocational training was, to some extent, shifted to technical colleges. According to Vincent, "something like a national system was created, and by 1912–13, 180,000 men over the age of sixteen were studying science subjects after work. By the end of the period, day classes in vocational subjects were also available in the major cities in 'Central' and 'Junior Technical' schools" (117). Vocational training, however, ultimately failed to gain a foothold in the British education system. The number of youths training at technical colleges represented a very small percentage of the total, while the continued breakdown of the apprenticeship system meant that more and more were doomed to remain un-skilled or semi-skilled. Vincent notes how vocational training was deliberately kept out of the curriculum because teachers did not want to be associated with it: "The subsequent development of the National and British Schools Societies served merely to consolidate the exclusion of work training. As their staff sought professional status, they were naturally reluctant to acquire or display an ability to teach manual skills" (106). As David Wardle writes, "The emphasis remained very much on the three 'Rs', and science, manual work, cookery and drawing were 'extras' very liable to be cut in time of economy" (93). If a working-class youth wanted to become a skilled labourer, he or she increasingly had to turn to a course of night study or home study. Jeffrey Richards notes that working men formed "mutual improvement societies" (60), small groups in which instruction was given by the members themselves.[30] Consequently, one of the important figures to emerge in the nineteenth century is the working-class autodidact studying a subject in his or her spare time in order to compensate for the lack of formal vocational training and proper apprenticeships. At the same time, an enormous number of self-help publications were published in order to make up for the lack of practical training given to British youths. The self-help movement's solution to the breakdown of the apprenticeship system was not, however, to train adolescents to become skilled tradesmen. Instead, it was to train them to use the materials of the family home, the warehouse and the workshop as the abstract building blocks for social mobility, for finding a way out of the working classes.[31] The most exciting of these publications were biographies of famous inventors, which were devoured by youths searching for a way to avoid falling into the trap of unskilled labour.

The most well-known author of biographies of scientific discoverers and inventors was, as I have indicated, Samuel Smiles, whose many books tell one story after another of a great man who as a youth toiled away in a menial job until he could make the discovery that brought him fame and fortune and allowed him to leave behind the working classes.[32] His books are driven by a real sense of the despair felt by youths stuck in unskilled jobs with no hope of ever breaking out of them.[33] For example, in *Self-Help* (1859), he refers to an "unhappy youth who committed suicide a few years since because he had been 'born to be a man and condemned to be a grocer'" (153). He encourages youths to use their spare time to undertake a course of home study because, as he argues, the education system is of very little value to practical individuals:

Schools, academies, and colleges, give but the merest beginnings of culture in comparison with it. Far more influential is the life-education daily given in our homes, in the streets, behind counters, in workshops, at the loom and the plough, in counting-houses and manufactories, and in the busy haunts of men. (3)

He tells the reader how Michael Faraday made important early discoveries while working as an apprentice in a bookbinder's shop:

In like manner Professor Faraday, Sir Humphry Davy's scientific successor, made his first experiments in electricity by means of an old bottle, while he was still a working bookbinder. And it is a curious fact that Faraday was first attracted to the study of chemistry by hearing one of Sir Humphry Davy's lectures on the subject at the Royal Institution. A gentleman, who was a member, calling one day at the shop where Faraday was employed in binding books, found him poring over the article "Electricity" in an Encyclopaedia placed in his hands to bind. (73)

Faraday is celebrated by Smiles for the way he transformed the common items lying around the shop into the materials of scientific discovery. Self-help books made the idea of becoming an inventor and taking out a patent suddenly seem a real possibility. Any child with some study and ingenuity could, like Faraday, transform an old bottle into a patented invention.[34]

Smiles's interest in the scientific possibilities contained in everyday objects was almost certainly influenced, as I have indicated, by Maria Edgeworth's advice handbook for parents, *Essays on Practical Education* (1801), which discusses the importance of educational toys in a child's development. According to Edgeworth, the home is to become a kind of classroom in which playtime offers the child a course of study in practical subjects. She encourages parents to give children toys that are miniature models of the machines used in actual manufacturing processes:[35]

models of instruments used by manufacturers and artists should be seen; many of these are extremely ingenious; spinning-wheels, looms, paper-mills, wind-mills, water-mills, might with great advantage be shown in miniature to children. We have found that two or three hundred bricks formed in plaster of Paris, on a scale of a quarter of an inch to an inch, with a few lintils, &c. in proportion, have been a lasting and useful fund of amusement. (31)

As Teresa Michals notes, Edgeworth believed that toys should also have some connection to physical and natural science. These include "gardening tools, wooden blocks, pulleys, pumps, prints of familiar objects and animals, microscopes, pencils, paper, chemistry kits, modeling clay and paste-board construction sets, to name just a few" (Michals, 39). In order to provide a child with a proper childhood, Edgeworth's audience of parents is to construct the child's playroom as a practical classroom or a workshop in order to allow him or her to discover his or her ingenuity which, she argues, is an innate part of the child.[36]

In the final section of *Men of Invention and Industry* (1884), Smiles includes conversations with working-class autodidacts who have continued their home study into adulthood. He relates, for example, his conversation with a man named John Robertson, a railway porter who is also an amateur astronomer talented enough to have come to the attention of professionals in the field. Robertson tells Smiles, however, that despite his ability he has no intention of leaving his job with the railway:

> The company are very kind to me, and I hope I serve them faithfully. It is true that Sheriff Barclay has, without my knowledge, recommended me to several well-known astronomers as an observer. But at my time of life changes are not to be desired. I am quite satisfied to go on as I am doing. My young people are growing up and willing to work for themselves. (330)

Robertson possesses enough technical ability in the field to become a professional astronomer but he makes it clear that he has no intention of leaving the working classes. His course of home study is a regression back into childhood, an escape from the drudgery of being a porter. He is not, as an adult, to use his abilities to transcend his already well-established class position because, in Smiles's self-help books, scientific discoveries and inventions are the stuff of childhood. They are marked off as such because ingenuity is for Smiles embodied by the child rather than the adult. He does not want the social order thrown into chaos as grown men begin later in life to chase after social mobility. At the same time, however, a father like Robertson, a working-class autodidact, destabilizes the working-class home for his children. He is the perfect Edgeworthian parent, constructing his home as a practical classroom for his children, who will use it to discover the ingenuity and innovation that will allow them to transcend their class position. His continued education and relationships with professional men announce to his children that they are not to follow in the footsteps of a railway porter.

So intense was the excitement around inventors and inventions in the nineteenth century that some authors felt the need to throw cold water on the growing patent fever. In the tract, *The Apprentice*, an uncle tells his nephew, "The biography of practical men will be eminently useful. These and many other kindred studies, may profitably fill up a portion of your leisure time; nor will they unfit you—with proper caution on your part—for the common everyday business of life" (69). Towards the end of the century, however, the RTS tract, *Two Ways to*

Begin Life (c.1883) indicates that the popularity of biographies of inventors had gotten out of hand, that they were having a detrimental effect on the psyche of British youths. The idea of striving to come up with an invention is exposed as an excuse for not having to do any real work. The story's prodigal son, Harold, tells his scolding uncle that he does not have to work hard, that he simply has to invent something like his friend, Charley, has done: "I do not see why I should not invent something and take out a patent, and make my fortune, like Charley Roget; he is not such a very clever fellow after all: I can't think how he managed it" (6). For children worried about too much competition in the labour market, biographies of inventors offered them the hope that they could almost in an instant transform themselves into a figure of great worth but it was feared that children might begin to think themselves entitled to achieve fame and fortune without working hard and without accepting a period of training. Writers from the evangelical tradition began to worry that the inventor's biography had inflamed the passions of British youth and that employment was beginning to lose its disciplinary hold on them.

In nineteenth-century Britain, the clerk and the apprentice came to embody both the new spirit of social mobility and the alienating and unfulfilling nature of modern industrialized labour. At the same time that the clerk and the apprentice were figures who had moved out of manual labour into white-collar labour, they were trapped within the dull and abstract world of the factory, the warehouse, the office, and the retail shop. Young-adult literature of the nineteenth and early twentieth century became increasingly focused on promoting careers that would save the youth of Britain from the clerk's position, careers that would both allow the youth to circulate in the national economy and to enjoy a life of romance. The adventure story began to represent the middle-class professional as an exciting figure who, rather than spending his working days shut up in an office, does the exciting and often dangerous work of nation building. The biography of the inventor demonstrated that a home workshop combined with an entrepreneurial spirit could obtain for the youth a lucrative patent on a marketable product. Both stories depicted the labour market as an imaginative space in which British youths could give expression to their career ambitions and release their adolescent energy. The adventure narrative and the inventor's biography rendered the capitalist economy an entirely democratic space inside which the tools of childhood itself— rather than wealth and social position—allow any child to, in an instant, transform a dead-end job into an exciting career. If youth employment was imagined in the first half of the nineteenth century as the solution to the nation's youth problem, it was re-imagined in the second half as a process of self-discovery and self-invention as the nation's ingenuity and innovation became located at the level of the child. Temporary youth employment was eventually integrated into the larger narrative of social mobility, not as punishment for sin, but as a material context out of which the adventurous and ingenious youth could fashion a much better career. Those who remained clerks and apprentices were no longer victims of the capitalist economy—they were youths who had failed to discover the spirit of capitalism lying within every child.

2
Family Business and Childhood Experience: *David Copperfield* and *Great Expectations*

Elizabeth Gaskell's *Mary Barton* (1848) is designed, as its preface tells the reader, to expose the horrible living conditions of Manchester's textile workers during the severe economic downturn of the 1840s. While the workers' children starve to death one after another, the mill owner's children continue to live a life of luxury. But just as the novel is on the verge of arguing for a more equal distribution of wealth, John Barton, the novel's union agitator, assassinates the son of the mill owner. Rather than furthering the cause of the suffering textile workers, the crime puts the owner in a sympathetic light when his employees find to their surprise that he grieves very deeply for his lost child. It eliminates union organization as a possible solution to the problems of economic inequality and blurs the line between owner and employee as both are shown to have a deep connection to their families. The Victorian factory owner who does nothing to aid the children dying in horrendous poverty can, according to the narrative, be forgiven anything if it turns out that he loves his children. In the end, the novel offers no solution to the social injustices it explores.[1] It is enough to learn that business owners are family men too.

As the business historian Stana Nenadic writes, "the Victorian age is commonly represented as the age of the family firm" (par. 1). In nineteenth-century Britain, family-run businesses were considered the moral centre of the nation's economy. In an age when there was very little in the way of government oversight of business practices, firms that were built on the moral bedrock of the family were considered more trustworthy than firms run by self-made entrepreneurs who lacked any such claims to legitimacy. According to Nenadic, to thrive within a local community, business owners and their firms were expected to observe certain conventions of behaviour whereby the public integrity of the firm was built on the public integrity of the family. (par. 4)

The employment of family members, including "wives, children, and spinster sisters" (par. 25) not only helped give the firm a solid reputation but also provided owners "with a workforce that was cheap and easily controlled, especially where the family lived alongside the business premises" (par. 25). In the first half of the century, the small family firm provided business with an important moral grounding at a time when business practices were unregulated and when the pursuit of profit was considered ignoble; but, in the second half, it was increasingly seen as an impediment to free-market capitalism due to its conservative, paternalistic approach. Richard Rodger notes that the small family-run workshop drove production in "the initial phases of British industrialization" but that "so pervasive was the workshop mentality that subsequent economic failure after 1870 has been partially attributed to it" (78).[2] The family firm continued to function as the moral bedrock of Victorian business but it was increasingly seen as a millstone around the neck of the national economy because of its inability to remain competitive and innovative.

There are many portraits of family-run businesses in Dickens's novels, which argue that while parents as owners tend to benefit from the connection of the firm to the family, children as employees tend not to benefit from the connection of the family to the firm.[3] *Nicholas Nickleby* (1839), for example, contains a comic portrait of an owner of a travelling theatre company, Mr Crummles, whose productions are so inept they can only play in the most remote parts of England. His daughter represents his star attraction, the kind of child performer popular in nineteenth-century theatre, whom he bills as the "infant phenomenon". According to Marah Gubar, child performers were admired by Victorians for their "prematurely developed skills and much-vaunted versatility [that] enabled them to blur the line between child and adult, innocence and experience" (64).[4] It turns out, however, that Crummles's daughter is really 15 years old and has been kept artificially small by her father who administers to her regular doses of liquor. Nicholas is informed by one of the adult members of the company that she is also a terrible actress: "There isn't a child of common sharpness in a charity school that couldn't do better than that. She may thank her stars she was born a manager's daughter" (283). The infant phenomenon calls into question the health of the family-run business that relies on its children as exploitable labour. Both the child forced into a job for which she is entirely unsuited and the product produced by cheap labour are made to suffer in the family firm. The infant phenomenon represents for Dickens the fundamental problem and the ideological crux of nineteenth-century capitalism as it struggled to be enterprising and innovative within the confines of the small family firm. At the same time that Dickens's novels idealize family homes with businesses attached to them, they tend to satirize the family firm for the exploitation of its children and for the poor quality of its product.

It is the purpose of this chapter to explore the relationship of the child to the family business in *David Copperfield* and *Great Expectations*. The Dickensian hero in search of a suitable career can only find fulfilment when the career that is achieved is authenticated by a connection to both the family home and his natural talent. In *David Copperfield*, a novel that Grahame Smith aptly describes as "a record of the triumph of earnest self-help" (49), the middle-class child in search of a career suited to his or her talent is able to transform the raw materials of the family firm into a new, more lucrative business.[5] By transforming it into a rather different enterprise that will better allow him to use his natural abilities, David is able to both obtain an authentic career and escape the kind of exploitation experienced by children like the infant phenomenon. In contrast, the working-class child in *Great Expectations* is portrayed as lacking a natural talent. There are indications that working-class children are for Dickens just as talented and improvable as middle-class children but that they are not allowed to discover a natural talent because they are embedded in the labour of the family firm too early in life. Dickens's novels advocate for a kind of family capitalism in which children grow up within the family business with all of its fascinating sights, sounds, and objects but remain uninvolved in its labour and production until they can discover where their true talent lies. The young hero must escape being embedded in the dense materiality of the family firm even as the firm provides him with the imaginative possibilities necessary for innovation and invention. What this chapter will demonstrate is how Dickens's novels are situated at a point in British history when family capitalism was in the process of transitioning into corporate capitalism, at a point when the open market was threatening to disconnect the family from business and the business from family. If family capitalism was to survive as the basis of the British economy, it would have to find a way to accommodate the natural talents of its children.

The family firm and child development

Throughout David Copperfield's life story, he is envious of the Peggottys' house-boat for the way it combines so completely into one space the family's home and the family's work. David is captivated by the home precisely because it is a house that is also a real fishing vessel:

> If it had been Aladdin's palace, roc's egg and all, I suppose I could not have been more charmed with the romantic idea of living in it. There was a delightful door cut in the side, and it was roofed in, and there were little windows in it; but the wonderful charm of it was, that it was a real boat which had no doubt been upon the water hundreds of times, and which had never been intended to be lived in, on dry land. That was the captivation of it to me. If it had ever meant to be lived in, I might have thought it small, or inconvenient, or lonely; but never having been designed for any such use, it became a perfect abode. (41)

David's imagination is inspired by a home that is not just connected to the work performed by adults in the real economy but that is literally constructed out of the materials of the family's livelihood. Unlike his own home, which has no business attached to it, the house-boat is crammed full of romantic artefacts from the sea that inspire in him a desire to become a ship's captain. During his visits there, he is given a bedroom located at the back of the vessel, which he is amazed to discover is an authentic captain's quarters:

> It was the completest and most desirable bedroom ever seen—in the stern of the vessel; with a little window, where the rudder used to go through; a little looking-glass, just the right height for me, nailed against the wall, and framed with oyster-shells; a little bed, which there was just room enough to get into; and a nosegay of seaweed in a blue mug on the table. (42)

The toys contained inside the home are not consumer items purchased by the family for the children's amusement but actual artefacts from the family's fishing operation. David is also captivated by the home because it smells like the sea:

> One thing I particularly noticed in this delightful house, was the smell of fish; which was so searching, that when I took out my

pocket-handkerchief to wipe my nose, I found it smelt exactly as if it had wrapped up a lobster. On my imparting this discovery in confidence to Peggotty, she informed me that her brother dealt in lobsters, crabs, and crawfish. (42)

The house-boat can become a playroom for young David precisely because it retains a connection to the real work of fisherman. The fact that it also unites the romance of the sea with the reality of commercial labour means that it is for him the ideal family firm, one with a wealth of imaginative possibilities.

Later in the narrative, there occurs a scene in which David, having finished school, confers with his aunt about his employment prospects. Here, he shows his envy of the Peggotty home as he laments that, unlike theirs, his home has left him with little indication of what it is he is meant to do with his life:

> For a year or more I had endeavoured to find a satisfactory answer to her often-repeated question, 'What I would like to be?' But I had no particular liking, that I could discover, for anything. If I could have been inspired with a knowledge of the science of navigation, taken the command of a fast-sailing expedition, and gone round the world on a triumphant voyage of discovery, I think I might have considered myself completely suited. But, in the absence of any such miraculous provision, my desire was to apply myself to some pursuit that would not lie too heavily upon her purse; and to do my duty in it, whatever it might be. (282)

If he had grown up in the Peggotty house-boat, he might have been inspired to study navigation and become a ship's captain but his own home has denied him the materials out of which he can imagine a career for himself. Having grown up in a home that is unconnected to a business, David feels that any career he might choose will only be an arbitrary one. A boy who is not born a "Yarmouth Bloater" (40) like the Peggottys cannot hope to become a real sea captain but, at the same time, as a middle-class child he can, unlike its working-class inhabitants, recognize and articulate the romance and adventure contained within it. Unlike the Peggottys, he can see that there are many more possibilities than fishing contained in the home because he is not involved in its labour. He can imagine becoming a sea captain precisely because he is only a visitor to the home, a child who plays within it but who does not participate in the production of the family income. The idea that an individual must come by his or her career honestly is proven to David later in the narrative by Mr Micawber who is the novel's comic figure for the way he continues to search for his start in life well into adulthood. After his disastrous time as a clerk in Wickfield's law office, Micawber decides to emigrate to Australia where he believes his prodigious talents will be better appreciated.[6] Rather than simply go as a typical passenger, however, he dons the guise of a ship's captain in order to turn the trip into a romantic sea adventure. As David watches him leave, he is struck by the nature of the man's costume, which has been scrupulously chosen for its authenticity; so scrupulously, in fact, that it ends up rendering him a ridiculous caricature:

> He had provided himself, among other things, with a complete suit of oil-skin, and a straw-hat with a very low crown, pitched or caulked on the outside. In his rough clothing, with a common mariner's telescope under his arm, and a shrewd trick of casting up his eye at the sky as looking out for dirty weather, he was far more nautical, after his manner, than Mr Peggotty. (808)

In playing the role too well, Micawber only succeeds in drawing attention to the arbitrary nature of his dramatic transformation from clerk to sea captain.

Unlike David, who feels that the house-boat provides an ideal childhood, Emily Peggotty, who actually grows up in the home, experiences it as a trap rather than a path to a fulfilling future. She is born knowing that she must perform work as soon as she is able and that she will eventually marry a fisherman like generations of women have done before her. Emily's resistance to the family business leads her to become a female version of the wayward apprentice as she runs away to have an affair with Steerforth, the novel's aristocratic rake figure, and attempts to make herself into a lady, a more exciting woman than a fisherman's wife who can only wait patiently at home to find out whether her husband will come back alive. Emily's desire to become a lady represents a desire to escape the working-class labour that defines her and to set a new value for herself, one that is determined not by her labour but by her scarcity in the marketplace.

In *The Principles of Political Economy and Taxation* (1817), David Ricardo argues that commodities derive their value from two sources, "from their scarcity, and from the quantity of labour required to obtain them" (5). He notes, however, that the value of commodities that are in short supply is not determined by labour:

> There are some commodities, the value of which is determined by their scarcity alone. No labour can increase the quantity of such goods, and therefore their value cannot be lowered by an increased supply. Some rare statues and pictures, scarce books and coins, wines of a peculiar quality, which can be made only from grapes grown on a particular soil, of which there is a very limited quantity, are all of this description. (6)

For Emily, the aristocratic lady represents a rare and beautiful object like a statue or a fine wine, whose value is determined by its scarcity, not by the labour that goes into its production. But her problem is that no matter how hard she tries, she cannot hide the labour that goes into transforming herself from a rough working-class girl into a polished lady. According to Steerforth's lawyer, Emily puts in long hours of training in order to live the life of a continental lady: "The young woman was very improvable, and spoke the languages; and wouldn't have been known for the same country-person" (675). Steerforth is disgusted to find, however, that she continues to long for her family home and that she has been telling the local children of her common upbringing: "Mr. James was far from pleased to find out, once, that she had told the children she was a boatman's daughter, and that in her own country, long ago, she had roamed about the beach, like them" (677). Tired of the "low girl whom he picked out of the tide-mud" (679), he decides to marry her to another man who is "a very respectable person, who was fully prepared to overlook the past, and who was, at least, as good as anybody the young woman could have aspired to in a regular way: her connexions being very common" (676). She wants to be a lady, a "pearl of such price" (679) bearing none of the marks of her humble origins but as long as her common beginnings are visible, she cannot become a rare commodity. The fact that she becomes a fallen woman means that her value within the family business is also destroyed and thus she must emigrate to Australia with her uncle. Here, she does not remarry despite offers from wealthy suitors but instead devotes her life to serving others. Her uncle tells David that she is "[c]heerful along with me; retired when others is by; fond of going any distance fur to teach a child, or fur to tend a sick person [...]" (874). The girl who tries to deny the labour of her family by making herself into a lady chooses, in the end, to perform unpaid labour within a kind of self-imposed penitentiary space. Emily can only attempt in the colonies to regain her lost childhood home by remaining unmarried and by performing unpaid labour as she shuts herself back up in dead-end employment. Malcolm Andrews notes that Emily is a figure trapped in the past as she looks "back to her lost childhood, as if there were no way forward" (136). Because of the scarcity of women in Australia, she can marry well but she chooses instead to return to a life of labour in order to atone for her attempt to become a lady of the leisured class. As she longs to recoup her lost childhood, however, she remains a victim of a working-class way of life that embeds her in manual labour and that denies her the ability to deploy properly both her ambition and her sexuality.

At the age of ten, David finds himself similarly trapped in his stepfather's London warehouse, a decidedly unromantic business where he is made a "little labouring hind in the service of Murdstone and Grinby" (165).[7] He is bundled off by a resentful stepfather to a miserable warehouse where he must put in long hours washing old wine bottles. While the Peggotty family business is full of romantic artefacts, the Murdstone business holds no such imaginative possibilities. Instead, he is imprisoned in a space that erases the possibility of child development by refusing to acknowledge the talents of its exploited workers. Despite being a sensitive boy with great ability, a "child of excellent abilities, and with strong powers of observation, quick, eager, delicate, and soon hurt bodily or mentally, [...]" (164), young David is not put to honest labour but to a kind of prison labour that is entirely punitive. Unlike the wine bottles, which have "made voyages both to the East and West Indies" (165), he remains trapped in a kind of solitary confinement in a dilapidated old building filled with the disgusting remnants of a time during the first phase of industrialization in Britain when children were exploited:

> Its panelled rooms, discoloured with the dirt and smoke of a hundred years, I dare say; its decaying floors and staircase; the squeaking and scuffling of the old grey rats down in the cellars; and the dirt and rottenness of the place; are things, not of many years ago, in my mind, but of the present instant. (165)

David finds himself in a workplace that provides him with no moral guidance. He recalls, "From Monday morning until Saturday night, I had no advice, no counsel, no encouragement, no consolation, no assistance, no support, of any kind, from anyone, that I can call to mind, as

I hope to go to heaven!" (170). Lacking any kind of parental supervision, he worries that he is perilously close to falling into a life of crime:

> I know that I worked, from morning until night, with common men and boys, a shabby child. I know that I lounged about the streets, insufficiently and unsatisfactorily fed. I know that, but for the mercy of God, I might easily have been, for any care that was taken of me, a little robber or a little vagabond. (172)

Even as David is in danger of becoming embedded in the working class, his co-workers refer to him as the "little gent" because he is related to the owner and because he is rather more delicate than the others. With no hope of promotion and no working-class camaraderie, he is cast into the hell of dead-end employment, into a space that cannot be re-imagined. In an exchange with the Murdstones that takes place after David has run away from the warehouse, Betsey Trotwood scolds them for having put the boy to such miserable work in such a ghastly place. She asks them pointedly whether they would have treated a blood relative so shabbily. The sister replies that a relative would not have been so inferior: " 'If he had been my brother's own boy,' returned Miss Murdstone striking in, 'his character, I trust, would have been altogether different' " (221). The Murdstones are against David from the beginning because he is not a biological member of the family. He is not a blood relative and thus they refuse to make him an heir or give him better work. In an effort to protect their kinship circle, they control the threat posed by his talent and ambition by keeping him locked in a space that cannot be re-imagined, that does not admit the possibility of social mobility.

Just as the Murdstones infiltrate the Copperfield family, so the working-class Heeps infiltrate the Wickfield family in a hostile attempt to take over their family business. They manage, like parasites, to hollow out the core of the firm while maintaining the cover and protection of its good name. Uriah Heep immediately recognizes David, who lodges in the home while attending school, as "quite a dangerous rival" (579) who may one day assume control over the firm ahead of him. The reason the Heeps have been able to come so close to assuming complete control over the law firm is that, unlike Murdstone, Wickfield has neglected to protect his firm from outsiders. His idleness and drunkenness are the result of his excessive mourning for his dead wife: "My natural grief for my child's mother turned to disease; my natural love for my child turned to disease. I have infected everything I touched" (584). He is at fault for his predicament because his dissipated condition has allowed a non-family member to become intimately involved in a business that is attached to his home. He has led Heep, a genetically inferior figure described as a "red-headed animal" (389) with strange eyes of "red-brown" (229) to believe that he has the right to marry the employer's daughter.[8] Unlike the working-class Heep, however, the middle-class David fits so neatly into the home that he becomes very close to a biological member as he continually refers to Agnes as "a very dear sister" (579) but, despite his comfort in the home, David assures Heep that he has no plans to take over Wickfield's law practice:

> I said I was going to be brought up there, I believed, as long as I remained at school.

> "Oh, indeed!" exclaimed Uriah. 'I should think *you* would come into the business at last, Master Copperfield!'

> I protested that I had no views of that sort, and that no such scheme was entertained in my behalf by anybody; but Uriah insisted on blandly replying to all my assurances, "Oh, yes, Master Copperfield, I should think you would, indeed! [...]." (245)

On the first night that David encounters Heep, he has a dream foretelling the blackmail and extortion the clerk will use against his employer in order to usurp control of the business. Before retiring to bed for the evening, he shakes Heep's hand which feels to him "like a fish" (246), an association that then conjures up a dream about the clerk stealing the Peggotty's house-boat and embarking on a mutinous adventure. In the vision, Heep "had launched Mr Peggotty's house on a piratical expedition, with a black flag at the mast-head, bearing the inscription 'Tidd's Practice,' under which diabolical ensign he was carrying me and little Em'ly to the Spanish Main, to be drowned" (246). The dream conflates the two family businesses by placing Heep at the helm of the Peggotty's house-boat and, in doing so, reveals how the employee from outside the kinship circle is a dangerous threat to the ideal structure of the family firm. Using the learning he acquires from Tidd's legal textbook, Heep seizes control of the ship to become its captain but, just as David is not born to be a sea captain, so the working-class youth is not born to be a middle-class lawyer. The lesson of Heep's hiring is that genetically unqualified individuals should not be allowed into the family firm. His genetic inferiority, which makes him unable to revitalize the family's bloodlines, corresponds to his industrial inferiority, which makes him unable to revitalize the family's law firm.

One of the fundamental problems with the narrative is that it grants social mobility only to children born into family businesses, a situation that automatically forces ambitious working-class figures like Heep to prey upon families that have firms attached to them. As Mary Poovey argues in her discussion of the novel, we cannot help but have some sympathy for Heep, who is "the novel's conscience, the figure whose effects the narrator cannot contain" (*Uneven Developments*, 120). Despite his crimes, the narrative allows Heep to tell the sad story of his difficult education in a charity school, which was designed, as he describes it to David, to turn working-class pupils into cheap and exploitable labour. He tells David that humility is the only subject the school ever taught him:

> They taught us all a deal of umbleness—not much else that I know of, from morning to night. We was to be umble to this person, and umble to that; and to pull off our caps here, and to make bows there; and always to know our place, and abase ourselves before our betters. And we had such a lot of betters! Father got the monitor-medal by being umble. So did I. Father got made a sexton by being umble. He had the character, among the gentlefolks, of being such a well-behaved man, that they were determined to bring him in. 'Be umble, Uriah,' says father to me, 'and you'll get on.' It was what was always being dinned into you and me at school; it's what goes down best. 'Be umble,' says father, 'and you'll do!' And really it ain't done bad! (580–1)

The school is entirely devoted to turning its poor students into obedient workers devoid of ambition but, as Heep informs David, it also preaches the gospel of social mobility:

> Or as certain as they used to teach at school (the same school where I picked up so much umbleness), from nine o'clock to eleven, that labour was a curse; and from eleven o'clock to one, that it was a blessing and a cheerfulness, and a dignity, and I don't know what all, eh? (764–5)

The school is designed to disorient working-class children by sending them a mixed message. One half of their day is about becoming disciplined workers willing to perform manual labour, while the other half is about learning to despise manual labour and to want something better.[9] The problem with Uriah Heep is that he is the product of an institution designed to engineer a large-scale industrial workforce, one that operates almost entirely within abstract space. As Matthew Titolo writes of his social position, "He occupies uncharted social territory somewhere between the autonomous, middle-class professional and the deferential, hat-tipping worker. Uriah Heep anticipates the emergence of a new class of organization men who may never achieve autonomy in exchange for the working-class culture they have left behind" (187). The Heeps may not have natural talent like the middle-class David but the father is intelligent enough to turn the only subject the school teaches him, humility, into a parodic form of talent. The criminality of the Heeps can be read, therefore, as an understandable act of revenge against a society that promises social mobility to working-class children only to pry them away from their local communities and place them in dehumanizing and alienating jobs. While Uriah Heep is, like David, an outsider born without a family business, he is also a dangerous radical who almost succeeds in gaining control over a middle-class business and polluting the middle-class family with his genetic material. He performs a parodic version of middle-class industry in which he uses his talent for humility to assume control of a business but his biological inferiority means that he can neither procreate nor innovate.

At the end of the novel, Heep is thrown into prison but, as David finds when he visits, he cannot possibly be rehabilitated by the abstract space of the new Panopticon penitentiary.[10] Unlike Emily, who internalizes her punishment and who is humbled as she returns to her original class position, Heep cannot be humbled because humility is that which has made him a criminal in the first place. The charity school that has designed him for abstract space has left him lost in a liminal class position that denies him the dignity of labour and the dignity of social mobility. He does not have the materials out of which he can fashion his own enterprise because he has been uprooted from his material context. When he is thrown into prison, the narrative returns him, in effect, to his childhood home, to the kind of institutional space that has produced him. He stands for a new kind of socially engineered working-class child whose discontent is a parodic version of middle-class ingenuity that, once it is attached to the family firm, can only unmake capitalist society.[11] The narrative would appear then to argue that figures like Uriah Heep must not be engineered, that working-class children when they fail must be left to internalize their punishment. They must not be radicalized but must be left instead sexually confused by their inability to achieve mobility in the way that the wayward apprentice Emily Peggotty is left to feel guilty about her affair with Steerforth.

The fact that David is unsuited to a career in law, that he should not (as Heep predicts he will) take over a law firm, is clearly proven when he goes to work in the government's Prerogative Office. His aunt pays 1000 pounds to the lawyer Spenlow to make David a proctor, an arbitrary choice that is made only because he and his aunt can think of nothing better. It turns out to be an archaic patronage appointment, a make-work project for the useless sons of the aristocracy. Like Murdstone's warehouse, it is completely devoid of imaginative possibilities. Steerforth describes how the position is unsuited to a youth of energy and ambition, how it will destroy David's development leaving him old before his time:

> "Why, he is a sort of monkish attorney," replied Steerforth. "He is, to some faded courts held in Doctors' Commons—a lazy old nook near St. Paul's Churchyard—what solicitors are to the courts of law and equity. He is a functionary whose existence, in the natural course of things, would have terminated about two hundred years ago. I can tell you best what he is by telling you what Doctors' Commons is. It's a little out-of-the-way place, where they administer what is called ecclesiastical law, and play all kinds of tricks with obsolete old monsters of acts of Parliament, which three-fourths of the world know nothing about, and the other fourth supposes to have been dug up, in a fossil state, in the days of the Edwards. It's a place that has an ancient monopoly in suits about people's wills and people's marriages, and disputes among ships and boats." (352)

According to Steerforth, David has forsaken his most productive years to work with mouldy old documents and arcane points of law that have little relevance to modern Britain. When David suggests to Spenlow that the aristocratic space of the office might be improved by some middle-class industry, "that possibly we might improve the world a little, if we got up early in the morning, and took off our coats to the work" (485), he is told to dismiss the idea as "not being worthy of my gentlemanly character" (485). David also objects to the fact that the Prerogative Office, which collects thousands of pounds for the job of safely protecting wills, pockets the money and stores the documents in an "accidental building, never designed for the purpose, leased by the registrars for their own private emolument, unsafe, not even ascertained to be fire-proof [...]" (485). He wants to improve and modernize the office but Spenlow argues that the public does not want the truth about the office revealed: "It might not be a perfect system; nothing *was* perfect;

but what he objected to, was, the insertion of the wedge. Under the Prerogative Office, the country had been glorious. Insert the wedge into the
Prerogative Office, and the country would cease to be glorious" (486).
He believes, contrary to David's opinion, that Britain will be diminished
in the eyes of the public if they are to see the actual labour that goes
into building and maintaining a nation. He argues that the aristocratic
leisured class, which believes in itself as a rare commodity, is the proper
class to run the nation, not as an efficient administrative structure, but
as a glorious emblem of British superiority. According to Spenlow, performing labour within government will only reduce the nation to a
tawdry business enterprise. David eventually comes to feel guilty that
he occupies such a comfortable position while the clerks below perform
the only real work in the office. He reflects that "perhaps, it was a little
unjust, that all the great offices in this great office should be magnificent
sinecures, while the unfortunate working-clerks in the cold dark room
up-stairs were the worst rewarded, and the least considered men, doing
important services, in London" (486). The Prerogative Office is a con-
flicted space inside which untalented but well-connected gentleman are
rewarded with secure positions, while useful clerks are mistreated and
exploited as cheap labour. By not showing themselves to be industrious,
those in positions of power are, as David tries to teach Spenlow, only
inviting the lower orders to revolt. In the end, the office needs some
adolescent energy in order to transform it into a dynamic enterprise in
which every worker performs labour that adds to the value and the glory
of the nation.

Similarly, in *Little Dorritt*, Dickens paints a picture of a British government infiltrated by a family called the Barnacles, whose hold on
the Circumlocution Office resembles the hold that Spenlow has on the
Prerogative Office. So ubiquitous are they in British government that
"wherever there was a square yard of ground in British occupation,
under the sun or moon, with a public post upon it, sticking to that
post was a Barnacle" (378). The inventor, Daniel Doyce, continually
brings his plans for "something serviceable to the nation" (181) to the
government only to be rebuffed by the Barnacles who work to ensure
their own survival in government rather than the improvement of the
nation. The British government is so clogged up with idle gentleman
that industrious figures like Doyce can find no support; they are treated
instead like dangerous outsiders threatening the kinship circle of the
family business. If the government is a family business, then it is one
that is managed by incompetent and irresponsible aristocrats who invite
the lower orders to seize control, just as Wickfield's drunkenness invites

Uriah Heep to seize control of his law firm. According to the narrative, individuals with natural talent who do not fit comfortably into bureaucratic positions are needed to drive the phallic wedge into the business of government to release its potential and to allow it to evolve into a new enterprise.

At the same time that David searches for his proper career, he attempts to repair and re-establish a family structure for himself by marrying Dora Spenlow, the delicate, doll-like daughter of his employer. She is a pretty object produced by a father whose position at the top of the social hierarchy is, as we have seen, propped up by the work of the clerks toiling below him. She has grown up in a family home that denies the existence of labour, that makes its women into dolls, in order to justify its social position. Spenlow has fabricated a daughter with no utility in order to prove that his family belongs to a class that is too rare and beautiful to have its value determined by labour. Dora comes by her uselessness honestly, it can be said, because she is born into a family whose business it is to remain idle; but David inserts the wedge to reveal that she is, like the nation, only glorious because those below her in the social hierarchy must perform labour. When David first marries Dora, he believes that she can help build a home for him that will restore the moral centre missing from his life. She proves, however, to be a poor manager of the household, one whose mismanagement of the books ends up corrupting the servants.[12] Because the household accounts are not properly balanced, the servants are free to steal from their employers. David warns her,

> I am afraid we present opportunities to people to do wrong, that never ought to be presented. Even if we were as lax as we are, in all our arrangements, by choice—which we are not—even if we liked it, and found it agreeable to be so—which we don't—I am persuaded we should have no right to go on in this way. We are positively corrupting people. (700)

Their mismanaged household becomes a breeding ground for criminal behaviour because it presents its employees with opportunities for making off with property. The pretty wife who does not work invites the servants to reclaim some of the wealth they have produced for the class above. In an effort to teach her to be a better manager, David provides her with training in home economics:

> [...] I showed her an old housekeeping-book of my aunt's, and gave her a set of tablets, and a pretty little pencil-case and box of leads, to

practice housekeeping with. But the cookery-book made Dora's head ache, and the figures made her cry. They wouldn't add up, she said. So she rubbed them out, and drew little nosegays, and likenesses of me and Jip, all over the tablets. (611)

In trying to correct his wife, however, David comes perilously close to resembling his stepfather, Murdstone, whose cold-hearted corrections killed his delicate mother. He becomes a bad patriarch, who puts a family member to work at a job for which she is not born. He is aware that he is becoming like Murdstone when he recalls,

But, as the year wore on, Dora was not strong. I had hoped that lighter hands than mine would help to mould her character, and that a baby-smile upon her breast might change my child-wife to a woman. It was not to be. The spirit fluttered for a moment on the threshold of its little prison, and, unconscious of captivity, took wing. (704)

On her death bed, she tells him he is better off without her because she would never have been able to grow up:

I was very happy, very. But, as years went on, my dear boy would have wearied of his child-wife. She would have been less and less a companion for him. He would have been more and more sensible of what was wanting in his home. She wouldn't have improved. It is better as it is. (772–3)

Because she is completely embedded in idleness, hers is a childhood that can only be destroyed by the middle-class economy that David tries to impose on the household. The doll-like woman dies childless because she cannot possibly reach maturity in a narrative that equates procreation with middle-class labour.

During his time as a proctor and during his time married to Dora, David begins a course of home study in stenography. The job tends towards being a legitimate choice for him because it is, in some ways, an attempt to transform the materials that surround him as a proctor into a more worthwhile enterprise. The old documents suggest to him that he should acquire the highly specialized skill of stenography, which will allow him to report from parliament and to produce a much more useful and relevant document in the form of the daily newspaper. Lacking a family firm that can provide him with an authentic career path, David recognizes that he must sell his labour in the open market and that in order to do so he will have to possess a very rare skill indeed. Thus, he becomes much like a working-class autodidact, studying at night for a more rewarding career than the one he occupies by day. After putting in long hours of challenging study, he acquires a highly technical skill that clearly does not come naturally to him:

> The changes that were rung upon dots, which in such a position meant such a thing, and in such another position something else, entirely different; the wonderful vagaries that were played by circles; the accountable consequences that resulted from marks like flies legs; the tremendous effects of a curve in the wrong place; not only troubled my waking hours, but reappeared before me in my sleep. (551)

The scarcity of qualified stenographers means that, once he has completed his training, David is a much sought after labour commodity: "I have tamed that savage stenographic mystery. I make a respectable income by it. I am in high repute for my accomplishment in all pertaining to the art, and am joined with eleven others in reporting the debates in Parliament for a Morning Newspaper" (692). Because there are only eleven other qualified stenographers to compete with, he can obtain work in the field very easily. He does not have a natural talent for it but the fact that his labour is in short supply means that he is as in-demand in the marketplace as a patented invention.

Stenography proves to be, however, only a temporary occupation when, after another course of home study, David eventually becomes a professional writer. Before Dora dies, he publishes "a good many trifling pieces" (633) in magazines before he finally completes his "first work of fiction" (672). Just as he improves with his stenography by devoting long hours to mastering his craft, so he improves with his writing. He notes that "success had steadily increased with my steady application" (672). As a novelist, he no longer has to sell his labour. Instead he converts it into a product that is sold on the open market just like a patented invention. David's novel is a finished product with a high value in the marketplace that is the result of his labour rather than a denial of it. As Jennifer Ruth notes in her study of the Victorian professional, *Novel Professions*, there was in the nineteenth century "a widespread public perception of writers as 'idle,' the epithet associated with a leisured aristocracy" (319).[13] The memoir he narrates—the book we read titled *David Copperfield*—is, however, nothing if not an account of his industry and invention. According to Ricardian economic theory, it is a commodity whose value is derived from both the quantity of labour that produces it and its rarity. For Dickens, the novelist is part inventor and part artist, a figure who produces a highly marketable product that is as useful as it is scarce.

In *Victorian Heroines*, Kimberley Reynolds and Nicola Humble note that the goal of the abandoned child in Dickens's novels is to "recreate the nuclear family" (161) through "the replacement of lost parents with good surrogates" (161–2). David's goal is in fact to recreate not only a nuclear family but a family business. He fails miserably in his marriage to Dora Spenlow to find a proper family business but succeeds very nicely in his second marriage to Agnes Wickfield. David first recognizes that the Wickfields are a surrogate family when he lives with them as a schoolboy and discovers that Agnes is like a sister to him. Unlike the doll-like women in his life, Agnes is defined not by her physical beauty but by her industry. She is a proper moral authority and an excellent household manager. When David returns some years later, he finds that she has created her own family business in the home as he sits "down to dinner, with some half-dozen little girls" (846), pupils belonging to Agnes's school. His aunt is so impressed with the little school's ability to improve its pupils that she tells David, "If she trains the young girls whom she has about her, to be like herself [...] Heaven knows, her life will be well employed! Useful and happy, as she said that day! How could she be otherwise than useful and happy!" (842). Agnes is able to return the Wickfield home, where David was once a happy schoolboy, to its original state before it was so very nearly ruined by Uriah Heep:

> The books that Agnes and I had read together, were on their shelves; and the desk where I had laboured at my lessons, many a night, stood yet at the same old corner of the table. All the little changes that had crept in when the Heeps were there, were changed again. Everything was as it used to be, in the happy time. (843)

Agnes tells David that she has essentially given him back his childhood, at least the best part of it: "I have found a pleasure, [...] while you have been absent, in keeping everything as it used to be when we were children. For we were happy then, I think" (845). The childhood she has maintained for him is exact in every detail right down to the placement of his books. She has kept the home as a kind of testament to his success as a writer as she makes sure to exhibit his favourite volumes, ones that inspired him as a child. It is at this point that David recognizes how it was in the Wickfield home that he first discovered his talent for observation, a talent that he uses as a novelist to construct his literary characters:

> I stood in a window, and looked across the ancient street at the oppo-
> site houses, recalling how I had watched them on wet afternoons,
> when I first came there; and how I had used to speculate about the
> people who appeared at any of the windows, and had followed them
> with my eyes up and down stairs, while women went clicking along
> the pavement in patterns, and the dull rain fell in slanting lines,
> and poured out of the water-spout yonder, and flowed into the road.
> (843–4)

Until he can locate the emergence of his gift inside the family business, his legitimacy as a writer is in doubt. He discovers, however, that the Wickfield home with a law firm attached to it has, unlike his original home, supplied the proper materials and conditions for his develop-ment as a writer. While Andrews argues, like many critics do, that David has left his childhood "stranded in a shabby past" (181), his true child-hood is not located in the Murdstone's warehouse but in the Wickfields' home. David discovers that indeed he was not in the process of follow-ing in the footsteps of Wickfield as Uriah Heep had predicted. He was, while he lived there, in the process of transforming the law firm into a writer's workshop.

David reconnects not only with Agnes after achieving success as a novelist but also with his friend Traddles, whom he expects to find living the life of a prominent London lawyer. Rather than being a partner in a top firm, however, his friend runs a very modest practice out of the family's tiny apartment. When clients visit, the home is cleared of any evidence of family and when they leave it is cleared of any evidence of business. His wife is charged with pulling off the deception:

> 'But then,' said Traddles, 'our domestic arrangements are, to say the
> truth, quite unprofessional altogether, my dear Copperfield. Even
> Sophy's being here, is unprofessional. And we have no other place
> of abode. We have put to sea in a cockboat, but we are quite pre-
> pared to rough it. And Sophy's an extraordinary manager! You'll be
> surprised how those girls are stowed away. I am sure I hardly know
> how it is done!' (830–1)

The passage's sea imagery allows for a comparison between Traddle's home and the Peggotty house-boat. The life of a lawyer is hardly as fascinating as the life of a fisherman but the fact that the home is also a working law firm makes it tend towards the romance and adventure that David first found in the Peggotty house-boat. Traddles assures David that his home provides the family with an exciting connection to the larger world outside almost as if they are at sea. Lying just outside their "snug" (921) home are fascinating sights provided by the daily labour of London's working classes:

> 'We look into the glittering windows of the jewellers' shops; and I show Sophy which of the diamond-eyed serpents, coiled up on white satin rising grounds, I would give her if I could afford it [...] In walking home, perhaps we buy a little bit of something at a cook's-shop, or a little lobster at the fishmonger's, and bring it here, and make a splendid supper, chatting about what we have seen. Now you know, Copperfield, if I was Lord Chancellor, we couldn't do this!' (920)

As a middle-class lawyer, Traddles can appreciate the imaginative possi-bilities of the working-class neighbourhood—one that appears to have a connection to the fishing industry—because, while he is not embedded in it, he has not forsaken it to moulder in the leisured class as an idle government official. His practice tends towards the romantic ideal of the Peggotty house-boat—it is both a work space and a family space—and, as such, it allows him to work as an adult inside the imaginative landscape of his childhood. Inside his modest firm, which contains his wife and children, he is able to convince himself that he is not living the life of an exploited worker in a dull office, that he is in fact living out his boyish dreams of going to sea. Meanwhile, Sophy is described as both a model household manager possessing "punctuality, domestic knowledge, econ-omy, and order" (851) and her husband's "copying-clerk" (851). As his wife and clerk, she closes the circle around the family firm, denying entry to predatory outsiders.

After ten years of marriage, David and Agnes live in a new home in London, a space that is full of imaginative possibilities for both the nov-elist and his children. It is a space we discover that is able to produce stories. When Mr Peggotty returns from Australia after a long period of absence, he is described as arriving at their door in the night looking like a romantic stranger: "As this sounded mysterious to the children, and moreover was like the beginning of a favourite story Agnes used to tell them, introductory to the arrival of a wicked old Fairy in a cloak who hated everybody, it produced some commotion" (871). The children growing up inside an author's home do so in a space that appears to deny industry and hard work in favour of storytelling and fantasy but the creation of imaginative realms is precisely their father's business. Like the Peggotty house-boat, the home creates imaginative possibilities for its children who witness the labour that goes into it without becoming implicated in it. In his marriage to Agnes, David ultimately turns the Wickfield's family law firm into a much more exciting family firm, a writer's workshop. His identity is complete when he finds a career that utilizes his natural talent and that is authenticated by his childhood experience within the family home. He creates a family firm that perfectly collapses the dreams of his childhood into the work of his adulthood.

In *David Copperfield*, there is a certain amount of ambivalence towards the ideal of the family firm. At the same time that it supplies the materials necessary to stimulate the child's imagination, it threatens to trap and exploit the child as cheap labour. The reason that David ends up prospering within the structure of the family business is that he is never expected to follow in Wickfield's footsteps to become a lawyer. Because the working-class Emily's identity is embedded in labour from birth, because she is a little adult before she can even begin her development, the family home displays no imaginative possibilities for her. Likewise, because the upper-class Dora is embedded in idleness from birth, because she is made into a fashionable toy, the family home displays no industrious work habits for her. While Emily's lack of development causes her to become a fallen woman, Dora's lack of development causes her to remain a child-bride. Unlike the working-class child and the upper-class child, the middle-class child is able to mature properly because he achieves what the narrative argues is a necessary conflation of sexual activity and commercial activity. David marries and has children with a sober middle-class woman who is like a "dear sister" to him as the kinship circle remains closed to outsiders but open to innovation and ingenuity.

The wayward apprentice and the end of victimization

Patrick Brantlinger notes how nineteenth-century novels "by middle-class writers that feature working class heroes and heroines generally [...] offer some version of the main lesson learned by Pip in *Great Expectations*: aspirations to transcend or transgress class barriers—to leave the proletariat and rise into the bourgeoisie—are doomed to a tragic outcome" (95). It is understood from the very beginning of his life that Pip will grow up to work in Joe Gargery's blacksmith shop, which is attached to the family home. Once he sees Miss Havisham's estate and Estella's beauty, however, he cannot fit himself back into his role as a blacksmith's apprentice. Upon his return to the forge, Pip tells Joe, "I wish my boots weren't so thick nor my hands so coarse" (64). His humble origins fill him with such shame that he turns his back on the family business. Looking back on his time as Joe's apprentice, however, Pip recalls how he once saw his home and the blacksmith's shop as a space full of romance and adventure:

> I had believed in the best parlour as a most elegant saloon; I had believed in the front door, as a mysterious portal of the Temple of State whose solemn opening was attended with a sacrifice of roast fowls; I had believed in the kitchen as a chaste though not magnificent apartment; I had believed in the forge as the glowing road to manhood and independence. Within a single year, all this was changed. Now, it was all coarse and common, and I would not have had Miss Havisham and Estella see it on any account.
>
> How much of my ungracious condition of mind may have been my own fault, how much Miss Havisham's, how much my sister's is now of no moment to me or any one. The change was made in me; the thing was done. Well or ill done, excusably or inexcusably, it was done. (106–7)

Pip experiences the forge in the same way that David experiences the Peggotty house-boat. He is able to appreciate it as a space full of imaginative possibilities precisely because it is a space of adult labour. He is able to re-imagine it and thus there is an indication that as a boy Pip has a natural talent waiting to be discovered. Given the lavish prose he uses to rhapsodize about the forge, it may well have been the same as David's but he is never able to discover a talent for writing because he is always defined as the blacksmith's cheap and reliable source of labour. The role of the apprentice, which binds him in childhood to the work of his father-figure, erases his adolescence and denies him the ability to channel his sexual energy into his work in the forge.

In his discussion of childhood in Dickens's novels, James Kincaid argues that in the Victorian period, innocence is often "filed down to mean nothing more than virginity coupled with ignorance" (33). This is certainly the case with Pip who is seduced from the family business by his sexual attraction to Estella, a woman who is really a gypsy girl made into a lady. While Kincaid notes that Pip cannot comprehend his predicament, that he "cannot come up with a formula, a plot that would explain things" (39), it is suggested that he is another George Barnwell, another wayward apprentice.[14] Soon after Pip learns that Estella has just come back from abroad as an educated lady "far out of reach; even prettier than ever" (116), he is made by Mr Wopsle to read passages from Lillo's *The London Merchant*. Afterwards, Mr Pumblechook tells him, "Take warning, boy, take warning!" (117). Just as Pumblechook predicts, Pip soon comes to resemble Barnwell as he abandons his apprenticeship for the life of a gentleman, a role that he feels will allow him to win the fair Estella. Like little Emily, his search for child development and the release of youthful energy becomes a sexual fall from grace as he leaves the kinship circle of the family business. Pip is eventually made a gentleman but, once he loses the dense material context of the forge, he descends into idleness and profligacy as he is transported to the gentleman's apartment, a space that is utterly devoid of imaginative possibilities.

As he moves into the upper class, Pip is made into a fashionable doll by Magwitch, who becomes a second surrogate father to him. It must be remembered that the making of Pip as a gentleman is not an act of kindness on the part of Magwitch. It is not a reward for the boy's help during the attempted escape which opens the narrative but is instead the convict's twisted plan to exact revenge on the criminal court system. Magwitch burns with hatred for the judge who allowed his accomplice and co-defendant, Compeyson, to go free simply because the man was dressed as a gentleman:

> "And when it come to character, warn't it Compeyson as had been to the school, and warn't it his schoolfellows as was in this position and in that, and warn't it him as had been know'd by witnesses in such clubs and societies, and nowt to his disadvantage? And warn't it me as had been tried afore, and as had been know'd up hill and down dale in Bridewells and Lock-Ups? And when it came to speech-making, warn't it Compeyson as could speak to 'em wi' his face dropping every now and then into his white pocket-handkercher—ah! and wi' verses in his speech, too—and warn't it me as could only say, 'Gentleman, this man at my side is a most precious rascal?' " (351)

Magwitch is given a harsh sentence of transportation because he bears on his body all the rough marks of his terrible upbringing. For this reason, he creates a gentleman out of a blacksmith's apprentice in order to make the point quite literally that the upper class has no innate value, that it is constructed by the labour of the class below. As Jaggers's law clerk Wemmick tells Pip, he will remain idle as a gentleman because he has not been "designed for any profession" (180). As Pip is released from the trap of the forge, he becomes deeply embedded in idleness as he begins to live out a destiny that has been fixed for him at birth by his Frankenstein-like creator. In neither his working-class childhood nor his upper-class adolescence is he allowed to experience development.

Once Pip is a gentleman, the fact that he can never return to his working-class community is made abundantly clear to him when he trades his old clothes for a fine suit. Before he leaves town, Pip pays a visit to Trabb's store in order to arrive in London in suitable attire. As he is busy being fitted for his new clothes, Trabb's boy who is at work in the store sweeping up makes it clear to Pip that he is a traitor who will not be welcomed back:

> Mr. Trabb's boy was the most audacious boy in all that countryside. When I had entered he was sweeping the shop, and he had sweetened his labours by sweeping over me. He was still sweeping when I came out into the shop with Mr. Trabb, and he knocked the broom against all possible corners and obstacles, to express (as I understood it) equality with any blacksmith, alive or dead. (151)

The boy sweeps over Pip in order to re-embed him a working-class context. The fact that he is Trabb's boy, a child who follows in his father's footsteps within the family business, reminds Pip of the exploitation he is leaving behind but, as he smugly dismisses the boy, he has no idea that he is about to become Magwitch's boy. The fate of the blacksmith's apprentice and the fate of the upper-class gentleman are both determined by the labour of the father. In both cases, he is made by the father and as such he is denied a period of adolescence.

The narrative's interest in clothing as a class marker is continued later in a scene in which Joe visits Pip at his lodgings in London after an eleven-year separation. The blacksmith has replaced his work clothes with more formal attire in order to enter a gentleman's home. Because Pip's friend Herbert Pocket is present, the meeting remains a rather public encounter for Joe, who is made uncomfortable by the obvious difference in class. Joe feels that by putting on a different set of clothes he has betrayed his working-class identity. He tells Pip,

> You won't find half so much fault in me if you think of me in my forge dress, with my hammer in my hand, or even my pipe. You won't

find half so much fault in me if, supposing you should ever wish to see me, you come and put your head in at the forge winder and see Joe the blacksmith, there, at the old anvil, in the old burnt apron, sticking to the old work. (224)

Joe is so enclosed within his role as a blacksmith that he is made uneasy in a space where he must appear as something other than a working man. At the end of the novel, after Pip's sister is dead and Joe has married Biddy, Pip finds that Joe's new wife has tried to make him into an adolescent schoolboy as she tries to educate and improve him. She has taught him to read and write but, despite becoming literate, despite being given the tools of social mobility, the blacksmith remains unchanged. Pip can see, as Joe writes a letter at his desk, that his new-found literacy skills have had little effect on him:

At my own writing-table, pushed into a corner and cumbered with little bottles, Joe now sat down to his great work, first choosing a pen from the pen-tray as if it were a chest of large tools, and tucking up his sleeves as if he were going to wield a crowbar or a sledgehammer. [...] He had a curious idea that the inkstand was on the side of him where it was not, and constantly dipped his pen into space, and seemed quite satisfied with the result. (464)

Joe's inability to adjust to the inkwell being on his wrong side shows that all his learning is gained by rote, that it has not penetrated very deeply and that he has no natural talent for the subtle art of penmanship. He wields the pen just as he would the tools of his trade, indicating that he will always remain enclosed in his original subject position as a blacksmith. His identity as a working-class adult cannot be altered and improved and thus Joe himself cannot become the site of invention and ingenuity. This strange period of youth forced upon him later in life threatens to unlock in him some greater potential but Pip finds that the wedge of education cannot make much of a dent in the blacksmith.

When Pip forsakes the forge for the life of a gentleman, he also loses the sentimental value he had inside the closed circle of the family business. When he resigns his position as an apprentice, the deal is brokered by Jaggers who, as Magwitch's representative, is required to negotiate with Joe for the loss of an employee. The blacksmith's family business comes into contact with the open market as the lawyer asks him to name a price for the boy. Pip recalls how, at the time, Jaggers saw in Joe the "village idiot, and in me his keeper" (142) because Joe is foolish enough to allow sentiment to cloud his business judgement. The lawyer is disgusted when Joe tells him that he cannot possibly be paid for "the loss of the little child—what come to the forge" (141). Joe cannot put a price on Pip because he has formed a sentimental attachment to him and because he is invaluable to the family business as a trusted source of labour. The fact that Orlick, who is the only non-family member in the forge, is responsible for the death of Pip's sister proves that outsiders are indeed a threat to both the family and the business. The deal that forces Joe to sell a child indicates that once Pip leaves the protection of the family business, he will find himself in the space of unsentimental capitalism. While the family business cannot function without the child, the open market, controlled by completely self-made entrepreneurs like Jaggers, cannot function with the child. The child can only be accommodated in the open market when it is no longer a child but a labour commodity with a precise monetary value.

In contrast to the blacksmith who runs a family business, Jaggers is a successful lawyer because of his ability to purge both himself and his law practice of emotional and sentimental attachments. He is portrayed as an effective defence attorney who is in such great demand that he must continually turn away London criminals from his office door. When Pip dines with Herbert Pocket and Bentley Drummle in Jaggers's apartment, he finds that part of the lawyer's after-work ritual is to clean himself thoroughly of his latest case: "I embrace this opportunity of remarking that he washed his clients off, as if he were a surgeon or a dentist. He had a closet in his room fitted for the purpose, which smelt of the scented soap like a perfumer's shop" (210). Pip finds that despite the man's obsessive cleansing ritual, his apartment is not a denial of the labour of his law office but an extension of it:

> There was a bookcase in the room; I saw, from the backs of the books, that they were about evidence, criminal law, criminal biography, trials, acts of parliament, and such things. [...] In a corner, was a little table of papers with a shaded lamp: so that he seemed to bring the office home with him in that respect too, and to wheel it out of an evening and fall to work. (211)

The room is furnished with the same legal books occupying the shelves in his law office. Unlike David's friend Traddles, however, Jaggers has no family stowed away in his apartment. He is an entirely self-made individual whose apartment contains no sentimental artefacts, no traces of his past. It is as if he has had to obliterate any evidence of his family and childhood in order to enclose himself in his role as a lawyer, a job that has no connection to his childhood home. During dinner, Pip takes Drummle to task for being so unfeeling that he would never lend his friends money even though he borrows from them. Drummle replies, "You are right, [...] I wouldn't lend one of you a sixpence. I wouldn't lend anybody a sixpence" (215). While Pip is disgusted by him, Jaggers declares that Drummle is "one of the true sort" (217), meaning he will do very well in business with such an unsentimental attitude towards his friends. Jaggers operates entirely outside of the kinship circle such that his value is determined entirely by the open market. He is certainly successful in that market but in order to stabilize his identity he must blot out his childhood. In order to operate as a ruthless professional in the very unromantic settings of the law office and the criminal court system, he must obliterate anything remaining of himself as a child and of the romantic ambitions he had in his youth. He cannot hold onto artefacts from his past that will only remind him that his career as a lawyer is completely inauthentic, that it is not what he wanted for himself when he was a boy.

While Jaggers's success is built upon his denial of his family and childhood, there exists one legal case from his past, however, in which he allowed his emotions to affect his professional judgement. After learning of Estella's origins, that she is the daughter of Jaggers's gypsy housekeeper, Pip tries to confront Jaggers with the fact that he was moved by sentiment to intervene in the life of an abandoned child by placing her in the home of Miss Havisham. Speaking of himself in the third person in order to maintain client confidentiality and to avoid incriminating himself, Jaggers tells Pip that he saved Estella because his experience told him she would inevitably have ended up a criminal in the court system:

> Put the case that he lived in an atmosphere of evil, and that all he saw of children, was, their being generated in great numbers for certain destruction. Put the case that he often saw children solemnly tried at a criminal bar, where they were held up to be seen; put the case that he habitually knew of their being imprisoned, whipped, transported, neglected, cast out, qualified in all ways for the hangman, and growing up to be hanged. Put the case that pretty nigh all the children he saw in his daily business life, he had reason to look upon as so much spawn, to develop into the fish that were to come to his net—to be prosecuted, defended, forsworn, made orphans, be-devilled somehow. (413)

Jaggers rescues Estella as "one pretty little child out of the heap" (413) in an attempt to take her out of the open market where she has no value and to place her with a family where she will at least have sentimental value. Unfortunately, he gives her to Miss Havisham, who embeds the girl in her twisted plot to break the hearts of men as revenge for having been left at the altar. In rescuing Estella, however, Jaggers momentarily lifts the lawyer's mask to reveal a feeling person and, in doing so, he betrays a dissatisfaction with the ruthless professional identity he has made for himself. His desire to save a poor child betrays a desire not only to recoup his own lost childhood but to somehow accommodate the child within an unsentimental marketplace in which poor orphan girls have no value.

If Jaggers's home is an extension of the work he performs in the office, his clerk Wemmick's home in the London suburb of Walworth is a complete denial of it.[15] When Pip attends Wemmick's wedding to Miss Skiffins, the clerk reminds him that the occasion is "altogether a Walworth sentiment" (455) and not to be shared with Jaggers, who will only think that the man's "brain was softening, or something of the kind" (455). He scrupulously maintains a separation between the two spaces to the extent that the office is maintained as the dull place of business, while the home is maintained as a child's fantasyland. He has constructed his suburban home as a child's paradise to which he returns every day after working at his unfulfilling job. He creates an adult version of the ideal childhood by making his home into a play-ground complete with a castle and drawbridge. Despite living in the smallest house Pip has ever seen, Wemmick has transformed it into a castle with gun turrets and gothic windows. He tells Pip, "When I go into the Office, I leave the Castle behind me, and when I come into the Castle, I leave the Office behind me" (208). He even has enough live-stock and provisions to "hold out a devil of a time" (207) if the house is ever under siege. If his duties as a clerk require him to perform only one kind of monotonous work, his home allows him to perform many dif-ferent kinds of much more interesting work. He tells Pip, "I am my own engineer, and my own carpenter, and my own plumber, and my own gardener, and my own Jack of all Trades" (207). Wemmick builds his sub-urban retreat because his working life represents the complete absence of the romance and adventure to which he aspired as a child. The prob-lem with Wemmick's castle, however, is that it is not a real castle but a model. While the Peggotty house-boat captures David's imagination because it was once a real fishing vessel, Wemmick's castle cannot cap-ture the child's imagination because it is a retreat from and a denial of the real labour performed by adults. It is only a plastic model of an ideal childhood purchased with money made in the city while working at a thoroughly unromantic job. As Samuel Smiles tells us, John Harrison was able to transform an ordinary household item—the watch that sat beside his bed—into the solution to the problem of measuring longitude at sea but the extraordinary items that Wemmick includes in what amounts to a child's theme park have no connection to real industry. In the end, Wemmick's two worlds cannot meet because they invalidate each other. His home must be kept separate from the office because it reminds him that his working life has no connection to the dreams and ambitions he had for himself when he was a child and his office must be kept separate from his home because it reminds him that he has assembled a collection of stage props which, the more it tries to be full of imaginative possibilities, the more it is devoid of them. His home plays the part of childhood too well and, in doing so, becomes only a ridiculous stereotype of childhood just as Micawber becomes, in his adventurer's garb, a ridiculous stereotype of a sea captain.

After Pip learns the truth that he has been made a gentleman by the convict Magwitch and that, in the process, he has burned any bridges that might lead him back to the comfort of Joe's shop, he retreats to the home of Herbert and Clara Pocket, which functions as a surrogate for his lost childhood home. By remaining unmarried in the home of a married couple, the husband of which is also his business partner, Pip attempts to re-embed himself in his childhood spent inside a family business. He makes it clear, however, that their trading firm is only moderately successful: "I must not leave it to be supposed that we were ever a great House, or that we made mints of money. We were not in a grand way of business, but we had a good name, and worked for our profits, and did very well" (480). The trading firm resembles the same kind of middle-class success that David's friend Traddles achieves with his law practice but he cannot recoup, even as he tries to recreate the kinship circle of the blacksmith's shop within the Pocket household, the imaginative possibilities that the forge once presented and, in this way, his childhood falls victim to a commercial marketplace that is far removed from the dreams of youth. Pip's seduction plot indicates that working-class children who have been embedded in the family's labour and who have had their destinies predetermined are denied a period of adolescence in which they are able to discover their true talent and the spirit of ingenuity that exists within every child. While David makes the mistake of marrying Dora when he is a frustrated proctor, he is finally able to control his sexual desire when he marries Agnes and becomes a novelist. He can marry a wife who is a "dear sister" because he is satisfied in his work. Pip, in contrast, is a victim of both the family business and the open market because in neither is he able to find the talent that will allow him to perform ingenuity and innovation. He remains a youth in a dead-end job who cannot properly grow up because he has never found the talent that will allow him to translate adolescent sexual energy into ingenuity. If he had not been bound to Joe as an apprentice from the moment of his birth, the forge might have remained full of imaginative possibilities. He might have developed a new and exciting career out of the material context of the forge—one with an authentic connection to his childhood—if he had not been denied a proper childhood by the working-class home that implicates children in the production of the family income. In the end, however, just as the narrative records a loss for Pip, so it records a victory for society as the working-class boy who fails to achieve social mobility is not, like Uriah Heep, left a dangerous radical, one who knows all-too-well the lie contained within the mixed message of social mobility. Instead, he is left a wayward apprentice who is only able to blame his lack of success on his attraction to Estella.

In *David Copperfield* and *Great Expectations*, Dickens argues that only businesses and careers that are connected to the family, to the moral centre of Victorian society, are legitimate. But at the same time that the family firm represents the moral basis of nineteenth-century business, it also represents an impediment to capitalist innovation. It relies on family members both as a cheap and reliable source of labour and as a means of lending legitimacy to the firm's trade practices but, in doing so, it fails to utilize the natural talent of its employees. Dickens's novels argue that in order for the capitalist economy of the nineteenth century to be both legitimate and innovative, its family firms must be able to accommodate imaginative children like David and Pip. In order for this to happen, however, the child's position in the home must be reconfigured such that he or she is not embedded in the production of the family income but not removed from it either. In reconfiguring the relationship of the child to the family home, Dickens's novels articulate the means by which nineteenth-century family capitalism could become innovative without being victimized by the predatory nature of the open marketplace.

3

Adventure Fiction and the Youth Problem: *Treasure Island* and *Kidnapped*

Adventure fiction is closely linked to British imperialism and, since its inception, it has tended to be a rather disingenuous form for the way it sets about conquering and disciplining the "exotic" locales and "savage" peoples without which it cannot possibly captivate its readership. Often the hero in adventure fiction is a military figure who subdues foreign races in battle but he is sometimes a government bureaucrat who uses efficient management skills to control foreign territories. One of the earliest and best-known adventure novels is Defoe's *Robinson Crusoe* (1719), a book that is very much connected to British imperialism. As Crusoe claims a distant island for the empire, he imposes his administrative control on a frontier space. Anyone who has read Defoe's novel knows that the high adventure of the story—stormy seas, shipwrecks, and cannibals—is tempered by long passages in which Crusoe is an accountant figure meticulously tabulating and recording his available resources. As John Bender writes, "Defoe's pervasive listings—his accountings, inventories, census reports, bills of lading, logs, and diaries—fictionally reinscribe the origins of writing as the medium of power" (58). Crusoe is able to maintain, through writing and accounting, such a control over the island that he rises up through the ranks of the administration that he himself has built. It is strange that a shipwrecked man should be able to rise up in rank, but the sea keeps offering up individuals like Friday whom he can exploit within his administrative hierarchy:

My island was now peopled, and I thought myself very rich in Subjects; and it was a merry Reflection which I frequently made, How like a King I look'd. First of all, the whole Country was my own meer Property; so that I had an undoubted Right of Dominion. *2dly*, My people were perfectly subjected: I was absolute Lord and

Law-giver; they all owed their lives to me, and were ready to lay down their lives, *if there had been Occasion of it,* for me. (241)

Crusoe is able to take the liminal space of the island and transform it into an emergent nation-state because he first transforms it into an enclosed jurisdiction with an efficient bureaucracy. The colonial world becomes disciplined, therefore, as it is subjected to the shopkeeper's accurate account ledger. He operates as both an imperialist who conquers foreign lands and as an employer who makes the colonial subject Friday into his young clerk or apprentice.

As Marah Gubar has recently argued, the Stevensonian adventure novel represents, to some extent, a departure from the imperialist narrative that is so much a part of the "Robinsonade formula" (74). I shall argue in this chapter that, while his two most famous adventure novels are part of the larger imperialist project, they are also concerned with fixing the nation's youth problem, a problem that according to Stevenson is caused by the imposition of the shopkeeper's values on both the space of the nation and childhood. In his novels, wild spaces are not inhabited by foreign races but by pirates and highlanders who have run away from respectable society to set up alternative, outlaw societies. His pirate and highland societies are essentially comprised of wayward apprentices, figures who have rejected the shopkeeper's Calvinist self-restraint for an unrestrained and unfettered life beyond the shop. Although both societies are located in an eighteenth-century setting, they stand for any kind of outlaw gang a wayward child of the nineteenth century might find attractive.[1] For Stevenson, the youth problem is caused by the fact that the overly disciplined space of respectable middle-class society begets the overly undisciplined space of outlaw society. As middle-class self-restraint makes the shop unbearable, the young apprentice runs away in search of a lack of restraint only to find that he is once again restrained by the danger and neglect of the criminal organization. As Monica Flegel notes in her discussion of child protection, Victorian society could not properly account for the origins of its child criminals:

The juvenile delinquent was [...] a key figure in Victorian narratives of child endangerment precisely because the issue of that child's endangerment could not be easily ascertained. Was the child a criminal because of nurture, or because that child had been reared in a lawless culture or, worse, a culture that had laws entirely opposed to those of normative Victorian society? (147)

Stevenson, I would argue, turns the argument around to make the point that it is respectable society itself that produces child criminals. For British youths, argues Stevenson, the middle-class respectability and self-restraint of settled society are just as harmful to the child as the violence and disease of unsettled society.[2] The pirate and the highlander are, in fact, versions of the private self, which the middle-class shopkeeper must suppress in order to carry out his business. While they perform in the libidinal theatre of aristocratic society and the violent street theatre of working-class society, the shopkeeper tabulates receipts in the decidedly un-theatrical space of bourgeois society.

It is the purpose of this chapter to examine the emergence of the modern professional in *Treasure Island* and *Kidnapped* as a solution to the nation's youth problem. As we shall see, Stevenson's boy heroes are, as their stories begin, just as likely to become wayward apprentices as they are to become part of the nation's management class. Jim Hawkins is rescued from criminality to become a future civil servant, while David Balfour is rescued from criminality to become a future lawyer. As professionals in training, they combine the discipline and expertise of the settled world with the romance and adventure of the unsettled world not only to forge professional identities for themselves but to help construct a modern nation-state in which young lads like themselves are no longer made into juvenile delinquents. As professionals who combine the technical expertise of the settled world with the courage and bravery of the unsettled world, Jim and David break down the division between respectable society and criminal society to imagine a modern nation-state in which there is only one society that combines discipline and romance in equal measure. The modern professional, who reconnects the private and public self, represents the solution to both youth employment and youth crime as he combines the best of both societies—technical expertise and physical bravery—within a new collectivist state able to protect the child from the threat of both too much discipline and too much neglect.

The romance of the modern civil servant

Recent scholarship devoted to *Treasure Island* has argued that the novel is constructed by sophisticated arguments about economics, class, and power. Without over-allegorizing the novel, scholars have demonstrated that, within the rollicking adventure story set in the eighteenth century, there is a sophisticated commentary on the emergence out of Britain's lawless past of the modern industrial state. In her analysis of imperialism in the novel, Diana Loxley writes, "the movement from the 'reality' of the nineteenth-century world to a mythic plane of eighteenth-century piracy cannot be seen simply as a displacement of reading attention away from the struggles and deprivations of British society in a phase of high capitalism" (139). Similarly, in her analysis of the function of money in the novel, Naomi J. Wood argues that it "provides an extensive commentary on the mechanisms of capitalist profit" (61). In his analysis of class struggle in the novel, Troy Boone argues that, in its depiction of a pirate mutiny, the novel engages Victorian fears about "a unified agitation to seize power by working-class subjects" (77). In this chapter, I want to continue to uncover the novel's connections to the rise of the nineteenth-century industrial state by examining its connections to the emergence of the modern civil service and administrative classes of Britain. In her study of Victorian children's literature, J.S. Bratton argues that there was a burgeoning market in the second half of the century for books that would help make middle-class boys a part of the machinery of state: "The greatly expanded ranks of the industrial and administrative middle classes needed all recruits who could be persuaded to make the effort to rise into them" (111).[3] My argument is that *Treasure Island* grooms its hero Jim Hawkins to take his place in this emergent class. Through an analysis of the novel's interest in accurate accounting and the management of resources, I argue that in young Jim there emerges an image of a heroic civil servant, one with energy and spirit. He comes to embody the myth of a civil service that, in doing the work of state and empire, is a technically proficient, administrative class but one with a taste for romance—a class that can both keep an accurate accounts ledger and fire off a brace of pistols.

In the 30 years before the publication of the novel, the British civil service underwent a period of expansion and reform.[4] By 1870, the reforms of the Northcote-Trevelyan report of 1853 were being implemented.[5] The report called for the end of patronage as it argued for the appointment of men from the universities who could pass an examination. It also argued that university men should no longer begin at the lowest rank, that the civil service should be divided into two classes, clerks and managers, to allow for the rapid advancement of talented individuals. Trevelyan expected the new kind of recruits to be more robust than what he referred to as the "sickly youths" of aristocratic families. He writes, "It would be natural to expect that so important a profession would attract into its ranks the ablest and most ambitious of the youth of the country" (qtd in Hennessy, 39). The fear that the

British civil service would become a dumping ground for sickly youths
is one that can be found early on in its history. Peter Hennessy notes
in his study of Whitehall that, during the reign of Charles II, civil servants were thought to be too meek and mild to do the work of the
nation. Charles wanted "'rougher hands,' 'ill-natured men, not to be
moved by civilities'" (Hennessy, 24). Some had doubts, however, that
Trevelyan's men, those who could pass an examination, would fit the
ideal of the rugged civil servant. Sir James Stephen, for example, complained that the youths of the Colonial Office "possessed only in a low
degree, and some of them to a degree almost incredibly low, either the
talents or the habits of men of business, or the industry, the zeal, or the
knowledge required for the efficient performance of their appropriate
functions" (qtd in Campbell, 36). He also doubted that men of energy
and ambition would want to attempt to rise up in the ranks of the civil
service given the thankless nature of the job: "He must listen silently to
praises bestowed on others which his pen has earned for them" (qtd
in Campbell, 36).[6] The search for robust and literate men to fill the
ranks was to some extent more successful after the First World War when
large numbers of appointments were held for returning servicemen but,
according to Hennessy, the interwar period was still marked by compla-
cency: "By the late 1930s the Civil Service was a staid organization at
virtually every level" (86-7). He notes how the civil servant H.E. Dale
wrote that in this period, "he had only known four officials who displayed 'intense energy, great driving force and devouring zeal'" (75).
E.J. Hobsbawm writes in *The Age of Empire* that along with the emergence of the modern welfare state, and the enormous increase in the
number of public servants in the late nineteenth century, came a less
romantic and more disciplined national landscape: "the steamroller of
collectivism, which had been in motion since 1870, flatten[ed] the landscape of individual liberty into the centralized and levelling tyranny of
school meals, health insurance and old age pensions" (103).[7] According
to Hobsbawm, the rise of collectivism brought about the death of a
romantic age of individualism. In the nineteenth century, however, the
civil servant was constructed as the figure that could hold together
the competing claims of individualism and collectivism. The civil servant was constructed as a heroic individual working for the safety and
security of the state.[8]

The almost impossible balance between a life of office work and a life
of romance is one that Stevenson recognized in his own family. As civil
engineers, his grandfather and father built Scotland's lighthouses. While
they were not strictly speaking civil servants—they did not toil away in

government offices—they were appointed by a government body, the Northern Lighthouse Board. In his essays concerning the family firm, Stevenson is proud of the fact that his grandfather and father did not hold private patents for their lighthouse innovations: "holding as the Stevensons did a Government appointment, they regarded their original work as something due already to the nation, and none of them has ever taken out a patent" ("Thomas Stevenson", 107). His grandfather and father were, for him, defined by both their technical proficiency and their romantic sensibility. In "Records of a Family of Engineers", which contains part of his grandfather's account of the building of Bell Rock Lighthouse, he writes,

> I have many a passage before me to transcribe, in which my grandfather draws himself as a man of exactitude about minute and anxious details. It must not be forgotten that these voyages in the tender were the particular pleasure and reward of his existence; that he had in him a reserve of romance which carried him delightedly over these hardships and perils. (453)[9]

Although Stevenson did not continue on in the family business, having abandoned his engineering studies at Edinburgh University,[10] he continued to view the profession of civil engineer as a happy union of the romance of the sea and the drudgery of the office. In "The Education of the Engineer", he writes,

> It takes a man into the open air; it keeps him hanging about harbour-sides, which is the richest form of idling; it carries him to wild islands; it gives him a taste of the genial dangers of the sea; it supplies him with dexterities to exercise; it makes demands upon his ingenuity; it will go far to cure him of any taste (if ever he had one) for the miserable life of cities. And when it has done so it carries him back and shuts him in an office! From the roaring skerry and the wet thwart of the tossing boat, he passes to the stool and desk; and with a memory full of ships, and seas, and perilous headlands, and the shining pharos, he must apply his long-sighted eyes to the petty niceties of drawing, or measure his inaccurate mind with several pages of consecutive figures. He is a wise youth, to be sure, who can balance one part of genuine life against two parts of drudgery between four walls, and for the sake of the one, manfully accept the other. (385)

In his essay, "On the Choice of a Profession", however, Stevenson doubts whether others will achieve such a happy union of work and romance: "A choice, let us remember, is almost more of a negative than a positive. You embrace one thing; but you refuse a thousand. The most liberal profession imprisons many energies and starves many affections. If you are in a bank, you cannot be much upon the sea" (263).

Stevenson's family of engineers can be placed in the context of the other great development in the British civil service, the rise of the Victorian expert. While the model of the civil servant envisioned by Trevelyan tended to lean towards a liberal humanist model—his exams involved rather more Greek and Latin than mathematics and chemistry—people of technical ability became increasingly vital to the performance of government in the period. Roy MacLeod notes in *Government and Expertise* how individuals with specialized technical ability began entering the civil service in the last half of the nineteenth century:

> This executive capacity for "expertise" at first acknowledged, then embraced, and later routinised specialist knowledge, made useful to government by its relevance to "social problems." In this discourse, power passed increasingly to the "agents of knowledge," wearing the badge not of birth but of merit; acting beneath the flurry of domestic politics and foreign affairs, through a poppy field of new administrative boards, commissioners and inspectorates. (5)

Stevenson's grandfather and father were Victorian experts—men of specialized ability without whom the work of government could not be done; there could hardly be a family that more neatly fit the romantic ideal of the civil service.

The idea that Jim Hawkins is in training for a career in the civil service is best supported by the fact that he is mentored throughout most of the narrative by Doctor Livesey, who is the novel's civil servant figure. When the doctor first encounters the boy, he is waiting on tables in his parents' tavern, the Admiral Benbow. Just as Jim is trapped on dry land, so he is trapped in the family business where he is exploited as cheap and reliable labour. The lives of his meek and mild parents, we soon discover, are very much governed by the shopkeeper's account ledger. It is their accurate accounting, in fact, which keeps them a respectable family even as their criminal clientele threatens to overwhelm the business. As Jim listens to the pirate Billy Bones's stories of the sea, he has within him the potential to desert his post in the family business, which is far too restrictive given the romance of the sea that lies just beyond its door. If the castaway Ben Gunn went to sea because his evangelical mother told him he was on the road to perdition for playing "chuck-farthen on the blessed gravestones" (81), then Jim appears almost ready to go to sea because of his parents' quasi-religious devotion to the account ledger. But just as it appears that Jim might be ready to become part of the youth problem, his father dies of illness and the tavern is broken up by Pew's gang, forcing his mother to place him in the care of a surrogate father in the form of Livesey. She allows Jim to accompany the doctor on the treasure hunt, which means that he is released from his dead-end employment without having to run away from home as a wayward apprentice.

When Jim first encounters Livesey, he finds a respectable, educated man, a doctor, and a magistrate whose library is "lined with bookcases and busts upon the top of them" (56–7). He is also a man strong enough to stand up to the lawless pirate Billy Bones, who has taken up a residency in the Benbow:

> "And now, sir," continued the doctor, "since I now know there's such a fellow in my district, you may count I'll have an eye upon you day and night. I'm not a doctor only; I'm a magistrate; and if I catch a breath of complaint against you, if it's only for a piece of incivility like to-night's, I'll take effectual means to have you hunted down and routed out of this. Let that suffice." (7–8)

Livesey warns Bones that he will be under surveillance, that as long as he is in his jurisdiction he is inside settled society and must act accordingly. As the local magistrate, Livesey's job is to bring lawlessness and liminality under bureaucratic control and, in doing so, he must himself be physically strong and heroic. When the treasure map is discovered in Bones's chest, it is turned over to the doctor because he is considered the figure best able to manage it. Supervisor Dance, the local revenue collector who also shows himself to be a rugged civil servant when he saves Jim and his mother from the blind beggar Pew, turns the map over to Livesey on the advice of Jim:

> perfectly right—a gentleman and a magistrate. And, now I come to think of it, I might as well ride round there myself and report to him or squire. Master Pew's dead, when all's done; not that I regret it, but

he's dead, you see, and people will make it out against an officer of his Majesty's revenue, if make it out they can. (29)

Dance will file a report to absolve himself of blame in Pew's death—exciting events will be controlled and disciplined by bureaucracy—and the map will be handed over to a more senior official. Livesey operates at the centre of a network that is able to establish law and order in the community because it uses both administrative expertise and physical force.

In the commercial world of Jim's parents, expertise is important but it does not operate in conjunction with the physical strength or the collective spirit for which Livesey stands. When Pew's gang attacks the Benbow, Jim's mother remains meticulous in her accounting of the debt owed to the tavern by Bones: " 'I'll show these rogues that I'm an honest woman,' said my mother, 'I'll have my dues and not a farthing over' " (23). Jim, however, sees her obsession with accuracy as pathological when her stubbornness nearly gets them killed: "But my mother, frightened as she was, would not consent to take a fraction more than was due to her, and was obstinately unwilling to be content with less" (23). Her accurate accounting is what makes her an honest woman and an upstanding member of settled society but it also makes her blind to the larger issue of her own escape. Boone writes that "Jim represents the upwardly mobile lower-middle-class youth who identifies with middle-class notions of respectable culture" (73) but respectable culture, in this moment, comes perilously close to a kind of petty or blinkered individualism. The fact that there is no collective spirit contained within the middle-class commercialism of shopkeepers is a direct result of their lack of bravery. The townspeople who will not come to the rescue are referred to by Jim's mother as "big, hulking, chicken-hearted men" (21). The settled world may be respectable but with too much respectability comes a lack of heroism. Consequently, the townspeople come to admire the pirates for their bravery, the kind that "made England terrible at sea" (6), as they desire that which they have suppressed in themselves. When Jim first sees the doctor, he recognizes how the civil servant figure operates between the two societies:

> [...] I remember observing the contrast the neat, bright doctor, with his powder as white as snow, and his bright, black eyes and pleasant manners, made with the coltish country folk, and above all, with that filthy, heavy, bleared scarecrow of a pirate of ours, sitting far gone in rum, with his arms on the table. (6)

Livesey has the expertise and respectability of the settled world in combination with the bravery and daring-do of the pirates. This is not to say
that the narrative is not aware of its own problematic, the fact that it
needs the pirates more than the civil servant in order to be an exciting
adventure story. Indeed, when Bones tells his wild tales to the patrons of
the Admiral Benbow, the locals are enthralled: "People were frightened
at the time, but on looking back they rather liked it" (6). With such
great excitement comes a short lifespan, however, as Bones soon drops
dead from a stroke brought on by the fear of the black spot and by his
non-stop drinking. Livesey, in contrast, is a fastidious man who brings
a snuff box containing parmesan cheese with him into the wild.[11] He is
less exciting than Bones but because he is a medical man, he will live
a much longer and healthier life. He represents a compromise between
the townspeople, who lead completely unexciting lives, and the pirates,
who lead all-too-exciting lives.

The pirate society is chaotic and undisciplined and yet it has a parodic
version of government. The pirates may not know about health and
safety but they do have a legal system. They may not be literate enough
to compose a legal writ, preferring instead the black spot but, in their
alternative society, the same kind of accurate accounting that ensures
upward mobility in middle-class society also ensures it in pirate society.
In Bones's log book, which is discovered along with the treasure map,
romantic and mysterious phrases such as "Off Palm Key he got itt" (32)
are found alongside tables of numbers detailing the business affairs of
his many voyages:

> This is the black-hearted hound's account-book. These crosses stand
> for the names of ships or towns that they sank or plundered. The
> sums are the scoundrel's share, and where he feared an ambiguity,
> you see he added something clearer. "Offe Caraccas," now; you see,
> here was some unhappy vessel boarded off that coast. God help the
> poor souls that manned her—coral long ago.
>
> "Right!" said the doctor. "See what it is to be a traveller. Right! And
> the amounts increase, you see, as he rose in rank." (33)

The log book also contains "a table for reducing French, English and
Spanish moneys to a common value" (62). Bones rose up in rank because
of his accounting ability, his attention to detail, and his clear reporting.
His managing of accounts formalizes the business of pirating and, as

the doctor and squire see it, holds the key to his advancement. Ironically, the man who once terrorized the Admiral Benbow comes to be admired for his middle-class frugality: " 'Thrifty man!' cried the doctor. 'He wasn't the one to be cheated' " (62). Jim's mother is certainly more scrupulous than the pirates who do not mind taking what is not owed to them but, when the veneer of respectability is stripped away, we find that middle-class society is also motivated by profit. The narrative doubles Bones and Jim's mother in order to show that in neither commercial enterprise, legal or illegal, is there a cause greater than the bottom line. Both are maintained by the account ledger.

The most frightening aspect of Silver's character is his ability, unlike the other pirates, to infiltrate the middle-class world. As part of a society that incorporates the carnivalesque use of duplicity and disguise into its practice, he defies class boundaries throughout the narrative. He appears as a middle-class publican, as a working-class mutineer, and as an aristocrat with a public school education. When Squire Trelawney goes to Bristol to outfit a ship, he finds Long John Silver in the guise of a respectable member of settled society. His ability to manage the books is taken as evidence of his respectability:

> I forgot to tell you that Silver is a man of substance; I know of my own knowledge that he has a banker's account, which has never been overdrawn. He leaves his wife to manage the inn; and as she is a woman of colour, a pair of old bachelors like you and I may be excused for guessing that it is the wife, quite as much as the health, that sends him back to roving. (70)

The bank account is proof enough for Trelawney that Silver is trustworthy enough to be taken on the voyage. He sees himself in Silver, imagining that they are both members of settled society who go to sea in an attempt to escape enclosure and to recapture boyhood romance and adventure. Jim is not suspicious of Silver, that he is the one-legged man Bones has warned him of, because he appears to him as a kindly father figure. As Loxley writes, "The image of nurturing fatherhood is sanctioned [...] not only by Silver's fearsome bravery but by a wealth of internalised knowledge and wisdom [...]" (156). He has the same job as Jim's father and he has the same interest in accurate accounting. When Silver takes Jim on a tour of the Bristol docks, he presents himself as both an expert seaman and, as someone who can give a precise account of the work being done on the docks, an expert administrator:

On our little walk along the quays, he made himself the most interesting companion, telling me about the different ships that we passed
by, their rig, tonnage, and nationality, explaining the work that was
going forward—how one was discharging, another taking in cargo,
and a third making ready for sea; and every now and then telling
me some little anecdote of ships or seamen, or repeating a nautical
phrase till I had learned it perfectly. I began to see that here was one
of the best of possible shipmates. (45)

The doubling of both Silver and Bones with Jim's parents does not allow
us to read the pirates as simply the opposite of respectable middle-
class shopkeepers. Rather, the pirate and shopkeeper are two sides of
the same coin. Pirates are what happens when the profit motive of the
shopkeeper is allowed to operate outside the space of England, beyond
notions of respectability.[12] When the shopkeeper is transported to the
colonies, respectability falls by the wayside to reveal the libidinal drives
suppressed by the construction of a respectable public self.

Silver's ability to shape shift into Jim's father makes him a dangerous
alternative to Livesey when it comes to the mentoring of the boy.[13] He
is a much more permissive parent than either Jim's real father or Livesey
who, along with the stern captain Smollett, confines Jim to the role of
cabin boy. Silver tells Jim that on the island he will be released from
all social constraints: "Ah [...] this here is a sweet spot, this island—
a sweet spot for a lad to get ashore on. You'll bathe, and you'll climb
trees, and you'll hunt goats, you will; and you'll get aloft on them hills
like a goat yourself. Why it makes me young again" (63). He offers Jim
a pirate society that releases him from the drudgery and confinement
that denies him the possibility of rapid advancement. While he appears
to be a good parent who allows the son to have a proper childhood free
from hard labour, he also appears to be a bad parent who allows him to
play in a spot that, as it turns out, is not "sweet" at all but full of disease.
If Livesey is to hold onto Jim, to continue to function as his father-
figure, he will have to grant him more freedom from responsibility and
if Silver is to hold onto Jim, he will have to keep him from dying of
yellow fever.

Once on the island, Livesey takes on the role of local health inspector.
As the island's medical expert, he works to bring the island under control
by mapping its healthy and unhealthy sites. Anne Hardy notes that public health experts were brought into government in the middle of the
nineteenth century: "in the years 1855–1875 they also became administrators and generators of sanitary legislation; by the end of the period,

by force of government demand for their services, they had become professionals with specialist qualifications and career patterns" (129). Christopher Hamlin notes that the health of the London water supply was much debated in government in the 1860s, the cholera epidemic of 1866 in particular sparked many reports and inquiries (111).[14] Silver, who operates at the centre of pirate society, works directly against Livesey's control of the island. At one point, he deliberately fouls the water supply by spitting into the spring near the stockade: "Growling the foulest imprecations, he crawled along the sand till he got hold of the porch and could hoist himself again upon his crutch. Then he spat into the spring" (108). The doctor later informs Silver that the reason many of the mutineers are dying is that they have camped in a swamp:

> "That comed—as you call it—of being arrant asses," retorted the doctor, "and not having sense enough to know honest air from poison, and the dry land from a vile, pestiferous slough. I think it most probable—though, of course, it's only an opinion—that you'll all have the deuce to pay before you get that malaria out of your systems. Camp in a bog, would you? Silver, I'm surprised at you. You're less of a fool than many, take you all round; but you don't appear to me to have the rudiments of a notion of the rules of health." (165)

Because the pirates have no public health experts, theirs is an unsafe society. Because the pirate society has no body of knowledge upon which it can draw, to enter into it is to remain an isolated and vulnerable individual. This point is illustrated to Jim when he retakes the Hispaniola and finds the sickly mutineers have cut out pages from a medical book to light their pipes. Their lack of medical knowledge becomes responsible for the death of young Dick, who contracts yellow fever. While the pirates prove to be completely unsympathetic and neglectful to their young shipmate as they blame his fever on the fact that he has "crossed his luck and spoiled his Bible" (162) by cutting out a page, the doctor tries to save him by administering medicine. The pirate's superstition is a parodic version of the evangelical sermonizing that sent Ben Gunn to sea as a boy. The idea that the Bible is a magical object rather than a religious text mirrors Ben's mother's belief in the materiality of sin when she frightens him with the damnation that comes from defacing a gravestone.

One of the reasons that the pirate society exists in the first place is that the British government does not provide pensions for ex-servicemen in order to integrate them back into society. The implication is that when they returned from battle, respectable society turned its back on their scarred and broken bodies. Just as Wickfield's respectable law firm cannot accept the grotesque physical form of Uriah Heep, so eighteenth-century Britain cannot accept its grotesque military veterans. When the blind beggar Pew comes to the Benbow looking for Bones, he is described as a disabled veteran who has not been properly compensated by the government:

> He was plainly blind, for he tapped before him with a stick, and wore a great green shade over his eyes and nose; and he was hunched, as if with age or weakness, and wore a huge old tattered sea-cloak with a hood, that made him appear positively deformed. I never saw in my life a more dreadful looking figure. He stopped a little from the inn, and, raising his voice in an odd sing-song, addressed the air in front of him:
>
> Will any kind friend inform a poor blind man, who has lost the precious sight of his eyes in the gracious defence of his native country, England, and God bless King George!—where or in what part of this country he may now be? (18)

In his letter to Livesey concerning Silver, Trelawney writes that Silver will go on the treasure hunt because he has received no government support after serving his country: "Long John Silver, he is called, and has lost a leg; but that I regarded as a recommendation, since he lost it in his country's service, under the immortal Hawke. He has no pension, Livesey. Imagine the abominable age we live in!" (38). Clearly, the pirate society does not take care of its members but, as the squire points out, neither does settled society. The pirates, it turns out, are a product of settled society and its lack of public assistance. The point is that there would be no pirates if ex-servicemen were properly taken care of by a public welfare system.[15] It stands to reason, therefore, that if the pirate identity is created by the state then it can be taken away by the state. This proves to be the case when the mutineers are eventually defeated in battle and laid low by disease. They come to be described as charity cases when Livesey forces medicine down their throats: "they had taken his prescriptions, with really laughable humility, more like charity school-children than blood-guilty mutineers and pirates" (166). The pirates are defeated in battle but, more importantly, they are defeated by Livesey the civil servant who brings them under state control. Once they are placed inside the boundaries of Livesey's collectivist state, they are no longer criminals but well-behaved children.

The efficiency with which Livesey's crew wages war would certainly have resonated with readers familiar with Britain's many administrative blunders during the Crimean War. The victory over the mutineers is the result of administrative control working together with military might as they fight with both the pistol and the account ledger. Captain Smollett's log-book becomes vital to their success because it allows the good side to keep track of its manpower:

> Alexander Smollett, master; David Livesey, ship's doctor; Abraham Gray, carpenter's mate; John Trelawney, owner; John Hunter and Richard Joyce, owner's servants, landsmen—being all that is left faithful of the ship's company—with stores for ten days at short rations, came ashore this day, and flew British colours on the log-house in Treasure Island. Thomas Redruth, owner's servant, landsman, shot by the mutineers; James Hawkins, cabin-boy—. (98)

When Jim leaves his post to go explore the island, he exists outside the captain's log—outside record-keeping—and, therefore, outside the settled world. He makes it back just in time, however, to be reckoned in the account. Even before the mutiny begins, Jim gives an accurate accounting of manpower when he computes the numbers on the good side versus those on the bad: "In the meantime, talk as we pleased, there were only seven out of the twenty-six on whom we knew we could rely; and out of these seven one was a boy, so that the grown men on our side were six to their nineteen" (66). The ability to keep track of the other side becomes difficult, however, as the war rages. As the account grows imprecise, the good side's victory becomes threatened: "There had come many from the north—seven, by the squire's computation; eight or nine, according to Gray" (111). The chapter ends, however, with a reestablishment of order through an accurate accounting of manpower: " 'Five!' cried the captain. 'Come, that's better. Five against three leaves us four to nine. That's better odds than we had at starting. We were seven to nineteen then, or thought we were, and that's as bad to bear' " (113). Jim adds a footnote to the captain's words: "The mutineers were soon only eight in number, for the man shot by Mr. Trelawney on board the schooner died that same evening of his wound. But this was, of course, not known till after by the faithful party" (113). The reader comes to experience the battle not through wrenching descriptions of violence but through efficient calculations. If warfare, such as it was waged during the Crimean War, typically chewed up and spat out soldiers as so much cheap and disposable labour, then Stevenson's version of warfare relies on managing soldiers as a valuable resource.

When Jim deserts his post during the battle in order to take it upon himself to recapture the Hispaniola, he does so because he feels he is being exploited by the adult members who have called him "ship's boy" (51) one too many times. After the battle, he is made to wash the camp site, which is littered with putrid bodies. Jim soon becomes jealous of the doctor's superior position as his own working conditions have become vile:

> What I began to do was to envy the doctor, walking in the cool shadow of the woods, with the birds about him, and the pleasant smell of the pines, while I sat grilling, with my clothes stuck to the hot resin, and so much blood about me, and so many poor dead bodies lying all around, that I took disgust of the place that was almost as strong as fear. (118)

The sudden appearance of the doctor as an overly prim and proper member of respectable society is that which remakes Jim into a dirty and diseased member of criminal society. Livesey unwittingly produces the conditions that create the nation's youth problem because the very sight of his respectability, while Jim is embedded in the grotesque conditions of working-class labour, makes the camp unbearable for the boy.

It turns out, however, that Jim does not join the pirates but uses the adventure instead to take back the ship for the good side. In doing so, he finally proves to Livesey that he deserves to be more than a cabin boy. When Jim returns from his victory, the doctor is sensible enough to expand his duties as a reward for his bravery and as an acknowledgment of his own complicity in the boy's desertion. Having proved that he has what it takes to make England terrible at sea, Jim settles back into the drudgery of counting coins, a job that requires him to use the accounting skills of his parents:

> It was a strange collection, like Billy Bones's hoard for the diversity of coinage, but so much larger and so much more varied that I think I never had more pleasure than in sorting them. English, French, Spanish, Portuguese, Georges, and Louises, doubloons and double guineas and moidores and sequins, the pictures of all the kings of Europe for the last hundred years, strange Oriental pieces stamped with what looked like wisps of string or bits of spider's web, round pieces and square pieces, and pieces bored through the middle, as

if to wear them round your neck—nearly every variety of money in the world must, I think, have found a place in that collection; and for number, I am sure they were like autumn leaves, so that my back ached with stooping and my fingers with sorting them out. (186)

The counting is much more like drudgery than fighting to retake control of a ship, but Jim expresses great pleasure at performing the task. He is back inside the settled world of account ledgers and defined ranks but because he has proved his physical bravery and released his frustration, he is no longer a part of the society of shopkeepers. He has become a clerk in the treasury office, a space that is connected through the exotic coins he counts to the romance of the high seas. As Wood writes, the coins "call up all the romance of fabulous wealth and faraway places, the words suggesting not only buccaneering but also the hoards in the Arabian Nights" (70). By the novel's end, Jim is enclosed inside a hierarchical work space but it is a work space connected to the romance of the global trade network. Like the Dickensian hero, he transforms the family firm and his parent's accounting abilities into a bigger and better enterprise. Jim's adventure on the island is the catalyst for turning their small business into a career as a civil servant who may go on to take charge of the nation's treasury.

The treasure, with its wild and exciting history in the world of romance—"How many it had cost in the amassing, what blood and sorrow, what good ships scuttled on the deep, what brave men walking the plank blindfold, what shot of cannon, what shame and lies and cruelty, perhaps no man alive could tell" (185)—is, in the end, transformed from private capital into public capital. Disappointingly, perhaps, there are no scenes of characters rolling around on a big pile of money and no conversations about the conspicuous consumption of wealth. As Wood writes, "Stevenson shows the money gravitating to its 'proper' owners, those who will most nurture it in investment, rather than those who would squander it in a grand spree" (71). Ultimately, the reified and fetishized money that Jim counts is transformed into abstract capital; the individual nature of the coins disappears as they are funnelled into the collectivist state. Just as knowledge is collected in medical books for the advancement of society, so the money is collected in a national treasury for the benefit of returning servicemen:

All of us had an ample share of the treasure, and used it wisely or foolishly, according to our natures. Captain Smollett is now retired from the sea. Gray not only saved his money, but, being suddenly smit with the desire to rise, also studied his profession; and he is now mate and part owner of a fine full-rigged ship; married besides, and the father of a family. As for Ben Gunn, he got a thousand pounds, which he spent or lost in three weeks, or, to be more exact, in nineteen days, for he was back begging on the twentieth. (189–90)

Smollett uses the money as a retirement pension after his years of service, while Gray uses it as a start-up grant to become a ship's mate and owner. He rises in rank because he gains technical knowledge of his profession but the amount of money is not so great that it frees him from middle-class labour. Jim's accurate accounting of time—not 3 weeks but 19 days—indicates that Ben Gunn has lost his money because he cannot account for it properly. He is, in the end, "given a lodge to keep, exactly as he had feared upon the island" (190), proving that when the pirate is brought in from the colonial world he is indeed a shopkeeper.

Jim's final words are calculated to warn others away from the liminal world of romance:

Oxen and wain-ropes would not bring me back again to that accursed island; and the worst dreams that ever I have are when I hear the surf booming about its coasts, or start upright in bed, with the sharp voice of Captain Flint still ringing in my ears: "Pieces of eight! pieces of eight!" (190)

The story concludes with the sense that Jim will remain in the settled world, that he will become a rugged civil servant like his mentor Doctor Livesey. Undoubtedly, *Treasure Island*'s great appeal is that it is a wish fulfilment; it allows a young boy to leave home, to run away from both his mother's authority and the drudgery of waiting tables in his family's tavern; it allows young Jim to break free of social constraint into the world of romance where he can prove himself to a well-connected father-figure. When he negotiates his way back into the settled world, however, he does so as a figure that combines the heroism found in the adventure world with the technical expertise found in the settled world. He achieves a respectable career in which he works for the good of the nation but he is no longer destined to be a member of respectable society, the kind whose prim and proper appearance makes a young lad into a juvenile delinquent.

The romance of the modern lawyer

Kidnapped tells the story of David Balfour who, after the death of his father, is abducted and very nearly sold into slavery by his uncle Ebenezer, who wishes to maintain total control over the family estate known as the ancient House of Shaws. Stevenson writes his fictional hero into the history of Scotland as David is rescued by the swashbuckling outlaw, Alan Breck, who leads him through the highlands where they become embroiled in the 1751 Appin murder case in which James Stewart was wrongfully convicted of assassinating the King's Factor, Colin Campbell.[16] The bitter feud between Whig loyalists and Jacobite rebels forms the backdrop to both the murder case and the Balfour family history, which is marked by a feud between David's father, a prim and law-abiding schoolteacher and his uncle, a wild and dissipated former rebel. As the family legend goes, rather than maintain control of the estate, David's father allowed his brother, in their dispute over the hand of a woman, to take unlawful control of it. Speaking what is very nearly the moral of the story, the lawyer Rankeillor tells David that the whole dispute could have been avoided if his father had simply consulted his lawyer:

> The one man took the lady, the other the estate. Now, Mr David, they talk a great deal of charity and generosity; but in this disputable state of life, I often think the happiest consequences seem to flow when a gentleman consults his lawyer and takes all the law allows him. Anyhow, this piece of Quixotry upon your father's part, as it was unjust in itself, has brought forth a monstrous family of injustices. Your father and mother lived and died poor folk; you were poorly reared; and in the meanwhile, what a time it has been for the tenants on the estate of Shaws! And I might add (if it was a matter I cared much about) what a time for Mr Ebenezer! (203)

According to Rankeillor, in relinquishing his half of the estate in order to dispense with the feud, David's father created just as much chaos as his petulant brother and thus he is just as responsible for the sad state of the House of Shaws. The old bargain splits the estate along the same lines as the Scottish nation with David's father, a Whig loyalist, on the one side and his uncle Ebenezer, a Jacobite rebel, on the other. His father is described as a respectable schoolteacher, "a man of learning as befitted his position; no man more plausibly conducted school" (8), while his uncle is characterized by his "squalling, sentimental selfishness" (203).

The one is a prim and proper lowlander, a "weak, dolefully weak" man (203), and the other is a rough-and-tumble highlander who in his youth had a "fine, gallant air" (202). According to Rankeillor, the uncle ran away as a lad to join the rebels: "In 1715, what must he do but run away to join the rebels? It was your father that pursued him, found him in a ditch, and brought him back *multum gementem;* to the mirth of the whole county" (202). Just as the respectable society begets the pirate society in *Treasure Island,* so the priggish lowland society begets the wild highland society in *Kidnapped.* The uncle runs away in his youth to join an outlaw society because his brother is too much the scolding moralist. Like the House of Shaws, the nation is divided because the lowlanders are too prim and proper to admit the youthful exuberance of the wild highlanders. It is David's job, therefore, as a lawyer-in-training to put the two halves of his family and the two halves of the nation back together such that neither structure continues to manufacture juvenile delinquency and youthful rebellion.

What makes David Balfour such a fascinating hero, however, is that throughout his adventure he does not know that his job is to unite the two halves of his family and the nation. Because his uncle has him kidnapped and sold into slavery in America (the worst sort of dead-end employment), David identifies completely with his father's values and thus, as he travels across the space of Scotland after the shipwreck, he tries repeatedly to impose his Whig morality on highland culture as a kind of revenge against his uncle.[17] He argues continually that the solution to the family feud, to the murder case, and to highland rebellion is to impose a ruthlessly objective and unsentimental legal system across the space of the entire nation. He does not understand that the completely sentimental highland culture, which is governed by emotional attachment, is a parodic version of lowland culture, which is governed by the letter of the law and a strict code of morality. What he discovers at the end of the novel, as we shall see, is that he has been dead wrong throughout his adventure, that what Scotland needs is not more "Whiggishness" but a modern legal system that can accommodate the youthful rebellion of highland culture.

In what remains of this chapter, I want to discuss how David Balfour is, as he journeys through the highlands with the outlaw Alan Breck, training to become a lawyer. Stevenson himself had studied law at Edinburgh University and was eventually called to the Scottish bar.[18] The fact that David goes on to study law at the University of Leyden in *Catriona* (1893), the sequel to *Kidnapped,* indicates that his adventure with Breck does indeed create in him an interest in the profession.[19]

As David travels through the rugged highlands, he does so as a kind of lawyer-in-training, a figure who even as he befriends the rebels continually scolds them for their lawless and immoral conduct. What we find is that as he scolds the highlanders for their bad behaviour, he only exacerbates and intensifies the divisions between lowlander and highlander and, in doing so, gives himself a very poor legal education. It is left to Rankeillor, at the end of the novel, to provide him with a better model for the Scottish lawyer than the one he has imagined for himself. Like Livesey in *Treasure Island*, Rankeillor is able to break down the division between the two sides by incorporating the values of both of them into one professional practice.

During his journey through the highlands, David operates as a kind of state inspector who would subject the homes of the poor to middle-class standards of law and order just as Livesey subjects the space of the island to sanitary standards. His tendency towards a strict code of respectability, even as he is welcomed into the homes of the highlanders who shelter him while he is a fugitive, places him at odds with the rough highlanders who label him a "Whig" and a "Covenanter" when he scolds them for their bad behaviour. Even though he must rely on the highlanders, David steadfastly refuses to be won over by their culture that for him is entirely irrational. When he first encounters the highland hero Breck, he describes him as a kind of man-child wearing an elaborate theatrical costume: "And to be sure, as soon as he had taken off the great-coat, he showed forth mighty fine for the round-house of the merchant brig: having a hat with feathers, a red waistcoat, breeches of black plush, and a blue coat with silver buttons and handsome silver lace" (57). His attire marks him as a kind of carnivalesque figure for David, one whose gawdy appearance makes him out of place within the austere interior of a merchant's ship. He has many faults, according to David but "the worst of them, his childish propensity to take offence and to pick quarrels" (84). Despite his courage and physical strength in battle he is, as David sees him, an unruly child who is unfit for civilized company. More evidence of the carnivalesque nature of highland culture is uncovered by David when he notices that highland beggars are so full of pride that they give themselves ridiculous airs despite their poverty. Their performances are carried out in defiance of their social position:

> [...] I marked a difference from my own part of the country. For our lowland beggars—even the gownsmen themselves, who beg by patent—had a louting, flattering way with them and if you gave them

a plack and asked change, would very civilly return you a boddle. But these Highland beggars stood on their dignity, asked alms only to buy snuff (by their account) and would give no change. (102)

Compared to lowland beggars who know their place in society, highland beggars refuse to conform to the rules of begging by performing subservience. Like Breck, who is described as having a "dancing madness" (57) in his eyes, they conform to a dramatically irrational code that stands in opposition to the reservedly rational code of lowland society.

The highlanders resemble in many ways the young cabin boy, Ransome, who David encounters earlier in the narrative as part of the kidnapping plot and who is eventually murdered by his fellow shipmates before he can reach adulthood. As Ransome claims to lead a free life that is enviable for its lack of constraint, David sees only a scared little boy whose performance of bravado cannot disguise his isolation and desperation. Ransome tries to convince himself of the superiority of a life at sea by sneering at the tradesman's apprentice, a figure who he sees as utterly enslaved: "He had a strange notion of the dry land, picked up from sailors' stories: that it was a place where lads were put to some kind of slavery called a trade, and where apprentices were continually lashed and clapped into foul prisons" (49). David, however, points out to Ransome that his life is more about exploitation than rugged individualism:

I asked him what trade could be so dreadful as the one he followed, where he ran the continual peril of his life, not alone from wind and sea, but by the horrid cruelty of those that were his masters. He said it was very true; and then began to praise the life, and tell what a pleasure it was to get on shore with money in his pocket, and spend it like a man, and buy apples, and swagger, and surprise what he called stick-in-the mud boys. (36)

Ransome sees the apprentice as having lost any sort of autonomy while he, free from the settled world, is a completed adult. David recognizes, however, that at the heart of the boy's devil-may-care attitude is a great deal of pain and suffering:

he swore horribly whenever he remembered, but more like a silly schoolboy than a man; and boasted of many wild and bad things that he had done: stealthy thefts, false accusations, ay, and even murder;

but all with such a dearth of likelihood in the details, and such a weak and crazy swagger in the delivery, as disposed me rather to pity him than to believe him. (35)

Like the pirates of *Treasure Island*, Ransome has left settled society because of the fear of being made an apprentice but, just as he cannot express his ambition on dry land, so he cannot expect any protection at sea. Like young Dick, he is a casualty of the youth problem in which neither settled society nor unsettled society can properly accommodate the child. Ransome's rebellion is so overwrought that it becomes a parodic version of masculinity performed to mask the frightened child that lies within. David fails to understand, however, that the boy's fear of a "kind of slavery called a trade" is as real as his own fear of slavery in the colonies. He does not understand that he also overcompensates for his own lack of protection by becoming a scolding moralist. If Ransome and the highlanders are too childish, then David is too "adultish" but they are both the result of a society that offers them little protection against both crime and punishment.

Like the young seaman, the entire group of Jacobite rebels are, for David, boastful children. The spirit of romance and adventure that they appear to possess is, for him, nothing more than a childish petulance produced by their refusal to be governed by disciplined logic. As David travels through the highlands on the run with Breck, he cannot help but try to reform the outlaw, to make him into a more rational and respectable figure. In the aftermath of the assassination of Colin Campbell, he believes that Breck may in fact be the guilty party and thus he is determined to question him. He is convinced that he should be told the entire story so that the truth can come out but he is soon baffled by Breck, who appears to use a child's obfuscation when he tells David that he did not see the assassin because, when the man passed, he was busy tying his shoes:

"I couldnae just conscientiously swear to him," says Alan. "He gaed very close by me, to be sure, but it's a strange thing that I should just have been tying my brogues."

"Can you swear that you don't know him, Alan?" I cried, half angered, half in mind to laugh at his evasions.

"Not yet," says he; "but I've a grand memory for forgetting, David." (123)

David argues that Beck should simply tell the truth so that the guilty party can be punished but the highlander counters that a boy who has experienced very little danger or hardship has no business judging: "Them that havenae dipped their hands in any little difficulty, should be very mindful of the case of them that have" (123). Despite remaining convinced that "Alan's morals were all tail-first" (123–4), David is impressed by the spirit with which "he was ready to give his life for them" (124). While he has a grudging respect for Breck's loyalty to a fellow fugitive, he ultimately believes that the cold, hard facts of the case, which have been obscured by the highlander's penchant for secrecy and intrigue, should simply be stated in open court.

The highland system of justice comes under David's scrutiny when he gets a very close view of it inside the hideout of the clan leader Cluny who holds court deep in the forest. David admires the chief's leadership but finds that he is too involved in family quarrels to be able to settle them disinterestedly:

> Disputes were brought to him in his hiding-hole to be decided; and the men of his country, who would have snapped their fingers at the Court of Session, laid aside revenge and paid down money at the bare word of this forfeited and hunted outlaw. When he was angered, which was often enough, he gave his commands and breathed threats of punishment like any king; and his gillies trembled and crouched away from him like children before a hasty father. (161)

The administration of law in the clan system is apparently too dependent upon one man, who operates as the law itself. David also judges Cluny's moral habits from the perspective of a priggish lowlander. He complains that the man is often drunk and that he gambles with his guests. When David tells him that he will not gamble because he once promised his father that he would not, the chief replies, "What kind of Whiggish, canting talk is this, for the house of Cluny Macpherson?" (162). The boy also objects to the way in which Cluny tabulates gambling winnings. His accounting practices, rather than being objective, are tainted by an old-fashioned code of hospitality. He tells Cluny, "if they lose, you give them back their money; and if they win, they carry away yours in their pouches!" (165). Cluny then openly accuses David of being heartless in his adherence to a rational code: "ye give me very much the look of a man that has entrapped poor people to their hurt" (166). While Cluny becomes fed up with the David's scolding, the boy presses on, arguing that the chief's adherence to the code of hospitality would be better served if he stopped gambling with his guests entirely. David would, like a good Whig, have the fun drained out of a night's entertainment in order to preserve the peace. Cluny tells him, "Mr Balfour [...] I think you are too nice and covenanting, but for all that you have the spirit of a very pretty gentleman" (166). As he tries to teach Cluny a lesson, David becomes precisely the kind of pretty gentleman whose religious cant drives a youth to join the rebellion.

More evidence of the irrationality of highland justice is uncovered by David inside the home of James Stewart, who offers the two fugitives temporary shelter and protection. He is alarmed to discover that because Stewart is the clan's leader he will have to "paper" them in order to prove to the authorities that he has not been aiding and abetting. David argues that much of the highland intrigue could be swept away if Stewart simply papered the real assassin: "But the plain common sense is to set the blame where it belongs, and that is on the man that fired the shot. Paper him, as ye call it, set the hunt on him; and let honest, innocent folk show their faces in safety" (134). Earlier, Breck tells David the history of the highlands and the ways in which the Campbells have, as representatives of the Crown, perpetuated clan feuds. They have used the modern mechanisms of the law to punish innocent people in their attempt to exact revenge on figures such as Ardishiel:

> Therefore he sent for lawyers, and papers, and red-coats to stand at his back. And the kindly folk of that country must all pack and tramp, every father's son out of his father's house, and out of the place where he was bred and fed, and played when he was a callant. (83)

As Donald McFarlan notes in his introduction to the novel, the actual trial of James Stewart for the murder of Colin Campbell did in fact convict an innocent man in order to make an example of a rebel for the sake of "the future well-governing of these distant parts of Scotland" (xx). A jury made up mostly of Campbells chose to believe "a mountain of perjured evidence" (xx) in order to send a message to the lawless regions. David argues that it is time for the rebels to grow up to realize that they are no longer in a battle against a rival clan, that they are at war rather foolishly with the machinery of state. He tells Breck that the assassination of Colin Campbell was entirely futile given that he was only following the orders of a faceless nation-state: "It's not this Campbell's fault, man—it's his orders. And if ye killed this Colin to-morrow, what better would ye be? There would be another factor in his shoes, as fast as spur can drive" (83). According to David, as an employee of the state Campbell did not possess any particular value or significance. Whereas the highlanders cannot see beyond their family feuds and clan rivalries, David sees the need for a Scotland with one administrative framework:

> "Oh!" says I, willing to give him a little lesson, "I have no fear of the justice of my country."
>
> "As if this was your country!" said he. "Or as if ye would be tried here, in a country of Stewarts!"
>
> "It's all Scotland," said I. (124)

David's journey as a hero, which takes him from one side of Scotland to the other, is, throughout the narrative, precisely about bringing the two halves of the nation together as one unified nation state. He believes that, even to the extent that he is willing to back the Campbells over the Stewarts, only through a complete and total adherence to objectivity can Scotland become a modern nation-state.

In the final scenes after the two fugitives have found their way to the lowlands, David goes to consult Rankeillor about Breck's escape to France and the restoration of his own inheritance. As a city lawyer, however, Rankeillor has no interest in becoming entangled in highland feuds. Rankellor insists that Breck is not worth protecting: "It would please me none the worse, if (with all his merits) he were soused in the North Sea, for the man, Mr David, is a sore embarrassment" (200). While he is no supporter of the rebel, he understands that David is in debt to him and that he is "quite right to adhere to him" because "indubitable he adhered to you" (200). The conflict between the heroic context in which David must acknowledge a strong debt of gratitude to Breck and the legal context in which David must disavow any connection to him in order to remain a law-abiding citizen represents the ideological crux of the novel's ending. It is left to the lawyer as a third party to find a solution. Even as Rankeillor knows that David has been involved with the notorious rebel, he makes sure the man's name is not actually mentioned in his presence. When David blurts out indiscreetly that he has been running from the authorities with Breck, Rankeillor insists he has not heard the name. David argues that he might as well keep using the name but the lawyer replies, "Not at all [...]. I am somewhat dull of hearing, as you may have remarked; and I am far from sure I caught the name exactly. We will call your friend, if you please, Mr Thomson—that there may be no reflections" (199). Later, when Rankeillor must meet Breck, he conveniently forgets to bring his glasses in order to avoid incriminating himself. Breck, we will remember, used the same kind of convenient trick by claiming that he did not see the assassin because he was tying his shoe when the man passed by him. He practices, in effect, the same kind of legal deniability as Rankeillor. The fact that David cannot name Breck in front of Rankeillor also recalls the highland tradition of maintaining complete secrecy around notorious rebels by never uttering their names. If the heroic context and the legal context are in conflict, then Rankeillor resolves the conflict precisely because he only knows as much of the story as he needs to know in order to serve his client. Built into the confidential relationship between lawyer and client is, as the connection between Rankeillor and Breck suggests, an ancient highland custom of not telling the entire story. If David has continually criticized the highlanders for not revealing the entire truth, he finds to his surprise that the modern professional uses the same strategy. The attorney emerges as a figure with a duty to serve the interests of his clients, even those who may be on the wrong side of the law, as David and Breck are in the Appin murder case. The lawyer can have a rebel for a client and remain at all times a law-abiding professional. This is as close as the novel comes to making the lawyer into a heroic figure—more than a scolding Whig moralist—one whose job is not to colonize the nation for a ruthless code of objectivity but whose job it is to advocate for his client. In Rankeillor's trick, there resides a modern version of Scottish law that is able to incorporate both lowland and highland legal codes of practice.

David's fortune is rescued, in the end, because he does what his father should have done and takes the advice of his lawyer. Rankeillor advises him to reach an out-of-court settlement with his uncle so that Breck's name does not come out in court: "[...] my advice (upon the whole) is to make a very easy bargain with your uncle, perhaps even leaving him at Shaws where he has taken root for a quarter century, and contenting yourself in the meanwhile with a fair provision" (204). The deal accommodates both the lowland and highland sides of the family and heals the damage done by the old bargain that left David poor and unprotected. Rankeillor's contract with Ebenezer is based on Cluny's model of hospitality, which David once criticized so strongly. Just as Cluny does not take all the gambling winnings owed to him in order that his guests should leave happy, Rankeillor does not take the entire estate for David but leaves Ebenezer with the manor house in order to keep him from bothering the boy in the future. David describes how the deal is struck between his lawyer and Ebenezer:

> They stayed there closeted about an hour; at the end of which period they had come to a good understanding, and my uncle set our hands to the agreement in a formal manner. By the terms of this, my uncle bound himself to satisfy Rankeillor as to his intromissions, and to pay me two clear thirds of the yearly income of Shaws. (214–15)

David's share in the estate is both old-fashioned and modern as it is produced by the landlord's rent but held for him as money in the bank.

In the final pages, he is also absorbed back into the modern city life of Edinburgh while his highland adventure fades into memory. As his narration concludes, David has a nagging feeling that despite getting back his father's share of the estate and despite no longer being a fugitive, his story is not a complete success:

> [...] I let the crowd carry me to and fro; and yet all the time what I was thinking of was Alan at Rest-and-be-Thankful; and all the time (although you would think I would not choose but be delighted with these braws and novelties) there was a cold gnawing in my inside like a remorse for something wrong. The hand of Providence brought me in my drifting to the very doors of the British Linen Company's bank. (219)

While he does not clearly state what the "something wrong" is, it is undoubtedly the suspicion that while he was travelling with Breck he was too much the priggish lowlander. As he walks the streets of Edinburgh, the exciting "braws and novelties" of city life remind him of how he was a scolding moralist throughout his adventure, of how he was a ridiculous "stick-in-the-mud" boy.

Prior to Stevenson's novels, the solution to the nation's youth problem was typically framed in terms of imposing middle-class standards on the poor and working classes. His solution, in contrast, effectively erases the boundary between the poor and working classes and respectable middle-class society. Just as the poor and working classes need to have technical expertise imposed upon them in order to protect children from death and disease, so the middle classes need to have a lack of restraint imposed upon them in order to protect children from too much discipline and punishment. Indeed, it is out of this double gesture of colonization that Stevenson's collectivist state is born. Because Dickens's novels make the family firm the centre of the Victorian society, they cling tenaciously to bourgeois respectability in order to shut out the grotesque physical bodies of working-class usurpers like Uriah Heep. But because Stevenson's novels make the collectivist state the centre of Victorian society, they jettison respectability in order to accommodate the private, carnivalesque self that was once victimized by capitalist society. But while his adventure novels are remarkably sympathetic to the marginalized and outcast figures that are demonized by middle-class values, they are fundamentally about the career aspirations of their middle-class heroes, figures who are still the right sort to run the nation. What we find is that Stevenson's imaginative child must combine the technical expertise of modern society with the carnivalesque spirit and libidinal energy of an older society to become a modern professional whose appropriation of aristocratic and working-class codes of conduct makes him an effective social actor, one who can hold together competing versions of society within the larger nation-state. If respectable society must purge itself of the private self, of any hint of the grotesque and the carnivalesque, then Stevenson relocates this repressed private self at the level of the modern professional who must do the dirty and dangerous work of nation building and at the level of the ambitious child who must use duplicity and disguise in order to break out of dead-end employment. In the next chapter, which examines E. Nesbit's novels, I argue that the repressed private self of the respectable middle classes became incorporated into the imaginative play of its children. If duplicity, disguise, and physical aggression are suppressed by middle-class business practices, then they are allowed into Nesbit's construction of the imaginative play of children in order to keep the respectable middle-class family competitive in the market economy.

4
Commercialism and Middle-Class Innocence: *The Story of the Treasure Seekers* and *The Railway Children*

In *Oliver Twist* (1838), Bill Sykes asks Fagin why he wants to use a delicate and sensitive boy like Oliver as a pickpocket when he can easily recruit one of the "fifty boys snoozing about Common Garden every night" (326). Fagin replies, "Because they're of no use to me. [...] their looks convict 'em when they get into trouble" (326). Fagin knows that Oliver has a sentimental value not possessed by the other boys. He understands that if he could somehow combine a pitiable figure like Oliver with a cunning figure like the Artful Dodger he might have the perfect pick-pocket, one who can continue to steal without ever being convicted. While the sentimentalized child of the workhouse is a figure like Oliver and his friend parochial Dick who is happy to die young before he is ever forced to earn a living as a criminal, the un-sentimentalized street child is a figure like the Artful Dodger who is a perversion of childhood innocence, a boy dressed in adult clothing and wise beyond his years.[1] Fagin knows that finding a child who is a combination of these two kinds of children is a virtual impossibility. In the figure of the inno-cent pickpocket, however, there lies a mythology about a middle-class hero who can be involved in a mercenary enterprise and yet still remain uncorrupted. One of the reasons that the child became such an impor-tant figure and that childhood became such an important structure of feeling in the nineteenth century is that middle-class society became increasingly concerned with the erosion of its innocence inside com-mercial society. By continually portraying itself through children like Oliver Twist, it could see itself as an innocent child put to work in a com-mercial society by forces ultimately lying beyond its control. It could see itself, in other words, as Fagin's perfect pickpocket, a child involved in the mercenary pursuit of profit whose looks will never convict him.

In this chapter, I examine E. Nesbit's novels *The Story of the Treasure Seekers* and *The Railway Children*, both of which depict middle-class families that suddenly experience a dramatic downturn in their social and economic position. In Nesbit's novels, when the middle-class family's position is threatened, its children are in danger of becoming mixed up with and mistaken for criminal subjects. Nesbit's children who temporarily occupy the position of the poor and the working classes are not mistaken for poor or working-class subjects, however, because it is always understood by those who witness their activities that they are only playing at being poor and playing at producing the family's income. As Jenny Bavidge has argued, Nesbit's novels are fundamentally about the "belief in the necessity of imaginative play" (140).² Her delightfully precocious and imaginative children are able to achieve a kind of agency that allows them to be sentimentalized even as they resort to some rather dubious business ventures in order to escape poverty. Child's play ensures that while they are involved in the commercial world—the all-too-realistic world in which adults must struggle to earn a living—they remain uncorrupted.

As I have previously discussed, in *Essays on Practical Education* Maria Edgeworth instructs her audience of middle-class professionals and industrialists to erase the boundary between the child's playroom and the industrial landscapes of Britain. In her conceptualization of childhood education, the tools of industry must become the toys of children as the child's playroom is filled with little models of the machines used in manufacturing processes:

> spinning-wheels, looms, paper-mills, wind-mills, water-mills, might with great advantage be shown in miniature to children. We have found that two or three hundred bricks formed in plaster of Paris, on a scale of a quarter of an inch to an inch, with a few lintils, &c. in proportion, have been a lasting and useful fund of amusement. (31)

Edgeworth believes that once children have become accustomed to such practical toys, they are ready to visit an actual workshop where they will not be "bewildered by the sight of wheels and levers" (31) or by "the explanations of the workmen" (31). Teresa Michals argues that the large-scale manufacturing of toys emerged at a time when children began to occupy their own separate sphere apart from adulthood but, even as the toy industry was involved in creating an imaginary world for children, it threatened to implicate them in consumerism. She writes, "In the eighteenth and nineteenth centuries, children's toys and education became deeply entwined with buying and selling. They also reflect the middle class's anxiety over its commercial consumption" (29). In Nesbit's novels, children's play is connected to rescuing the middle-class family from poverty and, as such, it is implicated in commercialism. As the children take over the role of the parents in the production of the family income, however, there emerges the middle-class myth that the family itself is only playing at earning a living, the myth that the middle classes can become involved in the aggressively competitive world of earning a living and chasing after profits without becoming corrupted. Children needed to play with toys connected to industry and invention, not only so that they would be trained to take their place in the labour market but so that the adult's involvement in commercialism would appear innocent. Tiny microscopes and tiny spinning wheels, in other words, functioned to make the larger industrial economy appear as so much innocent child's play.

Child's play and co-operative economics

Edith Nesbit was a founding member of the Fabian Society, a biographical fact that might lead the reader to look for the socialism at work in her novels.[3] Certainly, there are parts of *The Story of the Treasure Seekers* and *The Railway Children* in which the ideas of charity and co-operative economics become important to the narrative but the socialism of her novels is counterbalanced by a great concern for the economic well-being of the middle-class family. Fabian socialists of the nineteenth and early twentieth century were, as Nesbit's husband Hubert Bland writes in his section of *Fabian Essays in Socialism* (1889), committed to the definition of socialism as "the common holding of the means of production and exchange, and the *holding of them for the equal benefit of all*" (212). But even as the essays argue for the end of private capital, they demonstrate a definite commitment to paternalism and the interests of what Bland refers to as the "cultivated middle class" (210). As a writer of children's fiction, Nesbit is, despite some use of socialist ideology in her narratives, more interested in the economic well-being of the middle classes than a radical redistribution of wealth or a change in the ownership of the means of production. In his contribution to the collection, George Bernard Shaw criticizes a large portion of the British middle classes for living in constant fear of the working-class mob: "The section which is blinded by class prejudice to all sense of social responsibility, dreads personal violence from the working class with a superstitious terror that defies enlightenment or control" (192). Nesbit's children are undoubtedly depicted as enlightened and responsible members of the middle class who are not blinded by class prejudice. However, her middle-class children, who often temporarily occupy working-class positions, are also depicted as better at playing the role than working-class subjects themselves. Rather than focusing on social justice and economic equality, her novels are about the special ability of middle-class children to adapt to the vagaries and vicissitudes of the capitalist economy. Imaginative play grants them both the ability and the right to use whatever means are necessary to get out of poverty and, at the same time, saves them from the appearance of corruption.

In *The Story of the Treasure Seekers*, the upper-middle-class Bastable family is in danger of losing its position in society because of the death of the mother and the failure of the father's trading firm. Consequently, the six children (Dora, Oswald, Dicky, Alice, Noel, and Horace Octavius) take it upon themselves to restore "the fortunes of the ancient House of Bastable" (11) by attempting a great number of money-making ventures. At first they try their luck in the imaginary realm by digging for buried treasure in the back garden and by pretending to be highwaymen robbing travellers on the village common, but when these adventures fail to produce any real income the Bastable children venture into the commercial realm where they soon become involved in a series of questionable schemes. For example, they try to sell poetry to a sleazy newspaper editor who is much more interested in buying gossip about their friend, Lord Tottenham. They also make their way through the dangerous streets of London to borrow from a Jewish money-lender, Mr Rosenbaum, who charges 60 per cent interest.[4] Perhaps the most alarming and ridiculous attempt to restore the family fortunes occurs when they try to sell plonk sherry to adults, who are horrified to find children mixed up in the alcohol trade. As the Bastable children become involved in such schemes, however, they are never punished because ultimately the adults who come into contact with them find them to be charmingly precocious rather than cunning and deceptive. Because they have, from the start, conflated their activities with the romance and adventure of hunting for buried treasure, they are always interpreted as children at play. As such, they are rewarded not for the scheme itself but for the quantity of imagination they have put into it. Their play, which is often quite public, tends towards a public performance but it is never equated with the performances of child street performers who solicit money from passersby. Monica Flegel describes how Henry Mayhew, in his description of the impressive "tumbling" performed by crossing-sweepers in the streets of London, dismisses the poor children's physical antics as "just a glorified form of begging" (93). While the begging of street performers is a corrupt display of the physical body, the imaginative play of the Bastable children is an innocent display of their ingenuity. The Bastable children do not beg and they do not steal money from a parent's pocketbook. Instead, they concoct schemes, such as making and selling their own cold remedy, that are well beyond the scope of ordinary children. Their kind of performance does not involve spectacular forms of physicality but spectacular forms of ingenuity. Indeed, the more spectacular the imaginative child's involvement in commercialism is, the more charmingly precocious he or she becomes.

Ultimately, the Bastables have, because of their innate ability to play properly, the ability to transform the ugly reality of poverty into an imaginative landscape. When the family falls on hard times, the children discover that their home is in danger of being drained of its aesthetic beauty:

> And the silver in the big oak plate-chest that is lined with green baize all went away to the shop to have the dents and scratches taken out of it, and it never came back. We think Father hadn't enough money to pay the silver man for taking out the dents and scratches. The new spoons and forks were yellowy-white, and not so heavy as the old ones, and they never shone after the first day or two. (12)

As the lack of money causes the family's household items to lose their beauty, the house is in danger of becoming a working-class home. The children, however, are able to find in the books they have read romantic corollaries to their all-too-realistic circumstances. They turn their economic hardship into child's play as they imagine themselves as characters in the stories they have read. As Gubar notes, "The hyperliterate heroes and heroines of E. Nesbit's children's stories are promiscuous readers par excellence, having read everything from didactic tracts to adventure stories, from novels by Dickens and Thackeray to children's books by Kipling and Grahame" (129). When, for example, the children have nothing but mutton for dinner, Oswald rescues them from the ugliness of their situation by pretending that they are characters in Frederick Maryatt's novel *The Children of the New Forest* (1846), which tells the story of the orphaned Beverley children and their descent into poverty during the English Civil War:

> It was a wet day, I remember, and mutton hash for dinner—very tough with pale gravy with lumps in it. I think the others would

have left a good deal on the sides of their plates, although they know better, only Oswald said it was a savoury stew made of the red deer that Edward shot. So then we were the Children of the New Forest, and the mutton tasted much better. No one in the New Forest minds venison being tough and the gravy pale. (160)

The Bastable children are able to accept their poverty in a way that demonstrates their sympathy for the poor but that also works to displace the poor as sentimental objects worthy of pity. They are not like upper-class children, so entitled and haughty that they cannot endure their change of fortune, and they are not like working-class children, so untalented that they can only passively succumb to poverty. Because they are so well read and can play so well, they overcome the bleakness of poverty by turning it into an imaginative project.

In contrast, adults and non-middle-class figures tend to be defined throughout the narrative by their inability to play properly. When the children first come upon the idea of digging for treasure, they cannot imagine why adults do not attempt that which always proves so successful in fiction. Oswald, as the narrator, comments, "I couldn't help wondering as we went down to the garden, why Father had never thought of digging there for treasure instead of going to his beastly office every day" (20). He cannot understand why an adult would choose a life in an office over a life as a treasure seeker. Their foppish neighbour, whom they dismissively refer to as "Albert-next-door", also appears to them to be lacking imagination. He is described as a "very tidy" (23) child who wears "frilly collars and velvet knickerbockers" (23) and who "doesn't care for reading" (23). The fact that he is too prissy to dirty his clothes and too out of touch with the imaginary realm of fiction means that he "cannot play properly at all" (23). The Bastables have such a complete lack of sympathy for Albert that they only include him in their games so that they can bully him and prove their superiority. When he will not climb into a tunnel they have dug, Oswald tells him, "Take your turn like a man" (25) and when he refuses they "make him" (25). When the tunnel gives way and the boy is buried in dirt, they blame him and conclude that he is "a horribly unlucky boy to have anything to do with" (27). The treasure dig even begins to resemble a crime scene:

We would have dug him out all right enough, in time, but he screamed so we were afraid the police would come, so Dicky climbed over the wall, to tell the cook there to tell Albert-next-door's uncle he had been buried by mistake, and to come and help dig him out. (27)

When Albert's uncle, who shares the Bastables' lack of sympathy for Albert, asks how he came to be buried, they reply that it was not through physical force but "moral force" (28) that they were able to make him crawl inside. The uncle can only laugh at the children for the precociously philosophical way in which they are able to rationalize their bullying. Even as the scene is played for comedy, it demonstrates the serious idea that the middle-class child is better than the upper-class child because he or she has an ability not only to endure dirty and dangerous situations but to make them into a pleasurable fantasy. The fact that the children are understood to be playing grants them permission to be ruthless towards individuals who are not part of their imaginative circle.

The children encounter another upper-class child who, like Albert-next-door, is also unable to play properly. They meet a girl in the park who, when Noel tells her he is a prince, replies that she is a princess. They are surprised because "it is so seldom you meet any children who can begin to play right off without having everything explained to them" (73) but when it turns out that she really is a princess, a fifth cousin of Queen Victoria, they realize that she has not been playing at all. She expresses her envy of the Bastable children, who are able to play on the heath and ride the donkeys with "white saddle covers" (77), because, unlike them, she has "two prim ladies with little mouths and tight hair" (78) watching over her. As a princess, she cannot engage in child's play because she is too tightly guarded and because she already inhabits a fairytale realm. As Oswald remarks, "I might have known such a stupid-looking little girl would never have been able to pretend, as well as that" (80). While Noel, who has married her in a pretend ceremony, holds onto the idea that she is a romantic figure, the rest are unconvinced: "He says now that she was as beautiful as the day, but we remember her quite well, and she was nothing of the kind" (80). The princess is not qualified to be in such a select group of imaginative children. She has not developed an ability to play because her great wealth leaves her with no reason to transform her world or to construct an alternative identity for herself.

In a scene in which the children think they have caught a thief in their house after bravely drawing down on him with a toy pistol, poor and working-class figures prove to be just as unable to use their imaginations as upper-class figures. Rather than a common criminal, they find they have caught a man brimming with imagination who tells them about the grand adventures he has had, including robbing the Lord Mayor and living in a bandit's cave.[5] The children eventually discover that their interesting burglar is not a real criminal but an old friend of their father's but, in the mean time, they are captivated by his stories and moved to feel sympathy for him: "I never liked a new man better than I liked that robber. He told us he had been a war-correspondent and an editor, in happier days, as well as a horse-stealer and a colonel of dragoons" (191). Even though he is a criminal, the children want to let him go because he has lived an exciting life and has exciting stories to tell. Shortly thereafter, an actual robber breaks into the house but proves to be an entirely uninteresting figure with a coarse Cockney accent. The children are disappointed to find there is nothing at all romantic about him: "He did not look as if he could ever have been a pirate or a highwayman, or anything really dashing or noble, and he scowled and shuffled his feet and said: 'Well, go on: why don't yer fetch the pleece?'" (194). The burglar then attempts to convince their father's friend that he should be freed because he has children at home:

> Let me off, sir. Come now, I've got kids of my own at home, strike me if I ain't—same as yours—I've got a nipper just about 'is size, and what'll come of them if I'm lagged? [...] Don't be hard on a cove, mister; think of the missis and the kids. I've got one just the cut of little missy there, bless 'er pretty 'eart'. (194–5)

Alice is convinced that he should be freed but before a decision can be made the man escapes out the window. With a wink he tells them, "I'll give yer love to the kids and the missis" (196). The fellow's conventional sentimental appeal for sympathy for his children is, as the father's friend decides, more than likely a fabrication. When the father returns home and reveals that the first robber is his old chum Foulkes, the real burglar is soon forgotten as the children redirect their attention to the pretend burglar. As Foulkes leaves for the evening, Alice asks him whether any of his adventure stories were true and he replies, "I tried to play the part properly, my dear" (200). The real burglar, in contrast, has not played the part well at all. His attempt to portray his own children as just like the Bastable children is unconvincing precisely because he cannot compose exciting stories. If his children were really like them, then their father would be a much more interesting figure like Foulkes. By the end of the scene, the actual robber, who has been pushed into his trade by very real poverty, gets very little sympathy while the imaginary robber, who claims to have once been a war-correspondent, gets a great deal of sympathy. The narrative argues that it is not the actual poor who deserve sympathy but imaginative middle-class individuals who can transcend class boundaries when they fall on hard times. The inability of the poor to play their roles properly—the fact that they tell their same old sob stories with very coarse accents—disqualifies them from receiving it.

The key to understanding how charity works in the novel is to recognize how the Bastable children are able to turn the unpleasant circumstances of their poverty into profitable schemes. Giving money to the poor will not change their lives, so the argument goes, because they do not have the proper invention and industry to use it for upward mobility. The middle-class child displaces the poor child as the proper recipient of charity because he or she is able to put it to use to improve the family's class position. At the beginning of the story, Dicky finds an advertisement promising that for only two shillings instructions will be mailed out detailing how "ladies and gentleman can easily earn two pounds a week in their spare time" (19). He points out that because they are not in school they can "easily earn twenty pounds a week each" (19). While the notice is not taken very seriously, it does show how the children are determined to take what little money they do have and turn it into even more money in order to achieve social mobility. Later, Dicky argues that they should try to earn money by marketing their own cold remedy. He tells the other children, "Every one in the world wants money. Some people get it. The people who get it are the ones who see things. I have seen one thing" (162). The one thing that he has seen is the fact that medicine bottles can be purchased for only one cent while the packaged cures can be sold for "nearly always two-and-ninepence the bottle, and three-and-six for one nearly double the size" (162–3). When Dora argues that it is "the medicine that costs the money [...] look how expensive jujubes are at the chemist, and pepper-mints too" (163), Dicky counters that they will pay ruthless attention to the bottom line by using only inexpensive ingredients: "That's only because they're nice, [...] nasty things are not so dear. Look what a lot of brimstone you get for a penny, and the same with alum. We would not put the nice kinds of chemist's things in our medicine" (163). He then tries to catch a cold by walking home in his wet clothes so that he can test the product on himself but the more delicate and sensitive Noel catches one instead. In his state of poverty and in his sick bed, Noel is perilously close to becoming another parochial Dick, the sentimen-talized child who deserves pity because he is so sweet and innocent in his dying condition. Rather than sentimentalize their brother, the chil-dren use him for medical research as they test various concoctions made up of ingredients such as "gruel", "licorice-water", and "the juice of the red flannel that Noel's throat was done up in" (167). Albert-next-door's uncle is appalled by their lack of sympathy for the patient: "Health is the best thing you've got; you ought to know better than to risk it. You might have killed your little brother with your precious medicines" (172). But despite the fact that the children have been rather callous towards Noel, shortly thereafter all is "forgiven and forgotten" (173). The point of the scene is that rather than see Noel as a passive individual who may die soon, the children see his poor health as a chance to cure both him and the family's finances. The children deserve our sympathy not because Noel looks so sweet on his deathbed but because his brothers and sisters have turned a bad situation into an opportunity for social mobility. In *The Wouldebegoods* (1901), the sequel to *The Story of the Treasure Seekers*, Oswald goes so far as to announce his contempt for sentimental forms of charity. He sneers in particular at Maria Louisa Charlesworth's *Ministering Children* (1854), an overly sentimental story about children who help the poor. He declares, "I'm not going to smooth the pillows of the sick, or read to the aged poor, or any rot out of Ministering Children" (17). The sentimental subject is not the poor dying child but the precocious child who tries to emulate adult actions and who fails so charmingly to do so. The children's attempt to peddle bogus medicines never implicates them in crime because they do it with such style. The idea of sweet little children peddling fake cures is so audacious, it becomes evidence of ingenuity rather than criminality.

The displacement of the poor as the traditional recipients of charity is made quite literal when Oswald dresses up as a street vendor in order to make money to help Alice, who is in a great deal of emotional distress because she has, as she admits to him, knowingly passed a bad sixpence at the telegraph office. When the writer Mrs Leslie gives him flowers to take to poor Noel, he decides that they will be of more use to Alice, who is desperate to avoid being branded a criminal:

> He put on his oldest clothes—they're much older than any you would think he had if you saw him when he was tidy—and he took those yellow chrysanthemums and he walked with them to Greenwich Station and waited for the trains bringing people from London. He sold those flowers in penny bunches and got tenpence. (175–6)

The woman who is given the pennies at the telegraph office refuses them at first but eventually tells Oswald that she will "put them in the plate on Sunday" (177). The tale of Oswald as a street vendor is deemed so heroic by the others that Noel composes a verse to commemorate it:

> *The noble youth of high degree*
>   *Consents to play a menial part,*
> *All for his sister Alice's sake,*
>   *Who was so dear to his faithful heart.* (177)

Oswald's ability to see the value in the flowers beyond their use as a sentimental gesture towards a sick child and his ability to play properly the part of a vendor ensures that his sister's reputation is rescued. More importantly, however, Oswald has been able to turn a profit. After giving the lady in the telegraph office six pennies, he has four left over, which he uses to buy the "peppermint bullseyes" (177) he shares with the others. His play acting demonstrates the ability of the middle-class child to turn the job of street beggar into a lucrative business. The scene does not extend sympathy to the poor vendor who, in order to receive charity, forces his audience to confront the reality of the social structure, but to the middle-class child who, in playing the role better than an actual poor person, allows his audience to deny the existence of social inequality.

At the end of the narrative, the children return to their upper-middle-class status when their wealthy uncle returns to England from India. Because they hear him referred to as "the Indian Uncle" (214), they connect him to their reading, to "Lo, the poor Indian" from Pope's *Essay on Man* (1732–4). They confuse him with questions about "wigwams, and wampum, and mocassins, and beavers" (224), thinking that like Pope's character he is a North-American Indian rather than a British imperialist. At the same time that they mistake the uncle for a charity case, their father plans to ask him for money to help his failing business. During their conversation at dinner, the father broaches the subject of investing in the firm, which "only wanted a little capital" (215) but is quickly cut off: "The Uncle said, 'Pooh, pooh!' to that, and then he said he was afraid that what that same business wanted was not capital but management. Then I heard my Father say, 'It is not a pleasant subject: I am sorry I introduced it. Suppose we change it, sir' " (215). Later, however, when the children tell the Indian Uncle that they would like to give him their pocket money because he is poor, his attitude changes. He is impressed with the children's charity but he is more impressed with stories of their money-making schemes. He will "take the three-penny bit" (224) but he wants to know how they got "the money for this most royal spread" (224). When the children relate to him their adventures, he is won over:

> We told him all about the different ways we had looked for treasure, and when we had been telling some time he sat down, to listen better and at last we told him how Alice had played at divining-rod, and how it really had found a half-sovereign. Then he said he would like to see her do it again. But we explained that the rod would only show gold and silver, and that we were quite sure there was no more gold in the house, because we happened to have looked very carefully.
>
> "Well, silver, then," said he; "let's hide the plate-basket, and little Alice shall make the divining rod find it." (224–5)

The uncle is so charmed by the children's ability to make money through their play that he cannot help but join them. Their refusal to be passive charity cases and their ability to turn a profit from their business activities eventually convinces him that he should invest in their father's business. The children overhear the conversation between the two men:

> I say, Dick, I dined with your kids yesterday—as I daresay they've told you. Jolliest little cubs I ever saw! Why didn't you let me see them the other night? The eldest is the image of poor Janey—and as to young Oswald, he's a man! If he's not a man, I'm a nigger! Eh!—what? And Dick, I say, I shouldn't wonder if I could find a friend to put a bit into that business of yours—eh? (230)

The uncle can broach the unpleasant subject of the father's business because the children's imaginative play elides the differences between his finances and theirs and proves to him that the Bastables are the right sort of family in which to invest. Their play indicates to him that the father possesses the same ability to be inventive and to turn a profit as his children. Working-class fathers with children at home who are in need of assistance might be able to secure charity by using sentimental appeals but precocious children are able to secure investments by performing for adults the imagination and ingenuity contained within the family home. The imaginative child operates, therefore, as a valuable commodity in the home, one that by performing ingenuity and innocence allows the family in its disadvantaged position to acquire the faith, goodwill, and capital of the outside world. They receive a kind of charity that is not charity as the economic potential stored in the family overcomes the unequal economic relationship between the giver and the receiver.

The uncle is so charmed by the children, he eventually invites the whole family to come to live with him in his manor house, where he bestows upon them the colonial treasures he has accumulated. Gubar writes, "the fact that the Indian Uncle's immense wealth is signified by and associated with the booty he brings back from abroad implies that to be a colonist *is* to be a 'professional treasure seeker' " (145). The treasure is made up of beautiful artefacts from all over the world, which are turned into toys once they are transferred to the children:

> There were toys for the kids and model engines for Dick and me, and a lot of books, and Japanese china tea-sets for the girls, red and white and gold—there were sweets by the pound and by the box—and long yards of soft silk from India, to make frocks for the girls—and a real Indian sword for Oswald and a book of Japanese pictures for Noel, and some ivory chess men for Dicky: the castles of the chessmen are elephant-and-castles. (231–2)

The colonial treasure that is gained by British imperialism becomes equated with the imaginative money-making schemes of the Bastable children. Their possession of the treasure shows that they are capable of being colonial managers like their uncle and that imperialism itself is an act that, because it produces such imaginative booty, is as innocent as child's play. In what amounts to a kind of imperial money laundering scheme, ill-gotten wealth is cleansed of its corruption when it is converted into toys for children. In chivalric romances, women are typically used to redeem the warfare of their knights as gold and jewels are removed from the ugliness of the conquest and placed at the feet and on the body of the beautiful lady. The Bastable children perform the same function for the uncle as they legitimize his colonial conquests. But for some vague references to "Native Races and Imperial something or other" (216), we are not told how the uncle has acquired his wealth in India. But, no matter what he has done, his actions are innocent because romantic corollaries for them can be found in children's games. Just as the Bastable children can bully Albert-next-door, so the British Empire can bully the colonies.

The narrative closes with the emergence of a new class of individuals who are the right sort, the imaginative kind who, though they may be adults, are still able to play properly. The children are included in a similar group of like-minded souls made up of adults who will help ensure their future success. In order to complete their story, the children want to hold another dinner party and to invite all the characters with whom they have come into contact during their time as treasure seekers:

> Presently, when we had seen the house, we were taken into the drawing-room, and there was Mrs Leslie, who gave us the shillings and wished us good hunting, and Lord Tottenham, and Albert-next-door's Uncle—and Albert-next-door, and his Mother (I'm not very fond of her), and best of all our own Robber and his two kids, and our Robber had a new suit on. The Uncle told us he had asked the people who had been kind to us. [...] (239)

The network of invited guests consists of those who have helped the Bastable children because they have recognized their imaginative capabilities. The guests do not include the wrong sort of people, figures like the money lender and their father's butcher. The racial Other and the working-class Other are not part of the network because they are too much a part of the realistic pursuit of profit rather than the imaginative pursuit of profit. As the network encloses around the Bastable children, it marginalizes those who cannot be romanticized and stabilizes the children's identities within a class of individuals that not only shares their imaginative capabilities but can help them find suitable careers:

> Mrs Leslie often comes to see us, and our own Robber and Albert-next-door's uncle. The Indian Uncle likes him because he has been to India too and is brown; but our Uncle does not like Albert-next-door. He says he is a muff. And I am to go to Rugby, and so are Noel and H.O., and perhaps to Balliol afterwards. Balliol is my Father's college. It has two separate coats of arms, which many other colleges are not allowed. Noel is going to be a poet and Dicky wants to go into Father's business. (240–1)

A well-developed imagination becomes the mark of a new kind of class superiority that excludes the priggish aristocracy and the coarse and common poor. Ultimately, the imaginative child becomes a sign of the family's wealth of middle-class ingenuity, the kind that can build a business and turn a profit. The imaginative child is turned into a public display of the family's industry and invention so that it can secure investments from the outside world even as it continues to appear too sweet and innocent to be implicated in anything as crass as business. As the imaginative child displaces the working-class child as an object of sympathy, he or she becomes a code that when deciphered by the outside world allows the family to enter into a kind of secret society based on a middle-class version of co-operative economics. Crucially, it is not a space that can be threatened by predatory outsiders because it is kept well hidden from Jewish money lenders and working-class butchers.

The industrial landscape and the child's playroom

In *The Railway Children*, a middle-class family's fortunes are transformed when the father, a Whitehall civil servant, is wrongfully convicted of espionage after a co-worker plants incriminating documents in his desk.[6] The family moves from being an urban middle-class family to a poor rural family in which the mother and children are the only breadwinners. The mother manages the home frugally and makes a bit of money publishing children's stories while the children spend their days playing at the railway station and befriending the local working-class villagers. As they threaten to become embedded in the working-class neighbourhood, however, it is their ability to play their way out of poverty that proves their father's innocence and that restores the family to its former position. If the father's reputation as a civil servant lies in ruins, his children are able to restore his innocence not because they beg and plead his case to authority figures but because their imaginative play demonstrates to authority figures that his children have within them the noble spirit of public service.

At the beginning of the narrative, the implication is that the family's isolation within its suburban villa is responsible in some way for the father being found guilty. He makes the same mistake, it would seem, that Dickens's law clerk Wemmick makes when he completely separates his work and his home. The description of the father is of a man who has turned his house into an imaginary realm disconnected from the actual work he performs in his government office. The children's toys, including the locomotive engine that functions as the narrative's central symbol, are certainly practical but they have no connection to their father's work. He is a jack-of-all-trades figure who can fix their broken toys, which correspond to all sorts of jobs, none of which are civil servant:

> All Peter's hopes for the curing of his afflicted Engine were now fixed on his Father, for Father was most wonderfully clever with his fingers. He could mend all sorts of things. He had often acted as veterinary surgeon to the wooden rocking-horse; once the poor creature was given up for lost, and even the carpenter said he didn't see his way to

do anything. And it was Father who mended the doll's cradle when no one else could; and with a little glue and some bits of wood and a pen-knife made all the Noah's Ark beasts as strong on their pins as ever they were, if not stronger. (5)

When the knock from the police comes, the family's first instinct is to seal off the home. The father remarks, "Who on earth! [...] An Englishman's house is his castle, of course, but I do wish they built semi-detached villas with moats and drawbridges" (6). The children reiterate the father's desire to close the family off: " 'I wish we *had* got a moat and drawbridge,' said Roberta; 'then, when we didn't want people, we could just pull up the drawbridge and no one else could get in' " (7). When the police take the father away to prison, the imaginative middle-class family is suddenly faced with the reality that both its income and its reputation lie in ruins. Part of the reason he is convicted is due to the fact that he has not properly displayed his children to the outside world, that he has closed them off in an imaginary realm entirely dislocated from his office. The implication is that had the father allowed his children to be connected to his work and to be seen by his co-workers as the delightful and imaginative children that they are, he certainly would not have been found guilty. When the children are relocated to the railway village, their imaginative play is able, as we shall see, to make up for the father's unfortunate separation of family and business. As Susan Anderson has noted, "The technology of the railway, rather than embodying a depersonalization of their lives, enables them to connect more closely with others" (313). Their playroom is suddenly not the snug parlour of a suburban villa but the entire landscape of an industrialized Britain. In this new landscape, they unconsciously incorporate their father's work as a civil servant into their imaginative play and, in doing so, prove to the railway director who enjoys watching them that their father must certainly be an innocent civil servant.

The Railway Children can be said to be more precisely concerned with the issue of gender and gender roles than *The Story of the Treasure Seekers*, as the family's descent into a working-class community means that its female members are allowed, because of the liminality of their position, to imagine non-traditional, non-domestic careers for themselves. Before they are even transferred from the suburban home to their working-class home, the two girls, Roberta and Phyllis, who are given the male nick-names "Bobbie" and "Phil", have already been imagining non-traditional roles for themselves. As they play with the toy engine before their father's arrest, Peter asks him if girls can work on the railway with boys:

"*Can* girls help to mend engines?" Peter asked doubtfully.

"Of course they can. Girls are just as clever as boys, and don't you forget it! How would you like to be an engine-driver, Phil?"

"My face would be always dirty, wouldn't it?" said Phyllis, in unemotional tones, "and I expect I should break something."

"I should just love it," said Roberta—"do you think I could when I'm grown up, Daddy? Or even a stoker?"

"You mean a fireman," said Daddy, pulling and twisting at the engine. "Well, if you still wish it, when you're grown up, we'll see about making you a fire-woman. I remember when I was a boy—." (6)

While Phyllis is meant for a more traditional gender role as she finds male jobs too dirty, Roberta is perhaps meant for a career outside the home. When the father tells Roberta that he will see about making her a firewoman, it becomes clear that their enjoyment of the train engine has already destabilized the gender and class positions of the children. Child's play, which demands that children imagine different identities for themselves, has already prepared the girls for the necessity of having to make money by non-traditional means and to occupy working-class roles in order to rescue the family from its decline.

As the family departs for the country, the mother stresses to them that their time in exile will only be a continuation of their play time in London. The children are soon alarmed to find that their mother has had to sell all their pretty household items and that they are left with only practical ones:

"We can't take everything," said Mother.

"But we seem to be taking all the ugly things," said Roberta.

"We're taking the useful ones," said Mother; "we've got to play at being Poor for a bit, my chickabiddy." (14)

The mother stresses that they are not going to be the actual poor, but that they are only playing at being poor. She recognizes that it is the children's ability to play properly that will insulate them from poverty and allow them to overcome it. When they are soon forced to employ the services of the local doctor, however, it becomes clear that the family is very much in danger of becoming embedded in their poverty. They are forced to ask Dr Forrest whether they can join, like the other indigent members of the village, the "Doctor's Club", a Friendly Society that sub-sidizes health care for the local villagers. The doctor is disappointed to discover the family is so poor that it will not be able to pay the full price for his services:

> "You see, she told me what a good doctor you were, and I asked her how she could afford you, because she's much poorer than we are. I've been in her house and I know. And then she told me about the Club, and I thought I'd ask you—and—oh, I don't want Mother to be worried! Can't we be Club too, the same as Mrs. Viney?"
>
> The Doctor was silent. He was rather poor himself, and he had been rather pleased at getting a new family to attend. So I think his feelings at that minute were rather mixed. (69)

Once the family is the same as Mrs Viney, they are almost indistin-guishable from the rest of the working-class community. Any of the old connections they have to the middle class are in danger of disappearing as they begin to resemble the actual poor.

Because their father is a convicted criminal, the family is viewed with some suspicion in their new community even as it is recognized for its gentility. The children soon come perilously close to destroying their middle-class status, however, when they pretend to be a gang of robbers. They construct a narrative for themselves that comes rather too close to confirming the suspicions about them: "Peter was the bandit, of course. Bobbie was his lieutenant, his band of trusty rob-bers, and, in due course, the parent of Phyllis, who was the captured maiden for whom a magnificent ransom—in horse-beans—was unhesi-tatingly paid" (33). Playing at crime turns into real crime when Peter decides to steal some coal from the railway yard because the fam-ily cannot afford any during "three wet days" (33) in June. Peter has already been warned by the station master that a white mark on the coal pile is there to "mark how much coal there be [...] so as we'll know if anyone nicks it. So don't you go off with none in your pock-ets, young gentleman!" (31). The station master clearly recognizes the instability of the boy's position, that he can easily transform from a gentleman into a criminal given his father's incarceration. When Peter steals some coal, he tries to justify it by pretending he is only mining it. He even creates an imaginary coal business: "Here's the first coal from the St Peter's Mine. We'll take it home in the chariot. Punctuality and despatch. All orders carefully attended to. Any shaped lump cut to suit regular customers" (36). When he is caught, he claims to be unaware he was stealing:

> I was almost sure it wasn't. I thought if I took from the outside part of the heap, perhaps it would be. But in the middle I thought I could fairly count it only mining. It'll take thousands of years for you to burn up all that coal and get to the middle parts. (40)

The fact that Peter only half believes his story means he deserves punishment but his attempt to turn his theft into a story about mining shows him to be a cut above the average criminal who could not have played so well the part of an operator of a coal business. The station master is, therefore, willing to forgive and forget.

Just as Peter is very nearly branded a criminal when he steals coal from the railway yard, so Roberta is very nearly branded a criminal when she finds herself a stowaway on the locomotive. Roberta ends up inside the locomotive engine as she tries to get the attention of the men inside who she believes can help mend the toy engine. Before she ends up on the train, she thinks she is getting Peter's toy engine for her birthday but finds he is only giving her the sweets that are placed in it: "she was disappointed at not getting the engine, as because she had thought it so very noble of Peter, and now she felt she had been silly to think it" (74). The idea that the girl might get control of the train engine is constructed as transgressive, as a theft of the boy's rightful position in the industrial economy. When Bobbie takes the engine to the train engineer to get it mended, she accidentally ends up on the train as it pulls out of the station and becomes the "Engine-burglar" (84). Once on the train, however, she is treated kindly and is given an Edgeworthian lesson from a tradesman as she visits his workspace. She learns from the engineer the names of the parts of the engine and how they work:

> "That's the injector."
>
> "In—what?"
>
> "Injector to fill up the boiler."
>
> "Oh," said Bobbie, mentally registering the fact to tell the others; "that is interesting."
>
> "This 'ere's the automatic brake," Bill went on, flattered by her enthusiasm. "You just move this 'ere little handle—do it with one finger,

you can—and the train jolly soon stops. That's what they call the Power of Science in the newspapers." (82)

Part of her being an engine burglar is her theft of the technical knowledge normally given to boys but, because of the liminality of the family's class position, the girls are able to explore alternative identities for themselves. If their playtime once suggested that a girl might become a firewoman on a train, their playtime on an actual train suggests that a girl might even become an engineer. Later, Dr Forrest gives Roberta lessons on a different kind of engineering when they observe the canal as it runs over a bridge:

> "It *is* grand, isn't it?" she said. "It's like pictures in the *History of Rome*."
>
> "Right!" said the doctor, "that's just exactly what it is like. The Romans were dead nuts on aqueducts. It's a splendid piece of engineering."
>
> "I thought engineering was making engines."
>
> "Ah, there are different sorts of engineering—making roads and bridges and tunnels is one kind. And making fortifications is another." (70)

As she steals technical knowledge of male occupations, she begins to move up in rank from a train engineer to a civil engineer. She begins to assume the position of a middle-class professional like her father.

Even as the girls appropriate the position of boys, there are indications that their theft will only be temporary, that the narrative will eventually return them to more traditional gender roles. At the same time that she becomes the engine burglar, Roberta is struck by how dirty railway jobs can be. She finds the train guard's job to be quite revolting:

> She asked the guard why his van smelt so fishy, and learned that he had to carry a lot of fish every day, and that the wetness in the hollows of the corrugated floor had all drained out of boxes full of plaice and cod and mackerel and soles and smelts. (83)

The smell of the fish threatens to ruin the thrill she gets from temporarily occupying a male position in society. And, despite her appropriation of technical knowledge for boys, she continues to learn domestic knowledge from her mother. She makes sure to criticize Phyllis for not doing the washing properly:

> "Oh, no!" said Bobby, greatly shocked; "you don't rub muslin. You put the boiled soap in the hot water and make it all frothy—lathery—and then you shake the muslin and squeeze it, ever so gently, and all the dirt comes out. It's only clumsy things like tablecloths and sheets that have to be rubbed." (123)

The girls may assume non-traditional roles because of their poverty but their gentility and domesticity ensures that they do not fit into them comfortably.

The mother occupies a transgressive role as well when she becomes a published author. Economic necessity grants her the opportunity to make money composing the same kinds of stories that she told to the children when they were at home in London. Her influence widens considerably when she becomes a professional writer who uses the postal system to send her stories to editors:

> Mother, all this time, was very busy with her writing. She used to send off a good many long blue envelopes with stories in them—and large envelopes of different sizes and colours used to come to her. [...] At first the children thought 'the proof' meant the letter the sensible Editor had written, but they presently got to know that the proof was long slips of paper with the story printed on them. (44–5)[7]

Poverty releases her talent from the home and connects it to the larger commercial economy. Her role as an author eventually connects her to the Russian writer who mysteriously arrives at the railway station. He has fled Russia because, as the mother tells the children, "he wrote a beautiful book about poor people and how to help them" (97). While he is a vocal critic of Czarist Russia, the children and the mother remain strangely uncritical of the grave injustice that has been done to their own imprisoned father. In trying to reconnect the Russian with his family, the mother plays the same influential role as the old gentleman on the train, the director of the railway, who eventually secures the release of her husband. As she takes up the search for the writer's family, she comes dangerously close to becoming implicated in his political cause but she is not so much concerned with politics as she is with her own cause which is to reunite a father with his family:

> Mother wrote several letters to people she thought might know whereabouts in England a Russian gentleman's wife and family might possibly be; not to the people she used to know before she came to live at Three Chimneys—she never wrote to any of them—but strange people—Members of Parliament and Editors of papers, and Secretaries of Societies. (100)

As the mother's influence grows, she resembles her civil servant husband but, by remaining apolitical and uncritical, she proves that he cannot possibly be a threat to the government. She proves that he cannot possibly be a treasonous agitator who has stolen government secrets in order to overturn the existing social order.

If the father is a civil servant in the British government, the children and their mother during their time of playing at being poor end up assuming his former position as they take control of the railway village. As Troy Boone has argued, the middle-class children eventually assume their rightful place in the community as they become involved in the "surveillance of the working classes" ("Germs", 97). In *Fabian Essays in Socialism*, certain industries are identified that should be nationalized and managed by a centralized body of administrators: "The post, the telegraph, the railways, the canals, and the great industries capable of being organized into Trusts, will, so far as we can see now, be best administered each from a single centre for the whole kingdom" (153). By the end of their time in the working-class community, both the children and their mother have become actively involved in these industries. As the children's play time at the railway station turns from criminality to heroism, they begin to resemble railway managers. When the line is blocked, the children save the train by cutting up the girls' red petticoats and using them as signals: " 'How lucky we *did* put on our red flannel petticoats!' said Phyllis" (117). They are able to transform themselves from middle-class girls with red petticoats into heroic signalmen. The children are given commendations by the railway, which then seems to grant them the right to act as railway inspectors. When, for example, they find a signalman asleep in his signal-box, they give him a good scolding for his dereliction of duty. The children are able to boss and control the adult:

> "My hat!" cried Peter; "wake up!" And he cried it in a terrible voice, for he knew that if a signalman sleeps on duty, he risks losing his

situation, let alone all the other dreadful risks to trains which expect him to tell them when it is safe for them to go their ways. (222–4)

The signalman replies with the excuse that he has a sick child at home but, like the Bastables, they are not impressed by such a story:

> I know'd well enough just how it 'ud be. But I couldn't get off. They couldn't get no one to take on my duty. I tell you I ain't had ten minutes' sleep this last five days. My little chap's ill—pewmonia, the Doctor says—and there's no one but me and 's little sister to do for him. That's where it is. The gell must 'ave her sleep. Dangerous? Yes, I believe you. Now go and split on me if you like. (225–6)

The children are disgusted when the signalman attempts to give them money so that they will not betray him to the authorities. He is like the burglar in *The Story of the Treasure Seekers* and, like him, his sad story about his suffering children makes him a figure of derision. If adversity makes the middle-class family come to life and spring into action, then it makes the working-class father more passive and corrupt as he complains about an unfair social structure.

The children take over as managers and inspectors of the canal system when, in another display of heroism, they rescue a baby from a fire that breaks out on one of the barges moored on the canal. While the "bargees", as they are referred to, are drinking in the pub they abandon their infant onboard but the children soon detect the fire and are able to execute a dramatic rescue. Bill the Bargeman turns out to be responsible for the fire but he impresses the children greatly when he owns up to his guilt and refuses to blame his wife:

> But it wasn't she. It was Bill the Bargeman, who had knocked his pipe out and the red ash had fallen on the hearth-rug and smouldered there and at last broken into flame. He did not blame his wife for what was his own fault, as many bargemen, and other men, too, would have done. (153)

Bill is honourable enough to admit his own fault, unlike the signalman who shifts the blame for his sleeping on duty onto the railway company and his children. Because Bill proves to be noble, he becomes part of the children's network just as they become part of the bargees' network: "he said he'd tell all the bargees up and down the canal that we were the real, right sort, and they were to treat us like good pals, as were we"

(154–5). Previously, the bargees showed themselves to be distrustful of outsiders when they yelled at the children for fishing in the canal but now the children will "each wear a red ribbon" (155) when they go to the canal so that they will automatically be recognized by the bargees as the right sort. Their time spent as near criminals hanging around the canal eventually pays off for the children as they achieve a kind of professional status among the bargees. They are allowed entry into their secret society as friendly social workers.

The children also come to set up their own Friendly Society in the neighbourhood as they expand on the work begun with Forrest's Doctor's Club. When they solicit gifts for their friend Perks, the station porter, they end up pulling the local community together within a new co-operative economics. When the proud working man finds that the people have given him gifts, he is shocked that the children have spoiled his good name around the neighbourhood by begging for him. Roberta tells him that the reason the presents are given on his birthday, however, is that the people of the village know he does not need the presents:

> *He* said he respected a man that paid his way—and the butcher said the same. And the old turnpike woman said many was the time you'd lent her a hand with her garden when you were a lad—and things like that came home to roost—I don't know what she meant. And everybody who gave anything said they liked you, and it was a very good idea of ours; and nobody said anything about charity or anything horrid like that. And the old gentleman gave Peter a gold pound for you, and said you were a man who knew your work. (172)

The children argue that he is a recipient of charity not because he cannot pay his way but precisely because he can pay his way. They impose middle-class values on the villagers as they try to transform them into a collection of like-minded souls who will support and invest in each other. Unlike the middle-class family of social actors who can change their class position, however, Perks remains unchangeable as a railway porter. He proves intractable as he refuses to even look at the sentimental notes attached to the gifts:

> "I don't want to see no labels," said Perks, "except proper luggage ones in my own walk of life. Do you think I've kept respectable and outer debt on what I gets, and her having to take in washing, to be give away for a laughing-stock to all the neighbours?" (170)

He relents finally when he is told the word charity was not used by any of the gift-givers. The children's gesture is chalked up to the community's "friendliness" (174) and "loving-kindness" (174). The children teach Perks that he has something very valuable in "the kind respect of our neighbours" (173) and, in doing so, they bring the working class together as a Friendly Society based on mutual respect rather than pity. If Perks ever needs a helping hand, he will be able to receive one because his neighbours know he will not squander it. The children end up transforming the concept of charity in the community as they teach the local inhabitants about the power of investing in each other. As members of the cultivated middle classes, the children extend the concept of collectivism to a village that has been, up until their arrival, based solely on individualism.

The choice of profession offered to Roberta is ultimately that of nurse, a job performed outside the home that remains connected to domesticity and care-giving. Roberta becomes a heroic nurse when she rescues Jim, the grandson of the railway director, from the train tunnel during the grammar school's paper-chase game. She is forced into the position of Red Cross nurse as she must help him with his broken leg before the train arrives:

> She tried to pull off his stocking, but his leg was dreadfully swollen, and it did not seem to be the proper shape. So she cut the stocking down, very slowly and carefully. It was a brown knitted stocking, and she wondered who had knitted it, and whether it was the boy's mother, and whether she was feeling anxious about him, and how she would feel when he was brought home with his leg broken. When Bobbie had got the stocking off and saw the poor leg, she felt as though the tunnel was growing darker, and the ground felt unsteady, and nothing seemed quite real.
>
> "*Silly* little girl!" said Roberta to Bobbie, and felt better. (217–18)

Roberta is able to suppress her revulsion in order to do what needs to be done in a time of crisis. As his grandson convalesces in their home, the old gentleman promotes their mother to the position of matron of Three Chimneys hospital. While Peter is afraid her role as matron will keep her from earning an income as a writer, the railway director, who is in the process of winning the release of her husband, takes it upon himself to begin to manoeuvre her back into a more domestic role.

Peter and Dr Forrest also conspire to return females to more traditional gender roles. They make the temporary jobs that the females of the household have been working at into dead-end employment. Peter becomes a kind of apprentice to the medical man and together they attempt to control the girls' as they play at being both doctors and nurses. Peter announces that he will train them to be nurses but is disgusted to find that despite Roberta's bravery in the tunnel, she is too squeamish for the gruesome reality of the medical profession. He tells them:

How are you going to be Red Cross Nurses, like you were talking of coming home, if you can't even stand hearing me say about bones crunching? You'd have to *hear* them crunch on the field of battle—and be steeped in gore up to the elbows as like as not [...]. (231–2)

Roberta then places herself in the role of doctor rather than nurse: "I'll be the doctor and Phil can be the nurse. You can be the broken boner; we can get at your legs more easily because you don't wear petticoats" (233). Dr Forrest, however, arrives on the scene to put an end to their play by telling Peter that he is wrong to have discussed the gory details of the medical profession with girls. The boy replies, "It was only that I kept on talking about blood and wounds. I wanted to train them for Red Cross Nurses. And I wouldn't stop when they asked me" (235). Peter and the doctor emphasize that women in general are not made for dangerous occupations. By the end of the novel, the two have formed a society of professional men that excludes the girls. The doctor tells Peter of the "scientific facts" (239) about females: "girls are so much softer and weaker than we are; they have to be you know, [...] because if they weren't, it wouldn't be nice for the babies. And that's why all the animals are so good to the mother animals. They never fight them, you know" (238). He also shares his theory of gender differences: "you know men have to do the work of the world and not be afraid of anything—so they have to be hardy and brave. But women have to take care of their babies and cuddle them and nurse them and be very patient and gentle" (237). Coming near the end of the narrative, his words indicate that the girls must face facts and give up imagining non-traditional careers for themselves.

The doctor, however, does appreciate the efforts of the females within their temporary jobs as he applauds the ability of middle-class women in particular to rise to a challenge. He tells Peter it is middle-class women who, when forced into dangerous and unpleasant circumstances, are able to accomplish important things. He argues that while professions such as nursing are not quite appropriate for respectable girls, it is only respectable girls who have the ability to make them into heroic professions:

> "Think of Bobbie waiting alone in the tunnel with that poor chap. It's an odd thing—the softer and more easily hurt a woman is the better she can screw herself up to do what *has* to be done. I've seen some brave women—your Mother's one," he ended abruptly. (238)

Women are, according to Forrest, weak and in need of male protection but, when the cultivated woman loses such protection and is placed in adverse circumstances, she has the ability to rise to the occasion and to play the part properly. Only the heroic deeds of a genteel woman like Florence Nightingale who served so valiantly in war could have transformed the public image of the nursing profession so dramatically. The middle-class woman has more capacity for heroism than the working-class woman, as the doctor's argument goes, because the working-class woman is inured to her poverty and is, therefore, unable to struggle against it effectively. The middle-class woman in struggling to regain her lost position ends up discovering a hidden wellspring of courage and ingenuity.

When it becomes clear that the railway director will be able to win the release of the father, it also becomes clear that the mother's writing career will end, that she has only been playing the role of a writer temporarily. While she is quick to inform him that she will keep writing after she is finished being the matron of the hospital, the railway director implies that she may not have to because her husband will soon return:

> "We shall see," said the old gentleman, with a swift, slight glance at Bobbie; "perhaps something nice may happen and she won't have to."
>
> "I love my writing," said Mother, very quickly.
>
> "I know," said the old gentleman; "don't be afraid that I'm going to interfere. But one never knows. Very wonderful and beautiful things do happen, don't they? And we live most of our lives in the hope of them." (247)

The mother will be rescued from the necessity of earning a living with the return of the father. Once the economic hardship that has made her a published author no longer exists, she will return to being a traditional housewife as the original structure of the family is reconstituted. While temporary employment does not help the female members of the family find independent careers for themselves, it does restore the father's reputation. While the father can have no effect on his own position— he cannot appear innocent if he pleads his own case—they can, through imaginative play, write themselves into an adventure narrative, one that proves the spirit of heroic professionalism resides within the family.

In the final scene of the narrative, the happy home is restored as the father returns to his position as the head of the household and the reader, as a kind of intruder, is asked by the narrator to leave them in peace:

> I think that just now we are not wanted there. I think it will be best for us to go quickly and quietly away. At the end of the field, among the thin gold spikes of grass and the harebells and Gipsy roses and St John's wort, we may just take one last look, over our shoulders, at the white house where neither we nor anyone else is wanted now. (266–7)

The story ends by shutting the family back up in the home but it is clear from the way the children have won the father's release that the family will no longer be locked away from the outside world behind a castle drawbridge. At the beginning of the story, the home is a suburban retreat closed off from the actual work of the labour economy but, by the end, it is a new space that conflates the child's playroom with the railway industry. The toy locomotive becomes a real locomotive as the children are released from their isolation to play by the actual railway. In the process, they end up rescuing their father's reputation and winning his release because the charming nature of their imaginative play as little civil servants proves that he must also be an innocent civil servant. The fact that it is the children who prove that their father is not guilty of the crime indicates that the middle-class family's reputation in society can only be maintained by the public performances of its imaginative children. While the respectable adult must suppress any hint of duplicity and deception in order to be considered innocent, his children can incorporate it into their play in a way that is active enough to win his release but that does not make the family appear to threaten the social order. The imaginative child is, in the end, a subject with the unique ability to transcend class position in order to achieve mobility precisely because he or she never draws attention to economic inequality and social injustice.

Novels likes Nesbit's that are about special children with well-developed imaginations and a delightful ability to play and to see the world as an imaginary realm became vital to the golden age of children's literature, to the readership's sense of itself as part of a larger network of the right sort of people, the sort that while it must operate within commercial society is concerned with nobler and more imaginative pursuits. The middle classes coded into their children both their aggressive involvement in and their superiority over crass commercialism. The imaginative child emerged as a figure that displays middle-class ingenuity and invention and that renders entirely innocent middle-class involvement in the commercial world. Nesbit's novels demonstrate that adults need the imaginative child to be playing with toys with a connection to industrial and commercial activity in order to prove to the outside world and to themselves that they are also innocent children playing with practical toys. Child's play, in her novels, does not simply train the child to be able to negotiate the frequent and inevitable ups and downs of the capitalist economy. Rather, it is made synonymous with the ability to survive and prosper in an unstable and inequitable marketplace without having to criticize the social structure. Indeed, her middle-class children are often paid for acting as apologists for the capitalist economy as their performances demonstrate to respectable society that there is no excuse for remaining poor. Poor children who appear to have been victimized by the capitalist economy are not victims at all—they are children who have not developed their capacity for imaginative play. The moral of the story is that if a child cannot escape poverty he or she is simply not playing properly.

5
Educational Tracking and the Feminized Classroom: *A Little Princess* and *The Secret Garden*

The first half of Charlotte Bronte's *Jane Eyre* is a Cinderella story set in a charity school that uses oppressive methods of discipline and control to maintain its pupils as a subservient underclass. Within the walls of Lowood Institution, which is run by the evil Mr Brocklehurst, children who are the product of poor families are trained to become docile and obedient so that when they leave they will take their place as servants within the homes of the wealthy. Because Jane is unlike the other pupils, because she is from a family of middle-class professionals, she has a strong sense of pride that makes her better able to resist the school's brainwashing and better able to acquire the skills that eventually allow her to become a schoolteacher. It is not only her own strength of character that helps her to regain her lost social status but the benevolent Miss Temple who brings a kinder, gentler educational philosophy to the school, one that allows a gifted student like Jane to realize her potential.[1] If Lowood forces Jane into the role of a servant, the care and sympathy of her female teacher allows her to acquire the skills necessary to achieve social mobility. In this way, Bronte's fairytale plot replaces the fairy godmother with a career woman who inspires the long-suffering Cinderella figure to aspire to an influential social role. Throughout the nineteenth century, the British school system continued to be based upon the kind of social control experienced by Jane—the directing of children into social roles based on race, class, and gender or what is now referred to as tracking or streaming.[2] The British system, a hotchpotch of various types of institutions including public schools, grammar schools, proprietary schools, high schools, technical schools, and charity schools, had a school for every type of child from the richest down to the poorest. The curriculum of the school varied according to the social position of its students, with wealthy children receiving a classical education and poor children receiving an education in obedience. If public schools were designed to give children a gentleman's education suitable for making them into politicians and heads of state, then charity schools were designed to give working-class children basic literacy skills and a great deal of punishment.

In many of the public school stories of the nineteenth-century, poor scholarship students represent a threat to traditional class boundaries. While stories often include them as a nod to the possibility of social mobility, they are typically dismissed as unfit for the public school curriculum. As Michael J. Childs argues, the scholarship student was not proof that the education system had extended social mobility to working-class children but rather proof that it had denied it to them. The scholarship student, he argues, is the result of the failure of secondary education in the nineteenth century:

> The "broad highway" to secondary education that the progressive educators and working-class leaders wished to construct was replaced by the elitist concept of a "scholarship ladder" favoured by the middle-class, the board of education mandarins, and such promoters of national efficiency as the Webbs. A chance to create a wide network of secondary schools responsive to the needs and experience of the working class as a whole were ignored, while the foundations of such a system, gradually built up by the urban school boards since 1870, were destroyed. (31)

Working-class students were not able to pursue social mobility within their own secondary education system—one geared towards their own needs—but within the foreign territory of the public or grammar school. In Talbot Baines Reed's *The Adventures of a Three-Guinea Watch*, for example, George Reader wins a scholarship to Randlebury school, only to become a sick child who dies before he can use his education to better his lot in life. He is obsessed with his studies and denies his physical health unlike the robust middle-class students at the school who are well rounded enough to succeed at both their studies and their sports. He is, in effect, punished for his single-minded intent to hold onto his scholarship, his desperate need to win enough money to continue his studies. George dies because he is not suited to the public school curriculum, which includes, in addition to academic subjects, vigorous physical exercise and violent sporting contests. Rather than accommodate the working-class child on his own terms, the scholarship system forces him to sink or swim within an alien environment. The scholarship student represents both the failure of the nineteenth-century education system to address adequately the problems involved in tracking children according to their class position and the problems involved in putting children from different socio-economic backgrounds into one classroom.

Undoubtedly, poor and working-class children were subject to harsher forms of discipline than middle- and upper-class children but, as Jenny Holt notes, by the 1850s even public schools had undergone "an increase in adult supervision, a tightening of the curriculum to limit free time and the modification of buildings both for hygienic and disciplinary purposes" (120). Because the British public often looked back upon its time spent in Victorian schools with a real sense of fear and loathing, educational reformers began at the end of the century to argue for a kinder, gentler education system. As a pupil-teacher recalled of his time in school, "I never remember seeing my headmaster in school when he had not a cane hanging by the crook over his left wrist. [...] There were no backs to the desks and backs of boys were straightened by means of a stroke of the cane" (qtd in Simon, 115). Elizabeth Gargano has shown in *Reading Victorian Schoolrooms* how there was indeed a widespread concern that education in Britain had become too rigid and mechanical, too geared towards making young children obedient. She describes how this concern was reflected in the school stories of the period: "As education became increasingly institutionalized throughout the century, numerous Victorian school narratives portrayed harsh, excessively regimented classrooms, contrasting the looming specter of educational standardization with a supposedly nurturing tradition of domestic instruction that dated back to Rousseau's *Emile* (1762)" (1). According to Gargano, the "school garden movement" (89) emerged as a reaction to the institutionalized classroom. Its goal was to give children from all walks of life a more fulfilling education. Just as the movement looks back to the methods of Rousseau, so it looks forward to the independent and self-directed learning styles that have been incorporated into more recent teaching methodologies.[3] Gargano notes that by including a garden, "a space for cooperative work and communal games, fostering both body and spirit" (89) the kinder, gentler school could "reintegrate the lessons of nature into the institutional domain" (89). The school garden was designed to take the child out of not just the confinement of the classroom but the confinement of his or her socio-economic position so that he or she could be socialized within a more natural space. Gargano notes that while it was generally privileged children who benefited from the movement, poor urban children were increasingly offered gardening as part of the curriculum: "By the end of the century, 'nature study rambles,' roof gardens, and the reclamation of urban land for workable school gardens were becoming popular pedagogical devices in London schools" (94). The garden classroom released children of all classes from their socio-economic contexts and returned them to a common body of knowledge and a more natural state of being.

Gargano's analysis of the school garden movement also indicates, however, that despite the claim that the garden as a classroom would free children from mechanical forms of socialization, it was just as implicated in the perpetuation of class and gender boundaries as the Victorian school. While placing children in a garden appears to return them to a natural state, once the process of studying it begins they organize and interpret it according to their already established subject positions. In order to be studied, a garden must be compartmentalized, dissected, or broken down into its smaller components. The selection involved in such a process can never be done so from an ideologically neutral position, meaning that one garden quickly becomes many gardens as its totality is divided and reduced according to the various perspectives of the individuals studying it:

> While the boys' garden shapes a public identity, linking the development of individuality with work in the external world, the girls' garden emphasizes a veiled and private identity, linking individuality with interior and domestic spaces. As boys are schooled to tame nature, in order to become the proud possessors of property, girls are trained to see themselves as property under cultivation, taming their own wild spaces through self-regulation and self-control. (Gargano, 96)

Even as the school garden idealizes the child as part of the natural world, it continues to construct the boy's identity as social and the girl's identity as domestic. While the boy's garden is a training ground for social dominance and entrepreneurship, the girl's garden is a training ground for motherhood and household management. The child's experience of the garden cannot be free from ideology, therefore, because he or she interprets it and is encouraged to interpret it according to class and gender roles that are, by the time the child enters the garden classroom, already well established.

I want to demonstrate in this chapter how the idea of a common curriculum is at work in Frances Hodgson Burnett's *A Little Princess* and *The Secret Garden* and how these educational narratives attempt to overcome the heavy-handed methods used in Victorian schools to track or stream children which, by the end of the nineteenth century, had become an obvious impediment to the promotion of social mobility. What I want to demonstrate here is not that her novels eliminate the educational tracking methods used in the disciplinary classroom but that they render them much more discreet by coding them into the natural classroom. The independent learning performed in Burnett's natural classroom connects children of all classes to the same curriculum within which they are allowed to adopt a self-directed learning style. Boys and girls from different socio-economic backgrounds are accommodated within one classroom but it soon becomes many classrooms as the children interpret it according to their different subject positions. What happens, in effect, is that the children begin to track or stream themselves according to the class and gender positions that are established in the family home before they enter the classroom. In the case of both novels, a progressive argument about the need for a more natural and independent form of learning is inextricably linked to a regressive argument about the inability of young children to transcend their original subject positions. The lesson of Burnett's novels is that the organic approach to childhood education that replaced the more mechanical approaches was in fact a kinder, gentler form of educational tracking.

Female capitalism and the princess figure

Like Bronte's *Jane Eyre*, Burnett's *A Little Princess* combines a Cinderella story with a school story to produce a narrative that explores the influence of class position on the child's educational development. When Sara Crewe endures a miserable period of poverty and neglect imposed upon her by the evil Miss Minchin as punishment for no longer being a wealthy asset to the school, she still manages to hold onto the fantasy that she is a princess. Despite the fact that she no longer has a playroom, fancy dresses, and a doll collection, she manages to remain the same child she was when she was rich. In doing so, she proves that a child has a natural character that is not the product of class position. She tells Becky, the poor scullery maid who works at the school, that they are no different despite the remarkably different households into which they were born: "Why [...] we are just the same—I am only a little girl like you. It's just an accident that I am not you, and you are not me!" (41). Sara argues that the wealthy are not superior, that they do not occupy a position at the top of the social hierarchy because of a divine right. Every child is born with his or her own unique character, meaning that a child from a wealthy family may have very modest abilities while the child from a poor family may be quite gifted. For this reason, the novel argues against the use of tracking in schools, against tailoring the form and content of the child's education to his or her class position.

It may be difficult for the reader to accept Sara's progressive and democratic moral, however, given that the story does not actually provide an example of a child born into poverty who is as intelligent and imaginative as she is. The story's democratic sentiments are counterbalanced by a fairytale structure that is concerned only with restoring the once wealthy Sara to the top of the social hierarchy. The only child plucked from obscurity to become a prominent member of society is the girl who is originally born into wealth. Even as it argues for a more equitable education system—one that respects the natural character of every child—it refuses to identify a talented working-class child. To be fair, the novel is highly critical of the kinds of discipline and punishment used in Victorian schools to maintain class boundaries but it tends to re-enforce these boundaries by allowing only the upper-class child to transcend them. There is something disingenuous perhaps about a novel that holds out the promise of a more equitable education system only to have the wealthy child emerge as its only success story.

When Sara is placed at Miss Minchin's "Select Seminary for Young Ladies", her natural character is immediately in danger of being co-opted by the socio-economic context of the school. She becomes the school's prized student as Miss Minchin uses her as part of her marketing campaign to impress the parents of prospective students. She is a "beautiful and promising child" (8) with a "rich father who was willing to spend a great deal of money on his little daughter" (8). Captain Crewe insists that she be supplied with far more privileges than the usual "parlour-boarder" (9) including a "pretty bedroom and sitting-room of her own" (9) and "velvet dresses trimmed with costly furs, and lace dresses, and embroidered ones, and hats with great soft ostrich feathers, and ermine coats and muffs, and boxes of tiny gloves and handkerchiefs and silk stockings [...]" (10). Sara remains, however, completely unaffected by her wealth and the attention she receives. She does not buy into the false flattery heaped upon her by Miss Minchin, who she believes is a liar for calling her a beautiful child when she knows she is "one of the ugliest children I ever saw" (9). If Sara does not allow wealth to change her, then Becky the scullery maid, in contrast, has allowed poverty to change her considerably. Her class position in the school has been written on her body: "She blacked boots and grates, and carried heavy coal-scuttles up and down stairs, and scrubbed floors and cleaned windows, and was ordered about by everybody. She was fourteen years old, but was so stunted in growth that she looked about twelve" (38). While we are to sympathize with Becky's plight, we are also to interpret the effect poverty has had on her as a weakness in her character. Unlike Sara, she has not properly resisted her class position but has allowed it to transform her horribly.

Just as Sara remains unchanged by her wealth and preferential treatment, so she remains unchanged by the education she receives at the school. Miss Minchin's school is clearly not good enough for Sara who when she arrives is both a delicate, sensitive child and a precociously advanced child. Despite the fact that the school comes highly recommended to her father by Lady Meredith, it is not appropriate for a girl with a fanciful imagination:

> It was respectable and well-furnished, but everything in it was ugly; and the very arm-chairs seemed to have hard bones in them. In the hall everything was hard and polished—even the red cheeks of the moon face of the tall clock in the corner had a severe varnished look. (7–8)

When Sara arrives, she is already described by her father as a gifted learner and a voracious reader: "The difficulty will be to keep her from learning too fast and too much. She is always sitting with her little nose burrowing into books" (9). Her doting father has allowed her to take charge of her own education such that she is already an independent learner who must not be subjected to mechanical teaching methods designed to socialize her. She is "always inventing stories of beautiful things and telling them to herself" (7) to the extent that she is an almost completely self-directed and self-enclosed pupil. Miss Minchin's teaching philosophy for Sara is devoted entirely to making sure she does not report back to her father who pays the bills that she is unhappy at the school. Thus, she treats her more as a "distinguished guest at the establishment than as if she were a mere little girl" (27). In not wanting to upset Sara, Miss Minchin refuses to challenge her in any way or to put any obstacles in her path:

> Accordingly, Sara was praised for her quickness at her lessons, for her good manners, for her amiability to her fellow-pupils, for her generosity if she gave a sixpence to a beggar out of her full little purse;

the simplest thing she did was treated as if it were a virtue, and if she had not had a disposition and a clever little brain, she might have been a very self-satisfied young person. (27)

Sara's first French lesson turns out to be unnecessary because her deceased mother was French and the language was spoken at home. As a fluent speaker, the girl is completely unchallenged by the rudimentary nature of the lesson:

> She looked at the first page with a grave face. She knew it would be rude to smile, and she was very determined not to be rude. But it was very odd to find herself expected to study a page which told her that "*le pere*" meant "the father, " and "*la mere*" meant "the mother". (17)

Miss Minchin forms "a grudge against her show pupil" (19) when she is told by Monsieur Dufarge that the girl's French is perfect and that her "accent is exquisite" (18). He cannot teach her French, he tells the school's proprietor, because "she *is* French" (24). The French language is part of her character rather than the result of the training she might receive at an upper-class finishing school. Miss Minchin wants to promote Sara as her prized student, to make her the school's prodigy, but she grows to despise a child over whose educational development she has no control.

Sara's classmate Ermengarde, in contrast, is a completely untalented student who has no capacity for learning or imagination. Ermengarde is an unexceptional child who is described as "the monumental dunce of the school" (22) even though her father was once a brilliant scholar. She is proof that a child can have a character completely different from that of her parents:

> Miss St John's chief trouble in life was that she had a clever father. Sometimes this seemed to her a dreadful calamity. If you have a father who knows everything, who speaks seven or eight languages, and has thousands of volumes which he has apparently learned by heart, he frequently expects you to be familiar with the contents of your lesson-books at least; and it is not improbable that he will feel you ought to be able to remember a few incidents of history, and to write a French exercise. (22)

Her father insists that she must be "*made* to learn" (29) because he cannot stand the thought of allowing his daughter to be a "fat child who did not look as if she were in the least clever" (20). As a result, Miss Minchin turns on Ermengarde and repeatedly corrects her for the tiniest infractions. She yells at the girl, "Remove your elbows! Take your ribbon out of your mouth! Sit up at once!" (20). Even a wealthy child like Ermengarde is subjected to severe punishment when she does not fit into her defined class position.

For Sara, storytelling represents an alternative to the mechanical teaching methods used by Miss Minchin. She claims that storytelling, as the basis of self-directed learning, improves a child's imaginative capabilities and allows her to retain knowledge. Storytelling has a "Magic" (130) contained within it that dramatizes school lessons so that even a pupil like Ermengarde can commit them to memory: "She remembered stories of the French Revolution which Sara had been able to fix in her mind by her dramatic relation of them. No one but Sara could have done it" (79). Storytelling also represents for her a common curriculum that is available to children of all classes. When Lavinia asks her "whether your mamma would like you to tell stories to servant girls," Sara replies that her mother knows that "stories belong to everybody" (37). Jesse and Lavinia, however, heap scorn on her storytelling:

> "One of her 'pretends' is that she is a princess. She plays it all the time—even in school. She says it makes her learn her lessons better. She wants Ermengarde to be one, too, but Ermengarde says she is too fat."
>
> "She is too fat," said Lavinia. "And Sara is too thin."
>
> Naturally, Jesse giggled again.
>
> "She says it has nothing to do with what you look like, or what you have. It has only to do with what you *think* of, and what you *do*." (66–7)

According to Sara, storytelling can be used by any child to overcome her class position because the materiality of the world is only an illusion. It is only a narrative, which, as a construction, can be broken down and reconstructed. She tells Ermengarde, "*Everything's* a story. You are a story—I am a story. Miss Minchin is a story" (89). She believes that if a young girl thinks she is a princess and performs the role at all times, then she is a princess. It is not the class position of the girl but her ability to commit herself to the role that makes her an authentic princess. Sara's storytelling allows the child to rewrite or re-imagine her class position such that she creates an identity for herself that cannot be touched by discipline and punishment.

When Captain Crewe loses his fortune and dies, Sara uses the power of storytelling to resist being changed by the poverty into which she descends. Once she is no longer a prized asset to the school, Miss Minchin forces her to earn her keep as a scullery maid like Becky. Sara sets out to prove, however, that she can use her imagination to remain uncorrupted by drudgery and starvation. The unwavering belief that she is a princess has the ability, according to the narrative, to defeat hunger and neglect. Sara declares to Becky,

> 'When things are horrible—just horrible—I think as hard as ever I can of being a princess. I say to myself: "I am a princess, and I am a fairy one, and because I am a fairy nothing can hurt me or make me uncomfortable." You don't know how it makes you forget—with a laugh'. (120)

She believes she can save herself and Becky from hunger by substituting stories for food:

> 'When she comes into the attic I can't spread feasts, but I can tell stories, and not let her know disagreeable things. I dare say poor chatelaines had to do that in times of famine, when their lands had been pillaged.' She was a proud, brave little chatelaine, and dispensed generously the one hospitality she could offer—the dreams she dreamed—the visions she saw—the imaginings which were her joy and comfort. (136)

If she can continue to tell stories, then she can continue to deny the very real circumstances of her social position. She draws strength from her stories of French chatelaines, wealthy ladies of the manor house who also had to endure poverty. The only hospitality she has to offer Becky are her dreams and visions, but somehow they are able to stave off hunger.

It is important to note that what Sara refers to as the "magic" of storytelling—its ability to protect her from her miserable living conditions—is not necessarily rooted in a religious tradition. Typically, the fairytale heroine is rescued because she has displayed such innocence and self-denial that providence, often in the form of a fairy godmother, intervenes to rescue her from distress. In the case of Burnett's novel, however, the heroine's ability to endure poverty is taken out of a traditional religious context and relocated within the context of early twentieth-century capitalism. Burnett was part of the Spiritualism movement that originated in the late nineteenth century and that is perhaps best-known for its use of seances to contact the spirits of the dead.[4] She was also part of the New Thought movement and Christian Science, out of which grew the populist concept, the "power of positive thinking".[5] By thinking positively, one could connect to the life force contained within the natural world and use it to both heal the body and bring prosperity. *The Secret Garden* contains her most direct statement on the power of positive thinking where, in a long passage in the voice of the third-person narrator, it is presented to the reader as a new discovery born out of the age of industry with benefits to society comparable to some of the period's greatest inventions:

> In each century since the beginning of the world wonderful things have been discovered. In the last century more amazing things were found out than in any century before. In this new century hundreds of things still more astounding will be brought to light. At first people refuse to believe that a strange new thing can be done, then they begin to hope it can be done, then they see it can be done—then it is done and all the world wonders why it was not done centuries ago. One of the new things people began to find out in the last century was that thoughts—just mere thoughts—are as powerful as electric batteries—as good for one as sunlight is, or as bad for one as poison. To let a sad thought or a bad one get into your mind is as dangerous as letting a scarlet fever germ get into your body. (241)

The above passage, I would argue, marks the point at which positive thinking began to replace hard work and ingenuity as the basis of the self-help movement. While hard work and ingenuity were still necessary, the capitalist economy in the new century suddenly required people to believe and have faith in it in order for it to work properly. Later in the twentieth-century, the positive thinking movement became particularly popular in the USA, where it reached its zenith in the 1950s.[6] Positive thinking appealed to capitalists and business leaders who were taken with the idea that there is no difference between playing the role of a wealthy person and being a wealthy person, that it is the act of believing in the role that makes it so. Positive thinking can also be detected within the concept of self-esteem, which educators of the 1970s began to promote as a force able to empower girls. Self-esteem has been left such a vague, depoliticized concept, however, that like the role of princess it does not necessarily challenge the traditional gender regime.[7] When Sara single-mindedly invests herself in the role of princess, her strategy is to force society to deal with her as a princess despite her loss of wealth. The storytelling that gives her the power to endure her hardship resembles religious faith but it is repackaged by Burnett as a new invention that will allow a child to achieve mobility within a society that uses educational tracking to maintain rigid class boundaries. At the same time, it is designed to place an enormous responsibility on the individual to believe wholeheartedly in capitalist society. If the individual loses faith only for a moment, then he or she has only his or herself to blame for not being rewarded with wealth and social mobility.

The princess is essentially a figure who cannot tell her story of suffering to others in order to gain sympathy—she cannot be a vocal critic of injustice—because, if she does complain about her mistreatment, both her innocence and her beauty are diminished. For this reason, Sara sees in her doll Emily an ideal model of passive resistance. She sees in the doll an example of how, by remaining stubborn and stoical, she can thwart any attempt to change her identity. Emily, she decides, is a better, more self-enclosed version of herself: "It's a good thing not to answer your enemies. I scarcely ever do. Perhaps Emily is more like me than I am myself. Perhaps she would rather not answer her friends, even. She keeps it all in her heart" (95). Sara identifies with her dolls to such an extent that she animates them in her stories and imagines them inhabiting a little fantasy world inaccessible to human beings:

> She told stories of the voyage, and stories of India; but what fascinated Ermengarde the most was her fancy about the dolls who walked and talked, and who could do anything they chose when the human beings were out of the room, but who must keep their powers a secret so flew back to their places 'like lightning' when people returned to the room. (24–5)

The dolls provide a method for avoiding the kind of drudgery that has almost ruined Becky. Because they never let on to people that they are animated and that they can perform labour, they can never be put to work: "You see, if people knew that dolls could do things, they would make them work" (15). The child who refuses to show any ability to work, who ruthlessly remains enclosed inside her own story, will never have to, according to Sara's philosophy of passive resistance, be anything less than a princess.

Marie Antoinette functions as another model of passive resistance for Sara, as a figure whose isolation and imprisonment makes her the perfect model of a queen.[8] In Sara's telling of the story, the queen is able to endure her hardship unlike the hostile mob, which turns to violence to overthrow the French monarchy:

> If I am a princess in rags and tatters, I can be a princess inside. It would be easy to be a princess if I were dressed in cloth of gold, but it is a great deal more of a triumph to be one all the time when no one knows it. There was Marie Antoinette when she was in prison and her throne was gone and she had only a black gown on, and her hair was white, and they insulted her and called her Widow Capet. She was a great deal more like a queen then than when she was so gay and everything was so grand. I like her best then. Those howling mobs of people did not frighten her. She was stronger than they were, even when they cut her head off. (105–6)

The queen is more impressive than the revolutionaries, according to Sara, because she maintains the same aristocratic bearing throughout her imprisonment. Unlike the mob, which turns angry and violent when faced with miserable living conditions, the queen remains the same regal figure throughout her ordeal. Rather than reacting negatively to poverty by attacking the monarchy, the French peasantry should have, according to Sara's reasoning, used the magic of storytelling and the power of positive thinking to resist it non-violently.

Both the death of Sara's father, which is caused by his inability to endure the loss of his fortune, and the illness of his friend Tom Carrisford, which is caused by his guilt over involving his friend in such a venture, are proof of the female child's ability to endure suffering better than the adult male. Both men are typical of the fairytale father who is too weak to protect the daughter from the evil stepmother whom he has allowed to infiltrate the family. Because Carrisford languishes in bed and lapses into mental illness having "given way under the strain of mental torture" (114), he allows Miss Minchin to gain control of Sara. He tells Mr Carmichael that he is ashamed of his own weakness and lack of bravery: "I don't reproach myself because the speculation threatened to fail—I reproach myself for losing my courage. I ran away like a swindler and a thief, because I could not face my best friend and tell him I had ruined him and his child" (114). Carmichael insists, however, he is not to blame: "You were in a hospital, strapped down in bed, raving with brain-fever, two days after you left the place. Remember that" (114). Sara's passive resistance is more powerful, it would seem, than the strength of a military man like Carrisford. While the adult thinks negatively, the child thinks positively and, in doing so, is able to better survive sudden changes of fortune. The child is a much better speculative investor than adult males who, when their deals go sour, die or give into brain-fevers. Sara invests in the role of princess so committedly, she has such faith in it, that she causes the diamond mines to become profitable again. Her quasi-religious faith demonstrates that if the modern individual gives his or herself over entirely to the capitalist economy, it will provide.

She is so invested in the role and so able to resist poverty that even in the midst of her own suffering she manages to give charity to the poor. When she finds a fourpenny piece of silver "with spirit enough left to shine a little" (118), she uses it to buy buns for a beggar child, who is described as almost completely uncivilized: "The little ravening London savage was still snatching and devouring when she turned away. She was too ravenous to give any thanks, even if she had ever been taught politeness—which she had not. She was only a poor little wild animal" (121). Like Becky, the girl has given in to poverty and allowed it to corrupt her. Sara herself becomes an object of pity when Carmichael's son, Guy Clarence, decides after reading a story about charity that he wants to commit a benevolent act. Despite the fact that she does not want to be considered a charity case, Sara is generous enough to allow the boy to give her money so that he can prove his goodness: "There was something so honest and kind in his face, and he looked so likely to be heartbrokenly disappointed if she did not take it, that Sara knew she must not refuse him. To be as proud as that would be a cruel thing" (93). The dignity of the girl is not lost on the rest of the family who recognize that her genteel response to Guy Clarence, that he is a "kind, kind little darling thing" (93), shows her to be more than a street child: "A beggar girl would never have said that,' decided Janet. 'She would have said, "Thank yer kindly, little gentleman—thank yer, sir," and perhaps she would have bobbed a courtesy" (94). Because Sara does not draw any attention to her plight or perform subservience, she is recognized as a very different type of poor person. Her complete commitment to her role as a princess ensures that others will be able to identify her worth and that, in general, positive things will happen to her.

There are moments, however, when Sara's resolve is sorely tested and she begins to waver in her belief that she can continue to play the role of a princess. The longer she remains in poverty, the more she is in danger of losing the education she accumulated when she was wealthy but, even as a scullery maid, she takes the time to educate herself after her work is done in the school's library:

> Her own lessons became things of the past. She was taught nothing, and only after long and busy days spent in running here and there at everybody's orders was she grudgingly allowed to go into the deserted school-room, with a pile of old books, and study alone at night.

> "If I do not remind myself of the things I have learned, perhaps I may forget them," she said to herself. "I am almost a scullery-maid, and if I am a scullery-maid who knows nothing, I shall be like poor Becky. I wonder if I could *quite* forget, and begin to drop my *h*'s and not remember that Henry the Eighth had six wives." (73)

She is in danger of becoming corrupted by her low status in the school and devolving into the ignorance of a child like Becky but, by studying in her spare time, she sets an example to all poor servants, that they can take control of their own life story and their own education in order to better themselves. When Sara's suffering is at its worst, however, she very nearly gives up on the imaginary realm as she turns on Emily: " 'You are nothing but a *doll*!' she cried; 'nothing but a doll—doll—doll! You care for nothing. You are stuffed with sawdust. You never had a heart. Nothing could ever make you feel. You are a *doll*!' " (96). She can only see Emily as a model of resistance if she can continue to animate her through storytelling, something which becomes increasingly difficult as she feels herself being dragged down and embedded in her poverty.

Sara is eventually rescued from poverty, however, because she is observed in her attic room in Miss Minchin's school by Carmichael's "Large Family" and Carrisford's Indian companion, Ram Dass.[9] The beginning of her rescue occurs when, just as she is very close to giving up on her fantasy realm, she remembers that she has some white hand-kerchiefs in the bottom of her old trunk. In what is her last attempt at maintaining the role of a princess, she uses the handkerchiefs as part of a pretend royal feast that she lays out for herself and Becky: " 'These are the plates,' she said. 'They are golden plates. These are the richly embroidered napkins. Nuns worked them in convents in Spain' " (142). When Ram Dass observes through his window the poor girl pretending to have a royal feast, he sneaks into her room and makes it real for her. He leaves her many luxury items including "new warm coverings and a satin-covered down quilt; at the foot a curious wadded silk robe, a pair of quilted slippers, and some books" (149). Becky is pleased to find that the transformation of the room into a "fairyland" (149) has renewed Sara's resistance: "The Princess Sara—as she remembered her—stood at her very bedside, holding a candle in her hand" (235). Sara's storytelling and her positive thinking ensure that the forces of the universe conspire to make wealth return to her.

Her innocent faith in the overall stability of the capitalist economy—its ability to reward investment in the long run—stabilizes what is an otherwise unstable system. It is her kind of positivity that would later float an enormous financial bubble in the 1920s. As I have indicated, hers is not the reward of the traditional Christian hero who nobly endures suffering. It is the reward of the twentieth-century capitalist whose wilful denial of poverty releases the individual from his or her material context and becomes itself the source of earning power. Ram Dass's treasures are only a precursor to the enormous fortune Sara inherits when her father's investment in the diamond mines eventually pays off. Carrisford's lawyer tells Miss Minchin, "There are not many princesses [...] who are richer than your little charity pupil, Sara Crewe, will be. Mr Carrisford has been searching for her for nearly two years; he has found her at last, and he will keep her" (179). Sara's wealth is a reward for never presenting herself as anything less than a princess while her time as a scullery maid gives her a tragic history that increases her value further: "The mere fact of her sufferings and adventures made her a priceless possession" (185). With her wealth restored, she asks the woman running the bakery shop about the girl she had once given her buns to and discovers she is named Anne and that she works as a shop girl in the bakery:

> She stepped to the door of the little back-parlour and spoke; and the next minute a girl came out and followed her behind the counter. And actually it was the beggar-child, clean and neatly clothed, and looking as if she had not been hungry for a long time. She looked shy, but she had a nice face, now that she was no longer a savage, and the wild look had gone from her eyes. (190)

Sara decides that the girl who has been elevated out of savagery and into honest labour should be the one to give out buns to other beggar children. The girl who was once a street child achieves an elevated social position but her rescue is entirely the result of Sara's charity rather than her own storytelling. Likewise, Becky is elevated to the position of Sara's personal servant, which is certainly a step up from being Miss Minchin's scullery maid, but her rescue is also the result of Sara's charity. While they have value within the sentimental economy as objects of pity, they have very little value in the capitalist economy and the speculative world of investments because they are not good storytellers.

In the end, *A Little Princess* argues that storytelling is available to every child and can be used to resist the material conditions of one's class position. The problem with the narrative, however, is that even as it argues that the imagination can save the child from his or her economic circumstances and from mechanical forms of social control, it is only the girl from a wealthy family who is depicted as having the ability to play the role of princess and who is able, therefore, to achieve social mobility. The narrative wants us to believe that wealthy Sara is just like the poor scullery maid Becky, that it is only an accident they are born into different social positions, just as it wants us to believe that talent does not respect class boundaries (it is the wealthy Ermengarde who is the school's dunce). The implication is that Sara's gift for storytelling is the result of a family home within which her kind-hearted father has allowed her to develop as a self-directed, independent learner. We are to read her home as an ideal classroom with the ability to turn all children into storytellers. Sara's ability to tell stories when her playroom props have disappeared and to educate herself when she is forced to work long hours, indicate that the self-directed classroom is always available to poor and working-class children, that it does not require an enormous investment of resources. The problem, however, is that Sara's storytelling is still very much the product of her original subject position. Hers is an upper-middle-class home in which an indulgent father has spent great sums of money in order to outfit his daughter's playroom with books, dolls, and fancy dresses. She can hold onto the belief that she is a princess, she can commit to the role so completely even in poverty, because her original subject position—the family home in which her father is wealthy enough to indulge her as a princess—cements in her imagination the idea that being a princess is not just a "pretend", that it is a real possibility. While Sara can invest herself in the role, a poor child like Becky cannot possibly be convinced to invest in it because, unlike the wealthy girl, she has no proof it will pay off. Despite the narrative's attempt to make storytelling into an educational strategy that transcends class boundaries, it relies on a form of positive thinking that can only be produced within the well-outfitted playroom. It promotes social mobility to every child even as it knows that poor children will not have faith enough to commit as completely as Sara does to playing the role of princess.

Gardens and laboratories

The Secret Garden is also about the establishment of a common curriculum for children but rather than locating it in the concept of
storytelling, it locates it in the natural world. The garden functions as an
entirely self-directed classroom that allows its pupils to discover, free of
adult supervision, the knowledge contained in the natural world. David
Wardle notes that while there were experiments with more democratic
classrooms in the nineteenth century, it was not until after the First
World War, when "it became common form to condemn 'authoritarian-
ism' in teachers" (97), that more "child-centred" (98) classrooms became
common. In the new approach,

> [a]ttention was transferred from the teacher to the learner, and teach-
> ing considered as a process of so shaping the child's environment that
> the optimum conditions were obtained for learning. So far as possible
> the child was to be put into the position of a discoverer rather than a
> receiver of knowledge. (Wardle, 97)

In Burnett's novel, the garden is accessed by three very different
children: a girl, Mary Lennox; a working-class boy, Dickon Sowerby;
and an upper-class boy, Colin Craven. While education in the nineteenth and early twentieth century meant that children as diverse as
Mary, Dickon, and Colin would have attended very different schools,
the garden deliberately ignores class and gender differences as it edu-
cates all three children within its walls. What we find is that within
the natural classroom Mary interprets the garden curriculum from
her position as a girl, Dickon interprets it from his position as a
peasant, and Colin interprets it from his position as a wealthy boy.
In this way, the garden becomes a model for the self-directed classroom as it allows its students to find themselves in their lessons and
to take from them the knowledge that is useful to their particular
positions. Even as it presents a common curriculum, the garden is as
much about self-tracking or self-streaming as it is about self-directed
learning.

Literacy studies have demonstrated the extent to which young children read according to their already well-established subject positions.
For example, in a study of the reading strategies of 10-year-olds, Hilary
Minns has demonstrated that children's reading becomes very selective
as they tend to focus on parts of a text that are particularly relevant to
their own lives. She describes how a boy named Clayton, the son of a

farmer, read *Charlotte's Web* for its information on animal husbandry and natural science:

> It is as if Clayton is transforming what could be a totally aesthetic experience into a factual exchange of data, and making them a part of his theory of how the world works [...]. Clayton's sense of himself as a reader appears to be related to his own developing masculine identity. Two things are of key importance to him: his father and the world of farming. They are the pivot on which his life turns, and, although he demonstrates a sensitive response to fiction, at the same time he feels pressured to construct a stereotyped masculine role in his public response, often on his guard against certain ways of reading. (qtd in Millard, 11)

According to Minns, Clayton's reading strategy pulls from the story useful facts he can apply to his future career as a farmer. He ignores much of the story, including its more sentimental scenes involving Charlotte's role as a mother, and chooses instead to focus on the parts pertaining directly to his father's employment. In a classroom in which reading is self-directed, children are often encouraged to find themselves in a text, to identify with particular characters they might resemble in some way. While such a reading strategy is certainly less rigid and oppressive than reading that is adult-directed and that privileges the teacher's interpretation over the child's, it does not necessarily encourage the child to read outside his or her subject position and thus it tends to discourage social mobility.

Before the children of *The Secret Garden* enter their natural classroom, they have not had much in the way of formal schooling. Mary is weak from her time spent in India and needs, as Mrs Sowerby tells Archibald Craven, to get stronger "before [she] had a governess" (104), Dickon is a semi-literate cottage boy who "can only read printin" (73), and Colin is the heir to Misselthwaite manor who has been locked away in his room as an invalid. For all three, the garden directly replaces formal schooling. What we find, however, is that while Mary and Dickon have a natural connection to the garden classroom, Colin does not. Inside the garden, Mary, as a girl, reconnects with mother nature and to her instinctive knowledge of mothering and care-giving. Likewise, Dickon, as a noble savage figure who lives in a cottage on the Yorkshire moor and who befriends wild animals, finds that the garden reiterates the knowledge he has already acquired in his natural

habitat. He has within him a peasant lore that all rural cottagers supposedly possess, just as Mary has within her a maternal lore that all
females supposedly possess. Colin, in contrast, is a figure who is alienated from the natural world of the garden classroom. He does not have
the girl's connection to mother nature or the cottage boy's connection to wildlife. The only knowledge Colin has acquired comes not
from experience but from the books he reads in his sick bed. Because
he is alienated from the natural world, he has a kind of detachment
from it that gives him a very different perspective than Mary and
Dickon. Because he does not quite belong in the garden, he can only
study it as a scientist does, from a detached and objective perspective. Because he cannot experience the wholeness of the garden, he
can only study its parts in an effort to discover how it works. While,
inside the garden, Mary finds her natural identity as a mother and
Dickon finds his natural identity as a peasant, Colin constructs for himself an entirely new identity. The tension between the wealthy boy and
the female garden is that which allows Colin to change from a sickly
aristocrat into an ingenious and innovative member of the productive middle classes. He is the one to achieve social mobility because
he is the only one who requires a transformation within the garden
classroom.

When Mary enters the garden for the first time, she automatically
begins to mother the tiny green shoots she finds poking up out of the
soil. She defies the social order of Misselthwaite by entering into a garden that has been locked for the past ten years by its owner, Archibald
Craven, but once inside she becomes enclosed in her proper gender
role.[10] When she first enters the garden, her social position is confused—
she is both an imperious gentlewoman who is used to being waited
on by her ayah and a penniless orphan who is completely ignored by
adults—but inside the garden she is returned to her natural state. Having
been removed from a bad home in India and returned to good English
soil, she quickly discovers her maternal instincts. Dickon is impressed
by her gardening skills and is surprised to learn that she has no prior
experience. She tells him, "I don't, [...] but they were so little, and the
grass was so thick and strong, and they looked as if they had no room
to breathe. So I made a place for them. I don't even know what they
are" (92). She understands instinctively that she should treat the little
plants as children who are in danger of being smothered. In personify-
ing the plants as children with "no room to breathe", she automatically
equates the garden with the infant's nursery. In this way, she emulates

Susan Sowerby who, when she was a student at school, converted her geography lessons into parenting skills:

> "When I was at school my jography told as th' world was shaped like an orange an' I found out before I was ten that th' whole orange doesn't belong to nobody. [...] What children learns from children," she says, "is that there's no sense in grabbin' at th' whole orange— peel an' all. If you do you'll likely not get even th' pips, an' them's too bitter to eat." (168–9)

If a girl like Mary is returned to her natural state, so the argument goes, she will automatically discover in the garden the good mother lying within every female.

In addition to mothering skills, the garden connects Mary to the domestic arts, to the beautification of the family home that was framed in the nineteenth century as both an aesthetic issue and a moral issue. The role of the good mother in the home was not only to manage household finances but to beautify the living space so that it might function as a respite for her husband from the corruption of the commercial world.[11] The garden, as the site of Archibald Craven's love affair with his wife, is a model for the perfect Edwardian home. For the Cravens, it once held the promise of an ideal marriage that was left unfulfilled when Mrs Craven died. Martha tells Mary the garden's tragic history:

> An' she was just a bit of a girl an' there was an old tree with a branch bent like a seat on it. An' she made roses grow over it an' she used to sit there. But one day when she was sittin' there th' branch broke an' she fell on th' ground an' was hurt so bad that next day she died. Th' doctors thought he'd go out o' his mind an die, too. That's why he hates it. (43–4)

The image of Mrs Craven growing roses over the bent tree, which corresponds to the bent back of Archibald Craven, a man who like his son is described as a "hunchback" (121), shows how her role in the family is to be a care-giver and a civilizing influence. The roses connect to the healing power of the natural world, to the aesthetic beauty of gardens, and to the kinds of domestic arts practiced inside the home by Edwardian women. They connect to the embroidery work popular in the period, which often combined images of flowers with homespun phrases like "Home Sweet Home" and to the flowered wallpaper used to brighten gloomy Victorian rooms.[12] The circumstances of her death—the fact that the bent tree gave out from under her—imply, however, that her attempt to bring a more natural and positive approach to their domestic life failed to lift the gloom from Misselthwaite manor, a household inside which a kind of physical and spiritual morbidity has been allowed to take hold because of Archibald Craven's negative thinking. Later, when Mary is ready to graduate from her domestic training in the garden, she is described by Dickon's mother as a rose, indicating that she will go on to fulfil the destiny of Mrs Craven. Mrs Sowerby tells her, "Tha'lt be like a blush rose when tha' grows up, my little lass, bless thee" (237). Mary will take up the role vacated by Mrs Craven and grow roses over the bent and broken bodies of the Craven males because she has been reconnected to the mother's lore in the garden classroom.

When Dickon enters the garden as a natural classroom, he automatically interprets it as a space that is no different than the wild landscape on which he has grown up. It is a space that Mary discovers is no different than the peasant boy's body: "As she came closer to him she noticed that there was a clean fresh scent of heather and grass and leaves about him, almost as if he were made of them" (84). Unlike Mary and Colin, he does not experience the garden as a classroom because the knowledge it has to offer has already been available to him on his rambles across the Yorkshire moor. As a noble savage, Dickon connects the rural peasantry to the animal world and argues, in effect, that the poor do not require formal education because they are perfectly capable of understanding and living comfortably within their environment without it. He does not know the proper scientific names for plants but he knows their common names, which is enough knowledge for him to function in his environment. He tells Colin, " 'I couldna' say that there name,' he said, pointing to one under which was written 'Aquilegia', 'but us calls that a columbine [...]' " (175). He does not require the garden to act as a classroom because as an English peasant he receives his education from real life experience. Dickon comes to represent, therefore, the experience of the working-class boy who leaves school at a very early age because it does not offer him the knowledge he needs to get along in his own environment. The knowledge given to him in the classroom is no competition for the knowledge he has already gained through experience on the Yorkshire moor.

The Sowerbys' cottage is so idealized, it appears to be the home of a family of animals rather than the home of impoverished human beings. Even though they have no money and live in crowded living conditions, they are always perfectly healthy and happy. Mary is surprised to find that such a poor family has the ability to buy her a present when she receives a set of garden tools from them: "How could a cottage full of fourteen hungry people give any one a present!" (62). Dickon's sister Martha attributes the family's health and happiness to its connection to the animal world:

> There's twelve of us an' my father only gets sixteen shilling a week. I can tell you my mother's put to it to get porridge for 'em all. They tumble about on th' moor an' play there all day, an' mother says th' air of th' moor fattens 'em. She says she believes they eat th' grass same as th' wild ponies do. (28)

The children never go hungry because, like the wild ponies, they can live off the abundance of the moor itself. The cottage, we are to believe, is a completely non-social space where the family's paltry income does not affect the amount of food on the table. According to Martha, the family can thrive and multiply just like the animals whose habitat they share.

In the nineteenth century, there was a great deal of theorizing about the correlation between the birth rates and the standards of living of the poor. Harvey J. Graff explains how education and the rise of literacy were championed as a means of controlling the population numbers of the poor:

> Many supporters of mass schooling believed that education would reduce the burgeoning birth rate among the lower classes. The fertility effect was supposed to arise in two forms: either as a simple correlation of education and infertility, or in the Malthusian guise as a means of leading the poor to an appreciation of the means of their own salvation. (315–16)[13]

Supporters of mass schooling believed that educating the poor would drive down their birth rate as they learned to have fewer children in a bid to increase their standards of living. In Burnett's novel, however, the working-class cottage is romanticized for its natural fecundity. The Sowerbys' cottage argues that when the rural poor are left unmolested by society, they have as many children as the natural world can sustain. It is the aristocratic home, in contrast, with its sickly children and its neglectful parents, that is in need of some form of intervention. As the Craven family demonstrates, if the wealthy are not reconnected to the procreative power of the natural world their homes will continue to produce only one sickly child. The health of the poor and working classes is used to argue that they should remain marginalized non-participants in the capitalist economy, that they have no reason to attempt to increase their standards of living because they can produce many healthy and happy children without any money. Ironically, it is Colin's ill health that pushes him to become a powerful member of society. Because his environment has failed him, he must be taken out of the aristocratic home and placed in the healing space of the garden classroom—a space that is alien to him—where he discovers he is a scientific discoverer and a middle-class man of industry.

It is not just his general health that is in need of repair, however, but his masculinity. If the girl and the peasant boy are in better health than the wealthy aristocrat, a redistribution of resources is required to address this imbalance. While Colin's wealth ensures that he can make those around him do his bidding (which is the case with Mary and Dickon, who are treated in the second half of the novel as his servants), the fact that his struggle to regain his health takes place within a classroom setting indicates that the state's resources must be used to ensure that the wealthy boy is restored not only to health but to his position of power. The health of the Sowerby family and the ill health of the Craven family show how the national crisis is not located in the homes of the poor but in the homes of the landed gentry. For this reason, Dickon transfers the health of the peasantry to the upper-class boy when he acts as Colin's physical trainer. He even does some research as he acquires an exercise regimen from a local athlete:

> Th' gentry calls him a athlete and I thought o' thee, Mester Colin, and I says, 'How did tha' make tha' muscles stick out that way, Bob? Did tha' do anythin' extra to make thysel' so strong?' An' he says, 'Well, yes, lad, I did. A strong man in a show that came to Thwaite once showed me how to exercise my arms an' legs an' every muscle in my body.' An' I says, 'Could a delicate chap make himself stroner with 'em, Bob?' an' he laughed an' says, 'Art tha' th' delicate chap?' an' I says, 'No, but I knows a young gentleman that's gettin' well of a long illness an' I wish I knowed some o' them tricks to tell him about.' (220)

Dickon does not require a course in physical education because he receives an abundance of fresh air and exercise on the moor. It is Colin, shut up in the manor house, who requires formal physical training.

In recent years, there has been a widespread concern among educators that the school system has failed boys because the modern classroom has become a feminized space that pathologizes masculinity.[14] The fact that boys trail girls in test scores has led to the idea that more classroom time and resources need to be directed to them. Colin's life story represents, in many ways, a point of origin for this argument as it focuses on the need to rescue the boy's masculinity and return him to his rightful place at the top of the social hierarchy. According to the novel, the aristocratic boy's masculinity can only be rescued by taking him away from his governess or out of the public school and placing him in direct competition with female and working-class subjects who threaten his power. Rather than destroy his masculinity, such competition forces the idle aristocrat to find his capacity for ingenuity and invention.

When Colin enters the garden as a natural classroom, he begins to see the scientific and technological knowledge contained within it. It quickly becomes a laboratory inside which he will perform experiments. One of his early experiments includes having all three children use the power of their thoughts to heal his frail body. He tells the others:

> Every morning and evening and as often in the daytime as I can remember I am going to say, 'Magic is in me! Magic is making me well! I am going to be as strong as Dickon, as strong as Dickon!' And you must all do it, too. That is my experiment. (206)

He soon announces that his experiments will be used to transform not just his body but society in general:

> "The great scientific discoveries I am going to make," he went on, "will be about Magic. Magic is a great thing and scarcely anyone knows anything about it except a few people in old books—and Mary a little, because she was born in India, where there are fakirs. I believe Dickon knows some Magic, but perhaps he doesn't know he knows it. [...] I am sure there is Magic in everything, only we have not sense enough to get hold of it and make us do things for us—like electricity and horses and steam." (204–5)

All three children are exposed to the same curriculum or subject matter—the unified body of knowledge that is the magic contained in the natural world—but, according to Colin, only he can harness it to advance the cause of human civilization. The wealthy English boy is destined, unlike the girl, the working-class boy, or the Indian fakir, to use the mysterious forces of the natural world to improve society. He will extract the magic from the garden just as Jim Hawkins extracts gold from the island and, in doing so, he will make his fame and fortune.

If Mary's interpretation of the garden is based upon her biological connection to the natural world, Colin's interpretation is based upon his lack of a biological connection to the natural world. It is the upper-class boy's alienation from the natural world that appears to put him in a position to become a "Scientific Discoverer" (254). Mary discovers that it is his lack of experience of the world outside his sick room that has shaped his attitude towards learning: "She found out that because he had been an invalid he had not learned things as other children had. One of his nurses had taught him to read when he was quite little and he was always reading and looking at pictures in splendid books" (111). Unlike Mary, who as a female is connected to mother nature and pro-creation, and unlike Dickon, who lives in a cottage on the moor where he interacts with the plant and animal world, Colin experiences the natural world only through representations of it. For him, it exists in the abstract and theoretical rather than the real. His alienation from the natural world means that he studies it as an outsider, a perspective that gives him a scientist's objectivity. He acknowledges his own detachment: "I had never watched things before and it made me feel very curious. Scientific people are always curious and I am going to be scientific" (205). His position as a wealthy invalid means he is shut up in a big house apart from the natural world but it also means he has a greater curiosity about the design and the inner workings of nature than children who are embedded in it. In Colin's case, the family home functions as a dead-end space that produces in him a talent for scientific curiosity, which he puts to use in the garden where he is eventually promoted to his proper position in society.

Before Mary's domestic identity is completed—before she is declared a "rose" by Mrs Sowerby—there is an interlude in the narrative in which she poses a threat to the social order by claiming ownership not only of the garden but of its medical knowledge (that is, traditionally male knowledge), which she uses to heal Colin who lies in his bed like a damsel in distress. In the first half of the novel, when Mary is still the hero of the story and Colin continues to languish in his sick bed, she aggressively holds her cousin down on the bed because he has become hysterical. Mary performs an examination of his back only to find he has no observable medical disorder: "If you did it was only a hysterical lump. Hysterics makes lumps. There's nothing the matter with your horrid back—nothing but hysterics!" (153). Mary comes to enjoy using medical jargon to gain control of her patient: "She liked the word 'hysterics', and felt somehow as if it had an effect on him. He was probably like herself and had never heard it before" (153). She takes the technical term "hysterics" and puts it into action to force Colin out of his sick bed. Whereas the adult doctor has placed braces on his legs and has allowed Mr Craven to turn his neglect of his son into a medical condition, Mary teaches Colin that he is unwell because people have told him he is unwell and that by using the power of positive thinking he can restore himself to health.

We are not to believe, however, that Mary will grow up to become a doctor because the medical knowledge she acquires is, like the garden itself, returned to its rightful owner—the boy. Just as he reclaims ownership of the garden, so he reclaims ownership of the classroom. In his invalid state, he is often quite jealous of Mary and Dickon and their exploits in the garden. His motivation, therefore, for taking back ownership is not only to heal himself but to make himself the centre of attention in a classroom in which children with a connection to the natural world are more comfortable. The magic, as a kind of female power connected to procreation, threatens Colin but this threat is needed to motivate him to take it out of Mary's control and to do something new and different with it in order to reassert his authority.[15] Just as the genteel woman in *The Railway Children* is able to accomplish big things when she is taken out of the comfort of the home and put in danger, so the wealthy boy is able to accomplish big things when he faces the discomfort of the feminized classroom. Colin announces that he will become a famous medical researcher:

> "The Magic works best when you work yourself," he said this morning. "You can feel it in your bones and muscles. I am going to read books about bones and muscles, but I am going to write a book about Magic. I am making it up now. I keep finding out things." (232)

Just as Mary uses the magic to heal Colin's back, so he uses it to heal Ben Weatherstaff's back. Colin will use the female lore to become a new kind of medical practitioner, one who does not use mechanical contraptions like the braces forced on his legs but who uses instead the nurturing power of positive thinking. His new kind of medicine will replace the bad medicine that Ben Weatherstaff's doctor has been using:

> "You said th' Magic was in my back. Th' doctor calls it rheumatics."
>
> The Rajah waved his hand.

"That was the wrong Magic," he said. "You will get better. You have my permission to go to your work. But come back to-morrow." (209)

Mary has only been holding onto the role of doctor until Colin can get well enough to claim ownership. She temporarily deploys the power of the garden as a doctor might but it is Colin who will go on to become a professional doctor and a medical researcher while she will return to her domestic duties.

While the female and the peasant boy are connected biologically to the natural world, the upper-class male in *The Secret Garden* is a completely social being who is alienated from the natural world. At the same time, however, his alienation produces in him a heightened curiosity about the building blocks and mechanisms of the natural world. The further the boy gets from cottage life, the more the natural world becomes fractured into separate discourses. But only when it has been converted into separate discourses can the knowledge contained in the natural world be put into practice. At the end of the story, Colin's identity is complete when he is described as "the Athlete, the Lecturer, the Scientific Discoverer" (254). He is restored to the same kind of robust health enjoyed by Dickon but, in the process, he becomes the master of a variety of different disciplines. Despite the fact that only Colin becomes a leader in society, we are not to conclude that Mary and Dickon have been victimized by his success in the capitalist economy. Because they are included in the same classroom and given the same curriculum, their lack of participation in capitalist production is not the result of an inability to accommodate their versions of childhood within capitalist society. Rather, they stream themselves into the roles that make them non-participants. Because Mary and Dickon are embedded in their subject positions while Colin has become dis-embedded from his, they are free to *find* themselves in the self-directed classroom while he is free to *invent* himself. If the boy who read *Charlotte's Web* only for its information on animal husbandry is any indication, self-directed learning has continued to encourage children like Mary and Dickon to find themselves in the text while the wealthy and powerful boy who is unembedded in the natural world is encouraged to look for ways to turn a subject like animal husbandry or gardening into a much more lucrative business.

A Little Princess and *The Secret Garden* are both about the emergence of a new form of organic education, one that turns the classroom into a space of self-discovery rather than a space of discipline and punishment. Burnett substitutes storytelling and the garden classroom for dreary lessons learned by rote and the cold, institutionalized classroom and, in doing so, she gives the children in her stories new tools for resisting attempts to control their education according to their class positions. As we have seen, the ideal classroom in *A Little Princess* is for the girl a princess's playroom full of books, dolls, and fancy dresses. In the late twentieth-century, the princess mythology became so mass-marketed by the toy industry that it has now become almost synonymous with female childhood. The modern girl's playroom is a space full of princess toys within which she is taught to play the role of princess, a role which, as it is handed down from Burnett's novels, empowers her to resist mechanical forms of social control. As part of the positive thinking movement, *A Little Princess* helped ensure that the concept of self-esteem, which Sara Crewe certainly has in abundance, would become central to modern thinking about the development and position of girls in society. While Jane Eyre's self-esteem—her famous pride—allows her to understand that she can acquire skills that will help her find a career as a teacher, Sara's self-esteem is a magical force in and of itself that is diminished only when a young girl stops believing she is a princess and begins to see herself as contained within a material context. While Jane is taught and encouraged by a benevolent female teacher, Sara is so self-enclosed she can only be taught by herself. Her solipsism may be an effective means of resisting Miss Minchin's oppression but it deliberately erases the idea that it is an independent career and the struggle to obtain one that will rescue girls from poverty. The princess has been able to maintain her control of the girl's playroom because, even as she remains a model of traditional femininity, she offers, thanks to Burnett's novel, a strategy of female empowerment and wealth accumulation within a capitalist economy. The princess continues to be relevant to female childhood because she is a girl's version of capitalist ingenuity, one that allows her to be rewarded in the marketplace while remaining a chaste, doll-like figure who does not threaten the traditional gender regime.

In *The Secret Garden*, the ideal classroom for the boy is his own back garden full of the hidden knowledge of the natural world. But it is only the wealthy boy, at a distance from the natural world, who can properly turn the garden into the space of scientific discovery. Once Colin is rescued from his aristocratic indolence and is restored to health in the garden, he discovers the spirit of middle-class ingenuity in the form of scientific experimentation. The wealthy boy's lack of connection to the natural world means that he cannot experience its totality and thus he pulls apart the natural world and dissects it to see how it works.

In the process, he ends up producing new and exciting technological achievements. His alienation within the female space of the classroom brings out his spirit of ingenuity and invention as he is determined to do things with knowledge that female students and poor students cannot. The male student inside the kinder, gentler classroom eventually comes out on top in both the sentimental economy and the labour economy because, rather than dis-empowering the boy, the feminized classroom, as my reading of Burnett's novels demonstrates, allows him to seize control of the classroom and to make the natural world unlock its secrets. The lesson for today's educational theorists who worry about the state of masculinity is that the feminized classroom was never designed to victimize the boy. It was designed to make the upper-class boy, who was previously not forced to compete, into a much better capitalist.

6
The Female Life History and the Labour Market: *Anne of Green Gables* and *Anne's House of Dreams*

It became increasingly common in late nineteenth-century novels featuring the New Girl or the New Woman for the protagonist to declare that she will choose a life-long career over temporary employment.[1] In Margaret Todd's *Mona McLean, Medical Student*, for example, Mona declares that her career as a doctor will preclude marriage and children: "how many plans I have in my head that no married woman could carry out. It seems to me that the unmarried woman is distinctly having her innings just now" (49). She argues, "Mothering is woman's work without a doubt, but she does not need to have children of her own in order to do it" (49). Despite the fact that the novel, as Kristine Swenson notes, "stands out among New Woman novels because of the educational and professional successes of its women doctors" (132), it is underpinned by an old-fashioned Cinderella story in which Mona, the talented medical student, is mistaken by Dr Dudley for a shop girl. Having failed one of her examinations, she decides to work for a time in her cousin's clothing shop in Scotland where she must not reveal to anyone that she is more than a common store clerk.[2] Mona cannot tell her sad story of thwarted ambition but must be discovered, like so many female protagonists before her, by a male character who is sensitive enough to recognize her true value. It is, as Swenson acknowledges, a "marriage-plot novel, and thus must assert that her relationship with Dudley is her most fulfilling" (143). Mona eventually marries Dudley and shares a medical practice with him but her ascension to such a position is brought about only after she proves she can be a passive figure who waits for her husband to find her.

In this chapter, I want to situate L.M. Montgomery's *Anne* novels within the context of career novels of the late nineteenth and early twentieth century. In doing so, I want to demonstrate that while her novels are characterized by the same kind of compromised strategy of a New Girl novel like Todd's, they add something quite new and important to the larger argument about female employment. Her novels are some of the first to allow the heroine to give voice to her experiences of suffering and to turn them into a valuable credential in the labour market. Penny Brown notes in her discussion of feminine autobiography that "displaying the private self to the public gaze was directly contrary to conventional prescriptions of female modesty and reticence" (114).³ Sally Mitchell describes how the evangelical tradition dictated that women had to direct their suffering into an intensified performance of self-sacrifice: "Evangelical religion in the nineteenth century was a compelling sanction for the construction of nurture and service as women's appropriate glory. Girls learned to project their anger and self-pity onto others, and were taught that female power was manifested as care for those who were weaker, poorer and younger" (163). As I shall argue, the *Anne* novels are important in the history of social mobility for the way they transform the traditional female story of suffering and self-sacrifice into a qualification for professional employment. Unlike other female stories underpinned by fairytale plots, Montgomery's novels are striking for the ways in which their female characters give voice to their own life histories and to the conviction that they will make suffering and self-sacrifice pay. They are allowed not only to tell their own stories but to treat them as a valuable commodity.

In *Anne of Windy Poplars* (1939), there is an incident in which one of Anne's pupils, a girl named Hazell Marr, is willing to invent a life history of suffering in order to prove she is suited to a career in nursing.⁴ Hazell recognizes how the life history of suffering is an important employment credential particularly within the medical profession. She believes she is too romantic and imaginative for married life:

> "I've always felt I'd love to be a nurse. It's such a romantic profession, don't you think? Smoothing fevered brows and all that [...] and some handsome millionaire patient falling in love with you and carrying you off to spend a honeymoon in a villa on the Riviera, facing the morning sun and the blue Mediterranean. I've *seen* myself in it. I *can't* give them up for the prosaic reality of marrying Terry Garland and settling down in *Summerside!*" (179)

Hazell constructs nursing as a romantic career that will save her from marriage but, as we discover, she does not come by her choice of profession honestly because she has not suffered enough. She continually tries to prove to Anne that she has a well-developed imagination born out of a life of tragedy but her teacher is able to recognize her as a fraud. Rebecca Dew agrees with Anne that the girl is "nothing but skim milk pretending to be cream" (182). Hazell deserves to marry a dull man and to live in a dull town because she has not experienced enough hardship to be qualified for a professional career as a nurse.

The life stories of the pioneering women in the medical profession were indeed marked by great suffering and illness. In the United States, Elizabeth Blackwell went to medical school after her father's illness, in Canada, Emily Howard Stowe went to medical school because her son John had contracted tuberculosis and, in Britain, Sophia Jex-Blake went to medical school after a childhood in which, as Margaret Todd informs us in her biography, *The Life of Sophia Jex-Blake* (1918), she was "encouraged to live the life of an invalid" (24). By the middle of the twentieth century, it became standard practice for medical school applicants to submit biographical essays outlining their life experiences and their reasons for wanting to become a doctor. Such essays are often used by candidates to discuss their own history of illness or that of a close relative in order to prove that their desire to become a doctor is authentic. While personal histories have not always been used by medical schools in precisely this way—they were used in the 1920s by some schools in the United States to deny entry to candidates based on religion[5]—they have become a means of justifying entry into professions by individuals who may be economically disadvantaged but who have a more sincere desire to practise medicine than individuals from more advantaged social positions.

Whereas a life history of illness and suffering usually meant that a Victorian woman experienced marginalization throughout her life, Montgomery's novels are responsible for giving the female life history great worth in an otherwise unsentimental marketplace. Mitchell describes how illness in the novels of nineteenth-century women writers is often used within a marriage plot. While her illness "softens the woman and frightens the man into realizing his love", his illness is used to "feminize—or humanize—the leading man, making him aware of his interdependence and of his need for care" (161). Illness is used in a startlingly different fashion in Montgomery's novels, where it is taken out of its usual domestic and sentimental context and given value in the labour market. As I proceed to examine the series, in particular *Anne of Green Gables* and *Anne's House of Dreams*, I want to acknowledge that there are limits to the freedom granted to women in the texts, just as there are in other career novels for girls from the period. Anne is certainly not a New Woman when she gives up her teaching career to marry Gilbert and to become known in the community of Four Winds as "Mrs. Doctor". I argue, however, that even with such limitations Montgomery's construction of the narrative of suffering as an employment qualification eventually transcended the novels themselves and came to shape the ways we think about women's career choices and professional credentials. As we shall see, Montgomery's novels add the final piece to the puzzle to the rhetorical strategy I have been examining as they argue that not even the victimized child can be considered a victim of the capitalist economy when victimization itself can be made to pay in the labour market.

Sentimental capital and the female life story

Anne's development over the course of the series follows, for the most part, the same pattern as female protagonists in other career novels of the period that are driven by marriage plots. In her schooldays, Anne challenges the social order by competing openly against the boys in her class. She wins the Avery scholarship ahead of her rival, Gilbert Blythe, and is determined to pursue not just a teaching certificate but a Bachelor's degree. When she turns her attention away from her successful teaching career to writing, she publishes in Canadian literary magazines. Her achievements, however, are in the end not about finding an independent career but becoming an accomplished married woman. Because she has been successful in the labour market, when she finally marries Gilbert she is very much a woman who has proven she can earn her own living. But despite the fact that she is a character in a marriage plot, Anne's life history is remarkable for its almost single-minded focus on her struggle to maximize her economic value. When she is brought to the Cuthbert home from the orphanage, she soon discovers that Matthew and Marilla are disappointed she is a girl rather than a boy who might have performed farm labour for them.[6] During her early history, she is reminded constantly that she is at the bottom of the social hierarchy because she is a skinny, freckled orphan. She is a girl whose value is not immediately appreciated and thus when Rachel Lynde argues that orphans are more than likely to burn down the house or poison the well, Marilla watches vigilantly for signs of Anne's criminality.[7] When Marilla and Matthew finally tell her they do not regret adopting her because she is worth a dozen boys, it is not because they have magically discovered that Anne is an upper-class girl disguised as a lowly orphan. It is because she uses her voice to speak up for herself and to tell her story of suffering. Unlike Sara Crewe, she cannot afford to suffer silently because she is not from a wealthy home and she is not conventionally beautiful. Ultimately, her identity becomes complete when she achieves a proper balance between her use value in the labour economy and her emotional value in the sentimental economy. If she proves too useful in the labour market, she will be put to menial tasks at too young of an age and if she proves too sensitive and romantic, she will, like so many Victorian orphans in literature, die before she reaches adulthood. What makes her such a remarkable heroine is that she deliberately controls her value in both economies by carefully crafting her life history for public consumption.

The first step towards establishing her value in the labour market is for Anne to abandon the idea that the natural world offers a viable alternative to society. She must learn the lesson of *Jane Eyre*, that the traditional female association with nature results only in economic marginalization. When Jane escapes to the moor after society has proven itself unkind to women and orphans, she wakes up cold and hungry after a night spent in the bosom of mother nature and realizes that in order to survive, she must "strive to live and bend to toil like the rest" (286). She must reject the romantic notion that the natural world offers an escape from the pain and suffering inflicted on the powerless orphan. Anne must learn not only Jane's lesson but that of her own parents, who died prematurely in poverty. They are described by Mrs Thomas as "a pair of babies and as poor as church mice" (39). She remembers her childhood home as having "honeysuckle over the parlor window and lilacs in the front yard and lilies of the valley just inside the gate" (40). The implication is that the romantic sensibility of the couple caused them to neglect their financial responsibilities and to leave their daughter a penniless orphan. When Matthew goes to the train station to collect the boy for whom they have sent, he finds Anne sitting on a box of shingles, an object which, like the poor orphan girl, is valued only in terms of its practical use. She tells Matthew that she was sure nobody would arrive to claim her: "I had made up my mind that if you didn't come for me tonight I'd go down the track to that big wild cherry tree at the bend, and climb up into it to stay all night" (13). The orphan's impulse, when faced with society's neglect, is to escape to the protection of mother nature but, as Anne must learn, romantic escape is really a death impulse.[8]

Matthew eventually turns out to be one of Anne's "kindred spirits" when he proves to be a male character who is aligned with the natural world rather than society. His death is caused by the failure of the bank to which he has entrusted his life savings. He is too sensitive to protect his money properly and to survive the shocks of commercial society and thus, in death, he returns to the natural world:

> "I was down to the graveyard to plant a rose-bush on Matthew's grave this afternoon," said Anne dreamily. "I took a slip of the little white Scotch rose-bush his mother brought out from Scotland long ago; Matthew always liked those roses the best—they were so small and sweet on their thorny stems." (281)

He breaks down the traditional association of women with nature and men with society as his history turns out to be a traditionally female one.[9] His death reminds Anne, however, that in order to endure she must have a value in both the labour economy and the sentimental economy. Matthew dies still holding onto an enormous amount of sentimental value but the labour value he has stored up in the bank is gone.

Anne must suppress not only her desire to escape into the natural world but her desire to construct herself as an aristocratic lady. As she pretends to be a romantic figure named Lady Cordelia Fitzgerald, she writes a melodrama for herself in which she is more than a penniless orphan but it is a story that has no practical value in the community of Avonlea. Mitchell describes how sensational stories were particularly popular with domestic servants looking to escape their drudgery:

> One nineteenth-century social welfare worker, complaining about sensational fiction, did notice that a girl with wages of £10 a year who spent nearly one-tenth of her income on serials "had to spend every evening alone in a kitchen that swarmed with black beetles". Is it any wonder that such a girl might choose an aristocratic romance with brightly lit ballrooms and tasty midnight suppers in preference to an earnest evangelical tale of domestic life? (146)

Like other domestic servants, Anne needs to escape into a story in which she is a glamorous woman in order to remind both herself and society that she is not just a servant but such stories cannot possibly integrate her into a community that appears to have no tolerance for them. When she first arrives at Green Gables, Marilla is intent on purging her imagination of such romantic stories. As Marilyn Solt describes Marilla, she has read only "religious and 'moral' literature in her childhood" (60), which leads her to tell Anne that she must not attempt to imagine different circumstances for herself: "I don't believe in imagining things different from what they really are. [...] When the Lord put us in certain circumstances He doesn't mean for us to imagine them away" (56). Anne very nearly gives up on her fanciful stories when, in the midst of "playing Elaine" (212), her boat sinks and she has to be rescued by Gilbert as she hangs from a piling. She declares that Avonlea is no place to be romantic: "I have come to the conclusion that it is no use trying to be romantic in Avonlea. It was probably easy enough in towered Camelot hundreds of years ago, but romance is not appreciated now" (215). She is horrified to find that her attempt to sail down the river in a boat has become laughably realistic and that Marilla might be correct in thinking that one cannot imagine away one's circumstances. It is appropriate, however, that her attempt to play Elaine should fail because it is a story about a woman who cannot tell her own story. In Tennyson's retelling of the Arthurian legend in *The Lady of Shallot* (1842), Elaine is discovered by Lancelot to be a woman of class and beauty but by then she is already dead. He discovers her identity not from her but from a message written on the side of the boat. Later, Anne's teacher Miss Stacy insists that her stories must remain connected to the actual life she leads in Avonlea: "Miss Stacy sometimes has us write a story for training in composition, but she won't let us write anything but what might happen in Avonlea in our own lives, and she criticizes it very sharply and makes us criticize our own too" (240). Anne's overwrought compositions involving upper-class romantic women serve the purpose of reminding her she is more than a lowly orphan but she must begin, unlike Burnett's passive princess figure, to tell her own life story if she is to integrate herself into society. The career woman tells her, in effect, that she will have to incorporate social criticism into her imaginative play if she has any chance of overcoming the community's fear of orphans.

As Anne begins to attach herself to both the Cuthbert home and the Avonlea community, she tells her life story of pain and suffering in order to rescue herself from being exploited as cheap domestic labour in the homes of poor families. By telling her life story, Anne is willing to spend the capital she has accumulated in the sentimental economy in order to let others know that she can be more than a domestic servant in the labour economy. At the risk of appearing too active and un-ladylike, she shares her suffering with Marilla so that she will not be considered only in terms of her use value. She tells Marilla of the misery she has endured taking care of "twins three times" (41) in the home of Mrs Hammond. She also tells of the abuse that occurred in the home of Mrs Thomas, whose alcoholic husband was often violent. Anne describes how the isolation she experienced in the home forced her to create an imaginary friend out of her own reflection in the broken glass of a china cabinet:

> "Mrs. Thomas kept her best china and her preserves there—when she had any preserves to keep. One of the doors was broken. Mr. Thomas smashed it one night when he was slightly intoxicated. But the other was whole and I used to pretend that my reflection in it was another little girl who lived in it. I called her Katie Maurice, and we were very intimate." (59)

The china cabinet represents the wife's attempt to store up wealth of her own in a violently anti-female household. Likewise, Anne's creation of an imaginary friend represents her attempt to acquire sentimental value by establishing an emotional attachment to a girl her own age. Mitchell describes how young domestic servants turned to girl's periodicals for some relief from their boredom and isolation:

> Servants seem to have consumed more fiction than factory girls. Factory and shop workers had more stimulation and companionship; servants (especially those in single places) not only craved excitement and romance to fill their lonely hours but also enjoyed the imaginary friends supplied by the letters and advice columns in cheap papers. (146)

When Anne tells Marilla of her miserable childhood, she spends the sentimental capital she has stored up in order to force the Cuthberts to set a higher standard of protection than the Thomases. Anne makes sure, however, not to spend all her sentimental capital at once as she holds back some of the details of her life history: "What a starved, unloved life she had had—a life of drudgery and poverty and neglect; for Marilla was shrewd enough to read between the lines of Anne's history and divine the truth" (42).[10] Anne has to tell her own story because she cannot rely on Marilla to play the role of sympathetic observer. As Mary Rubio writes, "she discovers that the good folk of Avonlea do not want *her*" (69). The community's deep-seated antipathy towards orphans and outsiders means that she cannot afford, like Sara Crewe, to remain silent.

As Anne spends her accumulated sentimental capital, she does so using her extraordinary and precocious rhetorical skills, which she uses to manipulate the practical and often hard-hearted adults in Avonlea. She continually uses a kind of passive-aggressive irony on adults in order to deploy her life story in such a way that it acquires social efficacy without drawing attention to the fact that she is a satirist. When Rachel Lynde insults Anne to her face, something she feels she can do because the girl is only an orphan, Anne flies into a dangerous rage shouting "I hate you" (64) repeatedly at her. Her fury comes close to proving Rachel's suspicions about orphans, that they commit arson and put "strychnine in the well" (9) but Anne makes up for the damage she has done by using a much more constructive form of resistance in her apology. She suppresses her rage by converting it into irony, as she tells Rachel:

> My hair is red and I'm freckled and skinny and ugly. What I said to you was true, too, but I shouldn't have said it. Oh, Mrs. Lynde, please, please, forgive me. If you refuse it will be a lifelong sorrow to me. You wouldn't like to inflict a lifelong sorrow on a poor little orphan girl, would you, even if she had a dreadful temper? (72)

She becomes a sweet and contrite little orphan girl even as she quietly reaffirms that she does in fact hate Rachel. Her repetition of the hyperbolic phrase "lifelong sorrow" combined with a rhetorical question finishes the apology by backing Rachel into a corner. She must begin to treat Anne with more respect or else reveal herself to be the type of person who enjoys mistreating orphans.

The second of Anne's many apologies occurs when she is scolded by Marilla for wearing to church a hat that is "rigged out ridiculous with roses and buttercups" (81). The adult community members believe that an orphan girl should not be allowed to take pride in her appearance and, in response, Anne wears the flowers to display symbolically her alignment with the natural world and her rejection of a society that demands she constantly perform gratitude and subservience. Her apology is able to thwart Marilla's need to punish her as it uses her own lack of power for satirical purposes. She tells Marilla:

> Lots of the little girls had artificial flowers on their hats. I'm afraid I'm going to be a dreadful trial to you. Maybe you'd better send me back to the asylum. That would be terrible; I don't think I could endure it; most likely I would go into consumption; I'm so thin as it is, you see. But that would be better than being a trial to you. (82)

If society wants her to perform her powerlessness, she will do so in a way that proves she is not powerless at all as she draws attention to society's prejudices using all of the charm and audacity of the imaginative child.

Anne once again plays on her opponent's sympathy by cashing in some of her sentimental value. The result is that Marilla cannot send her back to the orphanage because Anne cleverly demonstrates with her rhetoric that being a trial is not nearly as bad as sending a child to her death. Marilla replies, "Nonsense. [...] I don't want to send you back to the asylum, I'm sure. All I want is that you should behave like other little girls and not make yourself ridiculous" (82). Her apology forces Marilla to voice with some certainty the fact that she will not be sent back, that her place in the Cuthberts' home is becoming increasingly secure.

Anne's position in the home remains tenuous, however, because at the first sign of trouble Marilla reverts back to her belief that orphans are potential criminals. When her amethyst brooch goes missing, Marilla immediately accuses Anne of having lost it and forces her to confess her guilt. She is only willing to do so when Marilla promises that if she confesses she will be allowed to go to the community picnic. Because she is innocent of the crime, she deliberately drains her confession of any hint of sincerity:

> "I took the amethyst brooch," said Anne, as if repeating a lesson she had learned. "I took it just as you said. I didn't mean to take it when I went in. But it did look so beautiful, Marilla, when I pinned it on my breast that I was overcome by an irresistible temptation. I imagined how perfectly thrilling it would be to take it to Idlewild and play I was the Lady Cordelia Fitzgerald. [...] Oh, how it did shine in the sunlight! And then, when I was leaning over the bridge, it just slipped through my fingers—so—and went down—down—down—all purply-sparkling, and sank for evermore beneath the Lake of Shining Waters. And that's the best I can do at confessing, Marilla." (95–6)

Because she recites her confession with no feeling, Marilla is incensed that she has displayed no "compunction or repentance" (96) and thus she reneges on her promise to allow her to go to the picnic. In an instant, Anne becomes valueless once again as Marilla concludes, "Oh dear, I'm afraid Rachel was right from the first" (96). She is caught in the classic bind of the falsely accused when she cannot properly tell her story to an authority figure who has already judged her to be guilty. The innocent prisoner who will not admit guilt and perform remorse is treated as a hard case that cannot be rehabilitated. The lesson of the incident for Anne is that control of her own life story and the ability to tell it properly are her most precious commodities.

The brooch, it turns out, is connected to Marilla's repressed life history when she tells how it once featured in a romance she had with Gilbert's father, John Blythe. Marilla, whose value has been measured only in practical terms, is suddenly measured in sentimental terms when she reveals her own tale of suffering. As she tells Anne, " 'We had a quarrel. I wouldn't forgive him when he asked me to. I meant to, after awhile—but I was sulky and angry and I wanted to punish him first. He never came back—the Blythes were all mighty independent. But I always felt—rather sorry' " (282–3). Appropriately, it is Marilla's refusal to accept an apology that leads to her suffering. She falls victim to her own need to punish and control but, at the same time, she gains a sentimental story of heartbreak that increases her value greatly in Anne's estimation. Anne is pleased to find Marilla has "had a bit of romance" (283) in her life. Marilla replies, "You wouldn't think so to look at me, would you? But you never can tell about people from their outsides" (283). Because she is a woman who looks more like a scullery maid than a princess, her romantic past cannot be discerned by the sensitive observer and thus she must tell her own tragic history in order to be discovered as a kindred spirit.

As Anne becomes integrated into the Avonlea community, it is inevitable that her tragic life history as an orphan will begin to lose some of its ability to evoke sympathy. Her increasing security in the community means that the suffering in her past is, to some extent, offset by the much happier events she has experienced at Green Gables. She is also guilty perhaps of saturating the market with her story. In yet another apology, she tells Mrs Barry who, as a close neighbour, is well acquainted with Anne's story that she is sorry for serving alcohol to Diana instead of raspberry cordial. She attempts the same kind of apology as the one she used earlier on Rachel:

> Oh, Mrs. Barry, please forgive me. I did not mean to—to—intoxicate Diana. How could I? Just imagine if you were a poor little orphan girl that kind people had adopted and you had just one bosom friend in all the world. Do you think you would intoxicate her on purpose? I thought it was only raspberry cordial. I was firmly convinced it was raspberry cordial. Oh, please don't say that you won't let Diana play with me any more. If you do you will cover my life with a dark cloud of woe. (124)

Anne includes in her sentimental appeal hyperbolic phrases such as "dark cloud of woe" but the hard-headed Mrs Barry remains unconvinced: "She was suspicious of Anne's big words and dramatic gestures and imagined that the child was making fun of her" (130). Because Anne's goal is to become part of what is a largely working-class community, she must find another way to win over practical women who are not kindred spirits, who are not participants in the sentimental economy. Mrs Barry only forgives Anne when she eventually saves Diana's sister from succumbing to a bout of illness. When she takes charge of the girl's care and calmly administers ipecac to relieve the girl's whooping cough, she proves that she not only possesses nursing skills but, in general, can be practical and level-headed. The largely working-class community will not buy her story that she is Lady Cordelia but they will buy her practical medical skills.

Anne's final apology in the narrative is to Diana's aunt, Josephine Barry, on whose bed they jump while she is sleeping. Once again, Anne threatens to prove that orphan children are dangerous criminals as she startles another prominent woman with her un-ladylike behaviour. Her apology is again designed to draw attention to her orphan status:

> We didn't know there was anybody in that bed and you nearly scared us to death. It was simply awful the way we felt. And then we couldn't sleep in the spare room after being promised. I suppose you are used to sleeping in spare rooms. But just imagine what you would feel like if you were a little orphan girl who had never had such an honour. (150)

Anne refers to the fact that her lowly social position is used as an excuse by adults to break promises to her. Her rhetoric is designed to ensure that she achieves the same kind of treatment as other girls and that she is valued as highly as the non-orphan child. By the end of her apology, she has acquired in Diana's wealthy aunt another kindred spirit. Like Nesbit's Bastable children, she becomes integrated into a network of imaginative individuals who will look after each other. A community of Avonlea women forms because they share their life histories. If Sara Crewe remains an extraordinarily isolated figure because, as a princess, she cannot share her story, Anne becomes integrated into the Avonlea community of women precisely because she converts her sentimental capital into strong emotional bonds.

Given that Anne is allowed to tell her story of hardship and suffering, it remains to be seen how she will use it to qualify herself for a specific career. Anne's first career is that of schoolteacher but there are indications that rather than being drawn to it as a vocation, she is drawn to it only because her classmates are planning to become teachers. She shows the depth of her commitment to teaching when she declares, "It's been the dream of my life—that is, for the last six months, ever since Ruby and Jane began to talk of studying for the entrance" (228). Anne describes the plans of her classmates, who are part of the group Miss Stacy puts together "to study for the entrance examinations into Queen's" (228):

> Ruby says she will only teach for two years after she gets through, and then she intends to be married. Jane says she will devote her whole life to teaching, and never, never marry, because you are paid a salary for teaching, but a husband won't pay you anything, and growls if you ask for a share in the egg and butter money. I expect Jane speaks from mournful experience, for Mrs. Lynde says that her father is a perfect old crank, and meaner than second skimmings. (229–30)

For Ruby Gillis, teaching is only a temporary job before she begins her real life's work as a married woman. Jane Andrews, in contrast, will devote her life to teaching and will not marry precisely because she does not want a husband. Jane will never get married because she has had a family history dominated by an abusive and miserly father. While Jane's life history justifies, even to the conservative Rachel, that she should remain an unmarried career woman, Anne's life history does not necessarily qualify her for a particular career path. Earlier in the narrative, Anne shows an interest in nursing, a job for which she is perhaps suited given her success in saving the life of Diana's sister: "Oh, I would dearly love to be remarkable. I think when I grow up I'll be a trained nurse and go with the Red Crosses to the field of battle as a messenger of mercy. That is, if I don't go out as a foreign missionary" (180–1). Her desire to become a missionary demonstrates that while she is talented enough to pursue many different types of careers, her life history has not pointed her in a particular direction. The fact that she has many possible identities both troubles and excites her: "There's such a lot of different Annes in me. I sometimes think that is why I'm such a troublesome person. If I was just the one Anne it would be ever so much more comfortable, but then it wouldn't be half so interesting" (153).

When she eventually marries Gilbert at the beginning of *Anne's House of Dreams* and becomes known as "Mrs. Doctor", it is made clear that her true calling in life is to be a wife and mother. She falls, therefore, into the category of the woman who uses a temporary career to increase her value as a married woman. As she pursues her job qualifications in the first novel, however, she is intent on shunning Gilbert as a love interest. When they first meet as young schoolchildren, he is hardly a sympathetic observer as he insults her by calling her "Carrots", (107) a reference to her red hair, which is for her the feature that is entirely emblematic of her lack of value. Because of this initial insult, their eventual marriage can never be viewed as a union between the passive princess figure and the powerful admirer who spots her true value. The insult announces to her his superior position and makes her determined to prove she is in fact better than him. In the process, Anne becomes a reformer of the education system of Avonlea, which is intent on defining girls as romantic partners. Much to her disgust her first teacher, Mr Phillips, actively courts Prissy Andrews in the classroom. Anne is painfully aware of the fact that he is not interested in Prissy as a pupil: "She's got a beautiful complexion and curly brown hair and she does it up so elegantly. She sits in the long seat at the back and he sits there, too, most of the time—to explain her lessons, he says" (103). Phillips is determined to define Anne as the property of a male-dominated society when, as punishment, he forces her to sit beside Gilbert: " 'Anne Shirley, since you seem to be so fond of the boys' company we shall indulge your taste for it this afternoon,' he said sarcastically. 'Take those flowers out of your hair and sit with Gilbert Blythe' " (110). The match-making culture of the school is also enshrined in the ritual of the "take notice" postings in which boys and girls names are written together to show their courtship. Anne is mortified when she continues to achieve the same academic scores as Gilbert, thus ensuring that her name is written alongside his in the grades posting: "One awful day they were ties and their names were written up together. It was almost as bad as a 'take notice' and Anne's mortification was as evident as Gilbert's satisfaction" (131). When she wins the Avery scholarship, her name is again written beside Gilbert's because he has been awarded a medal.[11] Her struggle to keep her name from appearing beside his represents her struggle to transform the school into a space where the female is given the same education as the male student and thus she is determined to marry only when she has proven she is more gifted than him.

Unlike Anne, who has no precise career path, Gilbert is destined to be a doctor because he possesses a life history involving illness. As a classmate tells her, "Four years ago his father was sick and had to go out to Alberta for his health and Gilbert went with him. They were there three years and Gil didn't go to school hardly any until they came back" (105). He has already had his ambitions thwarted when he must miss three years of schooling because he has chosen to sacrifice for a family member. He also proves to be self-sacrificing when he gives up the position at the local school for Anne so that she can remain close to Marilla. As Marilla tells her,

> Of course he gave up the school just to oblige you, because he knew how much you wanted to stay with Marilla, and I must say I thought it was real kind and thoughtful in him, that's what. Real self-sacrificing, too, for he'll have his board to pay at White Sands, and everybody knows he's got to earn his own way through college. (288–9)

Like Matthew's, Gilbert's life history is a female one; it is one that was all too familiar to women of the period, who were invariably the ones to sacrifice their ambitions for ill family members and it is a history that is familiar to Anne at the end of the novel when she puts her desire to study for a BA on hold to care for Marilla, who is losing her eyesight. The fact that Anne and Gilbert share a similar history means there is a case to be made that Anne could have pursued a career in medicine. When Anne saves Diana's sister from dying of the whooping cough, the doctor believes she has a talent for medicine:

> That little red-haired girl they have over at Cuthberts' is as smart as they make 'em. I tell you she saved that baby's life, for it would have been too late by the time I got here. She seems to have a skill and presence of mind perfectly wonderful in a child of her age. (137)

Anne, of course, does not become a doctor. While the female narrative of suffering and hardship is constructed as a credential for becoming a doctor, it is used as such by Gilbert rather than Anne. At the end of the novel, she will sacrifice her desire for a powerful social role in society to remain in the domestic space of Green Gables:

> Anne's horizons had closed in since the night she had sat there after coming home from Queen's; but if the path set before her feet was to be narrow she knew that flowers of quiet happiness would bloom along it. The joys of sincere work and worthy aspiration and congenial friendship were to be hers; nothing could rob her of her birthright of fancy or her ideal world of dreams. And there was always the bend in the road! (291)

Gilbert goes on to deploy his life history in order to become a doctor while Anne remains tied to Green Gables by the emotional bond that has formed between her and Marilla. The novel makes the male doctor a figure who has known hardship and sacrifice like a woman but it resists allowing the female to become a doctor. Even as it makes the argument that a woman's story has economic value, it compromises it by allowing only Gilbert to make his life history pay. Just as Colin Craven regains ownership of the secret garden so he can put it to use as a scientific discoverer, so Gilbert appropriates the traditionally female narrative of suffering and self-sacrifice so he can put it to use to become a doctor. In the very moment that Anne maximizes her value in the labour market, her career ambitions are overwhelmed by the enormous amount of sentimental value she has acquired in Avonlea. Even as the novel gives a new value to female suffering, it shies away like other career novels of the period from allowing her to use it in a way that might disrupt the social order. It ends by reasserting the primacy of the marriage plot in the lives of women.

Thwarted womanhood and the labour market

Anne's House of Dreams chronicles the beginning of Gilbert's career as a medical doctor and the beginning of Anne's career as a wife and mother. As they settle into their happy home in the community of Four Winds, they meet a neighbour named Leslie Moore, an uncommonly beautiful woman whose life story is pure melodrama. Her abusive husband Dick has been brought back to Prince Edward Island after a shipwreck off the coast of Cuba that has left him with brain damage. While he proves to be far more docile and manageable as an invalid, Leslie remains a wretched example of "thwarted womanhood" (101) who must sacrifice herself to look after a man whom she despises. When it turns out, however, that Dick is not Dick at all but his look-a-like cousin George who accompanied him on the sea voyage and that her husband is dead, Leslie is free to marry Owen Ford, a prominent Canadian writer who is summering in Four Winds. As his wife, she finally ascends to her proper social position as she becomes part of a circle of nationally important people. Her tragic life history combined with her rare beauty makes her deserving of her place at the top of the social hierarchy. However, like Anne's, her life story of hardship and suffering is transferred to her husband who, as a writer, uses her as his muse. In addition to acquiring the rights to Leslie's life story, Owen also acquires the rights to the life story of a local sea-faring man, Captain Jim, which is replete with all sorts of adventurous and sentimental tales. Just as he appropriates the female subject's story of pain and suffering, so he appropriates the working-class subject's story of romance and adventure. While the novel gives value to the stories of both women and the working classes, it argues that it is only the educated male who can properly deploy them for monetary gain.

In trying to account for the success of Hesba Stretton's novel *Jessica's First Prayer* (1867), which tells the story of a child abused by her mother (who is a disreputable actress), Mitchell describes how young female readers must have loved the book for the way it reveals what every young person knows, that the family home is often not the happy place it is supposed to be:

> Almost at once the book provides a glimpse of one central fact that girls knew but culture's voice denied: mothers were not always loving; family's could be the site of violence and pain. The knowledge is made safe by locating it in an outcast class; readers may therefore pretend to be looking from outside, feeling sorry for Jessica, and moved by acceptable charitable motives. (153)

In Montgomery's novel, however, the ugly reality of family life is located not in an outcast class but in a class of respectable landowners who have been rooted in the community for generations. Leslie's miserable life lifts the mask off the typical Canadian home to reveal how even fine young girls are abused. When Anne first meets Leslie, she finds a woman whose life history is even more tragic than her own. She recognizes how Leslie's suffering has given her great value in the sentimental economy:

> The girl's beauty and sorrow and loneliness drew her with an irresistible fascination. She had never known anyone like her; her friends had hitherto been wholesome, normal, merry girls like herself, with only the average trials of human care and bereavement to shadow their girlish dreams. Leslie Moore stood apart, a tragic appealing figure of thwarted womanhood. (101)

Leslie has endured both the suicide of her father, a "clever and shiftless" (92) man who, according to Cornelia Bryant, hanged himself "right in the middle of the parlour from the lamp-hook in the ceiling" (94) on the anniversary of his wedding to her mother Rose, a "lazy, selfish, whining creature" (92) and the death of her brother Kenneth who was killed by falling from a hay cart. Leslie is able to endure her brother's death silently:

> But she never screeched or cried again about it. She jumped from the loft on to the load and from the load to the floor and caught

up the little bleeding, warm, dead body. [...] She never mentioned Kenneth's name—I've never heard it cross her lips from that day to this. (93)

Leslie suffers through her family's tragedies by stoically refusing to ever speak of them and, consequently, her stock in the sentimental economy rises dramatically. As the novel's Cinderella figure—a woman even more beautiful and tragic than Anne—she does not have to tell her own story in order to be appreciated.

The history of Leslie's marriage to Dick Moore is just as pain-filled as her early childhood. Because the Moores hold the mortgage on the West family farm, she is forced to marry Dick in order to avoid foreclosure. She is completely at the mercy of the family finances as her mother trades her for the family farm. Cornelia tells Anne, "Dick just went and told Mrs. West that if Leslie wouldn't marry him he'd get his father to foreclose the mortgage. Rose carried on terrible—fainted and wept, and pleaded with Leslie not to let her be turned out of her home" (96). When the Moore family is bankrupt, Leslie is left with only the original West family farm where she lives as a figure isolated from the rest of the Four Winds community:

Old Abner Moore died soon after Dick was brought home and it was found he was almost bankrupt. When things were settled up there was nothing for Leslie and Dick but the old West farm. Leslie rented it to John Ward, and the rent is all she has to live on. Sometimes in summer she takes a boarder to help out. But most visitors prefer the other side of the harbour where the hotels and summer cottages are. Leslie's house is too far from the bathing shore. (76)

Her marriage to Dick is marked by abuse and neglect until eventually she is forced, after he comes back from the sea voyage brain-damaged, to be his nursemaid. As a passively beautiful woman, Leslie has the course of her life determined by others throughout the narrative. Such is the case when Captain Jim takes it upon himself to go to Havana to bring back her husband Dick. Cornelia, in her retelling of the story to Anne, is appalled by male interference in a woman's life:

He thought he'd poke round a bit—Captain Jim was always meddle-some, just like a man—and he went to inquiring round the sailors boarding houses and places like that, to see if he could find out any-thing about the crew of the *Four Sisters*. He'd better have let sleeping dogs lie, in my opinion! Well he went to one out-of-the- way place, and there he found a man and he knew at first sight it was Dick Moore, though he had a big beard. Captain Jim got it shaved off and then there was no doubt—Dick Moore it was—his body at least. His mind wasn't there—as for his soul, in my opinion he never had one! (98)

Captain Jim mistakenly brings back Dick's cousin as his act of kindness backfires and forces Leslie to become nursemaid to the wrong man. Cornelia, who throughout the narrative is consistently critical of husbands, tells of the persecution that has made Leslie an outcast:

She can't get away so very much—she can't leave Dick long, for the Lord knows what he'd do—burn the house down most likely. At nights, after he's in bed and asleep, is about the only time she's free. He always goes to bed early and sleeps like the dead till next morning. That is how you came to meet her at the shore likely. She wanders there considerable. (100)

Like Anne, who in her childhood dealt with society's mistreatment of her by running away to the natural world, Leslie seeks solace in the sea, which, as a romantic setting, provides an imaginative release from her drudgery. At the same time, however, the sea, which claimed the life of Captain Jim's bride-to-be, "lost Margaret", is associated with death. Until she can make her life story pay, Leslie is a marginalized figure whose escape from society into the natural world is, just as Anne's is in the first novel, a death impulse.

If the sea captain's interference dramatically alters Leslie's life history for the worse, then Gilbert's interference as a doctor dramatically alters it for the better. The women of the community object to his recommendation that the brain-damaged Dick might benefit from a new surgical procedure because they are afraid that if he is restored to fitness, Leslie will once again have an abusive husband on her hands. Anne tells Gilbert, rather unkindly, that the older doctor of Four Winds who is against the procedure is more qualified than him: "I do think, Gilbert, that you ought to abide by the judgment of a man nearly eighty, who has seen a great deal and saved scores of lives himself—surely his opinion ought to weigh more than a mere boy's" (224). As Anne tells Cornelia, however, "Gilbert believes that a doctor should put the welfare of a patient's mind and body before all other considerations" (175) and thus he insists on the operation despite their objections. Throughout the novel, Gilbert is characterized as a modern doctor with a cutting-edge knowledge of medical innovations. He saves Mrs Allonby, for example, using an experimental procedure. He tells Anne, "I tried an experiment that was certainly never tried in Four Winds before. I doubt if it was ever tried before outside of a hospital. It was a new thing in Kingsport hospital last winter" (55). The fact that the surgery on Dick leads to the revelation that Dick is in fact George and frees Leslie from her servitude proves that the objective male professional is in the best position to manage a woman's life story.

Because Leslie has had to become Dick's nursemaid, she logically decides when she is free of him to go to Montreal to study to become a professional nurse. Anne says, "She is going to Montreal to take up nursing and make what she can of her life" (258). Leslie already has the life experience to become a nursing student, having performed the job for 13 years under tragic circumstances but, rather than entering the job market, she marries Owen, who will take her away from Four Winds and introduce her to Canadian society. She will move in important social circles because she is more beautiful and has a much greater share of suffering than the "wholesome, normal, merry girls" (101) of the community. Owen is destined to marry Leslie because he is the typical sentimental observer figure who can recognize value in the suffering princess figure without her having to tell her story. He tells Anne,

> And she is so richly fitted for life. [...] Her beauty is the least of her dower—and she is the most beautiful woman I've ever known. That laugh of hers! I've angled all summer to evoke that laugh, just for the delight of hearing it. And her eyes—they are as deep and blue as the gulf out there. I never saw such blueness [...]. (200)

He loves her because of her ability to endure her misfortunes silently. He understands it is the tragedy of her life that intensifies her beauty:

> She is bound forever to that poor wretch—with nothing to look forward to but growing old in a succession of empty, meaningless, barren years. It drives me mad to think of it. But I must go through my life never seeing her, but always knowing what she is enduring. It's hideous—hideous! (199–200)

Leslie tells Anne that her only real value is within the sentimental economy and that she will transfer it to her husband who will make her life pay: "I hated my beauty because it had attracted him, but now—oh, I'm glad that I have it. It's all I have to offer Owen—his artist soul delights in it. I feel as if I do not come to him quite empty-handed" (287). Leslie deserves to be married to a famous man because her combination of beauty and suffering qualifies her for the position. Because she is a princess figure, her value in the sentimental economy is so great she does not attempt, as Anne must, to increase her value in the labour market.

The fact that Leslie comes to be prized, in the narrative, as the perfect wife calls Anne's value into question. She is forced to acknowledge that Leslie is better suited to the role of princess than she is:

> 'Oh, I once dreamed of a palace, too,' said Anne. 'I suppose all girls do. And then we settle down contentedly in eight-room houses that seem to fulfil all the desires of our hearts—because our prince is there. *You* should have had your palace really, though—you are so beautiful. You *must* let me say it—it *has* to be said—I'm nearly bursting with admiration. You are the loveliest thing I ever saw, Mrs. Moore.' (85)

Before she was forced to marry Dick Moore, Leslie had planned, like Anne, to become a teacher: "Leslie had made up her mind to pass for a teacher if she could, and then earn enough to put herself through Redmond College" (94–5). Her combination of beauty and suffering, however, transforms her into such a valuable sentimental commodity she does not have to have a career in order to boost her value in marriage. Captain Jim tells Anne flatly that because she has not suffered as much as Leslie, she is not worthy of the same social status. When she laments her inability to feel close to Leslie, the captain tells her they have experienced different levels of hardship: "You've been too happy all your life, Mistress Blythe. [...] I reckon that's why you and Leslie can't get real close together in your souls" (134). Anne, however, replies that her "childhood wasn't very happy" (102) but he insists that she still has not suffered enough to be a kindred spirit of Leslie's:

> "There hasn't been any *tragedy* in your life, Mistress Blythe. And poor Leslie's has been almost *all* tragedy. She feels, I reckon, though mebbe she hardly knows she feels it, that there's a vast deal in her life you can't enter nor understand—and so she has to keep you back from it—hold you off, so to speak, from hurting her." (134–5)

Unlike Leslie, who silently endures the loss of family members, Anne has had to continually use her status as an orphan to gain sympathy. She cannot afford to suffer in silence but must become a vocal critic of a society that has mistreated her. She must tell her own story because, as an unattractive child referred to as "Carrots", she lacks a sympathetic observer. Anne ultimately increases her value because she understands that the princess role is not suited to her. She cannot operate entirely within the sentimental economy, where it is impossible for her to compete with a woman as beautiful as Leslie.

Aware of his wife's excellent academic credentials, her status as a published author and her former engagement to the wealthy Roy Gardner, Gilbert worries that perhaps Anne has married beneath her, that she deserves to become a society figure like Leslie. He acknowledges his insecurity to her:

> And some people might think that a Redmond B.A., whom editors were beginning to honour, was 'wasted' as the wife of a struggling country doctor in the rural community of Four Winds. [...] If you had married Roy Gardner, now [...] *you* could have been "a leader in social and intellectual circles far away from Four Winds." (114–15)

She claims, however, that being his wife is exactly where she belongs, that she has not been thwarted in her ambitions. Anne's value is also compared to that of her old classmate Jane who, even though she was to have remained unmarried because of her father's meanness with money, has gone on to marry a millionaire. Diana tells Anne that Jane's mother is proud "Jane married a millionaire and you are only marrying a 'poor doctor without a cent to his name'" (5). Jane is qualified to pursue a millionaire because she has endured a mean and miserly father. She does not become a millionaire herself, however, but marries a man who completes her story for her just as Owen does for Leslie.

The book that Owen writes while in Four Winds is a novelization of Captain Jim's journals, which he publishes as *The Life-Book of Captain Jim*. The centerpiece of the book is the captain's story of "lost Margaret", the woman he loved who fell asleep in a boat and drifted out to sea:

> Then Captain Jim told the story—an old, old forgotten story, for it was over fifty years since Margaret had fallen asleep one day in her father's dory and drifted—or so it was supposed, for nothing was ever certainly known as to her fate—out of the channel, beyond the bar, to perish in the black thunder-squall which had come up so suddenly

that long-ago summer afternoon. But to Captain Jim those fifty years were but as yesterday when it is past.

"I walked the shore for months after that," he said sadly, "looking to find her dear, sweet little body; but the sea never gave her back to me. But I'll find her sometime. Mistress Blythe—I'll find her sometime. She's waiting for me." (159)

Owen writes Leslie into the captain's story as the model for Margaret and, in doing so, tells the stories of both the female subject and the working-class subject. Captain Jim and Leslie come to resemble each other as the working-class male, like the female, is made more beautiful by his suffering:

It could not be denied that Captain Jim was a homely man. His spare jaws, rugged mouth, and square brow were not fashioned on the lines of beauty; and he had passed through many hardships and sorrows which had marked his body as well as his soul; but though at first sight Anne thought him plain she never thought anything more about it—the spirit shining through that rugged tenement beautified it so wholly. (36)

He may be a wizened old sailor but his life history is a female one. He exists entirely within the sentimental economy as his story, like Leslie's, is written not on the page but on his body. When the captain tells his story to listeners he is pleased when they are moved to tears:

"I like to see folks cry that way," he remarked. "It's a compliment. But I can't do justice to the things I've seen or helped to do. I've 'em all jotted down in my life-book, but I haven't got the knack of writing them out properly. If I could hit on jest the right words and string 'em together proper on paper I could make a great book." (79)

Like Leslie, he requires an educated male writer to package his sentimental stories for public consumption. While he can evoke tears in the listener, he does not have the skill to turn his story into a marketable book.

When Anne hears of the captain's life-book, she comes to the same conclusion as Owen—that it should be written down and published. Gilbert suggests that Anne takes on the job but she claims she is, as a female writer, unsuited to the task:

I only wish I could. But it's not in the power of my gift. You know what my forte is, Gilbert—the fanciful, the fairylike, the pretty. To write Captain Jim's life-book as it should be written one should be a master of vigorous yet subtle style, a keen psychologist, a born humourist and a born tragedian. A rare combination of gifts is needed. (139)

Like the mother in *The Railway Children*, she can only write pretty children's stories suitable for the home and nursery. It will take a male writer to package the captain's story for the mass market. Owen, in fact, turns Jim's story into the great Canadian novel: "He knew that he had written a great book—a book that would score a wonderful success— a book that would *live*. He knew that it would bring him both fame and fortune [...]" (196). The captain is given credit on the book's frontispiece as Owen's collaborator but he dies without profiting from it. While Leslie is saddened by the fact that he does not live to receive public acclaim, Anne is wise enough to know that he did not want fame:

It was the book itself he cared for, Leslie—not what might be said of it—and he had it. He had read it all through. The last night must have been one of the greatest happiness for him—with the quick, painless ending he had hoped for in the morning. I am glad for Owen's sake and yours that the book is such a success—but Captain Jim was satisfied—I *know*. (295)

When Captain Jim holds his completed life story in his hands, he is able to die and be reunited with his lost love in the afterlife, in "the haven where lost Margaret waited, beyond the storms and calms" (294). He remains entirely within the realm of romance and adventure as his legendary status remains untainted by profit.

Anne's House of Dreams finally sees the completion of Anne's life history when she becomes, as I have indicated, a wife and mother. Whereas her other pursuits—teacher and writer—have not been sanctioned by tragic credentials, motherhood becomes an occupation for which she is authentically qualified when her first child, Joyce, dies shortly after birth. Like Leslie and Captain Jim, her suffering becomes written on her body: "there was something in the smile that had never been in Anne's smile before and would never be absent from it again" (157). When Anne gives birth to her next child, a boy, Marilla tells her rather insensitively that Joyce will now be replaced. Anne replies, "Oh, no, no, *no*, Marilla. He can't—nothing can ever do that. He has his own place my dear, wee man-child. But little Joy has hers, and always will have it" (253). The deceased child becomes Anne's "lost Margaret" as she waits to be reunited with her in heaven:

> If she had lived she would have been over a year old. She would have been toddling around on her tiny feet and lisping a few words. I can see her so plainly, Marilla. Oh, I know now that Captain Jim was right when he said God would manage better than that my baby would seem a stranger to me when I found her Beyond. I've learned *that* this past year. I've followed her development day by day and week by week—I always shall. I shall know just how she grows from year to year—and when I meet her again I'll know her—she won't be a stranger. (190)

While previously Anne lacked a life story that would qualify her to become a teacher or a writer, the suffering caused by the death of her first child finally gives her the credentials she needs to ensure that motherhood is her true calling. She finally has as much tragedy in her life as Leslie and Captain Jim.

In Montgomery's *Anne* novels, a tragic early history of suffering allows the woman to enter into society so that she can make her life story pay. A woman who has suffered is justified in becoming a rather mercenary figure, like Jane Andrews who marries a millionaire in order to make up for a childhood spent in poverty. While the novels do not necessarily allow their female characters to make their life histories pay directly—they tend to be deployed in society by male characters—their elevation of the life story to an employment credential is important to the history of female social mobility. Because Anne is not a princess but an unattractive orphan, she must prove her value to society by telling her own story. If she suffers in silence as Sara Crewe does in *A Little Princess*, she will not be rescued. In Burnett's novel, passive resistance allows Sara to remain unaffected by economic hardship long enough for people to recognize that she is more than a servant. In Montgomery's *Anne* series, however, the orphan child tells her story using a satiric and ironic strategy that forces society to recognize its cruel treatment of powerless women and children. In telling her story, she gives the life history of the marginalized female a new social value. As Anne tells her story using all the precocious skill of the imaginative child, she proves to the community she deserves a much higher social position.

In the novel *Anne of Windy Poplars*, a fellow teacher of Anne's named Katherine Brook tells her story of thwarted ambition, one that has made her an embittered and acerbic figure. Because she despises teaching in a small town, she has allowed herself to become an isolated and unlikeable woman with no emotional attachments in the community. Anne discovers, however, that beneath Katherine's misanthropy lies a kindred spirit, a woman with a superior intellect and a well-developed imagination. When Anne succeeds in humanizing her by taking her to the warmth and comfort of Avonlea, Katherine is determined to leave teaching. She declares, "Life owes me something more than it has paid me, and I'm going out to collect it" (193). She becomes a professional secretary to an member of parliament (MP), a position that allows her to become a world traveller. Anne is pleased to learn that she has found a suitable career:

> I had a long letter from Katherine last week. She has a gift for writing letters. She has got a position as a private secretary to a globe-trotting M.P. What a fascinating phrase 'globe-trotting' is! A person who would say, 'Let's go to Egypt,' as one might say, 'Let's go to Charlottetown ... and *go*! That life will just suit Katherine.' (255)

Katherine collects what is owed to her as she finds a position that allows her to circulate freely in the world. She is qualified to become a globe-trotting career woman because her life history has earned her the right to want such a position. Katherine is perhaps the only example in the series of a female character who is able to profit directly from her life history. The reason might be that by 1939, when the novel was published, the independent career woman was considered less of a threat to the social order than she was in 1908, when the first novel in the series was published.

Despite the fact that Montgomery's novels are often driven by traditional marriage plots, her female characters do indeed pose a threat to the social order, a threat that the author herself makes sure to mitigate by allowing only her male characters to be in financial control of the female life story. By dissolving the boundary between a woman's life history and the labour market, Montgomery brings the female subject in from the cold, in from the isolation and marginalization of the natural world, so that she can achieve a prominent social position. When the individual who has had a life of illness is recognized as more qualified to become a doctor than an individual who is simply born into a wealthy family that can afford to send him or her to medical school, then the social order is indeed under threat. It is for this reason that Montgomery makes sure that the middle-class male professional like Gilbert Blythe and Owen Ford are in control of the stories of female and working-class subjects, that they are the only ones who can tell their stories properly. It can also be argued that Anne, who is originally born into a middle-class family, maintains a middle-class control over the life history of the suffering orphan, that she alone can tell the story and play the part properly. But even as Anne—the quintessential imaginative child of the Edwardian period—gains entry into the community of Avonlea, she does so using a form of imaginative child's play that has contained within it a fair amount of ironic social criticism. As Montgomery accommodates the suffering female child within the capitalist economy, she comes close to accommodating the child as social critic within the capitalist economy, meaning that her imaginative child is more troublesome and much less of an apologist for the capitalist economy than those we have seen previously in this study. However, by packaging victimization as a commodity for use by the middle-class heroine in search of a suitable career, the novel ultimately blunts the social criticism of her imaginative child who is rewarded for being able to displace the poor and working-class orphan by playing the part much more effectively. As the tragic life history is elevated to the level of a qualification, it is no longer possessed solely by those groups that have been traditionally marginalized. Indeed, it can only be commodified by the cultivated middle classes who are in possession of the rhetorical skills necessary for packaging a tragic life history for public consumption. As it is given currency in the marketplace, the tragic life history can even be appropriated and counterfeited by individuals who have not suffered at all. However, despite the fact that Montgomery's novels are concerned only with the economic well-being of a middle-class heroine, they must be given enormous credit for the fact that men are now forced to compete for prominent positions in society with women who are able to tell their stories of illness, suffering, and marginalization.

Conclusion

At the end of the eighteenth century, the miserable working conditions of children within Britain's ugly industrial landscapes gave rise to British romanticism's representation of the child as a noble savage, a figure whose innocence is inevitably corrupted or destroyed when he or she is taken out of the natural world. At the end of the first industrial revolution, capitalist society had inflicted so much suffering on poor factory children that its public image was in dire need of rehabilitation. Indeed, its survival depended upon the emergence of a new relationship with the child. At the beginning of the nineteenth century, authors such as Maria Edgeworth argued that rather than being victimized by commercialism, children were in fact the living embodiment of the spirit of capitalism. Children were re-imagined as possessing an innate curiosity and capacity for ingenuity such that they became the point of origin of capitalist innovation. Samuel Smiles devoted numerous self-help books precisely to the idea that every famous inventor made his initial discoveries not as an adult but as a child playing with practical toys and everyday objects inside the family home. The self-help movement argued that there can be no such thing as imaginative play that is performed outside the bounds of the real commercial spaces of Britain, just as there can be no real innovation and ingenuity that is performed outside the bounds of childhood. Out of this movement emerged the idea that because children are defined by an innate ingenuity they are subjects with a special ability to resist being embedded in a particular socio-economic context; the capacity for ingenuity allows the child to transform his or her material circumstances into new and more exciting enterprises. Once such an argument was made, even the most miserable circumstances became an opportunity for performing ingenuity. Ultimately, what this study has shown is that once the child became defined in terms of ingenuity and invention, he or she could no longer be victimized by a capitalism that was no longer an external force corrupting innocence but an internal force granting even the poorest child the ability to discover boundless opportunities for social mobility.

This study has also demonstrated that as the middle-class child began to displace working-class and aristocratic versions of the child, childhood emerged as a performance of the relationship of the individual to the commercial marketplace. The imaginative child emerged as a figure who could reconcile for capitalist society the nobler pursuits of the mind and spirit with the baser pursuits of the commercial world. By holding together such seemingly irreconcilable forces, the child became the site where capitalism was transformed from the space of exploitation into the space of the imagination. In other words, the imaginative child emerged as a figure who could dissolve the boundary between the child's playroom and the nation's industrial landscapes such that they became part of the same imaginative project.

This study also suggests that the emergence in the Victorian period of the so-called "golden age" of children's literature must be re-examined in the light of its production of the figure of the imaginative child. By the Edwardian period, authors believed that the goal of children's literature was not simply to entertain young readers but to cultivate their imaginations such that childhood itself would become a public performance of the imagination with popular children's texts providing the script. Constant claims were made by authors of the period that the only children who could perform childhood properly were those who could also play properly. Consequently, imaginative play with its ability to reconfigure the child's material environment became equated with the ability to achieve social mobility and thus the child emerged as a subject that must by definition be granted the ability to imagine unlimited social mobility. If the golden age of children's literature was about cultivating the imagination, then it was about cultivating a kind of imagination that, even as it appeared to be unconcerned with the tawdry business of acquiring wealth, was profoundly implicated in a kind of aggressive competition within the marketplace. The obsession with the imaginative capabilities of children, which was so much a part of the golden age of children's literature, was bound up in the need to render the child as something that cannot be victimized by capitalism. What this book indicates is that further study is required in order to better understand the reasons why the child's imagination has become such an important commodity in western society and the precise nature of the role played by children's literature in producing it as a commodity.

What then is the legacy of the argument with which this study is concerned, that children are innately ingenuous and inventive and that they embody the spirit of capitalism? While this study situates its argument within a specific time and place and within a discrete period of literary history, it provides, to some extent, a framework for understanding some more recent developments in the relationship of the child to capitalist society. Many commentators today have expressed the fear that childhood and child development have become too involved in economic production. Kiku Adatto, for example, has argued that modern childhood has become virtually synonymous with the cynical business of résumé building: "Childhood itself has become a preparation for the selling of the self. This is because parents, anxious for their children's success, see their children as products to perfect and encourage their children to configure their lives as 'living resumes'" (38). She claims that the obsession with career training has reconfigured the relationship of the child to the home: "For purposes of resume building, a child doesn't get 'credit' for helping in his own home, but he does for volunteering in a nursing home. He doesn't get credit for cooking for his grandmother, but he does for caring for someone else's grandmother in a volunteer program" (39). Certainly, there are still some experiences available to children that are not about career training but children are, as Adatto argues, increasingly taught to value more highly life experiences that will lead in some way to the fulfilment of career ambitions.

Similarly, the concept of self-branding has emerged at the beginning of the twenty-first century as a form of self-help designed for young workers who, much like their Victorian counterparts, are deeply anxious about their ability to compete in the job market. According to Alison Hearn, self-branding is a kind of self-exploitation in which human experience is rendered completely subservient to an economy that demands "constant innovation and flexibility" (198). She describes how the branded self is to be constantly worked on and improved such that it becomes both the site of and the performance of capitalist innovation: "Perpetual activity on the part of workers is highly dependent on their flexibility and adaptability to change. The motivation for this activity must come from within and reflect personal innovation and autonomy" (203).[1] While self-branding is held out to anxious workers as a strategy for remaining employable in a difficult marketplace, it is, more importantly, a means of perpetuating a much larger narrative of social mobility in which enormous pressure is placed on the individual to be 100 per cent committed to the performance of capitalist innovation.

It supposes a point at which the self is so thoroughly devoted to capitalist society that it becomes something like a marketable brand. Even as the self-branding movement is marketed as a self-help strategy, it is, like the narratives of social mobility with which this book has been concerned, more often about assigning blame for failing to succeed in the capitalist economy. By demanding a total commitment to and a steadfast belief in the marketplace, it places the blame for a lack of success not on capitalist society but on the individual who, if only for a moment, allows doubt to creep in or who involves the private self in activities that are not connected to self-improvement in the labour market. In many ways, the self-branding phenomenon is an extension of the positive thinking movement such as it is found in Burnett's novels. The demand for complete faith in capitalist society operates in *A Little Princess* where, as we have seen, Sara Crewe is able to resist poverty because, unlike the other servant girls who work at the boarding school, she never for an instant believes she is anything other than a princess. Her complete commitment to the role is that which allows her to prosper in the end. The point of the narrative is ultimately to argue that those who remain in poverty do so because they have ruined the magic of positive thinking by allowing doubts about capitalist society and the possibility of social mobility to gain a foothold.

Perhaps the concepts of childhood as résumé-building and self-branding, which are characterized by an overtly mercenary rhetorical strategy, have emerged because of a change in attitude towards the capitalist economy. It may be that the educated classes no longer feel the need to apologize for their involvement in commercial activity as they once did in the nineteenth century. Consequently, the child's relationship to capitalist society may be, at this point in time, much less mediated by imaginative literature and imaginative play because of a greater willingness to accept the idea that childhood is about training for future employment. Capitalist society, however, will always require that it not be perceived as that which victimizes the child and thus résumé-building and self-branding will undoubtedly remain controversial forms of self-help as they dramatically flatten the landscape of childhood experience. Critiques such as Adatto's, which demand that the child be, in effect, rescued and returned to a more romantic version of childhood are proof perhaps that very few people openly subscribe to the idea that children should develop with only one goal in mind—success in the labour market. Ultimately, the problem with childhood as résumé-building or self-branding is that it threatens to break the delicate dialectical relationship between the child and the marketplace that emerged in the Victorian period. It threatens to re-define capitalism as that which can only victimize the child.

Perhaps the clearest indication that the imaginative child remains a powerful construct is the amount of cultural capital that continues to be invested in the question, "What do you want to be when you grow up?" Even as the question is evidence of a societal pressure to get children to think about their career prospects as early as possible, it is also an imaginative exercise that announces to children that they can be, as we so often tell them, "anything they want to be". It is often asked of school children as a writing exercise and, as a pedagogical device, it requires that they locate their imaginative capabilities within the bounds of the labour market. Adults are compelled to ask the question not only to encourage children to begin thinking about their career goals but to remind or even convince themselves that their own careers can be traced back to childhood. As this study has demonstrated, just as the child was re-imagined in the image of the capitalist economy, so the capitalist economy was re-imagined in the image of the child. Once the marketplace no longer appears to be driven by imaginative play—once it appears that the imaginative child is involved only in the cynical business of résumé-building—it is in danger of reverting back to that which exploits the child. In many ways, the question "What do you want to be when you grow up?" has become, for better or for worse, central to how we conceive of child development. It can be argued that it is *the* most important question in capitalist society, one that asks the child to become an apologist for both an unequal social structure and a decidedly unsentimental marketplace.

Notes

Introduction

1. Malcolm Andrews, in *Dickens and the Grown-up Child*, writes, "Rapid techno-logical sophistication, increasing specialisation, growing complexity in the power structure, social confusion in the large, packed cities: it was no won-der that people felt the impulse to retreat imaginatively to what they vaguely remembered as the simplicity of childhood or to sentimental pastoralism, neither of which had ever properly caught up with the great age of progress in the nineteenth century" (25).
2. See Mary Woodall, *Thomas Gainsborough*.
3. Studies that are concerned with the development of child protection legis-lation include Hugh Cunningham, *The Children of the Poor* and *Children and Childhood*; Laura C. Berry, *The Child, the State and the Victorian Novel*; and Monica Flegel, *Conceptualizing Cruelty to Children*.
4. For an overview of the Factory Acts and the issue of child labour, see Hugh Cunningham's chapter, "The Response to Child Labour 1780–1850", *The Children of the Poor*.
5. Flegel is quoting from Viviana A. Zelizer, *Pricing the Priceless Child*.
6. For the evangelical tradition, see also Hugh Cunningham's chapter, "The Search for Order 1680–1810", *The Children of the Poor*.
7. For the evangelical tradition in literature, see Brown's chapter, "Sinners and Saviours: The Child of Faith", *The Captured World*. For the Romantic tradition, see Judith Plotz, *The Vocation of Childhood*. See Marah Gubar's introduction to *Artful Dodgers* for an excellent discussion of the Victorian reaction to romanticism and the idealization of the child.
8. The idea of the "cult of childhood" in the nineteenth century begins with George Boas, *The Cult of Childhood*. Malcom Andrews, *Dickens and the Grown-up Child*, has also recognized the type of child described by Gubar: "He had to be the embodiment of innocence, spontaneity, romance and imagination; but he also had to be a respectable little citizen, wholly differentiated from his juvenile kin in the lower classes, especially children of the very poor, who were in many instances reverting to a savage state" (21). See also Joseph L. Zornado, *Inventing the Child*.
9. Monika Elbert (ed.), *Enterprising Youth*, is a recent collection of essays that examine American children's texts in relation to the so-called age of invention.

1 Avoiding Dead Ends and Blind Alleys: Re-imagining Youth Employment in Nineteenth-Century Britain

1. On the subject of female clerks in the nineteenth century, see Meta Zemmick, "Jobs for the Girls".

2. See also John Springhall, *Coming of Age: Adolescence in Britain.*
3. Harold Perkin, *The Rise of Professional Society*, notes that there was "segregation at every level and in every occupation" (83), which meant that young clerks would be lumped together as a group and largely ignored by senior workers.
4. David Wallace, "Bourgeois Tragedy", notes that Lillo's play continued to be performed throughout the nineteenth century and was subsidized by London merchants who made their employees attend as a warning to them should they consider stealing from employers.
5. On the connection between Weber and Lillo's *The London Merchant*, see David Wallace, "Bourgeois Tragedy".
6. Troy Boone, *Youth of Darkest England*, provides a useful history of the "penny dreadful".
7. Lauren M. Goodlad, "Middle Class Cut into Two", argues for a clear distinction to be made between industrialists and professionals.
8. Harold Perkin, *The Rise of Professional Society*, notes that the landed gentry and the millionaire industrialists formed "into one great capitalist plutocracy" (78) leaving the middle class as a diverse group of professionals, shopkeepers, traders, clerks all claiming middle-class status. He divides professionals into "higher" professionals and "lower" professionals. See also F.M.L. Thompson, *The Rise of Respectable Society*, and Dror Wahrman, *Imagining the Middle Class*. See E.P. Thompson, *The Making of the English Working Class*, for what is still a useful study of the working classes.
9. Harold Perkin, *The Rise of Professional Society*, describes the proliferation of professions from 1800 to the First World War: "To the seven qualifying associations of 1800—four Inns of Court for barristers, two Royal Colleges and the Society of Apothecaries for medical doctors the first eighty years of the nineteenth century had added only twenty more, for solicitors, architects, builders (not successful as a profession), pharmacists, veterinary surgeons, actuaries, surveyors, chemists, librarians, bankers (another unsuccessful attempt), accountants, and eight types of engineer. From 1880 to the First World War there appeared no less than thirty-nine, from chartered accountants, auctioneers and estate agents, company secretaries and hospital administrators to marine, mining, water, sanitary, heating and ventilating, and locomotive design engineers, insurance brokers, sales managers, and town planners. To these we should add the non-qualifying associations, such as the National Union of Teachers, The Association of Headmasters, and the Association of Teachers in Technical Institutions, the National Association of Local Government Officers, the Civil Service Clerical Association, and the Institute of Directors, which often combined professional aspirations with something of the character of trade unions or employers' associations" (86).
10. For the history of medicine see Noel Parry and Jose Parry, *The Rise of the Medical Profession*.
11. Harold Perkin argues that with such legislation "the client became in effect the whole community" (117) and that professionals became "much freer to act as critics of society" (117).
12. See Ellen Singer More, *Restoring the Balance*, for a history of women in medicine. See also Susan Wells, *Out of the Dead House*, and Jo Manton, *Elizabeth Garrett Anderson*.

13. For a history of the British civil service, see Peter Hennessy, *Whitehall*.
14. See Mary Poovey's chapter, "A Housewifely Woman", *Uneven Developments*, for a discussion of how Florence Nightingale imagined nursing as a domestic practice.
15. See Kimberley Reynolds and Nicola Humble, *Victorian Heroines*, for a discussion of the transformation of the governess in Victorian literature.
16. Samuel Smiles notes in *Character* that employers would often look at the character of a job candidate's mother: "[...]the managers before they engaged a boy always inquired into the mother's character, and if that was satisfactory they were tolerably certain that her children would conduct themselves creditably. *No attention was paid to the character of the father*" (42).
17. See Monica F. Cohen, *Professional Domesticity*.
18. Jeffrey Richards, "Spreading the Gospel of Self-Help", notes that in G.A. Henty's novel *Sturdy and Strong* (1888) the hero is sent to a good school by his employer as a reward for rescuing the business from a fire. He is "a civil engineer, and ends up happily married and going off to Brazil to survey a new railway" (58).
19. Tucker published her novels using the pseudonym "A.L.O.E.", which stands for "A Lady of England".
20. See Gilbert and Gubar, *Madwoman in the Attic*, for a discussion of female sexuality in *Jane Eyre*. See Nancy Armstrong, *Desire and Domestic Fiction*, for a discussion of the feminization of Rochester.
21. See Terry Eagleton, *Myths of Power*, for a discussion of the middle-class mythology of *Jane Eyre*. See Judith Leggatt and Christopher Parkes, "From the Red Room to Rochester's Haircut", for a discussion of Jane's colonization of Rochester on behalf of middle-class standards.
22. According to Sally Mitchell in *The New Girl*, working-class publications for girls promoted domestic service as an exciting career that could provide them with opportunities for both danger and romance. She writes that "just as the middle class typist has an exciting persona in a novel about a statesman's private secretary, the workgirls' papers offer glamorized versions of domestic service in serials about the shipboard stewardess, the 'Complexion Specialist,' the waitress in an elegant tea shop, or the detective under cover as a lady's maid" (32).
23. See Mary Poovey, *Making a Social Body*, and Linda Mahood, *Policing Gender, Class, and Family*, for discussions of the monitoring of the homes of the poor.
24. See Michel Foucault, *Discipline and Punish*, for the transformation of institutional and industrial spaces into abstract, grid spaces that took place during the eighteenth and nineteenth centuries.
25. Michael J. Childs, *Labour's Apprentices*, describes how the few working class children who rose into the middle class often looked back with regret: "Perhaps, looking back, a man who had accomplished the climb would envy his former schoolmate who 'always came top in arithmetic and [who] was leaving to become a van boy' " (43).
26. H.G. Wells felt compelled to comment on compulsory education in *Experiments in Autobiography*: "The Education Act of 1870 was not an Act for a common universal education, it was an Act to educate the lower classes for employment on lower class lines" (qtd in Simon, 97).

27. Michel Foucault, *Discipline and Punish*, argues that the internalization of rebellion and discontent is the key to discipline and punishment in the modern nation-state.
28. Hugh Cunningham, *Children of the Poor*, describes how the idea of "creating a ladder which would enable bright children to climb from the bottom to the top of the educational system" (195) emerged. In the interwar period, "the tools for an apparently fine-tuned categorization of the school population" (196) such as IQ testing were used.
29. See Childs, *Labour's Apprentices*, for a discussion of the breakdown of the apprenticeship system.
30. Richards also notes, however, that "the mutual improvement societies had rivals in the middle-class run Mechanics Institutes, whose aim was both mental and moral improvement of the working class and the diffusion downwards of middle class ideology" (60).
31. In her autobiography, Beatrice Webb recalls the self-help fervour of the middle of the nineteenth century: "It was the bounden duty of every citizen to better his social status; to ignore those beneath him and to aim steadily at the top rung of the social ladder. Only by this persistent pursuit of each individual of his own and his family's interest would the highest level of civilization be attained" (qtd in Richards, 52–3).
32. See Eric S. Hintz, "Heroes of the Laboratory and the Workshop", for a discussion of texts concerning American inventors of the period.
33. For a discussion of Samuel Smiles, see Jeffrey Richards, "Spreading the Gospel of Self-Help".
34. See Jack Meadows's chapter "School and Home", in *The Victorian Scientist*, for a discussion of the experimentation of tradespeople in their homes.
35. See Andrew O'Malley, *The Making of the Modern Child*, for a discussion of Maria Edgeworth and the concept of middle-class children and the envy of the upper classes.
36. As Monica Flegel, *Conceptualizing Cruelty*, argues, there was increased pressure on all classes to provide children with protective and nurturing homes and that it required "increased material demands upon parents" (14).

2 Family Business and Childhood Experience: *David Copperfield* and *Great Expectations*

1. Penny Brown, *Captured World*, notes that the novel takes a "curiously ambivalent stance to the problem" (76).
2. For the history of the family business, see also Leonore Davidoff and Catherine Hall, *Family Fortunes*.
3. In *Dombey and Son*, the sensitive child Paul Dombey dies as his father tries to make him the ideal business partner in the family firm. Malcolm Andrews, *Dickens and the Grown-up Child*, notes that the problem with the family firm of "Dombey and Son" is that "the two are not integrated. Mr. Dombey has chosen to give priority to one at the expense of the other" (121). See Laura C. Berry, *The Child, the State and the Victorian Novel*, for a useful discussion of Paul Dombey inside the family firm.

4. On child performers in Victorian Britain, see also Carolyn Steedman, *Strange Dislocations*, Monica Flegel, *Conceptualizing Cruelty to Children*, and Hazel Waters, " 'That Astonishing Clever Child' ".

5. Other critics have made this point about *David Copperfield*. See Mary Poovey's chapter, "The Man-of-Letters Hero", *Uneven Developments*, D.A. Miller's chapter, "Secret Subjects", *The Novel and the Police*, and Jennifer Ruth's chapter, "Becoming Professional", *Novel Professions*.

6. Despite the fact that he satirizes untalented rejects like Micawber, Dickens promoted emigration to Australia as a solution to the overcrowded British labour market in many entries in *Household Words*.

7. As has been noted by many scholars, David's employment at Murdstone and Grinby's warehouse is based upon Dickens's employment as a child at Warren's blacking factory. See John Forster's, *The Life of Charles Dickens*.

8. For a discussion of the physical description of Uriah Heep and its connection to race, see Tara MacDonald, " 'Red-Headed Animal': Race, Sexuality and Dickens's Uriah Heep". See also Goldie Morgentaler, *Dickens and Heredity*.

9. In his introduction to the novel, Jeremy Tambling writes, "Uriah Heep has grasped the divided nature of Victorian ideology. The Evangelical principle—which often, historically, supported charity schools—taught that labour was a curse, following Genesis 3.16–19; while the Utilitarian ethos, supported by Carlyle's 'gospel of work', preached in the 1840s in his *Past and Present* and influenced by the idea of 'self-help', made bourgeois happiness and domesticity dependent on hard work and duty" (xxxv). Christopher Herbert, "Filthy Lucre", notes that this divided nature is also at work in *Little Dorritt* where "the capitalistic cult of money-getting and the Christian cult of the holiness of the poor and the blessedness of the state of poverty coexist" (203).

10. See John Bender, *Imagining the Penitentiary*, for the role of the novel in the development of the Panopticon prison. See Michel Foucault, *Discipline and Punish*, for the history of panoptic discipline.

11. See Michel Foucault, *Discipline and Punish*, for the disciplinary mechanisms of the Panopticon prison. See also John Bender, *Imagining the Penitentiary*.

12. In *Character*, Samuel Smiles writes, "When the girl becomes a wife, if she knows nothing of figures, and is innocent of addition and multiplication, she can keep no record of income and expenditure, and there will probably be a succession of mistakes committed which may be prolific in domestic contention. The woman, not being up to her business—that is, the management of her domestic affairs in conformity with the simple principles of arithmetic—will, through sheer ignorance, be apt to commit extravagances, which may be most injurious to her family peace and comfort" (54). See Brenda Ayres, *Dissenting Women in Dickens' Novels*, for women who defy domestic ideology in his novels.

13. See Mary Poovey's chapter, "*David Copperfield* and the Professional Writer", *Uneven Developments*, for a discussion of the position of the writer in the commercial marketplace.

14. William J. Palmer, *Dickens and New Historicism*, describes the importance of *The London Merchant* to Dickens. See also William Axton, *Circle of Fire*. See Sarah Gates, "Intertextual Estella", for a discussion of Estella's connection to Lillo's play.

15. Monica F. Cohen, *Professional Domesticity*, discusses Wemmick's home in some detail. She provides an interesting reading of its playful nature by looking at its "camp" elements.

3 Adventure Fiction and the Youth Problem: *Treasure Island* and *Kidnapped*

1. Troy Boone, *Youth of Darkest England*, describes how Henry Mayhew observes alternative gangs and little societies within the London poor. Mayhew writes, "it would appear, that not only are all races divisible into wanderers and settlers, but each civilized or settled tribe has generally some wandering horde intermingled with, and in a measure preying upon it" (qtd in Boone, 21).
2. See Stephen Arata, *Fictions of Loss*, for a discussion of Stevenson's antipathy towards middle-class society.
3. Jenifer Hart, "Genesis of Northcote-Trevelyan", explores the question of whether middle-class access to the civil service was an influence on civil service reform, the idea that "middle-class desire for free entry to the public offices was a factor of no little importance in civil service reform; the older professions were overcrowded, and the middle classes were troubled about the future of their sons" (64).
4. Between the 1850s and 1890s, the civil service doubled from approximately 40,000–80,000 (Hennessy, 51). Between 1891 and 1911, it tripled (Hobsbawm, 103).
5. Peter Hennessy, *Whitehall*; Sir Norman Chester, *English Administrative System*; and Richard A. Chapman and J.R. Greenaway, *Dynamics of Administrative Reform*, provide useful overviews of the report. Jennifer Ruth, *Novel Professions*, also provides a good overview of civil service reforms.
6. Hennessy identifies one figure, however, who fits the ideal. Edward Bridges, who went on to become head of the civil service in 1945, was, he notes, "a war hero and a connoisseur of literature—the incarnation of the romantic ideal" (76). See Bridges, *Portrait of a Profession*, for his overview of the civil service. McKechnie, *Romance of the Civil Service*, has an intriguing title but does not discuss the romantic ideal of the civil servant.
7. See A.V. Dicey, *Lectures*, for a more contemporary view of the rise of collectivism in the late nineteenth century.
8. Diana Loxley, *Problematic Shores*, argues that *Robinson Crusoe* is in the tradition of "rational individualism" (144) as opposed to texts like *The Mysterious Island*, which are about "the new authority of the collective and collective destiny" (144). My reading of Defoe's novel is that Crusoe as administrator combines the values of the middle-class shopkeeper with the values of public service as he engages in nation building on his island.
9. In "Family of Engineers", Stevenson writes that others who have read his grandfather's account of the building of the Bell Rock Lighthouse have called it "The Romance of Stone and Lime and The Robinson Crusoe of Civil Engineering" (496).
10. See Graham Balfour, *The Life of Robert Louis Stevenson*.
11. On the construction of masculinity in Stevenson's writing, see Dennis Denisoff, "Consumerism and Stevenson's Misfit Masculinities".

12. Stephen Arata, *Fictions of Loss*, discusses Stevenson's attitude towards middle-class professionals in *Dr Jekyll* and notes that Hyde "acts out the aggressions of the timid bourgeois gentlemen" (39).
13. Troy Boone, *Youth of Darkest England*, argues that the political threat of the pirates as a working-class group is undone when Silver ultimately reveals himself to be violent: "they represent an organized working class group following an elected leader [...] who endorses a 'cool' restraint from violence as the means of subverting the normative division of labor" (75).
14. See Mary Poovey, *Making a Social Body*, for a discussion of sanitary legislation in the 1840s. She writes, "the sanitary idea constituted one of the crucial links between the regulation of the individual body and the consolidation of those apparatuses we associate with the modern state" (115).
15. The modern welfare state is, of course, a twentieth-century phenomenon, but in the 1880s when Stevenson's novel was published the idea of the public pension was prominent. Friendly Societies, for example, were operating as a precursor to government pensions. For a history of the rise of the welfare state, see Bentley B. Gilbert, *Evolution of National Insurance*.
16. For a thorough investigation of Stevenson's writing of Scottish history in *Kidnapped*, see Barry Menikoff, *Narrating Scotland*.
17. Barry Menikoff, *Narrating Scotland*, notes that the term "Whig" was used by highlanders to describe lowlanders with a superior moral attitude, not in a precisely political way.
18. See Graham Balfour, *The Life of Robert Louis Stevenson*, for Stevenson's biography.
19. *Catriona* is also published under the title *David Balfour*.

4   Commercialism and Middle-Class Innocence: *The Story of the Treasure Seekers* and *The Railway Children*

1. See Jeannie Duckworth, *Fagin's Children*. On the sentimentalization of deaths of poor Victorian children, see Gillian Avery and Kimberely Reynolds, *Representations of Childhood Death*, and Laurence Lerner, *Angels and Absences*.
2. See also Anita Moss, "E. Nesbit's Romantic Child", and Mavis Reimer, "Treasure Seekers and Invaders". For a discussion of play in Edwardian fiction, see Michelle Beissel Heath, "Playing at House".
3. For Nesbit's involvement in Fabian socialism, see Julia Briggs, *A Woman of Passion*.
4. Nesbit's money-lender is, of course, an offensive racial stereotype. Harold Perkin, in *The Professional Society*, notes that newspaper editors were "one of the few professions in which a poor boy could rise from the bottom" (90).
5. Gubar argues that as the children act out scenes from the literature they have read, the "art of thieving" (131) allows them to escape the "power that adults and their narratives wield over children" and to "commandeer more completely the scripts they are given, to revise rather than simply reenact them" (132).
6. See Chamutal Noimann, "Poke Your Finger", for a discussion of the father and political reform in *The Railway Children*. Kristen Guest, in "The Subject

of Money", provides a discussion of the middle-class subject in Victorian melodrama as both victim and victimizer in capitalist society.

7. See David Vincent, *Literacy and Popular Culture*, for the importance of the postal system in nineteenth-century Britain. Vincent explains how the "penny post" system played an important role in the rise of working-class literacy in Britain.

5 Educational Tracking and the Feminized Classroom: *A Little Princess* and *The Secret Garden*

1. For the influence of women in the education system, see Jane Martin, *Women and the Politics of Schooling*.
2. On the issue of educational tracking and how it is still a part of modern education, see Maureen T. Hallinan, "Tracking: From Theory to Practice", and William Ming Liu *et al.*, "White Middle-Class Privilege".
3. See David Wardle, *English Popular Education*, for the development of "child-centred" (98) teaching methods in the late nineteenth century. For an overview of recent theories on self-directed learning, see C. O'Mahony and W. Moss, "Self-Directed Learning".
4. See Ann Thwaite, *Waiting for the Party*, for Burnett's biography.
5. See Horatio Willis Dresser, *A History of the New Thought Movement*. See also Jane Darcy, "The Edwardian Child in the Garden", which touches upon Burnett's interest in New Thought.
6. Norman Vincent Peale's *The Power of Positive Thinking* (1952) represents the movement's most popular publication.
7. Maureen Stout, *The Feel-Good Curriculum*, is a lively discussion of the problems with self-esteem in girls' education.
8. Elisabeth Rose Gruner, "Cinderella, Marie Antoinette", notes that Sara is not the school's rebel but its "deposed monarch" (174).
9. For the colonial background of the novel, see Roderick McGillis, *A Little Princess: Gender and Empire*.
10. On Mary's role as a mother in the novel see Phyllis Bixler, "Gardens, Houses, and Nurturant Power", and Mary Jeanette Moran, "Nancy's Ancestors". Anna Krugovoy Silver notes that Mary's physical activity is a subversion of domestic ideology: "*The Secret Garden* subverts predominant Victorian child-rearing practices, which discouraged energetic physical activity for girls and segregated activities by gender" (198).
11. For the woman's role in the home, see Nancy Armstrong, *Desire and Domestic Fiction*.
12. See Danielle E. Price, "Cultivating Mary", for a discussion of flowers and the decorative arts in Burnett's novel and the period. See John Tosh, *A Man's Place*, for the male attitude towards the home.
13. On literacy and the working class in the nineteenth century, see also David Vincent, *Literacy and Popular Culture*, and Patrick Brantlinger, *The Reading Lesson*.
14. Christina Hoff Sommers, *The War Against Boys*, drew much attention to the state of boys inside the classroom. For an excellent critique of Sommers's

idea that the classroom robs boys of their masculinity, see Michael Kimmel, "A War against Boys?".

15. See Elaine Millard, *Differently Literate*, for a discussion of the boy's position in the classroom. She notes that many studies have shown that boys are very adept at controlling a classroom and reasserting their authority when it is challenged by girls.

6   The Female Life History and the Labour Market: *Anne of Green Gables* and *Anne's House of Dreams*

1. See Gail Cunningham, *The New Woman and the Victorian Novel*, and Sally Ledger, *The New Woman*.
2. Kristine Swenson notes that the motif was "the standard fare of musical comedy" (133) in the 1890s. She writes, "Ironically, working as a shopgirl is at once a penance for frivolling and a reaffirmation of Mona's moral fitness to minister the needs of other women—a fitness that had been called into question by her desire to become a woman doctor, that unwomanly, unsexed, and déclassé professional" (134).
3. In their chapter on feminine autobiography, *Victorian Heroines*, Kimberley Reynolds and Nicola Humble write, "The tendency to present the self in relation to/or through others is characteristic of femininity and is often identified as contributing to the repression of women" (135). On the subject of feminine autobiography, see also Domna C. Stanton (ed.), *The Female Autograph*, and Linda H. Peterson, *Traditions of Victorian Women's Autobiography*.
4. *Anne of Windy Poplars* is often considered the fourth book in the series because of its chronological position in the telling of Anne's life story. It covers her early career as a teacher before she marries Gilbert.
5. Charlotte G. Borst, "Choosing the Student Body", provides a discussion of personal interviews as part of the application procedure to US medical schools.
6. See Julia McQuillan and Julie Pfeiffer, "Why Anne Makes Us Dizzy" for a discussion of the fact that Anne does not perform farm labour for the Cuthberts. They argue that because Anne performs only traditional female labour she does not disrupt the social order.
7. See Kimberley Reynolds and Nicola Humble, *Victorian Heroines*, for a discussion of the orphan in Victorian literature.
8. Penny Brown, *The Captured World*, notes how Jane Eyre contemplates escaping oppression "either by running away or by starving herself to death" (141).
9. See Claudia Nelson, *Boys Will Be Girls*, and Catherine Robson, *Men in Wonderland*, for the ways in which gender roles are reversed in nineteenth-century children's literature.
10. See Hilary Emmett, "Mute Misery", for a discussion of "some notable scores on which Anne remains if not precisely *silent*, then, at the very least, tongue-tied" (81).
11. The same device is used in *Mona McLean* as Dr Dudley's name appears as the winner of the Gold Medal for anatomy alongside Mona's name as the

winner for physiology. Margaret Todd reports in *Life of Sophia Jex-Blake*, that the manipulation of scholarships awarded to female medical students at Edinburgh University was widely reported by British newspapers and became a scandal.

Conclusion

1. For examples of the kinds of books produced by the self-branding movement, see Stedman Graham, *Build Your Own Life Brand!*, and Peter Montoya, *The Personal Branding Phenomenon*.

Bibliography

Adatto, Kiku. "Selling Out Childhood." *Hedgehog Review* 5.2 (2003): 24–40.

Anderson, Susan. "Time, Subjectivity, and Modernism in E. Nesbit's Children's Fiction." *Children's Literature Association Quarterly* 32.4 (2007): 308–22.

Andrews, Malcom. *Dickens and the Grown-up Child.* Houndmills: Palgrave Macmillan, 1994.

Anonymous. *The Apprentice, or, Affectionate Hints to a Young Friend Entering upon the Business Life.* London: John Childs, 1845.

———. *Two Ways to Begin Life.* London: 1883.

Arata, Stephen. *Fictions of Loss in the Victorian fin de siècle.* New York: Cambridge UP, 1996.

Armstrong, Nancy. *Desire and Domestic Fiction: A Political History of the Novel.* New York: Oxford UP, 1987.

Avery, Gillian and Kimberley Reynolds, eds. *Representations of Childhood Death.* New York: St. Martin's, 2000.

Axton, William. *Circle of Fire: Dickens' Vision and Style and the Popular Victorian Theatre.* Lexington: U of Kentucky P, 1966.

Ayres, Brenda. *Dissenting Women in Dickens' Novels: The Subversion of Domestic Ideology.* Westport: Greenwood, 1998.

Balfour, Graham. *The Life of Robert Louis Stevenson.* 5th ed. London: Methuen, 1910.

Bavidge, Jenny. "Exhibiting Childhood: E. Nesbit and the Children's Welfare Exhibitions." *Childhood in Edwardian Fiction: Worlds Enough and Time.* Ed. Adrienne E. Gavin and Andrew F. Humphries. Houndmills: Palgrave Macmillan, 2009. 125–42.

Bender, John. *Imagining the Penitentiary: Fiction and the Architecture of Mind in Eighteenth-Century England.* Chicago: U of Chicago P, 1987.

Berry, Laura C. *The Child, the State and the Victorian Novel.* Charlottesville: U of Virginia P, 1999.

Bindloss, Harold. *True Grit: The Adventures of Two Lads in Western Africa.* London: S.W. Partridge, 1904.

Bixler, Phyllis. "Gardens, Houses, and Nurturant Power in *the Secret Garden.*" *Romanticism and Children's Literature in Nineteenth-Century England.* Ed. James Holt McGavaran Jr. Athens: U of Georgia P, 1991. 208–24.

Boas, George. *The Cult of Childhood.* Dallas: Spring, 1966.

Boone, Troy. *The Youth of Darkest England: Working-Class Children at the Heart of Victorian Empire.* New York: Routledge, 2005.

———. "Germs of Endearment: The Machinations of Edwardian Children's Fictions." *Children's Literature* 35.1 (2007): 80–101.

Borst, Charlotte G. "Choosing the Student Body: Masculinity, Culture, and the Crisis of Medical School Admissions, 1920–1950." *History of Education Quarterly* 42.2 (2002): 181–214.

Boyd, Kelly. *Manliness and the Boy's Story Paper in Britain: A Cultural History, 1855–1940*. Houndmills: Palgrave Macmillan, 2002.

Brantlinger, Patrick. *The Reading Lesson: The Threat of Mass Literacy in Nineteenth-Century British Fiction*. Bloomington: Indiana UP, 1998.

Bratton, J.S. *The Impact of Victorian Children's Fiction*. London: Croom Helm, 1981.

Bridges, Edward. *Portrait of a Profession: The Civil Service Tradition*. Cambridge: Cambridge UP, 1950.

Briggs, Julia. *A Woman of Passion: The Life of E. Nesbit, 1858–1924*. New York: New Amsterdam, 1987.

Bristow, Joseph. *Empire Boys: Adventures in a Man's World*. London: Routledge, 1991.

Bronte, Charlotte. *Jane Eyre*. Ed. Richard J. Dunn. New York: W.W. Norton, 1987.

Brown, Penny. *The Captured World: The Child and Childhood in Nineteenth-Century Women's Writing in England*. New York: St. Martin's, 1993.

Burnett, Frances Hodgson. *A Little Princess*. Ed. U.C. Knoepflmacher. London: Penguin, 2002.

——. *The Secret Garden*. Ed. Alison Lurie. London: Penguin, 2002.

Cain, P.J. and Hopkins, A.G. *British Imperialism, 1688–2000*. New York: Longman, 2002.

Campbell, G.A. *The Civil Service in Britain*. Harmondsworth: Penguin, 1955.

Carlyle, Thomas. *Past and Present*. London: Chapman and Hall, 1843.

Chapman, Richard A. and Greenaway, J.R. *The Dynamics of Administrative Reform*. London: Croom Helm, 1980.

Charlesworth, Maria Louisa. *Ministering Children: A Tale Dedicated to Childhood*. New York: J.C. Riker, 1855.

Chester, Sir Norman. *The English Administrative System, 1780–1870*. Oxford: Clarendon, 1981.

Childs, Michael J. *Labour's Apprentices: Working-Class Lads in Late Victorian and Edwardian England*. Montreal: McGill-Queen's UP, 1992.

Cohen, Monica F. *Professional Domesticity in the Victorian Novel: Women, Work and Home. Cambridge Studies in Nineteenth-Century Literature and Culture 14*. Ed. Gillian Beer and Catherine Gallagher. Cambridge: Cambridge UP, 1998.

Crouch, Marcus. *The Nesbit Tradition: The Children's Novel in England, 1945–70*. London: Ernest Benn, 1972.

Cunningham, Gail. *The New Woman and the Victorian Novel*. London: Palgrave Macmillan, 1978.

Cunningham, Hugh. *The Children of the Poor: Representations of Childhood since the Seventeenth Century*. Oxford: Blackwell, 1991.

——. *Children and Childhood in Western Society since 1500*. 2nd ed. Harlow: Pearson, 2005.

Cutt, Margaret Nancy. *Ministering Angels: A Study of Nineteenth-Century Evangelical Writing for Children*. Toronto: Five Owls, 1979.

Darcy, Jane. "The Edwardian Child in the Garden: Childhood in the Fiction of Frances Hodgson Burnett." *Childhood in Edwardian Fiction: Worlds Enough and Time*. Ed. Adrienne E. Gavin and Andrew F. Humphries. Houndmills: Palgrave Macmillan, 2009. 75–88.

Davidoff, Leonore and Hall, Catherine. *Family Fortunes: Men and Women of the English Middle Class, 1780–1850*. London: Hutchinson, 1996.

Defoe, Daniel. *Robinson Crusoe*. Ed. J. Donald Crowley. London: Oxford UP, 1972.

Denisoff, Dennis. "Consumerism and Stevenson's Misfit Masculinities." *Robert Louis Stevenson: Writer of Boundaries*. Ed. Richard Ambrosini and Richard Dury. Madison: U of Wisconsin P, 2006. 286–98.

Dicey, A.V. *Lectures on the Relation Between Law and Public Opinion in England during the Nineteenth Century*. London: Palgrave Macmillan, 1917.

Dickens, Charles. *Oliver Twist, or the Parish Boy's Progress*. 3 vols. London: Richard Bentley, 1838.

——. *Household Words*. London: Bradley and Evans, 1850–9.

——. *Hard Times*. Ed. David Craig. Harmondsworth: Penguin, 1969.

——. *Nicholas Nickleby*. Ed. Mark Ford. London: Penguin, 1999.

——. *Dombey and Son*. Ed. Andrew Sanders. London: Penguin, 2002.

——. *Great Expectations*. Ed. David Trotter. London: Penguin, 2002.

——. *Our Mutual Friend*. New York: Modern Library, 2002.

——. *Little Dorritt*. Ed. Helen Wall and Stephen Wall. London: Penguin, 2003.

——. *David Copperfield*. Rev. ed. Jeremy Tambling. London: Penguin, 2004.

Dresser, Horatio Willis. *A History of the New Thought Movement*. New York: T.Y. Cornell, 1919.

Drotner, Kirsten. *English Children and their Magazines, 1715–1945*. New Haven: Yale UP, 1988.

Duckworth, Jeannie. *Fagin's Children: Criminal Children in Victorian England*. London: Hambledon and London, 2002.

Eagleton, Terry. *Myths of Power: A Marxist Reading of the Brontes*. Anniversary ed. Houndmills: Palgrave Macmillan, 2005.

Edgeworth, Maria and Richard Lovell Edgeworth. *Essays on Practical Education*. Vol. 1. London: R. Hunter, 1815.

Elbert, Monika, ed. *Enterprising Youth: Social Values and Acculturation in Nineteenth-Century American Children's Literature*. New York: Routledge, 2008.

Emmett, Hilary. "'Mute Misery': Speaking the Unspeakable in L.M. Montgomery's AnneBooks." *100 Years of Anne with an 'e': The Centennial Study of Anne of Green Gables*. Ed. Holly Blackford. Calgary: U of Calgary P, 2009. 81–104.

Flegel, Monica. *Conceptualizing Cruelty to Children in Nineteenth-Century England: Literature, Representation, and the NSPCC*. Farnham: Ashgate, 2009.

Forster, John. *The Life of Charles Dickens*. Philadelphia: J.B. Lippincott, n.d.

Foucault, Michel. *Discipline and Punish*. Trans. Alan Sheridan. New York: Pantheon, 1977.

Gargano, Elizabeth. *Reading Victorian Schoolrooms: Childhood and Education in Nineteenth-Century Fiction*. New York: Routledge, 2008.

Gaskell, Elizabeth. *Mary Barton*. Ed. Shirley Foster. Oxford: Oxford UP, 2008.

Gates, Sarah. "Intertextual Estella: *Great Expectations*, Gender and Literary Tradition." *PMLA* 124.2 (2009): 340–405.

Gilbert, Bentley B. *The Evolution of National Insurance in Great Britain: The Origins of the Welfare State*. London: Michael Joseph, 1966.

Gilbert, Sandra M. and Susan Gubar. *The Madwoman in the Attic: The Woman Writer and the Nineteenth-Century Literary Imagination*. New Haven: Yale UP, 1979.

Goodlad, Lauren M. "'A Middle Class Cut into Two': Historiography and Victorian National Character." *English Literary History* 67.1 (2000): 143–78.

Graff, Harvey J. *The Legacies of Literacy: Continuities and Contradictions in Western Culture and Society.* Bloomington: Indiana UP, 1987.

Graham, Stedman. *Build Your Own Life Brand!* New York: Free Press, 2001.

Gruner, Elizabeth Rose. "Cinderella, Marie Antoinette and Sara: Roles and Role Models in *A Little Princess.*" *Lion and the Unicorn* 22.2 (1998): 163–87.

Gubar, Marah. *Artful Dodgers: Reconceiving the Golden Age of Children's Literature.* Oxford: Oxford UP, 2009.

Guest, Kristen. "The Subject of Money: Late-Victorian Melodrama's Crisis of Masculinity." *Victorian Studies* 49.4 (2007): 635–57.

Hallinan, Maureen T. "Tracking: From Theory to Practice." *Sociology of Education* 67.2 (1994): 79–84.

Hamlin, Christopher. "Politics and Germ Theories in Victorian Britain: The Metropolitan Water Commissions of 1867–9 and 1892–3." *Government and Expertise: Specialists, Administrators and Professionals, 1860–1919.* Ed. Roy MacLeod. Cambridge: Cambridge UP, 1988. 110–27.

Hardy, Anne. "Public Health and the Expert: The London Medical Officers of Health, 1856–1900." *Government and Expertise: Specialists, Administrators and Professionals, 1860–1919.* Ed. Roy MacLeod. Cambridge: Cambridge UP, 1988. 128–44.

Hart, Jenifer. "The Genesis of the Northcote-Trevelyan Report." *Studies in the Growth of Nineteenth-Century Government.* Ed. Gillian Sutherland. Totowa: Rowman and Littlefield, 1972.

Hearn, Alison. " 'Meat, Mask, Burden': Probing the Contours of the Branded Self." *Journal of Consumer Culture* 8.2 (2008): 197–217.

Heath, Michelle Beissel. "Playing at House and Playing at Home: The Domestic Discourse of Games in Edwardian Fictions of Childhood." *Childhood in Edwardian Fiction: Worlds Enough and Time.* Ed. Adrienne E. Gavin and Andrew F. Humphries. Houndmills: Palgrave Macmillan, 2009. 89–102.

Hendrick, Harry. *Images of Youth: Age, Class and the Male Youth Problem, 1880–1920.* Oxford: Clarendon, 1990.

Hennessy, Peter. *Whitehall.* Rev. ed. London: Pimlico, 2001.

Henty, G.A. *In the Heart of the Rockies: A Story of Adventure in Colorado.* Mineola: Dover, 2005.

Herbert, Christopher. "Filthy Lucre: Victorian Ideas of Money." *Victorian Studies* 44.2 (2002): 185–213.

Hintz, Eric S. " 'Heroes of the Laboratory and the Workshop': Invention and Technology in Books for Children, 1850–1900." *Enterprising Youth: Social Values and Acculturation in Nineteenth-Century American Children's Literature.* Ed. Monika Elbert. New York: Routledge, 2008. 197–212.

Hobsbawm, E.J. *The Age of Empire, 1875–1914.* New York: Pantheon, 1987.

Hodder, Edwin. *The Junior Clerk: A Tale of City Life.* 17th ed. London: Hodder and Stoughton, 1898.

Holcombe, Lee. *Victorian Ladies at Work: Middle-Class Working Women in England and Wales, 1850–1914.* Hamden: Archon, 1973.

Holt, Jenny. *Public School Literature, Civic Education and the Politics of Male Adolescence.* Farnham: Ashgate, 2008.

Hughes, Thomas. *Tom Brown's Schooldays.* London: J.M. Dent, 1906.

Jameson, Eva. *The Making of Teddy.* London: Religious Tract Society, 1904.

Jordan, Ellen. "The Exclusion of Women from Industry in Nineteenth-Century Britain." *Comparative Studies in Science and History* 31.2 (1989): 273–96.

——. "'Making Good Wives and Mothers': The Transformation of Middle-Class Girls' Education in Nineteenth-Century Britain." *History of Education Quarterly* 31.4 (1991): 439–62.

——. "The Lady Clerks at the Prudential: The Beginning of Vertical Segregation by Sexin Clerical Work in Nineteenth-Century Britain." *Gender and History* 8.1 (1996): 65–81.

Kimmel, Michael. "A War Against Boys?" *Dissent* 53.4 (2006): 65–70.

Kincaid, James R. "Dickens and the Construction of the Child." *Dickens and the Children of Empire*. Ed. Wendy S. Jacobson. Houndmills: Palgrave Macmillan, 2000. 29–42.

Kutzer, Daphne M. *Empire's Children: Empire and Imperialism in Classic British Children's Fiction*. New York: Garland, 2000.

Ledger, Sally. *The New Woman: Fiction and Feminism at the Fin de Siècle*. Manchester: Manchester UP, 1997.

Leggatt, Judith and Parkes, Christopher "From the Red Room to Rochester's Haircut: Mind Control in *Jane Eyre*." *English Studies in Canada* 32.4 (2006): 169–88.

Lerner, Laurence. *Angels and Absences: Child Deaths in the Nineteenth Century*. Nashville: Vanderbuilt UP, 1997.

Lillo, George. *The London Merchant. The Broadview Anthology of Restoration and Early Eighteenth-Century Drama*. Ed. J. Douglas Canfield. Canada: Broadview Press, 2001. 294–327.

Liu, William Ming, et al. "White Middle-Class Privilege: Social Class Bias and Implications for Training and Practice." *Journal of Multicultural Counseling and Development* 35 (2007): 195–206.

Loxley, Diana. *Problematic Shores: The Literature of Islands*. Houndmills: Palgrave Macmillan, 1990.

MacDonald, Tara. "'red-headed animal': Race, Sexuality and Dickens's Uriah Heep." *Critical Survey* 17.2 (2005): 48–62.

MacLeod, Roy. "Introduction." *Government and Expertise: Specialists, Administrators and Professionals, 1860–1919*. Ed. Roy MacLeod. Cambridge: Cambridge UP, 1988. 1–24.

Mahood, Linda. *Policing Gender, Class, and Family: Britain, 1850–1940*. London: UCL, 1995.

Manton, Jo. *Elizabeth Garrett Anderson*. New York: E.P. Dutton, 1965.

Martin, Jane. *Women and the Politics of Schooling in Victorian and Edwardian England*. London: Leicester UP, 1999.

Maryatt, Frederick. *The Children of the New Forest*. Ed. Dennis Butts. Oxford: Oxford UP, 1991.

Mayhew, Henry. *London Labour and the London Poor*. Vol. 2. London: Griffin, Bohn, and Company, 1861.

McFarlan, Donald. "Introduction." *Kidnapped*. Ed. Donald McFarlan. New York: Penguin, 1994. vii–xxii.

McGillis, Roderick. *A Little Princess: Gender and Empire*. New York: Twayne, 1996.

McKechnie, Samuel. *The Romance of the Civil Service*. London: Sampson Low, Marston, 1930.

McQuillan, Julia and Julie Pfeiffer. "Why Anne Makes us Dizzy: Reading *Anne of Green Gables* from a Gender Perspective." *Mosaic* 34.2 (2001): 17–32.

Meadows, Jack. *The Victorian Scientist: The Growth of a Profession.* London: British Library, 2004.

Menikoff, Barry. *Narrating Scotland: The Imagination of Robert Louis Stevenson.* Columbia: U of South Carolina P, 2005.

Michals, Teresa. "Experiments Before Breakfast: Toys, Education and Middle-Class Childhood." *The Nineteenth-Century Child and Consumer Culture.* Ed. Dennis Denisoff. Farnham: Ashgate, 2008. 29–42.

Millard, Elaine. *Differently Literate: Boys, Girls and the Schooling of Literacy.* London: Falmer, 1997.

Miller, D.A. *The Novel and the Police.* Berkeley: U of California P, 1988.

Mitchell, Sally. *The New Girl: Girl's Culture in England, 1850–1915.* New York: Columbia UP, 1995.

Montgomery, Lucy Maud. *Anne's House of Dreams.* London: Puffin, 1994.

——. *Anne of Windy Poplars.* USA: Seal, 1996.

——. *Anne of Green Gables.* Toronto: Penguin, 2006.

Montoya, Peter. *The Personal Branding Phenomenon.* Peter Montoya, 2002.

Moran, Mary Jeanette. "Nancy's Ancestors: The Mystery of Imaginative Female Power in *The Secret Garden* and *A Little Princess*." *Mystery in Children's Literature: From the Rational to the Supernatural.* Ed. Adrienne E. Gavin and Christopher Routledge. New York: Palgrave Macmillan, 2001. 32–45.

More, Ellen Singer. *Restoring the Balance: Women Physicians and the Profession of Medicine, 1850–1995.* Cambridge: Harvard UP, 1999.

Morgentaler, Goldie. *Dickens and Heredity: When Like Begets Like.* London: Palgrave Macmillan, 2000.

Moss, Anita. "E. Nesbit's Romantic Child in Modern Dress." *Romanticism and Children's Literature in Nineteenth-Century England.* Athens: U of Georgia P, 1991. 225–47.

Nelson, Claudia. *Boys Will Be Girls: The Feminine Ethic and British Children's Fiction, 1857–1917.* New Brunswick: Rutgers UP, 1991.

Nenadic, Stana. "The Small Family Firm in Victorian Britain." *Business History* 35.4 (1993): 86–114. *Academic One File.* Web. 23 Jan. 2011.

Nesbit, E. *The Story of the Treasure Seekers.* London: Puffin, 1994.

——. *The Railway Children.* London: Puffin, 2003.

——. *The Wouldbegoods.* Teddington: Echo Library, 2006.

Noimann, Chamutal. " 'Poke Your Finger into the Soft Round Dough': The Absent Father and Political Reform in Edith Nesbit's *The Railway Children*." *Children's Literature Association Quarterly* 30 (2005): 368–85.

O'Mahony, C. and Moss, W. "Self-Directed Learning: Liberating or Oppressive? Developing Autonomy in Open Learning." *Lifelong Literacies: Papers from the 1996 Conference, Manchester, England.* Ed. S. Fitzpatrick and J. Mace. Manchester: Gatehouse, 1996. 28–33.

O'Malley, Andrew. *The Making of the Modern Child: Children's Literature and Childhood in the Late Eighteenth Century.* New York: Routledge, 2003.

Palmer, William J. *Dickens and New Historicism.* New York: St. Martin's, 1997.

Parry, Noel and Parry, Jose. *The Rise of the Medical Profession: A Study of Collective Social Mobility.* London: Croom Helm, 1976.

Peale, Norman Vincent. *The Power of Positive Thinking.* Los Angeles: Fireside, 2003.

Perkin, Harold. *The Rise of Professional Society: England since 1880*. London: Routledge, 1989.

Peterson, Linda H. *Traditions of Victorian Women's Autobiography: The Poetics and Politics of Life Writing*. Charlottesville: U of Virginia P, 1999.

Plotz, Judith. *Romanticism and the Vocation of Childhood*. New York: Palgrave Macmillan, 2001.

Poovey, Mary. *Uneven Developments: The Ideological Work of Gender in Mid-Victorian England*. Chicago: U of Chicago P, 1988.

——. *Making a Social Body: British Cultural Formation, 1830–1864*. Chicago: U of Chicago P, 1995.

Pope, Alexander. *Essay on Man: The Best of Pope*. Ed. George Sherburn. New York: Ronald Press, 1940.

Price, Danielle E. "Cultivating Mary: The Victorian Secret Garden." *Children's Literature Association Quarterly* 26.1 (2001): 4–14.

Pue, Wesley W. "Guild Training vs. Professional Education: The Committee on LegalEducation and the Law Department of Queen's College, Birmingham in the 1850s." *American Journal of Legal History* 33.3 (1989): 241–287.

Reed, Talbot Baines. *The Adventures of a Three-Guinea Watch*. Charleston: BiblioBazaar, 2007.

Reimer, Mavis. "Treasure Seekers and Invaders: E. Nesbit's Cross-writing of the Bastables." *Children's Literature* 25 (1997): 50–9.

Reynolds, Kimberley. *Girls Only?: Gender and Popular Children's Fiction in Britain, 1880–1910*. Philadelphia: Temple UP, 1990.

Reynolds, Kimberley and Nicola Humble. *Victorian Heroines: Representations of Femininity in Nineteenth-Century Literature and Art*. New York: New York UP, 1993.

Ricardo, David. *The Principles of Political Economy and Taxation*. Mineola: Dover, 2004.

Richards, Jeffrey. "Spreading the Gospel of Self-Help: G.A. Henty and Samuel Smiles." *Journal of Popular Culture* 16.2 (1982): 52–65.

Robson, Catherine. *Men in Wonderland: The Lost Girlhood of Victorian Gentlemen*. Princeton: Princeton UP, 2001.

Rodger, Richard. "Mid-Victorian Employer's Attitudes." *Social History* 11.1 (1986): 77–80.

Rousseau, Jean-Jacques. *Emile, or, on Education*. London: Everyman's Library, 1974.

Rubio, Mary. "*Anne of Green Gables*: The Architect of Adolescence." *Such a Simple Tale: Critical Responses to L. M. Montgomery's "Anne of Green Gables."* Ed. Mavis Reimer. Lanham: Scarecrow, 1992. 65–82.

Ruth, Jennifer. *Novel Professions: Interested Disinterest and the Making of the Professional in the Victorian Novel*. Columbus: Ohio State UP, 2006.

Shaw, George Bernard, ed. *Fabian Essays in Socialism*. London: Fabian Society, 1889.

Silver, Anna Krugovoy. "Domesticating Brontë's Moors: Motherhood in *The Secret Garden*." *Lion and the Unicorn* 21.2 (1997): 193–203.

Simon, Brian. *Education and the Labour Movement, 1870–1920*. London: Lawrence and Wishart, 1965.

Smiles, Samuel. *Men of Invention and Industry*. New York: Harper & Brothers, 1885.

——. *Life and Labour*. Chicago: Donohue and Henneberry, 1888.

——. *Character*. London: John Murray, 1891.

——. *Self-Help*. Teddington: Echo Library, 2006.

Smith, Grahame. "Suppressing Narratives: Childhood and Empire in *The Uncommercial Traveller* and *Great Expectations*." *Dickens and the Children of Empire*. Ed. Wendy S. Jacobson. Houndmills: Palgrave Macmillan, 2000. 43–53.

Solt, Marilyn. "The Uses of Setting in *Anne of Green Gables*." *Such a Simple Tale: Critical Responses to L. M. Montgomery's Anne of Green Gables*. Ed. Mavis Reimer. Lanham: Scarecrow, 1992. 57–64.

Sommers, Christina Hoff. *The War Against Boys: How Misguided Feminism is Harming our Young Men*. New York: Simon and Schuster, 2001.

Springhall, John. *Coming of Age: Adolescence in Britain, 1860–1960*. Dublin: Gill and Macmillan, 1986.

Stanton, Domna C., ed. *The Female Autograph: Theory and Practice of Autobiography from the Tenth to the Twentieth Century*. Chicago: U of Chicago P, 1987.

Steedman, Carolyn. *Strange Dislocations: Childhood and the Idea of Human Interiority, 1780–1930*. Cambridge: Harvard UP, 1994.

Stevenson, Robert Louis. "The Education of an Engineer." *The Vailima Edition of the Works of Robert Louis Stevenson*. Vol. 12. New York: Scribner's, 1922. 375–88.

——. "On the Choice of a Profession." *The Vailima Edition of the Works of Robert Louis Stevenson*. Vol. 24. New York: Scribner's, 1922. 253–64.

——. "Records of a Family of Engineers." *The Vailima Edition of the Works of Robert Louis Stevenson*. Vol. 12. New York: Scribner's, 1922. 401–593.

——. "Thomas Stevenson: Civil Engineer." *The Vailima Edition of the Works of Robert Louis Stevenson*. Vol. 12. New York: Scribner's, 1922. 103–11.

——. *Kidnapped*. Ed. Donald McFarlan. New York: Penguin, 1994.

——. *Treasure Island*. Ed. John Seelye. New York: Penguin, 1999.

——. *Catriona: A Sequel to Kidnapped*. North Hollywood: Aegypan, 2006.

Stout, Maureen. *The Feel-Good Curriculum: The Dumbing Down of America's Kids in the Name of Self-Esteem*. Cambridge: Perseus, 2000.

Stretton, Hesba. *Jessica's First Prayer*. Minneapolis: Curiosmith, 2008.

Summers, Anne. *Angels and Citizens: British Women as Military Nurses, 1854–1914*. London: Routledge and Kegan Paul, 1988.

Swenson, Kristine. *Medical Women and Victorian Fiction*. Columbia: U of Missouri P, 2005.

Tambling, Jeremy. Introduction. *David Copperfield*. London: Penguin, 2004.

Tennyson, Alfred. *The Lady of Shalott: The Complete Poetical Works of Tennyson*. Ed. W.J. Rolfe. Cambridge: Riverside, 1898.

Thompson, E.P. *The Making of the English Working Class*. London: Penguin, 1968.

Thompson, F.M.L. *The Rise of Respectable Society: A Social History of Victorian Britain, 1830–1900*. Cambridge: Harvard UP, 1988.

Thwaite, Ann. *Waiting for the Party: The Life of Frances Hodgson Burnett, 1849–1924*. New York: Scribner, 1974.

Titolo, Matthew. "The Clerk's Tale: Liberalism, Accountability, and Mimesis in *David Copperfield*." *ELH* 70.1 (2003): 171–95.

Todd, Margaret (Graham Travers). *Mona Maclean, Medical Student*. 14th ed. Edinburgh: William Blackwood, 1899.

——. *The Life of Sophia Jex-Blake*. London: Palgrave Macmillan, 1918.

Tosh, John. *A Man's Place: Masculinity and the Middle-Class Home in Victorian England*. New Haven: Yale UP, 2007.

Tucker, Charlotte Maria. *The Lake of the Woods: A Story of the Backwoods*. London: Gall and Inglis, 1889.

Vicinus, Martha. *Independent Women: Work and Community for Single Women, 1850–1920*. Chicago: U of Chicago P, 1985.

Vincent, David. *Literacy and Popular Culture: England, 1750–1914*. Cambridge: Cambridge UP, 1989.

Wahrman, Dror. *Imagining the Middle Class: The Political Representation of Class in Britain, c. 1780–1840*. Cambridge: Cambridge UP, 1995.

Wallace, David. "Bourgeois Tragedy or Sentimental Melodrama?: The Significance of George Lillo's." *The London Merchant Eighteenth-Century Studies* 25.2 (1991–92): 123–43.

Wardle, David. *English Popular Education, 1780–1970*. Cambridge: Cambridge UP, 1970.

Waters, Hazel. " 'That Astonishing Clever Child': Performers and Prodigies in the Early and Mid-Victorian Theatre." *Theatre Notebook* 50.2 (1996): 78–94.

Watts, Isaac. "Against Idleness and Mischief." *Watt's Divine Songs for the Use of Children*. New Haven: J. Babcock, 1824.

Weber, Max. *The Protestant Ethic and the Spirit of Capitalism and Other Writings*. Trans. Peter Baehr and Gordon C. Wells. New York: Penguin, 2002.

Wells, H.G. *Experiments in Autobiography: Discoveries and Conclusions of a Very Ordinary Brain*. London: Faber and Faber, 1984.

Wells, Susan. *Out of the Dead House: Nineteenth-Century Women Physicians and the Writing of Medicine*. Madison: U of Wisconsin P, 2001.

Wood, Naomi J. "Gold Standards and Silver Subversions: *Treasure Island* and the Romance of Money." *Children's Literature* 26 (1998): 61–85.

Woodall, Mary. *Thomas Gainsborough: His Life and Work*. London: Phoenix House, 1949.

Wordsworth, William. "Ode: Intimations of Immortality." *The Complete Poetical Works of William Wordsworth*. London: Palgrave Macmillan, 1909.

Zelizer, Viviana A. *Pricing the Priceless Child: The Changing Social Value of Children*. Princeton: Princeton UP, 1985.

Zemmick, Meta. "Jobs for the Girls: The Expansion of Clerical Work for Women, 1850–1914." *Unequal Opportunities: Women's Employment in England, 1800–1918*. Ed. Angela V. John. Oxford: Basil Blackwell, 1986. 153–78.

Zornado, Joseph L. *Inventing the Child: Culture, Ideology, and the Story of Childhood*. New York: Garland, 2001.

Index

Note: The letter "n" followed by the locator refers to notes in the text.